Daniel Cailler
2007

Note for Librarians: A cataloguing record for this book is available from Library and Archives
Canada at www.collectionscanada.ca/amicus/index-e.html
ISBN 1-4251-0159-3

*Printed in Victoria, BC, Canada. Printed on paper with minimum 30% recycled fibre. Trafford's print shop
runs on "green energy" from solar, wind and other environmentally-friendly power sources.*

TRAFFORD
PUBLISHING

Offices in Canada, USA, Ireland and UK
This book was published *on-demand* in cooperation with Trafford Publishing. On-demand
publishing is a unique process and service of making a book available for retail sale to the
public taking advantage of on-demand manufacturing and Internet marketing. On-demand
publishing includes promotions, retail sales, manufacturing, order fulfilment, accounting and
collecting royalties on behalf of the author.

Book sales for North America and international:
Trafford Publishing, 6E–2333 Government St.,
Victoria, BC V8T 4P4 CANADA
phone 250 383 6864 (toll-free 1 888 232 4444)
fax 250 383 6804; email to orders@trafford.com
Book sales in Europe:
Trafford Publishing (UK) Limited, 9 Park End Street, 2nd Floor
Oxford, UK OX1 1HH UNITED KINGDOM
phone 44 (0)1865 722 113 (local rate 0845 230 9601)
facsimile 44 (0)1865 722 868; info.uk@trafford.com
Order online at:
trafford.com/06-1916

10 9 8 7 6 5 4

Thanks to Thomas Lewis for all your optimism and for the initial push that got it all going. If you didn't bother to ask me what I was writing on that first day, I'd not have gotten this far.

Thanks to Tina Tormey for your help with the editing process, and for your creative input.

Thanks to Frodo (my cat) for keeping my lap warm during those freezing Syracuse winter months.

And thanks especially to my love, Stefanie, for sharing my burden, and especially for your patience and support while my overstressed mind was trapped in a fictitious world.

This book is dedicated to Stefanie.

Waking

By Daniel Cailler

Chapters

'He who fights with monsters might take care lest he thereby become a monster. And if you gaze for long into an abyss, the abyss gazes also into you.'

— **Friedrich Nietzsche**, *Beyond Good and Evil*

Chapter 1 – The Waking

I call myself Child. I cannot bring to mind a single memory concerning the life that this body once lived, prior to my waking. Who I used to be, where I came from and what relationships I once held, are all irrelevant to me now, despite what few 'personal' facts I have stumbled across. This amnestic disposition is innate to my kind, I have learned; for all its apparent misfortune, it only helps me focus on what is now so important to me.

The only thing I can recall, from before my waking, seems unreal to me. In some unearthly place, there was a period of serenity and silence, and an empty void, filled with soft white light, spread outward all around me. Defined by no boundaries, I seemed to be everywhere, yet I took up no space, and though I saw not one neighboring soul basking in that warmth, I did not feel alone. I hovered in that place, in that realm, for I don't know how long; my memory of it lasts only a few seconds, it seems. I think back to that moment, from time to time, and it is merely like a thought within a dream – a perfect place I cannot avow with any sense of validity, since I sometimes wonder if it really was just a dream.

Dream or not, what happened next was a nightmare. The peace and light steeped into darkness and despair. Eclipsed from the warmth by some unseen evil, a foreboding penumbra widened around me, until the last of the white light was choked by a dark and ominous fog. It was during that dismal dawning, shrouded in a stagnant murk, that I first heard the voices. Shadowy figures, amorphous against the swirling blackness of that frigid void, whispered to me. At first, the vociferations were few, but as the last wisps of warm light succumbed to the assaulting darkness, a mesh of indecipherable calls and cries blossomed on all sides, like the clatter of a dark and crowded hall filled with the utterances of many men and women.

I screamed out, terrified and confused. I was unsure if I should fear or embrace the voices; it was not altogether clear. Then, a thunderous tone boomed, like a distant storm climbing the horizon.

"Another!"

As if summoned by that mysterious call, I began to fall, plummeting long and far, through blinding blackness; the raspy wake of a thousand whispers followed my rapid descent. The further I fell, the more I felt a stinging cold, a deep pain, rising up inside of me. I was crushed by the anticipation that soon I would break through the gates of hell, and find myself drowning in a lake of fire. Instead, I found myself lying on a dirty bed, in some small room, with no sense of self or time, pondering the strange fall which, by that point, had already seemed like a false memory.

That was my waking.

I remained still for a long time, lying on that bed, staring blankly at the ceiling, and coping with a pain I did not understand. Cold and weak, I strained to move. I hurt, yet my body was numb. Lying stiff and awkward on a mattress in the corner of a cramped room, I was positioned with my arms folded against my chest, with my hands reaching up for my throat. I was partially dressed, lacking only a shirt, and wearing jeans torn from overuse.

As I gazed around the messy room, I knew right away something was wrong. At first, I couldn't decipher what my senses were telling me. I thought I was having an out of body experience. There seemed to be too much information to take in. But with passing minutes, I adjusted and was able to focus.

I was in the bedroom, the main room, of a tiny apartment. White, naked walls were riddled with tiny cracks. There was hardly any furniture; everything was piled on the floor, which was carpeted with laundry. Pillars of stacked books and magazines shot up through the mess. A computer hummed from atop a desk, in one corner of the room; the desktop was muddled with scraps of paper, books, CDs, and trash. Behind the computer monitor, a lone window faced the wall of an opposing brick building not ten feet out. On the outer wall of that neighboring tenement, a parallel apartment was as equally robbed of a view.

A deep, voracious hunger urged me to get up, but I did not know what it desired, or how I should quench it. Despite the pain and numbness, I effortlessly sat up; my body groaned from stiffness when I straightened out my limbs. I stared, curiously, at the sickening discoloration of my flesh.

Am I ill? I wondered.

The sound of intense yelling took grip of my attention; I heard two voices remarkably clear through the stone walls of the building - a male and a young female. As sure as I heard their words, I felt anger and sadness, teaming with each of their exchanged cries, and it lured me to them, beckoning me to investigate. Driven to action, I rose from the bed.

There were only two doors in that room. One, by the bed, led to a bathroom. I trudged towards the other, where a sliding bolt, latch and chain were all unlocked. I had great trouble turning the knob; my numb hands fumbled as if I had never used them before. I pounded my hand into the door, waiting for some sensation to rise up, but a lack of feeling persisted.

What is wrong with me? I thought.

My entire body felt as if it were asleep, yet the peculiar pains of hunger intensified, and I felt as if I were encased in a block of ice, overwhelmed by a frigidness I wished to overcome. My vision ebbed, darkening, and I felt as if I would drop to the floor. Determined to find a hint of sanity, some explanation to what was going on, my limp fingers managed to twist the doorknob and open the door.

I was standing outside an apartment at the end of a hall, dimly lit, with a filthily stained, red carpet, kicked around into clumps. To my left was a small steel door leading to a stairwell. It had a bar-handle, a window of reinforced glass, and a '3' marked with faded paint. To my right, alternating apartment doors lined the narrow walls. At the end of the hallway, before it bent around a corner, a dying florescent bulb flickered. Lying beneath the strobing light, a raggedy-jacketed old man, wearing soiled, faded slacks, huddled over an old backpack as he slept silently on the floor. His long, grey hair covered his face, and he snored softly.

I stared at him for a few moments and outlandish thoughts entered my mind. I somehow knew that he could end my hunger. I kept hearing the words over and over - *Take him...Take him now.*

I did not understand the suggestion, pausing to decipher the unfamiliar urges before I acted upon them. Was I hungry, or was I a murderer? My morbid desires suggested both. I walked closer to the dormant denizen, curiously, but the yelling persisted from somewhere, further down the hall. An angry male continued to scream, burying a female's soft whimpers, and it took my attention from the vagabond. I passed over him, letting him rest peacefully.

I saw then, peering around the corner, just a few feet away, a small girl, no older than six years old, standing in partial view at the hall's bend. She observed me cautiously, with large, watery blue eyes. Her long, brown hair was tangled, which she tried to remedy with a cheap plastic comb. Her bare feet were darkened with the filth of the dusty carpet, and she wore a shirt which she had long outgrown, with tattered cotton pants exposing most of her calves.

I lumbered toward her, but she quickly receded from sight. After the turn, the hallway continued past more apartments, to a pair of elevator doors, one of which was open, revealing a cement shaft with a string of cables and chains down the center. Halfway down the hall, on the right, the young girl stood outside an open apartment door, pointing inside as if she wished for me to observe. The sounds of yelling and crying persisted from inside that place.

"No! You're not talking your way out of this one. Lance is already on his way over, so go get your stuff ready!" a grumbling male screamed.

"Please! Please!" a young woman's cries were desperate.

"No! Not unless you can match his offer." Throaty laughter sounded as if it belonged in a sty. "But you don't have any money, do you? You're worthless! But he'll put you to good use."

"I hate y…" Her frail words ended with a loud smack.

Her soft whimpering filled me with pity, but apparently, it eluded the riled brute's mentality.

"Shut up! I'm not getting kicked out on the street if I can help it."

I approached the door where the young girl from the hall looked in at the scene, careful not to stand in view of the opened door. Combing her tangled hair, she tugged at her knotted locks and held a small mirror in her other hand.

"Are you ok?" She pointed at my throat. "What happened to your neck?"

I patted my hand against the skin, but I felt nothing, neither my hand nor my throat. She handed me the pink, plastic mirror. I gazed into it, befuddled at what I didn't see. I saw neither the reflection of my face nor the wall's reflection behind me; the mirror seemed like clear glass mounted on a plastic head. Had she pretended it was a mirror, or had I overlooked something?

I handed it back, unsure if it was a joke, and then I turned and looked through the opened door of the neighboring apartment. Inside, a short, robust bulldog-of-a-man, in a dirty white tee-shirt and grey slacks, faced a woman in her mid-to-late teens. She knelt down before him in tears, with bruises on her arms and face.

The man grabbed her by the shoulder and pulled her up on her feet.

"Now, go in the bedroom and get your crap together! He'll be here soon, and I don't want him to see you crying like some brat!" The man pushed her towards a doorway and then reached to the floor, lifting a bottle, taking a violent swig of the clear liquid.

When the sweaty, overweight man turned, he saw me outside the door. His face crinkled up like an angry pug, and with glossy eyes and a furrowed brow, he scowled. His approaching stomps frightened the young girl standing beside me in the hall; she backed away from the angry man as he approached, but I stood motionless and stared at him.

"What are you looking at you…?" His sharp and annoyed expression melted into a concerned, almost shocked disposition. "What happened to *you*?"

He looked up and down my body, but took special notice of my eyes, which he blatantly stared at as if he were looking at me through the glass at a freak show exhibit. "You look *awful*, man." He glanced down at the girl who continued to watch and brush her hair. "Get outta of here you little rat! Don't you have parents? Go back to your hole!"

I felt his cruelty and nastiness seeping through me. I thought I might kill him where he stood, but I spoke first.

Watching the barefoot little girl step back from the man, I said to him, "Don't talk to her like that."

Something was queer about my voice which I could not place. My speech did not seem to come from within me, and from the look of the stout, balding man, he noticed something as well.

"Wha...?" he mumbled, seeming in awe. His eyes shifted left and right; it seemed his high blood alcohol content slowed his reaction and he shook his head, willing to ignore what he heard.

I continued to speak, "...and stop hitting your daughter."

He reeled his head back, insulted. "Mind your own business...you crack-head!" He raised his fist and flashed his yellow teeth, saying, "Unless you want some too."

Though he threatened me, I did not fear him. To my bewilderment, I felt each shift in his emotion, his anger, confusion, and even his doubt, with his fist shaking in the air by my head. I heard his heart pounding in his chest and I could not ignore the rhythm; it riled me so much, and I was almost unable to thwart off a horrific urge to attack and destroy him, but I was still so bewildered at the plethora of anomalous details governing my thoughts and perceptions, that I was hypnotized into temporary inaction.

The bottle fell from his hand and broke on the floor, and he stared at it with his mouth open. He became sad, only for a second, until his rage overwhelmed him. "No! Look what you did..." The man snarled, and with both hands, pushed me back against the hall. "Get lost!" He slammed the door.

I struck the wall hard, and being terribly weak, I fell limp and lifeless onto the dirty hallway carpet. The girl with the mirror squealed and fled.

Everything around me faded, darkening with the loss of consciousness. I began to dream. I felt weightless, hovering in the dark, still plagued with cold pains and intense hunger. I heard, again, ghostly whispers and voices all around me; they talked to each other, over each other, surrounding me with speech. I wondered if any talked to me specifically, but I could hardly understand them. Most were heavily distorted, sounding far away, but others were clearer, so close to me that I felt I could have reached into the darkness and touched some of them. Slowly, and with much effort, I managed to pick out single cries from among the endless sea of eerie converse.

"What's happening to me?" A female's voice seemed lost and troubled. "I'm not dead?" She screamed from within the dark.

"Come to us. Find your way here" A young-sounding man's voice repeated the phrase over and over, before he added, "We can protect you."

A desperate cry wailed in the distance. "They'll find you. He'll find you, and kill you!"

A booming male voice frightfully asked, "Are you there, now?"

Wanting to be known, I spoke, "I'm here."

An immediate response rang clearly. Another deep, male voice said, "You're close!" It sounded pleasantly surprised. "I will find you."

The conversation ended when I receded from that bizarre and spacious realm of darkness and voices. Had I dreamt it, was it real? I had little time to wonder; I regained awareness and found myself lying in the hallway where I had fallen and remained for some amount of time. I did not move, and stared up at two men.

In the doorway of the apartment was the doggish, perspiring jerk who appeared surprised that I was still in the hall. His brow was damp with sweat. With a can of beer in his hand, he stared down at me, with a look of shock on his face.

Standing over my body, from inside a pair of well-polished black shoes, a dark-skinned man wore a pinstriped, burgundy suit with a matching fedora, and flashed a white, toothy grin, speckled with gold caps. He held a unique-looking cane. It had a dark, slender mahogany staff with a polished, natural-wood texture. But the most striking feature was a silver octopus fashioned on the top; its bulbous cephalopod head served as the handle, and the eight silver arms spiraled halfway down, where the tips of the arms pointed outward.

I lay motionless; my eyes were open and unmoving.

Why are they looking at me like that? I thought. I couldn't understand why I was being viewed like an object, and not somebody in need. Somehow, I managed to remain calm and still. My nerves weren't shaken.

The arriver tapped his fingers upon his cane, and asked, "Did you kill him?"

From within the door to the apartment, the stout man nervously stomped in place, "No, Lance! I didn't!"

Lance chuckled, "Well, he is all messed up. Just look at his eyes." He knelt down for a closer look. "I've seen dead bodies

before, and this guy is dead. Been dead for days, I can promise you
that." He winked at me, oddly enough.

I'm not dead. He was mistaken.

"Looks like he was choked with something, see?" Lance stood
up. Using the tip of his cane, he lifted my chin to expose my neck
and then pointed downward, "See the mark? Some type of wire,
maybe."

"He has not been dead for days, Lance." He was so out of
shape that as he continued to stomp his feet in anger, he became
winded. "He *just* threatened me! So I pushed him!" He wiped his
sweaty brow with his hand.

Lance looked doubtful at his testimony. "Well, Charles, you
must have pushed him *hard* to make him look like *that.* How long
ago was this?"

"Twenty minutes."

Lance scratched the back of his neck. "You need to lay off the
juice, buddy." He looked up and down the hall, obviously nervous
about something. "Think anyone else has seen him here?"

"No! Just some dumb girl."

"Well, help me pull this fool inside for now. If someone got a
look at this while I was here, it would be a very bad situation for
me."

Lance handed his cane to Charles, who placed it inside the
apartment, by the door.

"You're not bringing that corpse in my apartment!" He sipped
beer from a can and continued, "He lives on this floor somewhere.
I've seen him a few times since I moved here."

"I know...I mean, well, I'm not dragging him all the way down
the hall to his place. Someone could see me. Too risky."

Lance gripped my ankles and dragged me into Charles's
apartment. My arms flopped lifelessly as I was towed onto a gritty
carpet in the center of the room.

"Man, this guy is cold! Your story doesn't make sense, Charles."
Lance let go of my ankles when I was in the center of the room, and
then wiped his hands against his suit pants. "Is there something else
you want to tell me?"

Charles shrugged.

Why did they think I was dead? I was definitely sick, or
perhaps injured, but I was aware, and though I was completely
numb, I felt something. Pain, cold, hunger... I wasn't dead! I denied
the impertinent suggestion.

Charles's apartment was devoid of any real furniture. Many
empty cans and bottles were littered about. Two folding chairs faced
a small, dusty television on the floor. A socket on the ceiling once

held a light, but now a small hole, tangled with cobwebs remained, and the lamp in the farthest corner did a poor job of lighting up the entire room by itself. An opened window on the back wall led to a black, rusted fire escape; the roars and squeals of semi-trucks came from outside. To my left a doorway led to a filthy, kitchen. The linoleum flooring was missing large pieces and the counters were covered in more beer cans and bottles.

I wanted to move, to react, but as of yet I was unsure of what I had become and what I would do if I let my instincts be realized. I passively stared up at the two men as they talked, and that dull throbbing pain became much more intense as I continued to resist action.

The young woman, whom Charles had cursed at and slapped, lay face down on a bed in an adjacent room, crying softly. If she had looked over, she would have seen my body on the floor.

Lance patted Charles on his shoulder. "Don't worry. I will help you remove the stiff after a little business?" Lance rubbed his fingers together as he reached into the front pocket of his suit, removing a wad of cash wrapped with an elastic band. "Here you go, Charles my man. Use this for rent this time. You've got nothing left to sell to me." Lance extended his arm with the money between two fingers.

Charles accepted it, thumbing the edge of the bills to see that he hadn't been gypped.

"Don't tell me what to do with my money, Lance," he sneered. "Just make sure she gets all her stuff! I don't want her junk taking up my space anymore!" He put the money in his pocket and walked into the kitchen, yelling back to his guest, "Good luck getting that brat to cooperate."

"Don't worry. I will take *good* care of her, like I do all of my ladies. Besides, my place is much nicer than this dump." Lance walked over to the bedroom, shutting the door behind him when he entered. "Hi honey. Get your things together, we're leaving."

I heard the girl beg Lance not to take her with him. Lance promised he'd treat her better than him, and make her into a lady. I wanted to help her, but I was struggling to understand my own lot. Had I died and returned to life? Why couldn't I remember anything before that night? I could not feel myself breathing; was it possible I was really dead? This pain, this cold numbness - I wanted it to end! I decided to let go of my inhibitions, and do what I felt driven to do. After all, instincts, by their nature, were often valid suggestions.

From the kitchen, Charles panted heavily as he searched through drawers. Stressed out and sweaty, he stomped back out from the kitchen with bungee cords and duct tape.

Standing over me, he gazed deep into my eyes and scratched his head before continuing.

"Whatever. Let's do this, eh?" He then turned to the bedroom to yell at Lance through the shut door. "Come out and help me..." His voice trailed off. "...you jerk."

With his back facing me, Charles knelt down over my legs. He pulled a strip of tape from the roll, preparing to bind my ankles together.

"Good thing it's garbage night tonight. You smell disgusting."

The heat of his body radiated and it sent me into a dazed frenzy. I was so cold and I was drawn to the warmth like a firefly to light. I sat up, silently, easily, without needing my arms to hoist myself, and without flexing my legs to support my torso, and with both hands, I grabbed Charles's head. My fingers hooked into his eyes, nose and mouth, anything I could get my hands to hold onto firmly.

Charles tried to scream, but I turned his head far to the side and he wheezed. I leaned in and bit his neck.

Everything darkened around me as I focused on that one, horrid act. The loud thumping of his heartbeat dominated my senses, perhaps like a child in the womb; the intense pounding grew faster and riled me. I could only assume what I was doing – feeding on his wasted life to alleviate my pain, but it felt right, and who was I to dismiss such a reward.

Charles struggled only for a moment, and then resigned all efforts. As his head fell from my grasp, I heard the final beat of his life dissipate into the air and then incredible warmth surged through me – the dull, agonizing throbs, and the hunger, had faded entirely.

I was now standing over the rapidly cooling corpse of a dead man. I had watched his involuntary spasms dwindle to a deathly halt, feeling no guilt.

What am I, a monster? Impossible! A murderer, maybe, I thought.

Perhaps, this was the twisted hallucination of a madman, doped and bound in a padded cell, a wonderful dream, an escape from what would be an even more disheartening reality. But unfortunately, everything was so clear, so convincing, devoid of any of the haze that borders the realm of even the most awesome of dreams. I was terrified at the thought, but like a serial killer's first murder, I knew it was the start of something new and exciting.

My senses were suddenly and dramatically elated, and I gazed upon the room with a tremendous clarity. My sight and hearing had enhanced beyond reason, it seemed.

The dimly lit room seemed as if its surfaces emitted a soft glow, defying the shadows that would normally obscure it. I stood motionless in the room, examining my surroundings with eyes that seemed to be everywhere, yet still – a panorama with my body in the center. At the mere thought, my eyes drifted to any vantage point. I could see things that intervening objects were physically obstructing from my line of sight – yet nothing was transparent. Colors were dull and faded, but everything else was so clear and extra-dimensional. Particles of dust fell as clearly as snow under a streetlight, even in the dark corners of the room. Tiny insects crawled on the carpet and ceiling and I could see their miniscule legs wriggling. Phenomenally, and with minimal effort, I could see all sides simultaneously – the exit door behind me, my own face, and even the back of my head, all concurrently discernable.

I stared at my stony face, at my dead eyes and pale skin. I saw, finally, what led them to think I was dead. A thin, deep line, crusted with dried blood, ran lengthwise across my throat; the skin around the wound was swollen and bruised. More definitive than a deathly scar were my eyes, and the expression they put forth. My face was swollen, and fluids had seeped out from my nose and mouth. I could not deny what I had become. I was a corpse.

To my relief, I quickly honed in on a new sensation altogether – something that ended the numbness that plagued my corpse, which until then, I had assumed was unwavering. I felt things, near and far from me, with what seemed to be a boundless and invisible hand, which seemed one and the same with my transcending eyes. The surfaces, textures and weights of all the objects in the room were comprehendible as if I used a living hand to examine them. I focused on objects, like the cool glass bottles lying all over the room, and it felt as if I held them in my hand. The rough, shaggy carpet, the steel folding chairs, and even the damp, sweaty shirt wrapped around Charles's corpse, were incorporable to my senses.

I quickly lost track of the time; I do not know how long I stared in awe around the filthy apartment, trying to understand what I beheld, and how I beheld it.

I heard Lance in the other room, loud and clearly, as if he stood directly next to me when I spoke.

"Come on girl, let's go. Hurry up and grab your things. I'm not going to hurt you."

Exploring my sensationally new vision, I peered towards the door. To my amazement, I saw into the bedroom as if I were a breeze passing through the wall. Like a presence hovering in the air, I saw the girl sitting on the edge of a messy bed, zipping up a backpack.

Lance pulled his shirt sleeve back to glance at a silver, gem-studded watch. He walked over to the girl, pulling on her arm. "Come on. We're going now! You're making your step-dad upset. I'm surprised he isn't yelling at us now." Lance put his hand on the doorknob, about to go back into the main room. "Maybe he's finally passed out."

I brought my focus back to where I stood. After wiping my lips with the back of my hand, I lowered back onto the floor, in a similar fashion as I had been when Lance saw me last. I did not panic. I couldn't panic; my heart was perfectly still.

The door opened slowly and soon Lance saw the new corpse in the room.

"Charles. Are you ok?" Lance ran over to investigate, and when he noticed the hole in Charles's neck, and saw the excess blood that had secreted from the wound, forming a dark-red puddle on the carpet, his heart increased in speed, pleasing me.

Without hesitation, Lance reached into the late Charles's pocket, retrieving the cash he had given him. Lance then removed a small, black revolver from inside his suit. He cautiously walked to the kitchen where it took but a glance to see that the tiny room was empty. He looked back at the scene, unsuspecting of the true culprit.

The girl emerged from the bedroom with her backpack in hand; her mouth hung open when she saw the corpses on the floor.

"I didn't do this! That one was already dead." Lance tried to convince her, and turned to the bedroom with desperate eyes. "And your step-dad was alive when I left him! "You saw, right? *Say* it!" Lance stepped closer to her, his gun waving around.

Her face welled up with tears and she took a step back and slammed the door, locking it almost simultaneously.

Lance knocked on the door, and then his attention turned back to me. He must have had a good memory because he seemed to notice something odd in my posture on the floor. I hadn't the time to adjust properly.

With his eyes fixed on me, he took a step forward and spoke, "Did *you* see what happened?"

He pulled the trigger, sending the bullet out the short barrel of the gun and into my chest.

I almost felt that.

Lance aimed the gun at my face and his finger twitched at the trigger.

I had to do something. I stared at the gun intently, seeing it up close. I felt as if I were an unseen fog, surrounding the pistol on all sides; it felt as real as if I had reached out and grabbed it with living hands, and with the smallest suggestion from me, the weapon slapped out from Lance's hand, landing on the floor nearby.

"What the…" He jumped back, breaking some bottles, sending a can rattling across the floor. He stared at his empty hand and his face displayed the fearful amazement which sent his heart racing.

I was surprised by the unimaginable power I had just discovered inside me. It took a moderate effort, and I was not completely sure how I had achieved such a telekinetic feat, but the possibilities were alluring.

I tried to strike Lance's face in a similar fashion, to knock him out, but I could not repeat the stunt, failing to feel his face as I had felt the gun, or the other objects in the room.

Lance pounded on the closed door, calling to the girl inside.

"Get out here! You're mine!" Lance walked over to retrieve his gun.

My mind raced as I tried to produce another reaction; and then focusing on the gun, inches from reentering Lance's grasp, the weapon slid across the floor as if it had been kicked.

How did I do that? I wondered, motionless on the floor.

Lance stared, wide-eyed, as the revolver careened to the furthest wall.

I quickly focused on the exit door, and with some effort, riled it into frenzy, rattling the hinges, causing heavy thuds when it shook inside the frame. The door sounded as if an enraged person attempted to break his way through.

Lance wasted no time running to the back of the room, where the opened window breathed fresh air. He quickly hunched through the opening and ran down the fire escape.

The door ceased its wild quaking, and without a limb to aid me, I rose to my feet. I had to leave, to go find answers, to think things over. I turned to the exit; beside the door, propped against the wall, was the unique octopus cane of Lance's. I took it with me.

Returning to the room that I woke in, at the end of the hallway, I searched through the mess on the floor. Books, magazines, and clothes…nothing useful. Nothing with a name to tell me who I was. I walked to the desk and sifted through piles of papers and photographs. My senseless, dead hand struck the keyboard, waking the computer from hibernation.

It was online with a message on the screen:

09/06 08:09pm – Olyvia138 – I'm on my way over. Don't go too far.

I don't know why, but I replied to the message, perhaps a little late. With clumsy, stiff and numb fingers, I typed:

09/09 11:55pm – dntfrchld6 – See you soon.

It had been three days since the latest message. *What happened?*
I turned my attention back to the desk and the photos thereon. I did not recognize any of the faces or places. Most of the pictures were taken on the streets, outside shops, and in parks. One photo, under the keyboard, was of me and some young woman standing on a sidewalk. I looked noticeably different...alive, but unmistakably the same body as mine. The woman next to me had blond curls and a huge smile. My arm reached around her black dress, my hand rested on her hip. We looked happy. Behind us, a yellow car awaited with a door opened. On top of the roof, a small sign read Taxxxi Cabs.
I turned the picture over. D&O was written with a marker.
'O' for Olyvia? I wondered. *Am I 'D'?*
A chime rang out from the computer. On the screen was a new message:

09/09 12:01am – Olyvia138 – who is this?

I thought about the answer for awhile. Another message came:

09/09 12:01am – Olyvia138 – hello?

Awkwardly, I typed:

09/09 12:02am – dntfrchld – I don't know

There has to be something in this room. I rationalized. *An I.D., wallet, anything!*
Papers fell from the desk and loose change clinked to the hard floor as I swiped my arms across the desk desperately.
I uncovered a pad of paper with scribbled coordinates on it.

1. e4   e5
2. f4   exf4
3. Nf3   d6
4. d4   Bg4
5. Bc4   g5

It went on and on for pages. Wedged between two of the sheets was a Polaroid photo. On the small, glossy print was picture of me and a bearded man at a chess table. We were both looking down at the board and disregarded the camera. We were inside a dimly lit room somewhere with finished wooden floors. I could not see any details.

I looked at the back of the picture, but there were no markings.

I felt a familiarity, a hint of some truth. I looked at the notes again and reexamined the picture. I had apparently played chess before I changed into whatever I had become. I was pleased at the clue I had stumbled onto. Finally, some sense of self, and of a past. It was a speck of light in my darkened mind.

I took the chess photo and the one with me and the young blonde.

I wanted to leave, to go find more about myself. I did not want to linger and risk another encounter, another murder, not before I understood what was happening to me.

I would need to cover up my grotesque appearance; my darkened veins were easily visible in contrast to my white skin. I picked up a wrinkled green shirt from the floor and slipped it over my head with stiff, blundering arms.

In the corner of the room, beside the mattress, a long, black coat, with a high collar, was lying in a pile. I picked it up, revealing beneath it, a long copper wire coiled on both ends. Traces of blood and flesh were dried to it. It seemed I was murdered, there in my bed, yet I was unsure if the killer had succeeded or not.

I slipped my arms into the sleeves of the jacket. It fell to my knees and the collar, when snapped up, concealed the nasty mark on my throat; I could not let that be exposed, nor any horrible feature. My eyes were unquestionably hideous, locked in a final, deadly gaze. Thankfully, a pair of sunglasses set atop a pile of books, did a decent job of hiding my festered stare. Taking the silver octopus cane with me, I exited the room, with all intentions of returning later for more answers.

The stairwell at the end of the hallway seemed a wiser option than the elevator. I extended my arm to push the handle, when unexpectedly, it clicked and swung open; it took me a moment to realize that I had opened the door. I felt the cool, metal handle with my mind whereas my dead, numb hands would not have. I would need to learn new ways to do old things.

I circled down three flights of stairs. My footsteps were so silent that my own heightened perception barely heard them scratching the concrete surface. An emergency door awaited me at the end of the stairwell. I escaped through the one-way door, into the deepening night, to discover what dark secrets the new world would expose.

Chapter 2 – No Aid for Southey

Robert Southey was a vampire hunter. He was fifty-three, but appeared much older. His shoulder-length hair was once bright as the sun, but years of stress had faded it slightly, and thinned it, revealing his spotty scalp through the wisps atop his head. He was lanky and stood over six feet tall, when he wore his brown, beaten steel-toed boots – the same trusty pair he had been toting for many years.

Robert Southey cracked his knuckles, pressing his fists against the wall in front of him. Smoke streamed down from his nostrils, his eyes were red and dry from many sleepless nights.

'Southey,' as his friends referred to him, was both a causer and a consequence of tragedy, and it was evident in the nasty and nefarious ways he would speak and act when stressed or pushed hard enough. His reputation as an easily angered codger, cited as being both delusional and dangerous, served to keep people from bothering him. He had a nasty quirk – when insulted or angered by someone, he would grin maliciously, displaying a wide, toothless gap in his yellow smile, and spit at their feet through his few missing teeth. When he spoke, phlegm and tar in his throat often chopped up his words.

Southey, especially in his later days, had an intimidating look to him, making it hard for him to gain people's trust. Scars scattered across the left side of his face were a fresh reminder from an incident just days before; unsightly cuts on his left ear, cheek, and chin had just recently started to scab over, but the skin was still pink and inflamed. Another wound, between his neck and shoulder, had healed into a small discolored lump; being a swollen, bulbous mass, it usually stole the attention of those who spoke with him.

From a large basement beneath an apartment complex he owned, a place he casually referred to as 'headquarters,' Southey led small bands of men, including his sons, on vampire hunts in the city. But it didn't always used to be that way; Robert Southey was once the city's police commissioner, but that was another life now, it seemed to him.

Southey stood in the large basement, staring at the concrete wall in front of him, on which, a large, wide satellite image of the city hung behind a thin sheet of damaged glass; a large, web-like crack was on the left side, and tiny bits of glass still remained where they had fallen free from the broken frame. In the overhead photograph of the city, roads and buildings were all clearly distinguishable, and if he pressed his nose to the map, tiny cars, and tinier people, frozen in that moment, were easily seen.

Dozens of small, round stickers formed two distinct clusters on the map. The eastern, and smallest cluster, was at the edge of a bay, between an airport and industrial park, not far from his apartments. The larger gathering of stickers was scattered along a series of roads, in the city's poorer, south-western side. On the northern rim of the map, the city's perimeter pressed along a thick forest.

Immediately behind Southey was a wide, metal desk where he planned his many searches and hunts. Speckled chips of old grey paint dominated the desk's heavily scratched and dented surface. Many small notepads, filled with names and addresses, were scattered atop the desk, amongst a glut of newspaper sections. A pile of drawings was in the center; the top sketch depicted some trees. An opened cigar box, in one corner of the desk, contained a silver butane lighter, dabbed with bloody fingerprints. Southey picked up a wristwatch that was buried on the desk; he groaned impatiently when he saw the time.

More than ten feet underground, there were no windows to let daylight in the basement, or through which to grant spying eyes a peek inside. A cold, concrete floor, speckled with cracks, swelled from many years of the settling foundation. Netted with large pipes, wires, and hanging fluorescent lights, the ceiling was high enough that Southey could not reach the choking layers of cobwebs. A few of the light bulbs were shattered, and occasionally, a working one flickered on and off.

The groans of generators and boilers sounded through an opened door to one side of him; 'Boiler Room' was labeled on that wall. On his other side was a smaller, arched door, made of heavy wood; on it, was a tiny circular window, through which a narrow and dark hallway could be seen.

Standing idly, far across the basement, were four men – three of which were much younger than Southey, being in their mid-twenties. One of those young men was Southey's only remaining of two sons, Jacob. The young men played cards as they sat on top of large, cracked wooden boxes and crates, stacked near a corner.

The older gent, Samuel Taylor, had been a hunting partner of Southey's for about ten years, but a friend for much longer. A graying man in his mid-sixties, Sam had a full head of salt-and-pepper hair, tied back in a small ponytail with a rubber band. Covering much of his mouth was a dark grey, bushy mustache, which he habitually stroked when thinking. Sam, a grandfatherly type of man, spoke softly – a sharp contrast to his partner – and interjected opinions sparingly.

Though he grew up on the streets, Sam had stayed clean and reliable, and was smart, though without a formal education. Charismatic, Sam was trusted by those who knew him. Through his experience on the streets, he knew the meeting spots, routines and evasive trickery – basically, the ins and outs – used by the criminal world. Sam's kindness extended toward even the unsavory criminal cliques, and as a result, he merited a long list of favors owed to him by the unruly patrons of the underground.

In another day, when Southey had been the city's police commissioner, he often tapped into Sam as an inside source of information, cashing in on his street-smarts to add momentum to his career; however word spread fast, and Sam lost his edge as a source of valid information when his criminal acquaintances became privy to his alliance with the commissioner.

When a heartbreaking tragedy turned Southey's world upside down, his eyes were opened to an unseen evil, and he focused in on a new obsession – vampires. All those years investigating crime in the defecated alleys and corroded sects of the city offered glimpses of the unexplainable. Cadavers sometimes disappeared from crime scenes without a trace. Missing persons, who had been declared legally dead, were reportedly seen walking around at night, as if in a trance, ignoring the calls and pleas of acquaintances. Sometimes, the corpses of missing persons surfaced, but only raised more questions: How could someone be dead for so long, and have such an abnormally low amount of decomposition? How come the corpses had injuries which were made postmortem? – There was no bleeding or healing in any of their wounds. Sometimes, the corpses had been administered make-up long after they had died, and others had undergone bizarre reparations. Oddly enough, when these corpses were found, it was usually face down in random streets and alleyways, not with some macabre collection in some lunatic's apartment.

At first it was rumored among police that some sordid serial killer was collecting bodies, playing doctor and dress-up with them, leaving them to be discovered. But every once in a while, a credible source, a clean citizen with a solid record, would testify something that just tilted the scales away from this serial killer theory and into the supernatural.

Now, Southey was a stubborn man, and saw things out to the end. As soon as he realized there were monsters that dwelt within the shadows, he used his resources, sending police guns-blazing after these creatures. Unfortunately for Southey's reputation, many street cops were killed by 'unseen aggressors,' producing no concrete proof to validate his claims. As far as the public was concerned, he had cracked, being overstressed from his recent tragedy. He was soon expelled from his seat as the city's police commissioner.

This setback did not hinder his ambitions, and determined to pursue the mysterious creatures he knew so little about, Southey purchased a small lot, where he built a few low-rent apartments, providing the funding for his continued pursuit of vampires.

Samuel Taylor paced near the footing of a narrow metal staircase. It climbed up to the only exit – a heavy steel door which led to the street, above ground. Under the canopy of the stairs, two large German shepherds slept silently in the shadow.

Reaching into the wooden cigar box, Southey removed the silver, rectangular lighter, and then opened a desk drawer, retrieving a fresh cigar from within. He lit it, holding in his first puff with satisfaction.

A muffled knocking hardly shook the heavy, metal door, and everyone except Southey turned to face the exit. Samuel, immediately making his way up the stairs toward the door, assured the two roused dogs that they needn't be concerned. He opened the door with a long, heavy screech.

A short, thin man, in a dark grey Armani suit, and a fresh haircut, waited on the other side.

"Hello Mr. Taylor," he said respectfully as he peered past Sam and down the stairs at the younger men. He clenched a briefcase in his left hand; a small, ruby ring glimmered on his middle finger, even in the dim, smoky room.

Sam nodded at the arriver, and turned back, leading the guest down the stairway, and into the basement.

Approaching the large metal desk in the back of the room meant cutting through a thick fog of cigar smoke, which created a swirling grey wake. The suited man coughed and fanned his hand in front of him, as if he would find a breath of fresh air.

Robert Southey clasped his wrists behind his back, continued to stare at the map, and awaited the words of his guest as he puffed furiously on his cigar.

"Robert," he sounded almost fed-up, "I got your message, and for some darn reason I figured I would hear what you had to say."

The well-dressed man sat in a wooden chair in front of the desk. He laid his briefcase on his lap and opened it. The initials A.P. glimmered in gold lettering from the top of the lid. Removing a small battery-operated fan from inside, he began to ventilate the air around him.

Still facing away, Southey said, "Well, Arnold…"

"Uh, Commissioner Paul, please...I'm on duty." He sneered.

"Well...it is *very* fortunate for me and perhaps for you too, that you have come." Southey turned and smiled, intentionally tilting the scarred side of his face towards the man. "It is getting worse out there." Southey pointed to his tattered cheek. "There aren't many left, but they are strong, and dangerous, and it is time you acknowledge the truth."

"What the *hell* happened to you?" Arnold leaned forward in his chair and pointed the small fan at Southey, making for a better visibility through the smoke which poured upward from a lit cigar, tilted in a marble ashtray on the desk.

Arnold Paul was the city's latest police commissioner, and hardly over thirty years old. He was not fond of the self-proclaimed 'hunter,' and their meetings were almost always at the request of Southey, whose inability to gather the men he needed drove him to seek additional manpower to strengthen his fading band of hunters. But as it were, Arnold Paul's visits were primarily to keep an eye on the locally-infamous troublemaker, and never to humor his wild rantings.

Southey narrowed his eyes. "I had *another* unpleasant encounter cleaning up the filth you seem overly apathetic about." He picked up the cigar from the ashtray and twisted it tightly in the gap formed by the adjacent missing teeth. With the cigar poking through his grimy grin, he breathed in and let loose a wave of grey-white smoke out through his nostrils.

"Perhaps you need to take a long vacation," said Arnold condescendingly. "My men got a number of calls the other night. There was a whole lot of commotion and screaming. It seems someone vandalized Oakwood Cemetery property, knocking things over and even completely destroying an antique greenhouse. That wouldn't be *your* doing, would it?"

Southey stared forward, motionless except for the smoke falling from his flaring nostrils.

Arnold flipped through a small file he had pulled from his case. "I was a bit surprised to find out about your son, actually."

"Colin," Southey shut his eyes. "How did you know?"

"I know." Arnold adjusted his black tie. "The guys down at the crematorium told me."

"Why are those grunts calling you?" Southey yelled. "No-good rats! Why do I even pay them? I just had Colin cremated last night."

"They called me because I told them to do so whenever you *sneak* a dead body in there to be burnt. You can't just go destroying evidence like that. You have to report it. There are channels to go through."

"Would those happen to be *your* channels?" Southey asked.

Arnold raised an eyebrow.

Southey spoke, almost below his breath, "You don't even believe in this stuff anyway. Why do you care?"

"It seems that Colin had a lot of glass stuck in his body...the same type that we found shattered all over that cemetery," Arnold Paul continued.

"I know it seems I have been a bit on edge recently, but things have slowed down. They're out there, I just...I have to follow any leads with extreme..."

"There are no *leads*...just your crazy theories. Keep your violent games out of my city! This is your final warning!" The commissioner looked over his shoulder at the four men who listened from across the basement. "You're all lucky I have got my hands full with relevant things, or I'd have you all..."

Southey interrupted, as if not to acknowledge the threat. "I have stumbled onto the whereabouts of a certain legend. Something even a skeptic like you must acknowledge." Southey paced behind the desk waiting for a reply; however, Arnold sat silently. "The missing men, in the woods?" He clarified, halting his pace.

More silence followed.

Southey, agitated at the dispassion of his guest, plucked the cigar from his teeth throwing it onto the cement floor, with a small, volcanic-like burst that scattered like fireflies. Loose scraps of tobacco hung from the cracks of his teeth which he attempted to spit out onto the floor before him.

"Say *something*!" he yelled. Saliva, darkened from the cigar, made its way onto the desk through the hole in his angry smirk.

Arnold stared with a blank expression.

Both hands resting on the desk, Southey's body was hunched over it; he looked strained and overtired, as if he were about to collapse.

Arnold shook his head. Breaking the silence, he explained, "Authorities have investigated those missing-persons cases many many times, and not once found a single shred of proof. Not a single corpse, scrap of clothing or drop of blood was ever recovered from those woods. Know why? Because it's a ghost story, an urban legend, something every kid in this town has had a nightmare about. The only evidence on file is the poorly written statements of terrified eye-witnesses of our so-called *witch*. Besides, I don't believe there has been an incident there for a long time now."

"Nothing *reported*." Southey snapped.

Arnold extended his arm, offering Southey the police reports and photographs which were bound in a neat file. He refused them and stood silently, his jaw moving in an unnatural manner.

This was the game they played. One of them would present data and the other would deny it. It had been going on for well over a year, ever since Southey first tried to persuade the newly elected commissioner to aid him with police power. Southey was determined to tap any resource necessary to find the vampires.

Arnold Paul would never bat an eye at Southey's testimonies, although he seemed to humor him with the occasional question. Because of this, and the fact that Arnold continued to visit, Southey suspected his accounts were given plausibility; however, Arnold was consistently doubtful and lucid.

"People disappear every day, Robert. There are a lot of questions I would like to be answered as well, but your personal mission continues to result in the deaths of innocent people...this time, it was your disillusioned son, Colin."

"I don't lie to my sons, you damned..." Southey pounded his fists on the hard, metal desk.

"My job is to protect the innocent. You *used* to keep your activities pretty quiet, but in the last few months, you've destroyed public property, risked innocent lives, carried guns around in public...like you are *above* the law." Arnold pointed his finger at Southey, "Well, you're *not*. You had better take it easy."

Arnold put the file back in his briefcase.

Southey began to beg, something very uncharacteristic of him. "Come with me just this once. You never have before, and if you do, I *promise* I will never ask you again. This won't be even close to the city, and you will not be disappointed." Southey was screaming on the inside, but spoke softly and respectfully. He hated humility. "Once you see it for yourself you'll..."

"I am a busy man, Robert." Arnold shook his head.

"If I fail to produce evidence, I will resign." Southey knew this was a blatant lie.

"No!"

"Then send some of those rookie street cops with me. They don't have to be in uniform. I need men and I am sure those bored blue-collars are aching for more action than petty misdemeanors." Southey's voice had grown aggressive again.

"I cannot do that. We'd need proof, and quite frankly, a ghost story is not proof."

"You've seen some of the vampires I've taken down." Southey's voice darkened with impatience.

"Yes...bodies torn apart by bullets and knives. The only thing tying those mangled corpses to vampires is your word, which is not as credible as you think." Arnold smiled.

"And the fangs?"

"They aren't that long, or sharp. Quite a few people have teeth like that...It's all genetic."

Southey turned and looked at the small, arched wooden door in the corner of the room – with the tiny, round window. He wanted to take Arnold Paul down that hall and show him the secret contained within, to show him the proof he needed, but Southey did not want to risk getting himself into trouble. He did not know how Arnold would react; the commissioner could end Southey's exploits at the drop of a hat. Southey would not risk losing, what might be, his greatest hunting opportunity to date.

Southey looked back to his guest. "What about that murder in my building over there – Mr. Preston? Your men were pretty hush-hush about it."

"What about it?"

"That was no typical murder! I'm not *stupid*. You were so interested in that incident, that you came down to check it out yourself. Why? Confused at what you found?"

With both hands, Southey leaned onto the desk, looking down at the smoldering cigar, breathing in the smoke that rose from the floor.

Arnold shrugged his shoulders. "Charles Preston was a drunkard who sold his physically abused step-daughter to that reprobate pimp Lance, in exchange for rent money. Besides, my men talked to Charles' daughter, and her testimony suggests that Lance played a role in it."

"That's bull!" Southey's voice was sharp and echoed throughout the cellar.

"Miss Preston's story had holes in it, sure, but what can you expect from someone who has been physically and mentally abused for years. Besides, Lance is a man with a shady past. I wouldn't put first-degree murder past him. The greedy lout probably killed Charles so he could keep his money. Robert, there are a lot of sick things done..."

"Shut up!" Southey interrupted.

"...done to people that is much worse than this. I have seen some crazy stuff and every time we followed the trails, some perverted human was responsible." Arnold paused and sneered. "There is a whole subculture of real people who dress up like vampires, you know that right?"

Southey rolled his eyes, insulted at the continued condescending tones from a younger man.

"Not only that!" Arnold sat up. With a big grin, he seemed to be holding back laughter. "These people pretend to be vampires and have fangs, even! Dentists can do that kind of thing nowadays. If crazy people go biting someone, am I supposed to assume it's some *monster* and not some psycho?"

Southey lowered his brow, "So you are saying he *was* bitten?"

Arnold snickered, "No, I'm just *saying*..."

Arnold sighed and shut his briefcase slowly, shifting his weight in the chair. "As for Lance, our purveyor of young girls, whom I am certain has run *far* from the crime scene...," he paused and looked into Southey's shifty eyes, trying to pick up any hint of deception. "...until we find him and question him ourselves, and assuming he can shed some different light on the subject, *he* will remain our primary suspect."

Arnold Paul stood up and sighed. "I know Lance has been around here...since then."

Southey raised his arms and shrugged. "Hey, so my tenants are a lonely bunch. They have needs, Lance provides it. I'm not their babysitter! They can buzz in to the buildings whoever they want, so long as my apartments don't burn down, what do I care?"

"Don't let me find out you know where Lance is. That's all." Arnold stared at Southey, who ignored the stern glance.

"Are you done now?" Southey snarled, looking over Arnold.

Southey, with his hands on his desk, lowered his head, gazing at Arnold from under a weathered and sweaty brow. As if he were trying to convince Arnold that he wasn't insane, Southey spoke calmly and softly, "I know that you must have seen them before. Maybe not too often, but you have. I have been investigating these phenomena since you were a hairless, prepubescent brat! There are a lot of unexplained disappearances and murders in this hole-of-a-town. If you did not grant me even one ounce of credibility, you would have stopped me by now. I know you *want* to."

Southey walked around the desk, next to Arnold, and spoke to his side; his chapped lips were just inches from Arnold's ear. "I have been in your shoes before. You've got nothing I haven't already tasted. I know you are keeping secrets, because you are a bad liar. However, I deal with problems you don't want to acknowledge, so you let me and my men suffer on our own."

Southey walked back to his desk, and pulled out a fresh wooden box of Cuban cigars from a drawer. His shaky hands worked for a few seconds to get the hinged flip-top lid open on his favorite Zippo lighter.

"Robert," Arnold paused long before continuing. "I know what is real and what is not. I have lived here my whole life too, so do not think my view on this is any less valid than yours. There are things which cannot be derived logically, that exist quietly outside the realm of acceptable science. What we are, no, you're dealing with here, and have been for some time, are self-containing problems. The bizarre events we read about in the papers have just enough substance to make the front page of the Enquirer. Whatever is going on remains quiet enough that no one of importance seems too concerned. When your primary set of witnesses consists of burn-outs, prostitutes, pimps, dealers and a plethora of unsavory folk, you find it hard to convince higher-ups to look beyond statistics. I can not send tax-paid officers on a ghost hunt... and *keep* my job."

Arnold raised an eyebrow at him. He usually made an effort not to bring up Southey's past as commissioner. He then glared at Southey with all the intimidation a small-framed, 'pretty boy,' like himself could muster.

"You see, Robert, the only time things *really* seem to get messy in this city, is when your little posse of bored, pissed-off delinquents go poking around in the shadows, looking for things that may very well best be left alone. I haven't totally disregarded your map on the wall there, and your lists of the dead and missing, but when I step back and look at the greater picture, I see a situation that is not increasing in severity."

"...because of my hard work!" Southey interjected.

Arnold continued, "It is like a snake eating its own tail, spinning on the dirt creating a small and insignificant cloud of dust that just may settle on its own if you would only give it the time."

Arnold took a breath, feeling light-headed. The smoky atmosphere was getting to him. Walking back towards the exit door, he stopped half way, looked back at Southey who stared angrily, and continued, "Being a father myself, I am sorry about your son, Colin. But you shouldn't have been messing around in that cemetery. I'd advise you to stop this futile mission, stop funding this little monster club of yours, and put some money back into your festering apartments. Your tenants are disgruntled because you have let those buildings erode to the point that anyone, like Lance, can get in and cause trouble. I think you may be causing more problems than you think you are solving." He looked up at the flickering light above his head. "I would hate to have this place condemned."

Arnold continued toward the stairs, climbing up to the steel door, and then he looked back. "Always a pleasure, Robert," he said and left.

Southey was frantically pacing, mumbling to himself loudly.

"That bastard!" exclaimed Southey. "He looked me right in the eye and fed me that pile of crap!"

Southey walked up to one of the younger men, putting his hand on his shoulder.

"You want to avenge your brother..." Southey patted his son, continuing, "...don't you, Jacob?"

"Yes sir," the younger man replied.

Jacob was lanky like his father, and had a full head of radiant yellow curls. His right eye was scarred, the pupil paled-over. White bandaging wrapped around his left and right arms, from his wrists to his shoulders, a token from the cemetery incident the day before.

"You bet you do." Southey raised his voice, speaking to the other two young men. "We are going to the top of the food chain on this one. I hope you all like the woods."

Southey pointed to Samuel, whose fingers combed through his mustache nervously. "Sam, load us up. One gun per person, as usual. We'll need the night vision, thermals, flashlights...the works."

Sam nodded and walked to a corner of the basement behind him, where shelves had been built into the concrete walls. Shotguns, long blades, and high-tech gadgets, all were fastened to the shelves by small leather straps and buckles.

Southey walked back towards the desk, sat down, and sucked on his cigar.

The small, arched wooden door in the corner opened up, and a short "gypsy" type woman came out and stood beside him. Her long grey hair was gathered in a tidy braid, with a string of beads and stones woven in, tying it back. Her loose and flowing charcoal colored dress, varied in texture, creating a series of intricate shapes, and a small brown satchel hung from her hip.

"We will be ok, even without the commissioner's help." Her voice was like a young girl's – anomalous to her older exterior. "We don't want police involved with us anyway...not with what we're about to do. They'd interfere with our project. Now that I'm here, you don't need lots of men. Just find that cabin, and look for the northern path. The witch in the woods is there. I promise!"

Chapter 3 – The First Night

When I stepped out from the apartment, I wanted to run away and ponder my lurid dilemma without distraction, to be in solitude until I recalled some memory, some sense of logic; that was the wisest choice, I thought, even if only a temporary solution to the madness. I felt any choice I made would be irrational. Nothing made sense, so how could I trust the soundness of any decision?

My thoughts were haunted by the man I had just killed; that repulsive, foul man is bound to cause a ruckus upon discovery – What drove me to such a ferocious, inhuman act? It seemed safe to assume I was in danger, should I linger there; my appearance would not escape the suspicious eyes of even the most unobservant, or intoxicated onlooker. If I wanted to return to that room in which I wakened, to search for more clues as to my identity, I would have to do so some other night. My only option was to flee, but I had nowhere to go…I did not know where I was.

Had I found, on the other side of that exit door, a vast expanse of grassy hills, or a throng of trees to hide amongst, I would have escaped into the placidity of nature to derive some course of action. I was not that fortunate.

Just outside the exit, sirens wailed high above the ambiance of distant cars' and trucks' humming. A piercing tone, a maddening electrical shriek, emanated down at me from nearby lighting, perched high upon poles.

A thick canopy of dark-grey sky extinguished all starlight. Rainfall was not far away; I felt the weight of a damp atmosphere around me, and air currents of an impending storm flowed near me, through me.

I stood still, and let my mind drift away from my body, gazing at my surroundings with eyes liberated from their cell of flesh – a perpetual out-of-body experience. When my psyche wafted like a free spirit, I occasionally found myself staring at my own deathly body, perceiving myself from many vantage points. That sickly-toned corpse of mine seemed more and more foreign to me, the more I got acquainted with it; for it seemed more like an anchor tied to my mind, instead of a vessel containing it.

Not far from the emergency exit, railroad tracks stretched past the building, and on the furthest side of the tracks, running adjacent to them, stretched a wide, industrial road. Beyond that road was a large paved lot, enclosed by a tall barbed fence. Inside the perimeter, a short, but very wide building was lined with dozens of sequentially numbered truck docks; many unattached truck trailers were parked outside the garage-type doors.

Massive lights illuminating the wide lot, and the adjacent road, exuded an intense electric buzz which I found most unpleasant. I was lost, helpless, and at the mercy of circumstance – trapped inside a bright, metallic wasteland. I wanted to run, but where to? A virtual labyrinth of walls, fences, and high-tension power lines, made it impossible to run far in any one direction. All around, the hum of electricity and machinery filled the air. Compelled to avoid the powerful electric buzzing, I turned to the dimmer block of buildings behind me.

The dark, red bricks of the three-story apartment I had exited were cracked and worn with age. A crooked, fire escape, many of its supports rusted through, looked as if it would fall one day soon. Layers of graffiti painted the lower wall with a slew of expletives, and strange symbols. Tenants standing in many of the curtainless windows were unaware of my ghostly eyes watching them from inches behind the grimy windows; they did not notice my body standing dozens of feet below, along the building's perimeter.

To one side, another similar-looking apartment stood close by; their two facing walls were cramped together, and a narrow one-lane road cut through the alley formed by the neighboring buildings.

On my other side was a dead-end street, laden with cracks and potholes. I stood at its end, where a metal guardrail severed the lone residential road from that wide, well-lit, main road, preventing traffic from crossing the railroad tracks to reach the other side. Faded and broken streetlights did a poorer job illuminating the dead-end road, as opposed to many of the surrounding blocks.

I walked from the emergency exit, followed the sidewalk along the road away from the guardrail, and headed past the main doors to my purported apartment. A tarnished metal sign embedded into the brick wall of the building read: Redbank Apartments, #2.

On the opposite side from where I exited was a small parking lot. Trash bags spilled onto the pavement, from inside an overloaded dumpster; litter escaped through tears in the plastic sacks. A half-dozen cars were parked there, and from inside one of the vehicles, a black utility van, I saw the spark of a flame, and an older man's face glowing softly from behind a smoldering cigar. Since his van faced opposite me, he did not see me creeping by.

I continued along the sidewalk, on edge of the shadows, tapping the cane I had acquired to justify the dark glasses I wore, as well as my awkward gait. Walking around felt much like gliding; though my legs were moving, I could hardly hear my feet hitting the pavement, and I did not feel them contacting the earth. There was no weight in my steps. The surroundings drifted past me; I watched them come and go simultaneously, with my new widened vision.

Further down the sidewalk, past the parking lot, was the third of three buildings on the small block; similar in appearance as its two neighboring apartments, it had one small difference – on the side facing the parking lot, near the occupied black van, was a large, metal door...perhaps similar looking to the kind found on a bomb shelter.

Some type of basement, I thought, and was about to curiously peek my eyes through the walls, when a black and yellow cab turned onto the dead-end road. When the vehicle slowed outside the front doors of that apartment, its headlights lit me up, and I halted my step.

The sign atop the vehicle read, 'Taxxxi Cabs.' I thought of the photo I had put in my coat pocket – the picture of me...alive...and a young woman with golden locks. I reached into the inner pocket, and when my numb hand clenched the photo inside, I removed it, only to find something else in my pale, clammy grasp. A small worn out notebook, with the dimensions of a deck of cards, was missing its cardboard cover, and strips of white lined paper were tangled in the spiraled rings where dozens of pages had been torn out.

On the first tiny page was penciled handwriting:

March 5 - 1:01am
I promised myself I'd write my thoughts down. Clear my head. I haven't felt right in so long I wonder if I ever felt right at all. Maybe I was just delusional. Or maybe I just forgot how to be optimistic. Could my frame of mind alone have changed the whole world? Oh well...it's just a phase...I will eventually die, after all.

I flipped through the notebook; there were at least fifty pages, each with entries ranging from a few words, to a few dozen. I looked at the photograph of that girl and me; I was wearing the same jacket. This little book had to have belonged to me. I had found something useful...a journal of scattered thoughts, perhaps things which would shed light on who I am, how I came to be this creature...answers I may never recall on my own.

The taxi's engine rattled idly, and then the backdoor opened.

A full-figured young woman emerged; her provocative attire advertised her profession. Her fishnet stockings accentuated the curves of her legs. The wide, platform heels of her black patent leather, knee-high boots, clopped along the pavement like a horse's hooves. Her hips swayed when she walked, and her black hair, bound into a long braid, swung like a pendulum across the small of her back. She wore a short dark-red vinyl skirt with a matching corset that laced up and down the entire length of her back. The interlacing of the corset was tied as such to reveal a tattoo of a long, slender, dragon; the narrow, pointed tail started at the small of her back, climbed up her spine, and curved into a figure-eight at her shoulder blades, with the dragon's head facing up the back of her neck. The black and red tattoo was a stark contrast to her fair skin.

She glanced at my presence, a few yards down the walk, but paid little attention before strutting up small cement steps to the building's front door, beside which, a metal plate read: Redbank Apartments, #1. She rang a buzzer outside the door and waited, stroking her long braid, and glancing at me peripherally.

I looked at the picture again, her and I, standing beside a Taxxxi Cab.

Had I frequented the services of a call girl? I wondered.

The cab in that picture did not prove she was a hooker…it could have been merely a backdrop. But based on the cute blonde's comparable attire to the woman I had just watched exit this cab, I assumed the worst.

The cabbie waited until the dark-haired seductress entered the building, and then leaned his head out of the driver's window, staring at me with a raised eyebrow. He kept looking down, at my feet, or perhaps my legs. I sensed his suspicion.

"Hey, you need a lift?" he asked.

The cab driver was broad-shouldered and muscular with a thick neck and large jaw, yet clean-shaven, donning a black suit and shirt, with a solid white tie. The gun in the holster beneath his right arm was exposed intentionally, perhaps to inhibit any desperate ideas he thought a guy looking like I did, in this part of town, might have. On the top of his left hand were four tattoos of a large animal's claws – one on each knuckle.

"Yes," I mumbled, accepting his offer without hesitation. He could take me somewhere, I hoped.

The driver reached back and slapped the rear door with his hand.

Aware of the intense scrutiny I was under, I avoided looking directly at him for fear of accelerating the inhibitions I sensed he felt. If he saw, more clearly, my death mask, he would be logical to mind his own business and leave me to wander the streets alone. As it were, shadows veiled my gruesome exterior where sunglasses and a high-collared jacket would have fallen short of sufficient.

The inside of the Taxxxi Cab was clean and accommodating. Ashtrays, cup holders, rear ventilation, leather seating. A small television slanted down from the ceiling. It was almost luxurious, but for a mesh fence dividing the front from the rear; the metal grating hadn't enough space between the links to put a finger through. It ran lengthwise to the floor – a little insurance against some unruly clientele, it seemed.

On the dashboard up front, a small screen displayed a roadmap with a blinking dot in its center. A clock read 12:39 am, and below that, a meter read $2.50.

The driver talked into a speaker phone, "I made the drop at Redbank, but I don't see him anywhere. You *sure* he was going to be here?"

The voice on the other line crackled, "Maybe he got caught-up. I'm sure he'll call when he's ready. Just head back, I guess."

"I'm giving a lift to somebody. I'll be there after."

"Okay."

The driver put the car into gear, and pulled forward, turning left into the small parking lot nestled between Redbank #1 and #2. As he passed the parked black van, I glanced at the hideous man idle in the front seat. He was a tall, lanky man with stringy long blonde hair. With narrowed eyes, the thin, grimy man turned his head, and through the smoky cabin, watched our cab drift by.

The cab turned right, after the small parking lot, and onto the narrow one lane road running between the place I wakened, Redbank #2, and the adjacent building, which I assumed was Redbank #3. After the short alley, the cab crossed train tracks, and merged left onto the wide, main industrial road with the intensely bright lights.

I placed the small notebook on my lap; I did not need to tilt my head down to read the handwriting on the pages, and I continued to stare forward as my ghost-eyes studied the journal entries.

March 6 - 11:05pm

Today I sat at my computer all day, facing the screen, the only window with anything promising on the other side. I need to get out more. Do things. But there's nothing out there for me. When I do leave my dirty hole, I'm driven to return. If it weren't so cold outside, I'd go to Bayview, set up my pieces, and wait for a challenger. Only a few months until it warms up. Maybe I'll head over to Crouse, see Jeremy, and learn some openings. Maybe not.

I continued to read as the Taxxxi Cab drove past factories.

Soaring smokestacks disgorged a black miasma against the solid grey sky. Other similar structures were scattered everywhere, forming layer after layer of disheartening metallic waste. Choked by the grimy, industrial infestation that stripped the landscape of anything earthly and good, the only traces of life grew from nooks and cracks of the neglected streets and sidewalks.

Many pages in the notebook had been removed. The next entry read:

March 15 - 9:33 am
I'll need a job soon. Being a nobody who does nothing costs a lot more than it should. A job...a job...a job...which of my values will I compromise for a buck. Wear this, say that, be this...F-that. My soul is not for sale. I will go buy a scratch ticket, and when I don't win, at least I won't be disappointed.

The driver had waited for my order, but I was rapt in the written words of a former me.

He spoke up. "So, where am I taking you tonight?"

His tone was rather friendly, but his head leaned a bit out his window and he took large, infrequent breaths.

Do I smell? I thought about it, realizing then that I could not detect any odors, good or bad. I failed in my attempt to pull air in through my nose and throat. My lungs were dead, like me.

"Hopefully, somewhere nicer than this." I looked at passing storage facilities and garages, fields of asphalt, and forests of poles and fence.

"Yeah, I hate this part of town too," he said. "But I need a destination, Mr..uh..."

I remained silent through a long pause as I read another entry.

March 20 - 4:21pm
I said I'd write everyday...it'd be good to vent, to release what pent-up frustration I have. But I can't write every boring, asinine detail of every monotonous, depressing day. Today was a bit different, though. I woke up and said that I would go out and be like others. I will buy stuff and talk about mindless crap with people I am socially obligated to care about and maybe if I am lucky I will find a comfortable niche to dwell in...a job...a hobby...a lover...a cleverly woven delusion of self-worth. Why can't life be more like my dreams? Maybe then I could stay awake.

The driver reached up to the rearview mirror, adjusting it to get a better look at me.

"Hey, I can't just drive forever." His voice grew stern.

"Why don't you just bring me somewhere you like?" With no sense of person, or place, how could I make such a decision?

"Not from around here, huh?"

"Not anymore."

He chewed on my cryptic reply and said, "How about...the park? Bayview?"

"Go there." I snapped back. Bayview...that name was written in my journal, and in retrospect to what I had seen so far, a park sounded splendid.

The cab veered up an onramp and climbed to an elevated highway, which traced the edge of a bay, huddled inside a crescent coastline. Markers and buoys in the water blinked in the night, a sharp contrast to the black wavy mass in which they floated. On the approaching side of the bowed shoreline, a growing city skyline had curiously escaped my attention, appearing abruptly and without warning, as if some confusingly thick fog had suddenly receded. Lofty buildings stood against the grey, cloudy night sky, like kindred black slabs, punctured with many grains of light. The mural of lit windows and streetlights should have been mimicked by the waters, which the buildings loomed over, but there were no reflections there – merely a dark, watery pit.

Though my body sat motionless inside the cab, I did not feel like a passenger inside the vehicle; instead, my eyes passed through the roof, hovering above the car, moving alongside it like a kite from an ethereal perch. The soothing night wind infused my soul with an energy, both soft and mighty, which I felt all around. Some wholly real, yet intangible force, pervaded me, and I felt my dimensions broaden until I could feel the air gusting in a wide radius around the vehicle. There was a new dimension to reality which I was unable to decipher. Time seemed to speed up and slow down at my command.

What have I become? I pondered. *A vampire? A god, perhaps...or am I just a corpse?*

I was mesmerized at how alive I felt when I beheld my surroundings. I was surely independent of that deadened flesh in the cab, which seemed only a terrifying token of a past life. I wanted to cut myself free, to abandon that physical curse, and wander up into the sky. I felt as if I could have, but as I floated higher, I felt a weakening brought on by the distancing of my spirit from that listless cadaver; I was compelled to return to it.

I brought my focus back to my corpse and became, once again, that ghoulish physical creature…and a passenger in a cab. I sat still, with the journal on my lap, the cane by my side, and my sickening face staring ahead from behind a pair of sunglasses, at the driver who was uncomfortable with my presence.

March 25 - 5:30pm
I got a job at one of the nearby warehouses, but I quit after a few days. All my coworkers seemed way too happy to be ants…walking around a maze of massive aisles, stacking boxes as fast as their muscles allowed them. Doing nothing with their lives to some other man's profit. Oh well, at least I will get a small paycheck to hold me for a bit longer.

A few miles later, the cab descended an off-ramp, and turned onto a freshly repaved road, following through a downtown district. Bars and restaurants, still active after midnight, buzzed with energy from behind wide sidewalks lined with caged trees. Patrons on patios and balconies laughed and chatted amongst each others' company. Inebriated night dwellers wasted away the hours with a showcase of gossip and fancy clothes; the contents of their wallets and purses emptied into wine glasses and hors d'oeuvres.

The car turned down a ravine of tall office buildings, banks and hotels. The driver whistled a tune as he watched passing people mingle on the sidewalk. I sat silently, hidden beneath my coat and glasses, clenching the cane on my lap.

"If you don't mind me asking," the driver broke the silence after a few miles, "…are you blind, you know, with that cane and all?"

Not only was I not blind, but I could see so much clearer.

"Yes, I am."

If I wanted to keep those glasses between my lifeless stare and a city full of suspicious people, I would need an excuse.

"Sorry. I was just asking because, uh…" He turned and glanced at me, to what he thought was eye-to-eye. "You see, I noticed your cane there. I know a guy who has one just like it," he said incredulously.

"Really? And here I thought I was the only one that eccentric."

"He had his custom made, actually." He paused and then continued, sounding suspicious, "In Mexico. Where did you get yours?"

"I found it, actually, lying around."

I realized the shaky situation I had gotten into. This man knew

Lance, whom I crossed paths with earlier and scared away, the man who really owned the cane. But worse yet, suggesting that a blind man would find anything merely lying about seemed a bit of a stretch. This driver was skeptical. Luckily, he ceased asking questions, and I watched his face crinkle up as he pondered the validity of my obvious lie.

The cab pulled to the side of the road, across from a large city park. The area was well-lit, both from the flashing bulbs of a nearby movie theatre and the numerous avenue lights. Looking as horrid as I did, and realizing I was soon to step out into a bustling part of town, I grew apprehensive, wondering if my presence there would go without incident.

A show inside the cinema must have ended; dozens upon dozens of people exited the front doors of the building, letting loose a surge of footsteps and excited voices, which poured outward like a wave, dissipating down the sidewalks and streets. The passers-by, and their collected body heat, spilt forward like the gush of hot air from a furnace. Many footsteps and heartbeats shook the air; the atmosphere seemed to get cloudy from the sudden rush in energy. As the numbers of people around the cab increased, I found the details of any one individual harder to sense. Focusing more on one person meant losing sight of others, causing obscurities in my perception.

I don't know how long the driver called to me before I brought my attention back inside the vehicle, away from the busied sidewalks.

"Hey? Hey! Sixteen fifty please." The driver rolled down his window, awaiting payment.

I put the journal back into my pocket, and stepped out of the vehicle to face the large, physically intimidating man.

"I have misplaced my wallet. I am sorry. If there is anyway I can repay you..."

The driver's mouth fell open when I guiltlessly admitted the truth. I could actually feel the shift in his emotion when his annoyance escalated into anger.

He reached down under the seat and pulled a small camera from somewhere below, quickly flashing a picture.

"Tell you what," his demeanor failed to exhibit the ire I felt coursing through his body. "I know whose cane that is. Give it to me now and I might forget this ever happened."

I was not prepared to negotiate, or to confront this man. I assumed his inaction was a direct result of the potential witnesses around the cab. I reluctantly handed over the cane.

The driver tossed the cane in the passenger seat, and then looked at the camera, inspecting the photograph he had taken. He lifted his gaze to me, as if to see with his own eyes, the gruesome details of my face which the camera's flash had highlighted.

"Stay out of trouble," he snarled out the window as he sped off down the road.

I walked from the cinema towards the large park across the street. A wide, concrete sidewalk circled the block alongside a tall, cast iron fence with high-reaching spears that curved outward to prevent scaling. The fence encircled the entire recreational area, breaking only for the entrances, appearing every few dozen yards along the perimeter.

I followed the sidewalk, where it veered into the tree-filled park, beneath a tall, stone archway, from which hung a bronze plate. It read: BayView Park, est. 1979.

A large grassy lawn formed the outer edge of the park. Towards the center, a dense assemblage of scattered trees and shrubs extended outward from a large ovular marble fountain. Four different paths, which bent and veered around the larger trees, originated at the base of the fountain and reached out toward four entrances at the edges of the park.

I strolled along one of the fours paths, toward the central fountain. Most of the trees were relatively young, reaching heights of no more than ten or fifteen feet. Between the breaks in foliage, lights from the soaring towers of glass, steel and concrete reached into the park's core, reminding those, whom might have ventured there to get away from the city, that their escape was just an illusion.

All classes of denizens strolled about; many of which turned back to look at me, after our paths had crossed, paranoid at the cold, stiff figure walking slowly past them. But I kept to myself, walking strategically to avoid crossing people's paths directly, perhaps even appearing a bit more suspicious that way.

Benches lined the central paths, and many were occupied by homeless citizens in ragged clothes who held out their hands to folks who refused to even offer a pitied look in their direction. When I passed these poor, panhandlers, they held their hands to their laps and awed at me with glazed eyes buried deep into their weathered faces.

The gurgling fountain was lit by bulbs submerged in the shallow water. The underwater lights convened on the centerpiece marble structure, which depicted three small children, huddled beneath a large mushroom, which served as an umbrella as water shot from the top of the fungus, and trickled down around the rim of the cap. Each child had one of their hands on the mushroom stalk while the other reached out, allowing water to fall through their fingers.

Protruding from the shallow pool were metallic sculptures of fish positioned as if jumping in and out. Bronze and silver coins lay still beneath the surface; they refused to dance illusively beneath the rippled water. These apparent deviations in reality piqued my curiosity as I struggled to comprehend what exactly was different with the world around me, and of my interpretation of it.

I followed through to the furthest end of the park; the scattered trees gave way to a clearing where a number of small steel tables with checkered tops were set between chairs, embedded into concrete slabs in the ground. I assumed it the spot I had written of in my journal. There was no one playing chess, however, and I continued to the furthest end of the park.

A short, brick wall at the rear of the park overlooked the ocean, hence 'Bayview.' Waves crashed upon a rocky beach, below the other side of the wall. A voluminous clatter of large pebbles clacking into each other followed every receding wave as they returned to the sea.

I turned back to the park and watched people stroll-about. I couldn't help but notice who was alone and approachable. I was not hungry, but I subtly felt the onset of a deathly chill returning, not even an hour after the kill. I remembered how good it felt when I took that man's life. As disgusted and shocked as I had been initially, the reward was fantastic; the freedom from that intense, throbbing pain, the clarity of thought and awareness. The longer I focused on the possibility, the more tempting it became to embrace my nature once more. I desired that warm rush of life which I could not feel with my body alone, a coldness elusive to the rather warm autumn night.

Like a predator observing the herd for the weak and vulnerable, I focused on the motion of those all around me; I honed on the presences of men and women, on all sides, tracing their movement near and far, and with an almost omniscient set of eyes, I spied on those who could not have seen me from where they stood.

Without hesitation, I found myself silently approaching one man, near the center of the park. Leaning against a tree, and facing the fountain, a young man, with light brown hair, and a tan complexion, stood just off one of the paths. He searched through a backpack strapped over his shoulder, standing in the shadows, where I could easily hide my presence from him.

As I neared him, and focused on his warmth, and as the details of the prey became as clear as if I were the air contiguous to his flesh, the surroundings darkened, and I could only see him. His breath sounded calm and steady, like the ocean waves, and his heartbeat pulsed calmly with a muffled thud.

After lifting his hands from inside the backpack, I heard a sound which stopped me in my approach: a lively melody burst into the air, as the man began to play his flute.

I halted in my murderous crave, listening to the notes flutter through the night. The musician was skilled and his song satisfying. A soothing pleasure eased my tormented mind, and having second thoughts, I turned away, almost ashamed. I felt an inhibition and fell back into the shadows of the trees, listening to the song, hypnotized, and observing him from a short distance. The flutist's body became one with the song; his heart, breath and movements were perfectly synchronized with his music. I found it hard to differentiate the music from the musician. There was something spectacular, of which, I could not intrude upon – an energy I had to allow to flow forth.

I cannot take this man's life, I thought.

My mind raced. I tried to justify what I had wanted to do. My corpse was cooling with passing minutes. I knew how to escape that deathly chill, but I also knew I could resist for the time being. Eventually, however, the hunger would return. I did not know when, but I knew I would be maddened from the pain when it finally reared its ugly head…and then, who knew what I would do?

Then, in my confusion, amidst a swirling storm of desire and inhibition, I felt a new sensation; something cold lingered in the air around me, and I knew somewhere that there was another inhuman presence.

A tall, bald man loomed far up the path, clad in a long, black raincoat with a strap tied around the waist. I studied him, suspiciously, in his silence and coldness. With chilling blue eyes, he faced me; his strong, chiseled expression, was like a Greek statue, but aged and wrinkled. The healthy tone of his skin, and his lively gaze, made me doubt, at first, his true nature. But his presence was commanding; I could not understand why those around me had not turned to see him.

His voice interrupted my frantic thoughts, speaking into my mind. *This is not the place, or the time, to quench your thirst*, it said with deep, soft-spoken words.

"Who are you?" I asked aloud, unsure what I was dealing with.

With each fluid and silent step toward me, it became clear that his heart, like mine, was still. When he finally spoke aloud, no breath came from his lips. His lungs were too, like shriveled raisins.

"I am Arthur," he mouthed the words so meticulously that I

could have read them from his lips. But he was careful not to open them too wide; I saw the short, sharp fangs hanging from his gums behind his cold, dry lips. "I know you have questions, but it is in both our best interests to leave now."

Not waiting for my reaction, Arthur turned and walked back down one of the paths, toward the avenue from which I had entered. I adamantly followed, a short distance behind him, determined to shed some light on what has happened to me.

Direct your thoughts at me, Arthur's words rang in my mind. *I can hear them, and we are then free to discuss anything we want.*

What have I become? I tacitly replied. As we conversed, we passed citizens who did not flinch at the silent words exchanged between us.

Like me, he thought to me, *you are no longer biological, and in that regard, you are dead. But, in some ways, you are more alive than ever before.*

The sense of relief from the discovery that I was not alone, far outweighed the uneasiness I felt from his verification that I was, in fact, dead. Despite that seemingly unfortunate and grim premise of my renewed existence, I could not deny that there were strange yet remarkable enhancements.

I followed Arthur through a small alley, across the street and adjacent to the cinema. He entered a concealed area, nestled between a few buildings – a dimly lit nook, containing dumpsters and backdoors. A fire escape ran up the side of one of the hotel-looking buildings, which had on its facing side, many lit windows, a few of which, still had air conditioners perched on their sills.

Arthur halted, waiting for me to catch up. We stood in the center of the small shadowed area and faced each other.

"I have an idea what I am." I thought of the cold, numb flesh I carried around, and of that intense hunger I experienced, which I relieved by killing that man. "...but I cannot understand how."

"Understanding is a luxury, and not a requirement in life, or death." He paced around me with mannerisms colorful and lively; and when he spoke, his lips shaped to each word carefully. "I imagine that you haven't got a clue *who* you were before this?"

"Not really," I touched the outside of my coat, behind which, a pocket held the small journal and the pictures I had taken from my apartment. "Just some notes and pictures."

"Well," Arthur continued, "the pressing issue is not in the past, but in the present. You are no longer organic...no longer a metabolizing, growing, reproducing member of the faunal kingdom. You are a spirit, a soul...and that corpse tied to you is merely incidental…a vehicle." Arthur knocked on my stiff flesh with his fist.

When I watched him closely, I failed to understand the aptness of his appearance; not only were his gestures fluid and lifelike, but his face was not a death mask like mine; it possessed healthy color…and his eyes were so lively.

"You are new, and you will find yourself in very precarious situations if you don't make some changes immediately." Arthur extended his arm and lifted the sunglasses from over my eyes.

"Changes?" I yelled, slapping his arm away. "What kind of changes? *Everything* has changed!"

Arthur turned around to face one of the dumpsters, and knelt. An alley cat emerged from a small pile of empty cardboard boxes. The feline rubbed against Arthur's extended hand. Its long, black and striped-brown fur was tangled and matted, and a patch of white lined its belly.

"You *look* like a corpse." His voice was stern, unsympathetic. Though his back was turned, I felt his spiritual eyes intruding the air around me, a definite presence I would grow used to. "Do not take it personally… we all do. But we are amidst a sea of living creatures."

He stood up and turned face to face with me. The feline nudged into his ankles and sat by his feet.

"And if you want to avoid unnecessary conflict, you must disguise amongst humans convincingly, and that means looking alive and acting alive when you are in their sight."

"What do you mean…?"

When Arthur spoke, his shriveled tongue remained idle between the blackened teeth of his dark mouth.

"You would do well to know that since you are dead, you lack in instincts and reflexes. Your lips don't naturally shape to each spoken word, nor does your expression shift with emotion. You will have to consciously move your mouth, and even your brow, when you wish to speak, or you will cause alarm. Even the motions of your walk are lacking, without a moderate effort on your part. You weren't swinging your arms when we walked, among other things."

Arthur's deep, blue eyes turned up and down, side to side.

"Your eyes are very important, perhaps above all things. They will not shift when you look out at the world with your spiritual eyes," he paused and added, "…and they will not blink. Your body is a corpse now. Things that were reflexive must now be intentional."

"Are those…" I watched them move around with vigor, and compared them to mine – those sunken, discolored sacs of fluid which had twisted into unnatural alignment.

"...not real. My original pair was as equally frightening as yours are now. These are prosthetic. They look phenomenally realistic. I'd suggest you get a pair, especially if you wish to intermingle among the living."

"I don't know *what* I wish yet."

Arthur lightened his tone, from a stern warning, to a welcoming optimism. "Don't regard these characteristics as only a curse, for they bring great possibilities. If you think you are alive, you are holding yourself back, and putting yourself at risk. Your eyes may be dead, but you can see much more without them. When you speak, it is not by the stale air in your lungs, but rather in the manner of ghosts...and capable of so much more. Your motions are not from muscles and nerve working together, but a supernatural force tugging at your dead limbs like a string pulls at a marionette." Arthur motioned a smile across his wrinkled, hardened face. "Your body has ceased to be your prison...and now, is your puppet. Don't fall into the illusion that you are contained within that wall of flesh."

Arthur leaned over, picking the cat up. "You would not be standing here now, so calmly, if you had not killed somebody already."

I paid close attention to my face, alternating the expression, and opening my lips with the words. It was not easy at first. "I had to kill him...I was driven to it, by the hunger and pain." My ventriloquism was less than adequate. Having these details brought to my attention led me to wonder who may have noticed my behavioral deviations.

Arthur held the cat close to his face, letting the feline rub against his chin. "When you were reborn as a vampire, you were pained with an intense hunger. Had you not fed soon after waking, you would have collapsed, died again, resigning to what lies beyond this world." He placed the cat down again, and stepped closer to me. "If you felt any lack of control over your actions then, it was only to your long-term advantage, similar to the person feeding from garbage to escape starvation, despite their disgust or reluctance. If you fail to kill, your strength will fade and your corpse will deteriorate. Honor this rule, and you can remain as you are now, perhaps forever."

I looked at my cold lifeless hands. "I can't die?"

Arthur laughed, "A vampire's existence is not as glamorous as fairy tales would have you believe. We are neither shape-shifters nor seducers, and we are certainly not free from destruction. We all can die...rather easily, I'm afraid. Injuries no longer heal, and will add up fast over time." Arthur circled around me, with a cold, expressionless gaze. "To look less like a vampire, and more like a human, takes effort and luck."

Arthur stopped moving, and his voice reentered my mind, unheard in the air around us.

I cannot stress this fact enough...you can't kill just anybody you desire, not anymore, not in the city. Things are monitored, recorded...noticed. Unnecessary deaths quickly merit investigation. It is dangerous for you out here, looking like that, reeking of death. I suggest you pay a visit to a friend of mine before you begin to seek more...answers. It is not far from here. Follow me.

Arthur led me out the other side of the alley. I followed him closely, struggling to decide which of many questions to ask.

As we walked, my mind kept wandering back to the waking, the comfortable darkness and the voices therein. Were those calls and cries other vampires like myself? How would I find them? Perhaps they would find me, as Arthur did.

"Are there many others like us?" I inquired.

"We are few, but that is to our advantage. Hardly anyone acknowledges vampires, and I prefer it that way. Unfortunately, there are a few who have taken notice and will not permit our existence. Hunters intently seek us out and destroy us, even at the mockery of a doubtful public. If they grow savvy to your presence, you will be targeted and extinguished. Adaptation and resourcefulness will keep you hidden. Just remember that you are inhuman, a force to be reckoned with! With practice and cunning, you can remain unseen to those who would do you harm."

We left the downtown, wandering by expensive homes in upper-class neighborhoods. Large, old trees, with thick, robust trunks, and tall, wrought iron fences, stood between the well-lit streets and the many wealthy houses tucked into the shadows of their expansive yards. Flawless green lawns, filled with flower gardens and shrubs, stretched far back from the paved road.

Arthur stopped outside an opened gate of one of the houses. The driveway was wide, meant for small amounts of traffic to enter and exit. He turned and walked onto the lot, heading up the driveway towards the large home. Lights embedded into the lawn shone onto a silver sign, reading: Tully Funeral Home.

Up the driveway, past a small, roofed covering, carpeted stairs climbed up to two wide wooden doors. We continued past the main entry, into a parking lot at the rear of the building; there, behind the house was a small, wide door which appeared to descend into a cellar.

Arthur turned to face me and spoke, "Her name is Lucia and she can help you. Be kind to her, as she is one of few I know we can trust."

He turned to leave me, almost as unexpectedly as he had appeared. I felt as if my only chance to answer a montage of questions was about to end.

"Wait!" I was angered. I had no desire to be stranded there, alone, to meet God-knows-who. "Where are you going?"

With his back still turned, his voice filled the air around me.

"I have survived as long as I have because I am very careful. I risked more than you realize by intervening in that park. Hunters comb the city almost every night. They were near, and you would have paid the price, had you given in to your urges and killed that man. If you wish to be in my company, you must first remedy that baleful appearance. Then, and only then, will I grace you with a firmer understanding of our nature."

"Where, later, can I find you?"

"When Lucia is done, go out into the city and I promise you our paths will cross again." Arthur nodded and before I could object to being abandoned, he was gone.

Though I felt fortunate to have found him, his prompt exit frustrated me; I did not understand why he led me there. I had other questions, and the things that Arthur told me were merely confirmations of what I had been denying.

The patter of rainfall surrounded me. The sound was so clear that I could have counted the droplets. Instead of feeling each raindrop strike my numb flesh, I felt their trajectories all around me, watching them plummet to the ground, bursting into many smaller fragments.

I stood outside the back door; a small window in the center, revealed stairs leading down into darkness. A metal plate, built into the wall beside the door, offered two small buttons and an intercom. I knocked; a light turned on next to me, emitting an annoying electrical buzz. I was in a small spotlight, differentiated from the surrounding darkness, so I took a step back into the light's margin.

Uncertain what to expect, and trying to take advantage of the situation, I peered far past the door to see what figure approached. All but physically present, I waited like a ghost in the dark hall, listening to the loudening footsteps.

A tall, slender woman came to the foot of the cellar stairs. Perhaps in her late fifties, she had faded blond hair, streaked white with age, and tied neatly up on her head.

She peered up at my motionless corpse, which lingered beyond the light's influence; she was unaware of my scrutinizing eyes hovering in the dark, inches from her warm skin.

I sensed her heat and felt her heartbeat shaking the air, listening to its slow, steady rhythm speed up when she noticed my figure standing outside…she was alive.

She removed protective gloves, and then reached to the wall, pressing a button on a metal plate.

"Who are you?" Her voice crackled through the speaker outside.

I brought my attention back to the physical, carefully forming the motions of my words. "Arthur sent me. I'm here to see Lucia." I removed my glasses and stepped into the light, not knowing what else to say.

"Arthur?" She seemed puzzled at first, but then smiled and nodded. "He told you his name was Arthur, huh?" She pressed another button and the door clicked, swinging outward. "Alright, come on in."

The woman turned and walked back where she had come from, managing through the pitch dark hall with ease.

I made my way out of the rain, and down the wide cement stairs.

"I'm Lucia. Have you got a name?" she asked. She was already in another room, but seemed to understand that I would see and hear her clearly, despite the thick wall between us.

I walked a short, twisting hall, to a doorway, entering into a large, cool room. Lucia stood by a stretcher, on which was a corpse, draped with a white cloth. A toe tag hung from a protruding foot. She wheeled it over to a large, windowless metal door in the back of the room. When it opened, a cool fog spilled out, creeping along the floor.

"I don't know my name," I said. "I am not even certain why I am here."

"Who on *earth* is?" Lucia laughed ever so briefly.

As it were that Lucia knew Arthur, I assumed she had no doubts that I was a vampire. Despite her and I being the only ones in that cellar, she did not keep a cautious eye on me, keeping her back turned as she finished her work.

Lucia disappeared into the cooler, pushing the stretcher towards its resting spot alongside other bodies, and continued to talk from inside.

"Arthur doesn't know his name either. I gave it to him when I worked on him the first time." She exited, and shut the door, staring at me from across the room.

She was not afraid of me. How she could be so sure of my quality, I did not know. Why she trusted me, even before I did, is a mystery.

Lucia walked towards me, stopping just a few yards away. "He dislikes names in general."

A waist-high aluminum table was built into the center of the room; its edges were raised a few inches, forming a shallow tub, and it sloped forward into a drain. Piping, beneath the basin, ran down through the floor. The concrete flooring was embedded with metal drains, located around the perimeter of the table.

Many bright lights shone down at the operating table. Hoses hung from two large pipes, in the ceiling, and suspended over the table, stained from recent use, were scales, like those found in a butcher shop.

A large machine beside the table looked like a vacuum; a series of tubes came out from the side. Visible in a large clear bag, hanging from the other side, was a reddish liquid – not blood.

Against one wall, on a large counter, were many surgical tools. Glass cabinets, with many varieties of bottles and tubes, also contained jars of unidentifiable matter, floating in tinted liquids. Two large steel sinks were in the center of the counter, and on the far end, by the cooler door, was a very large digital scale almost seven feet long and a few feet wide; a system of straps and pulleys might have been used for hoisting a corpse onto it.

Standing almost toe to toe, Lucia studied my face, pressing her gloved fingers against the skin. She lifted the collar of my jacket to study the wound on my neck.

"You were strangled." Her fingers spread apart the dried, bloody crease. "Some type of cord, or wire. Do you know how long ago it happened?"

"A few days, I guess."

"I can fix you up, if you want." She motioned to the metal table behind her. "This is why Arthur brought you here...because you would not last long out there, with your natural appearance."

"Anything you can do will be appreciated."

"I didn't want this to be another late night, but what the heck...this is what I do."

Lucia walked over to the counter and opened cupboards, shuffling through various items.

"What...help vampires?" I asked.

"Specifically, I make corpses look and smell nice. I can do autopsies too, but I don't think you want that, at least, not a full one."

I clumsily removed my clothes, discarding them onto the floor. Thankfully, my jeans were loose-fitting, falling off with the snap's release.

My corpse was a pale purple with blue veins showing through much of the skin. Fluids had leaked from my midsection and seeped down my inner thighs, coagulating on the skin. My waist was bloated, and small cysts had formed.

I walked to the steel table and laid back, slipping silently onto the surface, almost weightless.

Lucia gathered her tools, and then approached the side of the table. Getting her first look at my naked body, her eyes immediately noticed the bullet hole in my chest.

"This wound did not kill you." She protruded her finger inside, twisting it. "It was done much later. Perhaps someone wanted to make sure you were dead."

I thought back to Lance, and his dirty business in that now-dead man's apartment. "I was aware when it happened. It didn't hurt at all."

"That's good." She smiled and continued.

Lucia reached up and pulled down one of the hoses from overhead; she sprayed me and used a small sponge to wash the skin. The runoff from the water, stained with the filth of death, ran down the table to the drain at my feet.

"First," she explained kindly, "I will wash you thoroughly. You secreted fluids when you died and it smells rancid. Then, using a large needle, I will drain the fluids from your stomach and abdomen, after which I will make a small incision from your sternum down, exposing your insides. I will vacuum up any pooled blood and fluids, and then I shall proceed to remove a few organs, specifically of your digestive system. This will make you a bit lighter, but more importantly, if you sustain serious injuries in the future, you won't spill your bowels and liquids everywhere."

Lucia finished rinsing my corpse, and released the hose. "Do you realize that you can not heal on your own?"

"He told me."

"Keep that in mind. It is why you must be so careful out there. Take enough damage and you will drop dead...again. No more second chances." She cracked her knuckles and then lifted one of my legs from the table. "Any serious injuries should be patched up. You may not bleed, but it will lend to a gruesome appearance, walking around with holes or gashes in your skin. You'll only draw attention to yourself."

Lucia began massaging my leg, bending it at the knee, and kneading the muscles, kindly informing me of the reason. "This will reduce the stiffening of rigor mortis," she noted, moving on to the other leg.

She manipulated each joint, limb, and finger...and I felt

nothing, except for the heat of her body in the air. The feeling of her warmth did not change when her massaging hands moved from my legs, to my arms and then to my neck; it was as if I had one body part, unlike living persons, who can distinguish the same stimulus as it affects different areas of the body. Somewhere inside, or outside, of the corporeal host that I occupied, was something altogether unique – a soul, anomalously connected to the physical world.

"There. That should relieve tension in your walk. You were moving around like some kind of zombie. Irregularity of motion stands out in a crowd. People notice subtleties like that. It's instinctive."

Lucia grabbed a very large and thick syringe from under the table and sank it deep through my navel and into my stomach. As she pulled on the large rubber plunger, the empty plastic barrel filled with fluids and partially digested matter from inside my stomach.

Lucia's eyes narrowed and she blew air from her nostrils, placing the syringe beneath the table. "Gastric acid is vile."

I smelled nothing.

Lucia held a scalpel in her hand. "I will not be damaging any bones, since they are necessary to maintain a normal shape. But your organs are, more or less, unnecessary...just extra baggage to tote around."

Her blade neared my corpse, and knowing very well what I was about to behold, I was without worry.

Lucia cut a t-shaped incision downward from under my chest plate. A small burst of gas escaped from the opening as the skin was pulled back. With long, curved hooks attached to the sides of the table, she fastened the thick slab of skin and muscle open, exposing the insides.

"After all the surgical stuff, I'll take care of the aesthetics."

"Aesthetics?" It was now clear to me why Arthur appeared so alive, like the vampires of modern lore.

"Yeah, you know...make up." With her hands free from holding the skin open, Lucia sunk her fingers into the cold, slightly-liquefied organs inside me. "Your eyes are grossly discolored, and sunk into your skull, giving you a rather gloomy stare. I will put in a synthetic pair. And not only has your skin changed color, but so have your lips, fingers and veins. We'll touch that up after we attend to your wounds."

Lucia pulled the rancid cords of my large intestine from my exposed trunk. Holding them high with one hand, she used a large pair of scissors to cut them free from both the small intestines, and the colon.

"How many times have you done this?" I asked, watching numbly as I was disemboweled. The sloshing sound of gore filled the room, as liquids, not limited to blood alone, fell from the severed, tubular organ, and back onto the table.

"To vampires?" She thought for a moment, and continued, "Five times, including you. Arthur was the first one, almost thirty years ago. Since then, he has brought a few others...some of which are still around."

Lucia placed the intestines into a large receptacle beneath the table. Her stained gloves dove back inside me. With the scissors, she snipped the small intestine from its connection to the stomach. A wet smacking sound followed as she lifted the twisted mass of tube from inside my corpse and placed it into the bin.

I was numb from any pain; even my mind was still when I should have been panicked. I was silent during most of the procedure. I don't know if I was being rude, or considerate; it seemed that a talking corpse would only serve to shaken Lucia's nerves. However, even when my still lips uttered occasional words, her nerves remained still, her heart steady, with an unwavering concentration.

"How did it come about that you first met Arthur?" I asked.

Lucia stopped and stared off, recalling some memory. "I had just received my PhD in pathology, working for a coroner back in my hometown. The body of a five year-old boy came in. The autopsy revealed he had been poisoned...cyanide. He was mentally handicapped, and as it turned out, his father, a yuppie CEO, couldn't cope with the responsibility or embarrassment. Over the course of a few days, he had poisoned the child's food."

Lucia reached back into my corpse. Her wrists pressed close together so she could fit both arms through the small opening and deep up under my ribcage.

She hesitated, taking a deep breath, and continued, "I stared at the child for a long time before I mustered up the will to cut him. He looked adorable, and knowing that he was killed because of something he had no control over..." She paused, changing her thought. "It was the first child I operated on and it was under such cruel circumstances that I became emotional and for a while felt unable to work. I had dreams about it for a couple weeks. I was heartbroken."

Using a scalpel, Lucia cut free a large, dense mass, which she explained was my liver. After placing it in one of the scales hanging overhead, she continued talking.

"Not too long after the truth came out, the father went missing, along with a small fortune in cash. He even abandoned his wife, who was expecting. I became furious, fantasizing about what I would say and do to that man if he were there with me."

Her eyes gazed into space and her expression was intense, almost unladylike. "I imagined tying him to one of these tables and..." Lucia stopped, perhaps digging up buried demons.

She continued removing pieces, cutting free my pancreas and kidneys, which, like the other organs, she placed on overhead scales. When she was done, she put the scalpel down and stared off, again, in deep thought, continuing her story.

"I was sitting on a city bench, one evening, watching people walk by. My mind raced, obsessed with this sick bastard. I think I had a panic attack. I don't know why I cared so much."

Lucia smiled, a beautiful, womanly smile, like a goddess about to unveil a miracle. Her words were soft, and quiet, "And then I heard a whisper inside my head, as soft as my own conscience, saying to me, 'I have heard your thoughts. I know what plagues your dreams. The vengeance you want could be realized for a favor returned.' I was beguiled by his heavy voice." Lucia laughed, "I assumed it was the devil or God, perhaps. Anything seemed better than proposing I was crazy. The voice said that one night, a corpse would come through my work, unbeknownst to anyone except me. He listed things he wanted done to it, and said I should place it outside when I was done."

Lucia paused, looking up at the scales, noting the weight of the organs.

"I agreed because the favor was reasonable, and it didn't involve the selling of my soul or anything like that," she chuckled, but then her voice lost all hint of its kindliness. "That man deserved to die, and I was sick of being tormented by my own mind...on account of him!"

Lucia used a simple butter knife to cut a cross-section of each of the three organs. She placed the samples into clear plastic cassettes, submerging them in jars labeled 'formalin.'

After throwing the remaining liver, kidney and pancreas into the receptacle beneath the table, Lucia volunteered an examination of the saved specimens to see if any useful information concerning my demise should arise. I accepted the offer.

Lucia lifted a hose from beneath the table; its mouth was wide, and when she pressed a switch in the handle, the end began to suck the air. She traced the inside of my hollowed corpse, vacuuming the liquids that had collected inside when the organs were cut free. When there was hardly a stray puddle of gore, Lucia placed the vacuum back beneath the table.

"I will now put a filler inside of you, to keep the corpse from caving in, now that it is half-empty."

"What type of filler?" I asked.

Lucia walked over to the counter, talking back over her shoulder, "It's a light, yet firm, pillow of sorts, shaped kind of like an egg." Kneeling to reach into a lower cabinet, she removed an ovular, flesh colored object, with a plastic-like texture. "After installing this, I will sew you up and you will appear fairly normal. Your odor and weight will be reduced."

Lucia walked back to the operating table. With minor stretching of the skin, she squeezed the filler inside the empty cavity, turning it so it packed the empty space effectively.

As she unfastened the folds of skin, held up by the large hooks, she continued talking.

"So the father had disappeared without a trace, and many folks assumed he was fleeing the country. But just a day after I made that deal, his head was found by a citizen traveling north on the highway. The entire jaw had been removed, and the body was never recovered. That night, Arthur's corpse awaited me in the cooler."

Lucia stopped chatting, maybe getting tired of the sound of her own voice. Her concentration was now focused on sewing up the large incision on my gut.

I felt that she withheld information about the incident, perhaps facts which would make the situation more personal, but I did not ask. She seemed saddened, and I wished not to worsen it for her.

I found it hard to rationalize what I was experiencing. My insides were spilled on the floor, hanging from scales, and stained on Lucia's gloves and goggles. The thought of my voice emanating from a hollow corpse seemed too grisly. I found it hard to cope with the idea I was not defined by tangible elements.

"You know," she said, breaking the silence, but still sewing the flesh with thick thread, "...in my experiences, I have noticed consistencies among the host corpses of vampires. Those I have done this procedure to were cadavers in decent condition...no missing limbs, major cuts, holes or even broken bones. From what I gathered, through keen observation, the causes of death in most cases are overdose, heart failure, asphyxiation...as in your case, basically non-devastating injuries."

"Because we cannot heal," I suggested, "...perhaps its best."

"Maybe. I mean, each corpse goes through the initial decaying process, but during some point, the natural death process stops."

"What does happen?" I asked.

"Well, it all really depends on where the corpse is. Out in the heat, it will be unrecognizable within a day or two, whereas if a body is left in a cool, dry environment, like in a home, the presentation is much more intact. So, assuming a stable and sheltered environment, the first thing to happen is the muscles go limp, emptying the bowels and bladder. After an hour, the skin begins to change color, taking on a waxy feel from the lack of oxygen. Eyes sink into the skull, and lips turn whitish, as do the finger and toenails. Fluids seep into the body...this is when it begins to develop that unforgettable stench. Rigor mortis occurs within twelve hours and lasts a couple days. During the next few days, the flesh turns bluish and green and soon after, will bloat and swell up as gases escape through breeches in the skin."

Her somber words depicted for me a morbid portrayal of the moments leading up to my waking.

Lucia cut the thread one last time and sat back, examining the strength of the stitches with her thumb, which she pressed against my skin.

"Anything beyond this stage of decomposition serves to make the corpse unrecognizable in virtually all cases. Boils form and fluids start to leak from every orifice as it slowly liquefies. However, with vampires, the decomposition ceases prior to this point, and continues to, until the vampire dies."

Lucia wiped the splattered gore from my skin as she examined the shape of my corpse and the convincingness of the new insides I had adopted. She pressed down on my stomach, and the inserted filler bounced back, retaining my normal shape.

She stood over my head and using small, spoon-like scissors, began to dig out my eyes from their deep sunken state, cutting the optic nerves. Watching that happen, realizing I was almost totally independent of my retired sensory organs, was one of the most enlightening moments.

Lucia dug through a drawer in the side of the operating table "What color eyes would you like? I have blue, brown, and I think green somewhere in here."

My old, shriveled eyes rested on a tray, staring back next to a blood soaked spoon.

"Green is fine."

"Green it is then." Lucia held one of the eyes out and squeezed it. "These look, and feel, like real eyes. I got them for my special clients. Normally, we leave the eyes in and put small concave caps over them, so when the eyelid is shut, they don't appear sunken."

She put them in my sockets and adjusted the eye lids over them.

"There. Now all you need to do is work on moving them

around and you will fool most people. The pupils won't change size in the light, so that will be a dead giveaway. Keep it in mind."

With an almost effortless act of will, the new green eyes twisted back and forth, up and down, but blinking was hard, almost impossible. The skin covering did not slide easily over the smooth, dry orbs.

Lucia walked to the head of the table and rinsed my short hair with a small hose attached to the head of the operating table. She massaged shampoo into the scalp and rinsed. My hair dried fast with a towel.

She opened up my mouth and fingered inside for any foreign objects.

"Aside from the cessation of decay, the only strange change in the corpses of vampires is the elongation of the upper canines, which is bizarre since it is the only aspect that resembles growth. The tooth extends downward by about half a centimeter, but its roots grow deeper into the gums."

"How do you know that?"

"I have seen the corpses of dead vampires, and in most cases, the canines have fallen out by the time they get here. I usually see them in the back of the throat, or stuck between the cheek and molars."

"You have seen dead vampires?" I inquired, curiously.

"A couple, but I had already met Arthur at that point, so I was much less shocked about the idea. Anyway, I wasn't told they were once vampires. Immediately after death, vampires continue to rot at the normal rate, as if time resumes influence over them. The authorities merely said that they were bodies of long-missing or homeless folks."

"Did they know the truth?"

"Probably...the types of questions I was asked about some of the corpses were unorthodox, and given the poorly thought-up facts they tried to feed me, many of those corpses should have been in a worse state of decay."

"What had killed the vampires?" I asked.

"One had been struck by a car, and the torso was split in half. Another one had been charred beyond recognition. Many were decapitated...major spinal cord injuries seem to be fatal, for some reason. Anyway, all of them were killed by hunters. The vampires that I don't fix up are usually identified from among the living, and tracked to their death. I assume this has been going on since the dawn of civilization, but around here, one particularly cruel man exacts his crusade with painstaking perseverance."

Lucia examined the gash on my neck, thinking about what to

do.

"This will only need a light stitching and then we will begin applying some cosmetics to your corpse to make it seem less cold and lifeless. Okay?"

I wondered how often she talked to the corpses as she worked on them. Being alone with deceased people so regularly undoubtedly brings up questions about who they were, who they loved and who loved them. Lucia is faced daily with the grim fact that nothing is static and all things end, and it makes her stronger, wiser. Seeing so many minds reduced to matter probably makes a person numb. Talking breathes life into them one last time, it says: 'you are still a person, not defined by flesh, but by actions and relations.'

Lucia finished stitching my neck, and then using a towel, cleaned the splattered areas of my corpse. She then opened a drawer in the side of the table which contained a number of small, fancy brushes, crèmes and powders.

"Now we will try to make you look alive again. My favorite part."

Lucia opened a small tube labeled, 'filler,' and began to apply the crème to the sewed-up gashes of my neck and stomach. "This will fill all the scars. It will smooth it right out. I will use it on your chapped lips too."

"Everything has changed so fast." I had developed a trust in Lucia already, and knew she would listen to my words with compassion. "I don't feel alive, merely extra-aware of how dead I am. I am in this world, but not of it. I smell and taste nothing. To feel anything takes effort...it is no longer passive. With no memory of who I am, how can I assume I ever was? How do I know this is my body?"

"If you have no memory, then how do you know everything has changed? Maybe you have always been a vampire, just not in this particular body?"

"I do remember something before I awoke. But it's hard to recall well enough to adequately explain."

"Try me," she coaxed.

"I was somewhere peaceful, quiet. Time and direction seemed irrelevant. I could not see anything around me, but it was not dark. In fact, it was quite illuminated, but there was nothing around to be lit. Although nobody was with me, I did not feel alone." My words failed to sufficiently describe what I had experienced.

"I have heard other vampires speak of that place. It is like you are leaving the light at the end of the tunnel."

Lucia finished filling the cracks and cuts of my skin. Bouncing between a powder and a shallow jar labeled 'camel crème,' she applied a layer of healthy color to my dead skin.

"This stuff can come off, so try to keep that in mind when it rains or if you let people touch you. It can be rubbed off. It was made for corpses under the assumption they would only need to look good for a few hours."

I continued with my sordid rant.

"I am an existential outcast...doomed to anonymity if I hide well, else threatened with being hunted if I fail. What can a monster become, but smothered by an unwelcoming world? My needs are unethically obtained, and my survival requires that I kill. I do not imagine you find that thought too pleasant."

Lucia smiled subtly as she applied makeup. "Your needs are no more unethically obtained than the cheetah that preys on the weak or injured among the pack, or the trap door spider that hides in the shadows of the earth, ending the lives of passers-by in a split second. All life requires death and vice versa. Mankind, in his egocentricity, is too quick to deem something harmful to him as evil, or unnatural. Having a throne usurped from atop the food chain is not taken lightly."

Lucia seemed to suggest that vampires had a role, a function, which was a comforting thought. It seemed logical, at a glance. After all, could anything really exist without a purpose?

"Just keep in mind one thing," she added.

"What's that?"

"Not once have I seen a vampire with any signs of having been bitten by another vampire...meaning you were not put here by any man or monster you will find walking the earth."

"What are you saying?" Perhaps I was too pessimistic to find the conclusion myself.

Lucia cracked her knuckles and said, "Something else, perhaps divine, has chosen you."

I thought back to my waking, and in that swirling void of darkness and voices, I recalled hearing the words, 'another one,' prior to my decent. Were those the words of God, of the devil?... perhaps they are the same.

Lucia's voice adopted a hint of jealousy. "When I see a vampire, I do not see a person trapped in a body, as I do with many young and old people. Nor do I see a soulless cadaver waiting to rot into dust. I see a mind, freed from the boundaries of flesh, somehow, defying both life and death, and having an existence more pure and simple than a human can ever dream of."

I doubted the validity of her apparent envy. She did not know that horrid cold, throbbing pain of hunger I wakened to. Inevitably, it would return, and I would become a killer again.

"There are many things I can never enjoy as you do, Lucia."

"There are many woes you will never have to deal with either. You are free from disease, time, and earthly desires that corrupt the lives of millions. I am sure as you walk the earth at night and see how few of us are truly happy, you will realize you got off pretty easy."

She held her finger up, like an idea had just sprung to mind and then spoke from her memory.

"What joy it is, when out at sea the storm winds are lashing the waters, to gaze from the shore at the heavy stress some other man is enduring! Not that anyone's afflictions are a source of delight, but to realize from what troubles you yourself are free, is joy indeed."

"Who said that?" I asked, curiously.

"A Greek poet...Lucretius, I believe he was called. It has been years since I have read it, but some things just stick with you. All the times I have watched widows and widowers clench their chests in agony at the loss of their loves, or when I see parents blame themselves for the deaths of their children...people trapped in the emotional hell of their own lives...those words remind me of the sanctuary I have in the solitary life I have chosen."

Lucia, adding the final touches, painted a flesh tone on my fingernails, colored my lips, examining me with the same scrutiny she would if she expected loved ones to look upon my corpse and compare my appearance to their grieving memories.

She nodded and backed away from the table, removing her gloves.

"That should do it. I'm exhausted. It is going on 3:00am."

I looked over her work, like an out-of-body examination. There was a striking difference from before. My face, while not appearing full of life, was not stricken with death. However, Lucia had only painted my face, neck, and lower arms. My disguise was dependant on my staying covered-up.

I stood from the table. "I don't know how I can repay you."

Lucia handed me some used, clean clothes from a closet in the back of the room – a pair of wrinkled, grey pants and a black, long sleeved shirt, faded from use. She provided me with a pair of ragged sneakers, without laces. I kept my long, black coat and glasses.

After helping my numb, inept body slip into the clothes, she stood before me and held out a small vile of a clear liquid.

"You may not appreciate this," Lucia said, as she pressed two fingers over the opening, tilted the bottle, and dabbed the liquid onto my neck and arms with her fingers. "...but this cologne will cover what remaining odors you have. You are less foul now, but the fact of the matter is, you are a corpse. Put some on, now and then."

She placed the vile in the front pocket of my jacket.

"Take care. If you ever get really messed up, ring the buzzer at night. I work late often, usually alone."

Lucia turned and walked to a sink in the back and cleaned up. I stared for a moment, contemplating the bizarre faith Lucia seemed to have in me, in my kind. I thought about saying something, but instead, I turned and exited up the stairs and out through the back door, cold and alone.

Chapter 4 — The Witch in the Woods

Samuel Taylor combed his mustache with his fingers as he stared out at the empty highway. He drove the large, black van at Southey's request, who sat in the passenger seat, gazing out the window at the thickening leafy forest to his right. The autumn nights had transformed a once verdant and youthful canopy into a fiery realm of reds, oranges and yellows. Numerous breaches in the canopy offered glimpses of the forest floor.

The sun was still strong at 5:00 pm, and the sky was a soft blue, cloudless and serene. Few cars accompanied them on that drab stretch of highway, being that the area was overwhelmingly rural, and exits were far and few. Not a hint of a town or city would be evident until nightfall when the gritty orange haze of city lights would be visible on the horizon as they returned southbound on the I-95.

In the rear of the van, inside a large, steel cage, were two German shepherds, Cain and Abel – avid hunters and loyal pets. Their long, sharpened nails clicked on the floor of the cage, as the canines paced inside.

Seated around the cage, uncomfortably atop large duffel bags, were three young men:

Jacob Southey was twenty-two years old, and the most experienced of the three younger men. A brave and loyal son, Jacob, and his recently-deceased older brother, Colin, adopted the same prejudices as their father. Ever since the sons were young boys, Southey told them about the creatures hiding in the shadows of the alleys, sewers, and abandoned lots of the city; he would tell his sons about one vampire in particular, one whom Southey wanted dead more than any other. 'One day...' he would promise them, '...we'll be heroes, and make your momma proud.'

Dario Antonio had been a hunter for less than a year. A twenty-six year old Italian, with two hundred pounds of muscle, his day job was bouncing at a local biker bar – Fatty's. It was there, bouncing drunken ruffians, and chatting with the pedestrians of the lower-class community, that he heard the rumors...ghost stories that would not die. Being particularly religious, he did not need much convincing to believe that evil spirits existed – and when Samuel Taylor had scouted for volunteers to join a team of vampire hunters, Dario was one, of few, who accepted.

Rick Hardy, at only five foot five, was the shortest of the men in the van, and usually among others his age as well. Twenty-four years old, with no prior 'hunting' experience, Rick was an Eagle

Scout, and his knowledge of the wooded areas nearby was the sole reason Southey had asked him along. Rick claimed to know where a cabin was located, which local lore stated was the dwelling of the witch in the woods – the target for that evening.

The witch in the woods had been a staple in local lore since before Southey was born. As a child, he had heard the tales of the spirit of the witch that roamed the dense and dank forests of the north; he remembered the poem that was much older than him:

> Ashes to ashes, dust to dust,
> The witch in the woods feeds on us.
> The Queen of the trees travels on air,
> and plunders the sinners who wander in there.
> The will of the woods, it speaks of her name,
> through the tormented souls that were driven insane.
> Run 'til you die, run 'til you fall.
> Run from the daemon that captures us all.

Rick claimed to have been hiking in those very woods, with other scouts, three years ago, when they stumbled onto the deserted cabin during a hike. None of Rick's subsequent outings in that area ever resulted in anything supernatural, but almost every scout he knew claimed to know somebody who knew somebody who had disappeared.

As a result of the witch's infamousness, many folks shunned away at the thought of braving those trails – even those who laughed at the stories. Few campers and hikers actually reported anything at all; the only ones who ever had something to report were hunters, trappers and loggers, from all over the state, who spoke of their experiences in those woods with alluring consistency – if they were lucky enough not to be one of the many who had disappeared over the years.

Rick leaned closer to Jacob and Dario, initiating conversation.

"Her name is C, like the letter." Rick orated as if relaying a speech he had prepared beforehand. "She wasn't always a witch. A long time ago, she was studying to be a nun. One night, after returning to the convent from some charity work, she was assaulted by some guy waiting outside. He didn't hurt her too bad, but he did end all chances of her becoming a real nun if you know what I mean."

Rick laughed and nudged Dario in his side; immediately, Dario slapped his arm down.

"Anyway," Rick continued, "she was so distraught that she left some sappy little note saying she could no longer find God in this

world…and then disappeared.   Years later, she was discovered
living in a small cabin she had built by a stream in the mountains.
She devoted her life to nature, grew her own food and made her
own clothes."

"Hippie," Jacob interrupted.

"Hermit," Rick corrected.   "At night, campers in the mountains
would see her singing spells and dancing ceremonially around a fire,
tossing things in.   Sometimes, she was seen walking naked in the
forest, or wrapped loosely in ivy, or other plants.   She was known for
hiding in the woods, using a slingshot to scare away would-be prey
from hunters' sights.   This went on for years, and then one day, two
men went up there during hunting season.   One of them accidentally
shot her cabin while tracking a deer with his rifle.   Inside, she was on
the floor, bleeding in the furthest corner."

Rick stopped to take a breath.   His years as a Scout endowed
him with ample story-telling skills.   One could almost see the
campfire sparkling in his eye as he relayed the tale.

The van exited the highway, and was on a smaller, two-lane
road.   A steep descent ran along a hillside which overlooked a small
lake, so devoid of activity that it appeared as a hole in the earth
falling into more sky.   The van shook when the asphalt broke into a
dirt road; pebbles clanked from beneath the cabin.

Rick looked out the windshield, to see the change in direction,
and then continued, "Mortally wounded, she reached out to the
hunters and begged for 'help.'   But they panicked and left her to die
with a bullet in her gut.   A week later, when they finally got the
nerve to tell anyone, the two men headed back up there with some
officers.   She was gone!   Her stuff was inside the cabin, and a pool of
blood was right where they claimed she had been laying.   The area
was searched with no trace of her.   The two hunters got a slap on the
wrist, and continued to hunt in those woods…," he leaned forward,
"…once more anyway."   Rick stared off, having crept himself out.

The sun was well past its peak, and long shadows from the
trees reached through the windshield.

"Since then," Rick snapped out of his daze, "few have claimed
to see her chafed and weathered body, walking around, watching
visitors with an ominous and frigid gaze that haunts survivors with
crippling nightmares!" Rick nodded slowly, and then with a lowered
voice, he gazed back and forth between the noticeably concerned
faces of Jacob and Dario, whispering, "…some people say when she
is close to you, you can hear hell."

Southey turned his head back to Rick, annoyed.   "Rick, if you
keep talking like that, I am going to let you out here."   His left hand

was clenched tightly, and he said, "Witch or no witch, this clammy broad is a leech now."

"A *what*?" Rick asked.

'Leech' was the term Southey had coined, since 'vampire' sounded too fantastic for him. The creatures he hunted were very much unlike those written about in fiction, unlike the common assumptions of the general population. Southey opted to call them something different, something devoid of the seductive and often intimidating overtones the word 'vampire' carried.

Southey's voice crackled from excess phlegm in his throat, "When we find your witch, you will see that she is nothing more than a stiff corpse with a few cheap tricks. If there is one thing I have learned over the years, it is that leeches are more afraid of you than you are of them. As long as we stick together, when she comes out of her cabin or her tree house, we will tear her apart and make mulch of her."

"I don't know...," Rick sounded amused. "...*how* you plan on killing a ghost."

Southey sourly smiled at Rick, and turned back around in his seat. He pointed left, towards a clearing, telling Sam of their arrival.

Sam steered the van into a small dirt lot, parked, and exited promptly.

Southey lit one cigar for the hike, leaving the rest behind, and then rounded to the back door of the van.

The air was cool and crisp, and the smell of a lake nearby was a striking contrast from the city air; pine and earth filled the lungs.

"Rick better not be jerking me around," Southey said quietly to Sam.

Sam tugged at the point of his mustache. "I believe him. I just don't think he believes himself." Sam turned away from the van, peering at a grassy field separating the parking lot from the edge of the woods.

"What do you mean?" asked Southey, as he reached out to open the rear door.

"Rick thinks it is only a story."

"Well," Southey laughed. "He will be in for a rude awakening, won't he?"

Southey pulled the doors open; golden sunlight shone on the three men and two dogs.

Sam leaned in to the van, opened the cage, and attached leashes to the two dogs. When Cain and Abel were standing out on the dusty lot, Southey turned the cage so the boys could fit out through the back door.

Jacob, Dario and Rick each stepped out from the van.

"Ok, leave all unnecessary garments behind," Southey ordered. "No belts, necklaces or other accessories." The young men began removing their possessions as Southey continued to bark. "Since it will be very buggy, you can wear a shirt, but only one...and short-sleeved. I have some extras in the van if you need it."

"Why is this necessary, again?" Rick questioned.

Jacob replied, "Because your '*ghost*' can grab on to that kind of stuff and use it against you."

Jacob and Dario each took a duffel bag, in which contained guns, special customized blades, a small tent, some electronic equipment, minimal food and first aid.

Southey and Sam each grabbed hold of a leash, with the dogs sniffing their way through a small field of waist-high grass. Rick followed next to the older men; in his left hand, he held an electronic compass and pointed out the correct direction when the path branched off or became covered in underbrush.

A wide dirt path, matted with crisp, fallen leaves, was not yet sodden from rain; it led them beneath a thin canopy of glowing orange-yellow, which couldn't keep the blue sky from permeating through. The sun slumped in the west, but still shone strongly.

Southey, already choking down the cigar, talked low to Sam who nodded occasionally.

The path followed past small bends, turning north, then east, finally joining alongside a shallow stream, a few feet wide, which flowed down at them from atop an inclination. There, the path continued over the stream, across a small wooden board, serving as a bridge. Rick insisted it was quicker, instead, to go north, uphill alongside the brook. A slight ascent slowed the pace for fifteen minutes, until they turned away from the soothing gurgle of running water, and around a thick stretch of dense foliage.

Rick was hardly looking at his compass anymore, having oriented himself with his surroundings; he glanced around as if the trees wore familiar faces.

"We are not too far away," Rick spoke loudly so Jake and Dario, who lagged behind with the heavy bags, would perhaps get a second wind.

The five hunters, and two dogs, circled north, around a massive webbing of thorny shrubs, and continued uphill, with Southey, Sam and the dogs immediately behind him. The trees had thinned out a bit here, and a large half-moon hovered in a soft blue on the horizon, dancing on treetops.

Not ten more minutes passed when the band of hunters came up on the stream again, but they remained a ways away as they continued north. The men exhaustively pulled on small trees for support as they trudged uphill. The terrain soon leveled off, and the men turned east.

"Here it is," Rick announced.

Far ahead, in a clearing of about three acres, was a small, dark wooden cabin; it rested on four small supports which held it a few inches above the ground. A lean-to on its west side faced the approaching hunters.

Behind the cabin loomed a threatening wall of large evergreen trees which seemed to suck the daylight from the air like a black hole. White pines, black spruces and balsam firs stood hand-in-hand and stretched off into a void of dark greens and browns. The stream, now far up ahead, ran out from the dense forest, turning south, down the hillside.

It was approaching six-thirty and the trees and hills cast long shadows across the clearing, warning of an early dusk.

Southey handed Sam his dog's leash, and walked to the only door on the tiny cabin, leaning to see inside without entering it. The door itself was missing, the frame rotten and soft. The others were still back a few yards, gazing at the thick patch of forest ahead of them.

The cabin was very basic. A sole window in front had a spider web where once was glass. Two cots could fit inside with little floor space left over.

Southey stood in the doorway and looked around. The room was empty except for a pile of rags in the far left corner. In a crook by the missing window, empty shelves contained broken glass, mouse droppings and more spider webs.

Sam had circled the cabin with Cain and Abel sniffing the grass around and under the little shack. Sam kicked at a mound of moss and rotting firewood piled under the lean-to.

Southey dropped his cigar stump to the floor, crushing it with a twist of his boot. He had a keen eye and noticed that, on the floor, under the smoldering ash, was a faint footprint – small and slender. When he glanced closer, he realized there were a half dozen more, beginning at the door, and ended near the far left corner; there, on the floor, was a striking discoloration. Southey walked slowly toward the pile, stepping on each of the five footprints when, before he could react, his right foot broke through the soft wood in the corner.

"Jee-zus!" he yelled aloud. His foot was deep in thick black mud that lay beneath the cabin.

"You alright Southey?" Sam rushed to the door and helped pull him up.

Southey said nothing, and dragged his muddy boot across the cabin floor in an attempt to wipe it clean.

Southey and Sam exited the cabin and stood in the clearing.

"Well, Rick thank you for finding it." Southey said. He then turned and pointed at the evergreen forest many yards beyond the cabin. "We head north. There should be a path somewhere, so we will build our camp on the edge of the clearing. We will gear up and take it from there."

"How do you know that? I thought you haven't been here before," Rick inquired.

Southey turned to face him with an annoyed look on his face. "I know someone on the inside," muttered Southey and walked ahead.

"The inside of *what*?" Rick murmured.

It took Sam only ten minutes to set up the small tent; it was only meant to protect food and equipment from weather, and two people hardly fit inside. It was generally understood that no one would be sleeping that night, so no sleeping bags were taken.

Immediately behind the shelter, a narrow path, hardened with clay, cut deep into the shadow of the pines, running as far as could be seen. On both sides of the trail, the trees reached out from high overhead, and the sky could not be seen through the overhead canopy from most vantage points. The wooded realm was thick with large, twisted and knotty trees, and a sea of saplings was strewn in between. To veer from the path meant walking through a tangled mess of fallen branches, shrubs, and the occasional wreckage of a toppled, rotting tree.

The hunters would not have been able to see far, even in the day; and as the sun dipped somewhere in the west, the darkening horizon inside the woods appeared like a thick, blackness seeping toward the hunters from behind nearby tree trunks.

Hardly a sound came from inside the choking wooded realm; the quiet was occasionally broken by a squirrel scurrying overhead, sending debris falling to the earth, or the sharp creaking of tree trunks, hardly moved by the light wind. A murder of crows cawed as they circled in a black swarm, barely visible through the web of branch and needle, or against the distant murk of darkness.

The two older men divided the goods inside the duffel bags.

Southey enforced a 'one gun per person' rule, to avoid any lost weapons. He preferred something big, something he could hold tightly with both hands; his weapon of choice was a pump-action, 12-gauge shotgun. In the city, he used special slugs, as opposed to the scattering pellets; this prevented over-penetration and minimized ricochet – there were civilians, and angry authorities to consider, after all. However, as they were far from straying pedestrians, Southey had nothing to worry, and used shells.

Aside from a shotgun, each member of the group had a specially crafted blade fastened to their right arm – a weapon conceived a few years prior by the recently deceased, Colin Southey.

Colin knew both from his father's teachings and personal experience, that leeches had a tendency to knock weapons from one's hands, inexplicably. This often happened before a hunter was even aware of its presence, and on many instances, left hunters vulnerable to attack.

In his craftiness, Colin devised what he named, the Armblade. Similarly shaped to a shark's dorsal fin, but pointing forward, it was fifteen inches along its arc, and was welded to a curved metal plate which fit on top of the forearm. The plate was held to the arm by a series of straps and bands which hugged the wearer, from his wrists to his shoulder. A solid hook of the arm was all it took to send a head rolling to the ground – or a limb, lifeless to the floor. Also, it enabled the wearer to easily hold and aim a shotgun, without need to abandon the blade. All this cutting power sat comfortably on each hunter's arm, always ready for battle and better yet, impossible to drop.

Each hunter also received a heavy-duty flashlight, which could easily be clipped to the straps holding the armblade to the arm, so that the flashlight would point, more or less, where the shotgun was aimed.

Sam removed a set of heat-vision goggles from a bag, and handed them to Jacob – a favorite tool of the young hunter – who immediately strapped them to his head. Since vampires were cold-blooded, the thermals allowed the wearer to look at a crowd and detect a presence, indicated by the composition of cool colors. Very useful in the city, here in the woods, it would help Jacob see his comrades in the dark.

Two pairs of night vision binoculars were also taken, one for Sam and the other for Southey. Anything present in the darkness would be discernable through the goggles in various shades of pale green. The hunters rarely needed them, being there ample secondary light throughout much of the city, but out there in the thick woods was a different story.

It was now after seven and the stars were becoming visible, the night was crystal clear. The half-moon had moved across the sky a small ways and emitted a soft light over the clearing. The buzz of many insects rose slowly from all around, filling the once silent surroundings with their incessant chirps, and the air soon crowded with waves of mosquitoes.

Southey removed a rusty shovel from a bag, handing it to Dario, saying, "Here, you're strong.   Dig a pit for a fire, and then another deeper one, somewhere nearby."

Dario took the shovel and walked away from the tent.

Rick thought for a moment and asked, "What's the other hole for?"

Southey stomped the earth with his boot and said, "To bury it when we kill it."

"That's awfully respectful of you," Rick replied.

"It's not *respect*, it's a safety precaution, incase it is still alive. A leech can play possum very well." Southey narrowed his eyes, offended.   "You see, one way to kill a leech is to bury it in loose earth. That stops them much like licking your fingers and pinching a flame."

"I don't get it." Rick shrugged.

Jacob, overhearing the esoteric knowledge being divulged, joined in, "Listen, Rick, forget what you've seen in movies...that's all just an elaborated version of the truth."

A pit had been dug to hold a small fire which Rick insisted be made correctly. During his scouting career, he had won a number of 'one-match' fire building contests.   These contests tested fire building expertise. If built optimally, only one wooden match would set it ablaze.   Here, it was easier; he was given a regular lighter.

Dario and Jacob sat on a small log they rolled over to the shallow fire pit.   With their shotguns on the ground, and their feet planted firmly on top of the barrels, they chatted and shared a warm bottle of beer as they watched Rick scurry about to gather some final sticks for the fire.

Cain and Abel's leashes were tied to stakes in the ground, and they sat upright, keeping their gaze in the direction of the woods, which grew portentously dark.

Cricket calls had sprung to life all around, in dizzying numbers.

"Ok boys," Rick announced, with his shotgun in one hand, and a mass of twigs buried under his arm.   "We will have s'mores tonight!"   He chuckled and turned to Jacob and Dario, who had disregarded his words.

Rick knelt down to arrange the twigs along the base of the soon-to-be fire, placing his shotgun idle by his side. The lighter fell from his pocket, unbeknownst to him, and as he crawled around the teepee of sticks, his knee struck his weapon, pushing the beer bottle, which rested between Jacob and Dario's feet; a mouthful of beer spilled onto the lighter, surrounding it, for a moment, in a small muddy puddle which was soon absorbed by the ground.

Rick gasped silently; the lighter failed to light, and he tried to hide the fact he was using his shirt to dry the lighter.

Dario noticed the error. "How's that fire coming along, Cub Scout?" Annoyed, he picked up the bottle and sipped, spitting dirt from his lips; it was the only beer Southey had allowed them.

"I...I...am almost ready," Rick stuttered a bit.

It became clear to Jacob what happened. "Well, I hope we have something else to light it with," he said, standing up, looking toward the tent, a few yards away.

Southey knelt outside the tent, holding his gun in one hand and a set of night vision goggles in the other. Sam was inside, arming himself, and digging through a duffel bag for a case of shotgun shells.

"Can I see your Zippo," asked Jacob to his father. "Rick got the lighter wet."

Southey stood up, furrowing his brow as he glanced over toward Rick. "It's in the van, I never smoke when I am hunting."

Southey stomped towards Rick, who sat with his back turned as he clicked the lighter, desperately. "Did you get the lighter wet, you dumb piece of..." Southey kicked dirt.

Rick jumped out of the way; Southey was a nasty and threatening-looking man, and when Rick beheld his approach, with a large armblade fastened to his arm, and a shotgun in his hand, he could not help but react.

Southey looked down at the arrangement of sticks and twigs. "We'll be doing a lot better for ourselves if we have a fire. In fact, I would say that if we don't have one going soon, we're in for a *very* rough night." Southey was flashing his teeth, pondering spitting on the kid, but Rick was new, and for the sake of the team, he decided against extinguishing what confidence this pup had built up inside himself. "So tell me now, fire-master, are you going to have a fire within the next couple of minutes, or is somebody going to have to run really fast back to the van to get my silver one?"

Sam approached the scene, fastening the armblade to his right arm. "I will go," he clipped the flashlight to a strap on his arm. "I can take care of myself."

"Alright," Southey said, as he handed Sam his shotgun and the night vision. "Take these and I'll go get another from the tent. Be quick, it'll be dark before you head back."

"Uh-huh." Sam put the goggles on his head, but not over his eyes. With his flashlight pointed ahead of him, he jogged off – swifter than would seem possible for an older man – past the cabin and over the hill.

Rick sat awkwardly during the uncomfortable silence which

followed for the next twenty minutes.

It darkened so that a flashlight was necessary to see beyond each others' company. The crickets had sprung into full vigor; their chirps and clicks were so overwhelmingly abundant, that their multitudinous calls merged into a uniform hum which was impossible to shut out.

Jacob turned towards the shadow of the looming forest. With his thermals over his eyes, he glanced around. "There is a deer way off over there," he said, as he pointed east past the clearing. "There are a ton of bats overhead, too," he added. "But I can't hear them over the crickets." Jacob was less concerned about the growing darkness than seemed possible to the others.

Dario sat still, biting his finger, tense and impatient; his gaze fixed towards the path, behind the tent, that lead into the hellishly black wood. To him, that path was more foreboding than every grimy alley, condemned lot, and troubled neighborhood he had wandered through in the city; at least in the city, there were people to hear you scream if things got real bad.

The dogs had not averted their eyes from the woods for quite a while, and their suspicions were always taken with gravity, being their senses were so keen.

To the surprise of all, Rick's face lit up following a click of his dried lighter. Carefully, he leaned toward the fire pit, and within a few seconds, a subtle light grew stronger and a soft crackle became loud pops and fizzes as the fire erupted to life.

"Yes!" Rick smiled, feeling that his success negated his earlier mistake. "Did you see how *easily* it ignited?" When he remembered that Sam had not yet returned, he lowered his eyes.

Southey stood with his back to the fire, and peered into the woods – which now seemed much darker in contrast to the light behind him. In the surrounding clearing, they could see very well and had a comfortable margin of safety from that side, but all around them was a solid black wall of trees.

Cain and Abel began to growl, quietly. All eyes turned to the dogs; now, their noses pointed the other direction, toward the cabin, and they pulled on the leashes hard enough to wiggle the stakes in the ground.

Southey slowly walked away from the fire, towards the cabin. The flashlight clipped to his armblade lit a wide area in front of him. He turned and yelled back at Dario, Rick and Jacob, who watched him from afar, "Keep your damn eyes on the *woods*!"

The boys turned away, and combed the immediate area with their lights, pointing their shotguns into the surroundings.

Southey stood behind the cabin. He peered around, aiming his shotgun in the directions he was not facing, as if guarding his blind spot.

It was then, Southey heard it, perhaps what the dogs had picked up on – a faint male's voice was too far to understand. The crickets' buzz was covering the words. Perhaps he imagined it, he thought. He then thought of Sam, out in the darkness gone over thirty minutes now.

"It shouldn't take him *this* long," he whispered to himself. "I should have sent that idiot, Rick."

He walked a bit further past the cabin and towards the hill Sam had descended, where the stream bent south and flowed downhill.

Southey panned his flashlight across the woods; the shadows danced across the trees, creating the illusion that the trees themselves moved about in the thick darkness.

The cricket symphony continued, as Southey concentrated on the sounds buried beneath the veil of chirps and clicks.

Another faint male voice called softly from the dark, barely above the threshold of hearing.

"There she is," it seemed to say, over and over, slowly.

Southey aimed his shotgun into the darkness, towards where he thought the sound had originated. More whispery voices followed.

"I see her. Don't you?"

"Let's go. Now!"

It definitely wasn't Sam; Southey knew his voice well. However, it was a male, perhaps talking to someone else.

"Look...Do you see..."

"Where?"

The voices were many, and sounded like parts of larger sentences, as if bits of a recording. The calls came from the dark all around – up and down the edge of the clearing.

Southey's eyes were moving back and forth so fast they were getting sore, and he could not help but be concerned with the continued babble.

"The witch..."

"...behind the tree..."

"...coming closer..."

"I...see her....don't you?"

The voices seemed calm, and curious. There were words he couldn't make out over the crickets, but most were clear enough.

"Is someone there...?"

"...don't you?"

"Oh my god! Oh my god!" A male voice cried out forebodingly, and then a gunshot fired off in the distant night.

Southey jumped back, startled. That was not one of his shotguns, the sound was different – a rifle.

The crickets suddenly halted their song. The silence that followed hit Southey like a ton of bricks, a sharp contrast to the ambience from before. Even the voices paused, and in that brief halt, Southey heard the sound of a branch snapping, not far into the darkness.

Southey ran back towards the fire where the dogs were now viciously barking. Cain and Abel no longer were interested with the cabin. Their attention returned to the tenebrous woodland.

All the boys stood, back to the fire, awaiting an order.

"That wasn't one of *our* guns," Southey said, short of breath. "I hope Sam is ok."

Southey looked frazzled, but after a few deep breaths, he gained his composure. The silence ended as the chirp of the crickets slowly began to increase in vigor. The dogs settled down. Whatever disturbed them seemed to have left.

"What *was* that?" Jacob asked his father, almost annoyed.

"I don't know, but we are definitely *not* alone," Southey ran his hands through the hair on the sides of his head, a bit disheveled.

"Those were the souls of missing people," Rick said, as his voice stuttered.

"That's bull! There are no ghosts here! That is just vampire trickery. Where the hell is Sam?!" Southey walked towards the tent. He removed the flashlight from his arm, placing it on the floor so it pointed upwards, lighting the entire tent. He reached for a box of shells, inside one of the large bags.

To his horror, in the corner of his eye, he saw, not a foot away from where he knelt, a face, pressing into the tent from the outside. All its features were clearly visible: the small narrow nose, the recess of the vacant eye cavities, and the gaping mouth which widened ever so slowly. It pressed into the fabric, yet no shadow was cast from the fire, which burnt brightly from behind the frightful effigy. The face was still, facing Southey, even after he froze and it became evident that he was aware of the presence.

"There, I see her!" Jacob yelled from outside the tent, and without delay, the blast of the shotgun rang out.

Southey flinched, and fell on his backside; he had expected a swarm of metal to tear through the tent, to destroy the manifestation, but it didn't happen.

The face tilted down toward Southey, as if to observe him.

With the blade on his right arm, he gashed the side of the tent. The razor-sharp metal tore through the tent with ease. There was nothing on the other side.

Southey peered through the large hole to where Rick stood alone by the fire. Rick's shaking gun aimed at the mouth of the path into the dark wooded realm.

Southey grabbed his flashlight and ran at Rick, shouting, "Where did Jacob and Dario go?"

Southey turned to the direction Rick faced, holding his shotgun tightly with both hands.

Dario and Jacob were stopped, side by side, a few feet into the woods along the path, engulfed by the shadows which the fire sent dancing over them.

The dogs acted rabid, their leashes were tangled as they circled around each other, chewing at their restraints.

Southey unhooked their collars; Cain and Abel ran into the woods, in pursuit of their unseen prey. He then approached the edge of the wood with his night vision binoculars lowered over his eyes. Through the display, the trees and the two boys were visible in green hues. Southey could see far into the forest.

"Where did you see her, Jake?"

Southey panned back and forth with the binoculars, scanning for any motion. But there was nothing in sight.

Jacob pointed off of the path, "She was standing right there! I didn't get a good look though!"

"Crap!" Dario kicked the ground with his boot. He stared down the barrel of his gun, refusing to let his guard down. "You shouldn't have yelled out like that. It scared her away."

Southey was scoping for anything suspicious, when a hand touched his shoulder. It was Sam, a little frazzled, but unharmed.

"Sorry I'm late." Sam panted, a bit out of breath. His flashlight was cracked, turned off, and the night vision goggles were missing. "I got to the van fine enough, but on the way back I started hearing…things. At first I thought it was you guys, but the voices came from all around. I figured you hadn't resorted to splitting up, so I kept following the stream, since it was too dark to see, and then…"

Sam stopped as if to judge the credibility of his next few words.

"…the wind picked up, but it did not feel normal. The breeze came from all sides…."

Rick was losing it fast, listening to Sam's account of the strange wind.

"I looked around with my flashlight," continued Sam, "and I caught a glimpse of her far off, I think." He stopped to glance around.

The dogs were neither seen nor heard, and Jacob and Dario had backed a bit further into the light, having noticed Sam's return.

"What happened to your stuff?" Southey asked.

"It shattered, as if it were hit with a brick. The night vision too. These things can take a beating, or so I thought. Anyway, I used the stream as a guide back...in total darkness."

The crackle of the fire was the only sound for what seemed like a long time, and then Dario called out to the rest of the group.

"Do you hear that?" Off in the dark, the rustling of leaves and the crunching of branches rose up.

Everyone faced into darkness, guns aimed. Southey handed the night vision to Sam. "Here. Be our look out."

The rustling sounds were growing louder by the second.

"It's the dogs!" cried Jacob, when he saw their images in his heat vision, nearing the edge of the woods. "Don't shoot!"

The two dogs came tearing out of the darkness, side by side, running so fast that nobody could tell which dog was which; they darted past the tent, towards the cabin and over the hill, into the descending forest without slowing down.

Southey called to them, but it was hopeless.

"I never seen 'em, run from a leech before." Sam whispered to Rick.

Then, something bone-chilling caught everyone's eyes. Rick, who stared in awe at his shirt, watched as two hands pressed outwards through the fabric, in a similar fashion to the face Southey had seen in the tent. Long, bony fingers moved across Rick's chest, and down to his stomach.

Rick slapped the figures on the shirt with his hand the way someone might if they realized large bugs were crawling on them. He easily ended the manifestation yet felt nothing but the fabric itself. Then the phantom hands poked out from his side, repeating the same haunting game.

Rick screamed as he tore his shirt off and threw it onto the fire, which choked on the smoke produced from the burning fabric. The surrounding area grew darker, and Rick, having realized what he had done, yanked the shirt off of the burning logs. Unfortunately, the fabric caught on the wood, and the weakened structure collapsed on itself. The resulting fire was much smaller.

Southey cursed and turned back towards the woods. To his surprise he saw her – a pale figure standing behind a tree not twenty yards away. His flashlight was not pointed directly at her, and she did not seem to notice his discovery.

No one else saw her in the dark, and Southey began to talk low. "She is out there behind a tree. Sam, you and Rick stay here. Let me know where she goes."

Sam used the night vision to search the area, and he clearly saw what Southey had picked out. The slender figure of a woman leaned against the side of a large tree, which stood between her and the path. Her long hair flowed upward, as if a slow breeze orbited her head.

Southey motioned Dario and Jacob to follow him. They walked along the path, into the dark. Southey intentionally did not shine his light directly on her, waiting for them to get closer before he let her know.

Jacob, who followed directly behind his father, zigzagged his light from side to side at the boding black space around them. He had lifted the thermal vision goggles off of his eyes for the moment.

Dario, last in the line, glanced behind himself frequently, paranoid, and saw Sam and Rick by the smoldering fire.

The only real sound was of their heavy breaths and footsteps on the hard, clay earth.

A branch snapped loudly somewhere to the right, and Jacob and Dario spun to that side, pointing their flashlights, but they saw nothing. Southey knew it was a distraction, a trap to try to get them to turn; he knew the witch was to his left, waiting for them to wander closer. His nerves were strong still, and with the knowledge that Sam would tell him if she moved, he knew not to be concerned.

Sam had the witch in his view, but could not shoot her, since she stood behind a tree, and the three hunters stood in his line of fire. He watched as Southey approached. The witch did not move when he got within five yards of her; the boys, however, did not know exactly where she was, and had fallen a bit behind of Southey, startled by the breaking twig.

Then the pale figure ducked out of view and Sam yelled out, "She moved!"

A light breeze grew from the stillness of the air and swept Southey's hair in front of his eyes. His hand repeatedly needed to let go of the barrel of the gun so he could brush the hair away from his eyes. Annoyingly, it persisted as if it was toying with him.

A shot rang out from somewhere, but none of the men had pulled a trigger. Voices began to surround them from all sides, whispering from what seemed just a few feet away – from behind this tree, or that one. The ravings grew louder and more numerous as the seconds passed, shaking the three hunters' nerves. They could do nothing to stop the ghostly calls, only listen.

"Do you hear that?" One concerned voice began the chain.

"I see her!" replied another.

"Help…"

"...see..."

"...her."

"...coming...go!"

"Let's get out of here!"

"Run!" The last eerie voice was blood curdling, and so convincingly close by.

Without warning, Dario's flashlight shut off; and without attempting to fix the problem, he cursed out loudly, stressed from the impending murmurs, and turned and ran back down the path.

"No! Stay together!" Jacob turned to track Dario with his flashlight, but he could not see him, and no longer heard his steps – only a thud, a brief brushing of branches, and silence. Stupefied, he froze.

Sam had seen things more clearly with his night vision. When Dario had turned to run, the figure emerged on the edge of a path, hidden from Jacob and Southey's view. The witch in the woods tackled the frightened young man with ease. She then hunched over his squirming body, just off of the path and out of range of Jacob's spotlight, and pulled him into what appeared to be a hole in the earth.

Sam ran up to the path, yelling frantically at Jacob who was a few stones throw away. "She got him Jacob, turn around!"

Jacob had walked past where Sam had seen his comrade fall.

Sam aimed his gun and fired twice at the figure obstructed by the trees.

Southey, having heard the commotion, turned back. The whiz of bullets from Sam's shot was uncomfortably close to him, stopping him in his tracks. Pellets smacked into the trees nearby, cracking wood, adding to the confusion. Southey was disoriented from all the chaos; the voices still echoed from around him, calling out to the hunters. Southey found it hard to ignore the whispery and tormented cries – it dizzied him.

"...who are you..."

"...stay back!"

"...she's right there..."

"...there?"

Jacob cautiously followed back along the path, toward Southey, in search for Dario, combing the area with his light. To his shock, he inadvertently aimed the light directly at the witch, who stood off of the path to his right, just a few feet away, and staring right into his eyes. His body went numb for just a moment, and as his fingers loosened their grip on his shotgun, his weapon darted out from his hands, landing in the brush far behind the witch.

The witch was very old in appearance, and no more than five feet tall. Her pale-white skin had wrinkles deep like trenches. Patchy moss covered a significant portion of her naked body. Her eye sockets were empty cavities, her nose a narrow ridge of festering cartilage. The tight skin of her cheeks dipped inward like holes, and when her mouth opened up, insects scurried out and crawled into the crevices of her face, and into her nostrils and eye sockets. One second before Jacob's flashlight lens shattered, the witch smiled a black bloody grin.

When the dizzying darkness hit, Jacob swiped the air in front of him with his armblade, desperate to attack the creature before she could sink her toxic fangs into him. But he missed, having hesitated. She fled, silently, scarcely making a noise on the forest's debris laden floor.

Southey approached his son, and stood next to him, holding the only light left between the two of them. He searched the immediate area, but saw only trees and shadow.

"No way," yelled Jacob. Even with his thermal goggles, he could not see the still-warm body of his friend, hidden among the trunks. "Where did he go? Dario?" He yelled into the woods, but there was no reply. Dario was gone.

Southey panned the area again with his light. "Where is his body? Where?" Southey gnashed his teeth.

Jacob was stunned and speechless. Her frail, ghastly white image had burned into his mind, and the terror numbed his limbs. Only when his father nudged him did he turn and walk back out from the woods.

Sam had trotted a ways down the path, but was hesitant to abandon Rick, who had been cowering. He pointed west and yelled out, "I saw her in a tree!" She could be anywhere!"

Southey looked past Sam, toward the darkness once lit by their camp fire. "Is Rick still there?"

Sam ran back towards the camp, only to find a smoldering fire with no sign of Rick at all.

"Rick!" Sam called out.

Jacob and Southey had exited the path, and the woods, standing by the tent.

"Rick, come back!" Jacob yelled.

There was no response at first, but then something they hadn't expected replied. A crackled, raspy female voice whispered from the very sky above their heads, "Rick we need you. They need you." Then the voice deepened unnaturally, "I need you."

Southey, Jacob and Sam were all alone. Southey held the only flashlight, Sam the only night vision, and Jacob, without a gun, possessed the only thermal goggles.

Jacob, still optimistic that Dario might be alive, peered through his thermals into the woods. To his amazement, he saw a person, colored in yellow and orange hues, sitting behind a tree, perhaps hurt.

"It's him, he's alive!" Jacob yelled, thinking that it had to be a person; after all, leeches were cold.

He darted bravely and foolishly into the dark, at the half-concealed figure, with no light, except for what his father could illuminate from an increasing distance.

Southey and Sam did not hesitate to follow after him, and called for him to wait.

Jacob was a fast runner and had gained a good distance on the older men. As he neared his destination, and saw more accurately its petite, frail size, a doubt entered his mind. He realized, too late, that he was running at the witch, and not Dario.

Before then, the fact that leeches got warm after they fed had somehow eluded the hunters; Jacob was the first one to discover this – to his death.

It was hard to stop on a dime; Jacob's foot slid on the dirt as he tumbled head first into the trunk of a tree. His face broke when his skull collided with the thick, gnarly trunk. He was not conscious when the witch dragged his limp body off of the path.

Southey and Sam heard the smack of the tree, followed by the scuffle of twigs and cones. Older, and incapable of running as fast, they arrived with no knowledge of what happened to Jacob.

Southey cried out into the dark, "You bitch! Show yourself!" He fired into the air; debris fell from the canopy overhead.

Sam panned around with his night vision, but to his dismay, saw no signs of the witch or Jacob.

It was now just Sam and Southey, and as if their hearts were not pounding hard enough, the sounds of strange voices from the woods arose once again.

"he's not here…gone?"

"she got him…he's…"

"we're dead…"

The repeating voices were both close and far away, making the environment unnervingly surreal.

"…I want to go…"

"We're gonna die…"

"Run!"

Listening to the frightful wails, the two men were so tense, they would have shot each other if one of them yelled 'boo.'

Suddenly, Southey heard in his ear, as if whispered directly into it, her voice, taunting him, "You did not find me," she said with an old, scratchy voice. "You were sent to me. I'm the hunter in these woods you fool. They are mine, and now…you are too!"

Southey panicked.   For the first time in his life, he was genuinely terrified and acted out of emotion, not logic. He turned and ran deeper into the woods, his shrieks echoing throughout, meshing with the other tormented voices.

Sam listened to Southey's screams fade and watched his terrified friend dissipate into darkness with the only source of light.

Sam's head spun as he pondered their failure. With the night vision as his only means to see, he spun around and around. A tugging at his shirt and pants stopped his mad, desperate search, and he was lightly jerked back and forth, and side to side. It was then when he noticed, peering through his night vision, dozens of tiny spiders hanging from overhead branches. The arachnids he had brushed into were crawling all over his body. Clenching his shotgun with a mighty grip, he began to fire in all directions, desperately.

Southey had not run too far before he heard Sam's frantic shots. Courage rose up inside him, and after he rationalized that to split up meant his doom, he turned and ran back along the path as fast as he could. His flailing arms shook the flashlight, almost to the point of uselessness, and his legs were rubbery and numb with fear. He picked up on a soft sound as he returned; it was Sam, gurgling and trying to speak.

Southey pointed his flashlight to his side and saw the bare-white back of a woman, hunched over Sam's body. Patches of green moss covered the skin on her back, legs, and arms. Her shoulders and spine poked through the skin on her frail body. Her long, white hair ran down onto the soil and twigs – leaves and bark were entangled within, and moving all over her body, and through her locks, were hairy, black spiders.

The witch turned from feeding to face Southey who approached her slowly, no longer at the mercy of emotion, though his chest was tight and he found it hard to breathe.

Southey lifted his shotgun, looked into the dark pits which used to contain her eyes, and aimed at her head. Her face was so foul, so lifeless, that the warmth of his body seemed to spill into the air, leaving his limbs tight and rigid.

As he pulled the trigger back, an ear shattering wail shrieked so loudly, that Southey dropped his gun to the ground when he reflexively covered his ears from the painful siren. His eyes welled up with tears and his undergarments turned soggy and warm; never had he heard a sound so sour, so vile.

Having dropped his gun, standing with his eyes closed, Southey already resigned to his imminent demise. But before his worst fear was realized, Sam hooked his right armblade at his distracted predator, sending her head spinning into the air before it smacked the earth and rolled aside.

The decapitated corpse collapsed onto Sam, but its stumpy neck did not gush blood. The voices in the woods halted, and slowly, the rising chirps of crickets took over the darkness.

Sam sat up; his hand was pressed to the side of his neck as blood squirted through his fingers.

"I'll be ok," he croaked. "She barely got me." Sam's eyes were full of tears, and his face pale. He grabbed her severed head by its long hair.

Southey struggled to focus. He murmured, "We'll get you to a hospital...Hurry."

Southey grabbed the defeated corpse by its ankle and dragged it back to the clearing, where Dario had dug a shallow grave beside her cabin.

Southey tossed the headless corpse in, stepping on it to pack it in tightly. Sam dropped her shriveled head in on top. Her skin was teeming with night crawlers, beetles, and other flesh-hungry insects which seemed to come from nowhere.

Southey turned to face the woods. He wanted to go back and find the bodies, or perhaps just to grab some of his equipment, but Sam's face was turning pale, and the filthy bite of the vampire had to be treated fast. It could quickly turn fatal. Dazed and exhausted, the two men left everything they were not already carrying behind.

As if blinded by the flashes of one hundred cameras, the two men could not shake the image of her face, burnt into their sight, hovering in the darkness around them; and though no more voices spoke to them from the depths of the woods, their minds replayed the events over and over in their heads, refusing the men any sanctuary from their nightmare.

The only body found was that of Rick's, which lay face down in the stream along the way back. He had tripped when he fled, and struck his head off of a rock. He drowned in the shallow water, and just out of reach of his hand was his shotgun.

Southey stopped to take the shotgun, but he didn't have the patience to unfasten the armblade, and the flashlight was busted, the lens cracked like the others. Southey left Rick's body to rot.

Back at the van, Cain and Abel sat in the moonlight, awaiting their masters' return. The dogs wagged their tails as the two men approached.

Southey immediately opened the passenger door and lit a cigar.

The hunters had been decimated, Southey's kin eradicated – the price of killing a legend...of the witch in the woods.

Chapter 5 – The First Dawn

The hour had grown late. Lucia's work on my corpse was an immense improvement. My limbs hardly resisted when I moved them, and I felt lighter and swifter, as if my feet scarcely touched the earth. When I studied my face, my eyes and my skin, I did not look like the same deathly creature, though I felt it beneath the thin layers of crèmes and powders. I suspected there were many subtle elements to my less-than-lively mannerisms – in my speech, my expressions – which suggested my nature. Until I learned more about where, and what I was, I had to be cautious.

Without a destination, and ambivalent as to my direction, I wandered aimlessly about the city, studying the small journal I had found. Full of memories that I could not remember, the handwritten words failed to endow me with even the most fleeting sense of familiarity; yet the writer and I seemed to share an underlying dread, loneliness, a sense of displacement.

April 4 - 10:05 pm
What am I even doing here...in this city? I don't want to be here. It's ugly to me, and I feel ugly here. I have a couple more months' prepaid rent, but then I should leave. Somewhere out there is a place I care about, a place I have yet to discover. How do I find it? How do I get there?

I avoided main avenues whenever possible, passing through many surrounding neighborhoods, remaining unseen on the edge of shadow. Residential roads were more pleasant; the silence of the night sung to me, and the lessening of commotion all around deepened my vampire eyes and ears.

I easily heard the voices and actions of residents within the walls of their homes, and with little effort at all – a quick glance – those walls revealed their contents to me. From the streets and sidewalks, with spiritual eyes, no longer confined to flesh, I exercised the fascinating perversions of my sensory prowess.

At that late hour, most people slept soundly, unaware of my otherworldly presence hovering above them in their slumber, looking down at them from above their beds, feeling heat from their cuddled up bodies seeping up through their loosely swaddled bed sheets, as the soft drumming of life beat inside them. Once or twice, rapt at life's savory lure, I stretched my phantom hands across the bedding, towards their exposed necks, but their bodies eluded my spiritual touch, my grasp. I was able to pull the soft bed sheets and thick comforters off their bodies to expose their vibrant veins and arteries, but when I reached my ghostly hands toward their flesh, I felt nothing.

However, my actions were not entirely without effect; sleepers stirred and moaned in displeasure, and the rapidity of their heartbeats responded like an alarm, as if my hands reached through them, into their very thoughts, eclipsing their very dreams. When my malevolent curiosity would shake them from slumber, they sat up in their beds, breathing heavy; and though I was certain my presence was invisible, the wakened sleepers' eyes sometimes fixated on the space in which I lingered. I wondered if I was totally undetectable.

I walked a couple of miles, experimenting with my abilities, feeling the soft hum of life reverberating inside each passing home. When a rowdily barking dog, dismayed at my passing, incited his canine neighbors to join in a feral chorus, the ruckus brought onlookers to their front windows – and I moved on, fearful to be seen.

I passed through the quaint, nestled, suburban clusters, and along a well-lit, uninhabited road, which stretched past an airport. The high-pitched buzz of massive lights filled the area, clawing at my senses, and the muffled roar of an approaching flight screamed from above a miserably bland sky, shaking the air forcefully. Hastily, I moved away from there, until the airfield lights fell far behind me, and the shadows of the night covered every surface again.

Darkness did not inhibit my sight in the least; in fact, its stillness, its calm, clarified my perceptions altogether, and I knew I would find peace only in darkness. I roamed in the shadows, brooding over what I was to do with myself, with my time.

As I walked, I read more of that curious journal. Most entries in the journal were a collage of depression, angst and frustration – the manic melody of a lost soul...perhaps mine.

April 10 - 9:30pm
What nice weather. Sunny, warm. I went to Bayview, played chess for hours. That Russian kid beat me 4 out of 5 games, which would be ok if he weren't half my age. Where did a 13 year old learn to play like that?...and I am good with the King's Gambit too.

April 16 - 11am
I wonder what it is like to matter...to have a definite

role...not to be just a spare part of some larger machine. Currently, I am anonymous. Lots of people are. I shouldn't feel so bad. I should just learn to cope. That's what this little book is for...to cope, and so that when I am dead, someone can read it and laugh, and for at least that one ridiculous moment, I will be known.

April 20 - 4:30pm
There are two times when someone will get the recognition they deserve: When they've done something terrible, something ethically heinous, and when they are dead...yeah, a funeral...that is when people really stop and think about you...hold you inside them and taste your memory. But who would come to my funeral, except the few obligated to, crying perfunctorily because that is what people do at funerals. I'm nobody. I wish I could die and then have my ghost hang around just to see how people reacted...see how people really felt about me...

I read that sordid wish over and over, heeding its irony. *Was my vampirism random, a punishment, or a wish come true?* I thought, as I reread those last words. *There has to be a purpose to it all. Did I hope this deathly state onto myself?* I pondered, confused. That last line was only a coincidence, I was sure.

The quiet road stretched toward a development, where soothing darkness yielded to bright lights. Groupings of closely-knit apartments were strewn amongst small shops and businesses. Automobiles lined the edges of the widened road; there was hardly a lot or driveway to contain them. From the sidewalks, I peered into dark lanes, stifled by the crowded buildings. Alleys beckoned me to escape into their shadows; the gloomy sky had lightened noticeably, and night was transposing into the early phases of dawn. A sense of urgency welled up inside of me, a fear I did not yet understand.

"Hey brother." A rough, weakened male voice called out from between two of the apartments.

A dumpy, grimy man staggered into the light, walking lamely, as if one of his knees could not bend. He wore grubby blue sweatpants, and a torn, red windbreaker jacket. More hair hung from his chin than from the top of his head. His face contorted and twisted with some nervous spasm. His heartbeat was fast, anxious; I heard its palpitations as surely as a maestro detects a deviation in tempo. The man was weak.

"Help m'yout. Spare some change? Um hungry and homeless." His pasty, shriveled tongue licked his lips as he spoke, and he extended a greasy, calloused hand and continued to beg, mumbling incoherencies occasionally favored with a discernible utterance. His eyes bulged out with total desperation. His expressions were awkward, almost as if I offended him.

He breathed very hard and presumed no intrusion when he stood almost toe to toe with me, speaking, "I need a dollar, just a...I got nothing...help. Don't walk away."

"I do not have any money."

I looked into his eyes, and saw his pain. Behind that reddened, glossy, aimless stare, I sensed his fear, not of me, but of himself and what he had become, and how hopeless it was to change any part of it.

What crime had driven a soul so far into ungodliness, that I, even after all I have seen that night, could be repulsed?

"Anythin' please...a quarter? Help me. I'm sick." The beggar grabbed my arm, as if he were afraid I would turn – or perhaps he did not want me to see a figure approaching me from behind – and with his dirty fingers clenched to the fabric of my sleeve, he smiled, when it seemed to him that I was oblivious.

Creeping silently along the sidewalk was a younger, healthier-looking man, with a baggy sweatshirt hanging to his knees. He suspiciously held his hand in the front pocket. It was easy for me to see that his fingers were wrapped tightly around the hilt of a small knife. When he was only a few feet away, the attacker pulled his left hand from the pocket, and raised the knife over his head.

I pushed the rotund old man down onto the concrete; his head clopped off of the sidewalk, and he was still. In his helpless moment, I stood on his chest with both feet, and turned to face the aggressor.

The baggy-clothed offender lowered his knife and held his hand out by his side, preparing for a slicing motion.

I saw the surprise in his face, the uncertainty in his eyes when he realized I would not be duped into being backstabbed. I sensed his fear, and it riled me in a peculiarly gratifying way.

Cautiously, he inched toward me, his heart pounding as he sneered at me in some vain attempt to instill fear in me.

"Hand over your wallet and the blade stays clean," he spurted.

The knife-wielding thief was under the illusion that he had some sort of power over my emotions. Was I supposed to freeze? Panic? I felt as calm as I did when I watched Lucia removed my organs from my corpse and throw them away.

The old man clasped my ankle with his hand, trying to pry my foot off of his sternum. But I pushed my heel down, into his chest, and I twisted it into the bone.

"Get off! Stop! I'm sorry!"

I pointed my finger at the assaulter who stopped three feet from me. "I will be doing the only killing tonight!" With intentionally motionless lips, but a mouth hanging wide open, I spoke with a ghostly ambience innate to vampires; my words called to him unnaturally by his side, as if a breeze formed the words.

The goon jerked his head with a vigor that could have snapped his own neck. He expected to see someone there, but was soon reassured we were alone. His brow raised, his eyes widened. The unwonted manner of my voice had spooked him.

His heart pounded, and reacting out of fear, he lunged forward and swung the knife just inches from my throat. To avoid the blade, I hopped from the chest of the capitulated body, which had ceased its writhing under my feet. The crazy old man, no longer pinned by my foot, took the opportunity to roll to the side, out of our way.

With a desperate grunt – a feeble battle cry – the knife rounded back at me.

I felt the blade slicing through the air, heading toward my face in a backhanded stabbing motion. Somehow, without thinking, I knew what to do. I stopped the blade mid-swing, not with my hands, but my thoughts.

The mugger's elbow buckled from the sudden stop, as if he had stabbed an invisible wall.

"Ow! How the ...?" He clenched his elbow with his right hand, wincing in pain.

The blade had stopped a foot from my head, and his hand, still gripping it tightly, tugged at the hilt, but he could not pull the knife free from my influence.

I extended my arm, grabbed his wrist and squeezed as hard as I could, but he would not let go of the knife, even when I sunk my clammy fingers into his wrist.

"Let go!" he screamed. "Your hand is cold!"

With his free hand, the frightened thug made a fist and swung wildly. For some reason, I could not stop his punch as I had his knife, and he pummeled my jaw with alarming force. I staggered back, still gripping his wrist.

"Yeah, you like that?" He grew excited. "I got another one for you." The thug pulled at his constrained arm, but was unable to loosen my cold grip on his wrist. He made another fist, pulling his arm back for another punch.

Not making the same mistake, I focused on the knife, and not his fist. My mind wrapped itself around the blade, intimately perceiving it, feeling its shape, size and sharpness. When I felt as if I held the knife in my own hand, by my will alone, it twisted inside his palm.

His eyes, wide with disbelief, fixed themselves on the blade which rotated in his sweaty hand, against all logic, and though he used both hands, he still could not stop the twisting.

He let go of the weapon, and the knife fell with a metallic clank against the pavement.

I released his wrist and the thug staggered back a few feet. I stepped towards him, slowly, but he receded with every step I took, continuing to stare into my new eyes with a terrified curiosity. I rotated them so the whites filled my sockets, and pulled my lip up to express how offended I was.

He turned and ran. I let him escape, though I felt I should have punished him. The grimy, dumpy old man was hunched on his knees behind me. His hand was pressed to his chest, and he wheezed wildly. He attempted to stand, but fell down, short of air.

"I can't breathe, I can't breathe," he gasped as saliva fell from his mouth.

I stood over him. With no way to save the man, nor the inclination to do so, I took hold of his pudgy arm and dragged him into the shadows between two adjacent buildings. When I was far into the alley, I pulled the man's collar back and leaned closer.

I was not driven by hunger, as before, but depravity, selfishness. I was not maddened by that horrible cold, throbbing pain I wakened with. I knew very well what I was doing this time. I had to have that warmth again, that elation that I had felt when I first tasted life.

"What...are you...do...ing?" The man spoke between feeble gasps. His eyes were closed.

I only hesitated for a moment then bit his neck with a soft crunch.

The air around me became dark as I drained his life. Sick and weak, the strain on the old man's heart was too much. Hardly a moment passed before the beating stopped, and only a few mouthfuls of blood were taken. Five seconds after I bit him, that wholly satisfying warmth poured through me, the intense climax seemed to electrify my senses.

I stood up, watching him grow cold, hoping I had done him a favor. Perhaps, in that one selfish moment, when I bowed to my desire, I also freed him from his sickly and demeaning existence. I tried desperately to make sense of everything, trying to justify my actions. Was I merely a reaper of life, a slave to some evil will?

Would I be doomed to lead an iniquitous existence, spending my nights lusting over innocent sleepers… killing whoever crossed my path? I did not want to believe it. I was not without emotion – a mindless creature whose fate is left entirely up to chance. I knew I would need to find my place, my role, before I resigned to the madness that undermined my every desire…releasing some devilish creature from within.

I walked out from the alley, wiping my bloody mouth against my sleeve.

The sky was brighter. A new, threatening stimulus seemed to cloud my thoughts, piercing my soul with a new, frightening pain that could not be extinguished. A distant shrieking arose from the eastern horizon, like the torrid wails of a distressed goddess.

I ran down the sidewalk, searching for protection from the sky, which seemed to scream down at me. I needed to lie down, to hide. Something was terribly wrong. I was not welcome out there anymore, and I felt it in the air. I dashed west a few blocks, facing the still-darkened dawn's horizon, yearning for its protection. With the looming doom climbing at my back, the apartments and small shops fell behind me, consumed from my sight by the growing radiance.

The street tapered into a dirt and gravel road, and crossed a grassy clearing. There, a short, stone bridge arched over a small, gloomy pond, laden with the floating debris of nearby flora. On each side of the crossing, robed angels sculpted with jubilant expressions, silently played their slender trumpets.

I came to the perimeter of a massive cemetery. A plethora of graves were scattered along many large, rolling hills, cloaked by hundreds upon hundreds of old, towering trees.

Tombs and crypts, built into the sides of the grassy mounts, welcomed me with massive, steel doors atop marble and concrete steps, shouldered by blooming gardens. Dirt paths branched in every direction, each road twisting over and around the green, lush, swells, disappearing into an ocean of trees and headstones.

Entry into the many mausoleums and tombs proved impossible; padlocks, clamped over rusty corroded bars, kept the dark and inviting rooms out of my reach.

Each passing second, my torment grew. A bright, burning plague escalated overhead and I found myself running from hill to hill, trapped in a maze of decaying shadow.

Then, atop a tall grassy peak, I saw a pyramidal structure made of large stone blocks. A cross was mounted at its apex, where the four walls convened, almost twenty feet high. Grass and roots grew forth from the gaps between the massive slabs of granite, darkened with age.

Fate was kind. An opened door on the tomb exposed its inviting, shadowy core and I hurriedly clambered the earthen slope to the base of the elongated pyramid. The doorway was cast a few feet into the sloped wall, sheltered by a small covering.

Inside, beyond the warped metal door, was a tiny dank cell with no windows. A short pedestal in the center of the room held a large carving of an opened tome; upon it, written across two pages of rock, was the name Blavatsky.

With all the force I could gather, the metal door groaned loudly, swinging shut at my command, and scraping to a halt against the rocky frame.

In that dark, cool tomb, the painful wail of a looming sunrise had been muted; though its presence was not entirely without effect. The sun haunted me from outside, blinding me from perceiving what lay beyond the tomb's thick walls. My gaze could not pierce the intense light of day.

I was safe only in shadow, never again to roam in the light. I would need to find a convenient dwelling lest be cornered by sun one ill-fated dawn. For the moment, I was safe, granted the door remain closed. I had neither the energy nor the means to relocate, so I rested my corpse in the far corner. Succumbing to the exhaustion brought about by the change in atmosphere, I fell into a deep, deathly rest.

The rest was peaceful, and like the dream when I had been unconscious before, I seemed to float in darkness, though I did not hear voices calling out in the dark. I woke without pain, hunger, or the sense of urgency I had felt after my waking; in fact, I might have remained there and slept for many days had I not been so curious to what I would find out about myself.

When the sun faded outside the crypt walls, and I was able to see beyond, into the safety of the cemetery, I fell upward from the dank corner of the floor, lifting to my feet in a swift rising motion.

At the mere suggestion, with screeching hinges, hideously crying out, the warped tomb door hurtled open, slamming into the outer wall of the crypt.

Dusk's dim light bowed to evening's canopy – a palette of black and dark blues. I stood at the top of the hill, overlooking the landscape, still softly aglow from belated light.

Many crows woke from rest in the surrounding trees and flew over me like a storm; their raucous hollers chopped through the air as they flew far into the sky.

The air became silent, but filled with oft-overlooked sounds:

The trees told me to hush when the wind blew softly through their leaves; and the faint hum of a distant highway was cleverly hidden beneath the air's breath, only detectable during its lulls. Miles away, a ship boomed its call – much quieter than the buzzing of the mosquitoes, which flew past me, uninterested. Without a discernable sensation to be picked up by my numb and dead flesh, all those subtle sounds were pieces of my experience. It was easy to forget I was differentiated from all of it.

I strolled through the massive cemetery, observing scores of beautifully arrogant monuments, superfluous testaments of past lives, all futile attempts at a piece of immortality. But those century-old tombstones, eroded beyond identification, had outlasted the mourners whom once placed flowers at their bare, overgrown, earthen beds; whereas other graves were swallowed by the very ground they once stood upon.

All around me lay a vast spectrum of dying memories. I thought deeply about those buried below my feet, about those who had inevitably fallen to time.

What had these souls done with the piece of immortality they possessed when alive? Had any of their lives become stories, songs, or legends? How many lives had been wasted, or taken away…perhaps as mine had been?

I continued to stroll about the tomb-laden hillside, my mind racing with thoughts. *Right now, in the world…,* I contemplated to myself, *…someone is dying, someone is starving and another is drowning. Right now, others plummet, burn and are murdered. Are those people bound in a hospital or prison…lost in an institution, a war, or worse? Are they innocent victims of chance, or perhaps of someone's malevolence? I could just have easily been one of those unfortunate souls, to be there then, and not here now, to be in hopeless agony and pain, and not in admiration at the beauty of the night – a simple but priceless gift by comparison. And when my peace ends, and my suffering inevitably begins, who then will be happiest? Who then, will be enjoying that which people take for granted – freedom from pain?*

I could have remained dead, and murdered. Would that have been best? *What will change for better or for worse due to my new being?* I asked to myself, over and over with a fleeting hope. *Perhaps I will be forgotten like so many. Have I even yet mattered?*

I recalled the scribbled thoughts of the mysterious journal in my pocket. *How long would the wound of my former self's absence take to heal, or did it not even leave a scar? It is much harder to be a good memory, than to be a bad one…or none at all. What type of memory would I become this time around?*

After much thought, much deliberation, I reached the edge of the graveyard. Greeted by a tall Victorian gate, webbed in ivy, and shouldering neatly pruned hedges, I passed through the double-doors; intricate with lacings, they depicted a flock of geese flying into a sunset.

Beyond a flat stretch of lush grass, the towers of the city awaited me. A wide avenue, bustling with passing cars, and sidewalks crowded with civilians, stretched through a virtual canyon of buildings.

I entered a busy sidewalk. Hiding behind a long coat, false eyes and makeup, I walked alongside citizens, making sure to act like them, to hold my head up, to swing my arms with each step, and not to drag my feet like I was weightless. Whether or not my act was convincing, the strolling herds of people paid little attention to me as I wove through the crowd; they chatted on phones, read newspapers, or hung their heads down, refusing to look at their acquaintances. They had no idea a monster was among them.

Though I seemed to blend in, I felt like I stood out violently. I anticipated that, at any moment, one of the many faces would gawk at me, horrified, and scream for others to witness the creature among them. Thanks to Lucia, they did not; my guise proved effective.

I walked only a few blocks when I concluded it would be best for me to avoid being needlessly amongst a large group of people. Not only was I uncomfortable, feeling wholly unlike them, but I could not clearly watch them all at the same time, not with the onslaught of surrounding city hubbub; the multitudinous motion and clamor was overwhelming, blurring my perceptions.

Feeling at risk, I opted to leave the sidewalks, but I had no idea where to turn to escape. Then, rising above the clatter of humans' feet, piercing the gritty hum of numerous passing cars, I heard the hanging note of a flute. I followed the pleasant sound through the mechanical madness, to Bayview Park, where, leaning against its tall, black gate, was the flutist. The young man I had almost killed guided me to the only sane place I knew in this city.

I passed through one of Bayview's stony pillared gates, and sank deeper into the park.

There, I stumbled onto a curious scene; by the circular grouping of steel, checker-topped tables, men and women sat at the chairs, and stared at the black and white pieces scattered on the tables. Their hands clasped their heads in deep concentration while observers stood by turning from chess game to chess game with avid curiosity.

The only fact I knew about myself, prior to my waking, was that I had played chess, perhaps passionately. I approached one of the tables where a man and a boy shook hands over the completion of a game.

The older gentleman was in a grey business suit; he stood up, with briefcase in hand, and walked away, leaving his white king smothered in its own pieces, checkmated by a crafty black knight.

The victor was much younger – a boy. His hair was white-blonde, and his eyes light blue. He wore tan slacks and a black shirt and stared at the board as if there were subtle lessons to be deciphered from the arrangement of the few remaining pieces. In his mind, the game continued on.

He did not, at first, look up to greet me when I stood across from him, as if he were finishing an important thought. When he finally looked up, he nodded and smiled, saying, "Hello again."

The boy proceeded to move his scattered black pieces into their neutral positions, as I pondered his apparent recognition of me. But I did not speak, only nodding and smiling back. I did not want to frighten him, preventing the chance of him teaching me something about myself.

I sat across from him. He proceeded to set up the white pieces, tacitly inviting me to join. We played three games in a row; I lost each time, but the matches all were long and drawn out, tense and epic. I was puzzled and thrilled that I could recall the game, and knew right away I had found something…an escape, perhaps, a window into a different life.

A wide range of folks – men, women, and children - would stop in for quick matches among the other tables, while others spent many minutes, even an hour, pondering a single move. Everyone in Bayview shared one experience, one passion, united by a concept which transcended the wooden armies of black and white. There, amongst the living, breathing, would-be prey, I found a commonality, a correlation between the unimaginable differences that defined our existences.

Like the flutist who, with a hollow tube and moving air, stirred my soul, this game was not merely the sum of its parts. I was hypnotized at the dynamic symphony innate to chess – its subtle beauty, its operatic story. During each game, two unique minds, stripped of all prejudices, are placed in a battle of philosophies. How could something so silent be so powerful? You did not need ears, eyes, speech or strength to play; the only requirement was a mind.

Hours passed.

Few words were ever exchanged, and I kept my face down at the board. The serenade of the flutist lasted long, but as the night grew deeper, traffic of both cars and people lessened, until the final note fell into silence. Locked in thought, engaged in a splendid game, I was interrupted by a pedestrian's call.

"Dante?" A voice called a few times before I realized it was directed at me. "Is that you, Dante?"

An older gent in a flannel shirt, with a head of scruffy brown hair paired with a beard and mustache, stood by my side. His eyes glanced down at the board, curiously.

I stood and faced him, my attention lost from the game.

He smiled at me, his eyebrows quivering, perhaps noticing a change in my appearance. I had died, after all.

I made an effort to move my fake eyes, to pretend I was alive. I thought to move my mouth, not to project my voice, but to keep it nestled by my cold corpse's breathless lips.

"I am sorry. I had an accident, and suffered serious memory loss." I lied to him.

"That's horrible, Dante." The pitied man extended his arm, patting my shoulder. "I haven't seen you in so long I figured something awful had happened. I guess I was right!" He paused. "Oh, I'm sorry. I'm Jeremy."

"How long have you known me?" I asked, wondering what information this opportunity could offer.

"You *really* don't remember?" Jeremy clenched his chin with his hand, "...about a year. We play...played chess, frequently, at the club in Crouse Hall." He pointed over his shoulder, indicating the direction. He scratched his head, and then took a peek at his watch.

I pulled the picture from my jacket pocket – the one I found wedged between the pages of a notebook in my apartment. The man playing chess with me in the photo was Jeremy.

"I remember *that* day," he said, leaning over to see the photo. "That's over in Crouse, one of the first days we competed. After I beat you, we came here and I taught you some openings." His smile was encouraging, but faded with my silence.

"Don't you remember *anything*?"

"Not yet." My monotone voice must have given him the impression I was annoyed, or uninterested...but nothing was further from the truth.

He smiled and chuckled. "You remembered how to play, I see."

"Barely."

I glanced at the board, at a position I was glad to have abandoned. The young boy figured, wisely, to gather the pieces and leave.

"Want to see where the photo was taken? It is just around the corner. I have only a few minutes, but maybe it will help."

"Lead the way."

"Anything to help a friend," he said.

I followed Jeremy a short distance, over to a large cathedral-looking building made from rust-colored stone, and plastered with many small windows. Four steeples, with tapered roofs, climbed from the corners, and a bell tower extended upward from above the large, arched front doorway.

Jeremy gripped the railing and climbed a high set of dark marble steps.

"I don't want to sound...I mean..." Jeremy stuttered, "You seem a bit troubled. Do you need any help?"

"I will be fine. Everything is so...new, again."

Jeremy turned to look at me, and I knew I did not fully match his memory, physically and emotionally...but he was kind enough not to push.

Through tall, heavy wooden doors was a main hall, a large towering room with a ceiling many stories high. An ascending wooden stairway, with red carpeting and hand-carved hardwood railings, wrapped around and around the room, tracing the walls up until the top floor.

A gigantic library lay beyond an opened door, across from the entrance, and Jeremy hastily walked inside. Massive bookshelves lined the walls. Narrow, metal landings circled the perimeter of the library, accessible by stairways on each side.

In the middle of the room, librarians stood in the center of a large, circular desk. Many wide tables filled the floor space, laden with opened books, and occupied by people taking notes, or pouring over texts.

Jeremy nodded at one of the young folks sitting at a table, who looked at him, smiled, and said, "Back already? That's a record."

Jeremy laughed and threw his thumb over his shoulder at me. "Just showing my friend the chess room."

Jeremy turned in to one of many small rooms adjacent to the library. Inside awaited a study, with a tall ceiling, and walls paneled with intricate designs. Finished hardwood floors matched the rich, dark wooden walls, on which hung many framed photographs. A cold, ashy fireplace rested against a far wall. Folding tables and chairs were propped near an old blackboard on one side. A single window, which stretched all the way to the ceiling, looked down to the street below.

Jeremy walked over to one of the photos hanging by the fireplace and pointed at the men depicted playing chess.

"See? You and I won a team tournament late last year."

The black and white photo showed Jeremy and me holding a

trophy. The caption read: D. Fairchild and J. Silman.

Jeremy walked around, clicking his shoes intentionally on the hard floors.

"Once a week, every Saturday, a bunch of us in the city meet here, and we play. Sometimes someone brings in music, but usually it's just the soft patter of wood on wood." He looked out a window, in a deep stare. "I've been playing here for years. I've gotten to know some of the regulars very well, yet most of them hardly say a thing. You can tell a bit about someone by the way they play... their style."

Jeremy turned and sat on the wide sill, picking at his fingernails. I walked toward him, wanting to ask him anything I could to enlighten me about where I came from.

"...and what was my style?" I asked him.

Jeremy chuckled, and thought for a moment, and said, "Quiet...reserved. You didn't like to throw your men out there without a purpose. You waited for your opportunity, and then you pounced. Well, until I taught you the King's Gambit."

"...and then what happened?"

Jeremy shook his head. "Then you became aggressive, nurturing the initiative until it exploded in your opponent's face. It's a great opening. Risky, though. Bobby Fischer enjoyed it for many years."

"Bobby...?"

Jeremy laughed. "Nevermind. I'm rambling. Don't get me talking chess or I'll be late." He stole a peek at his watch again. "You came in here, Dante, early last fall. You had taken some books from the library, and on your way out, saw a bunch of us playing in here. You spied from the door, until I saw you and invited you in for a game. I won."

Jeremy laughed, and with minor effort, I returned a smile, which I am sure, he appreciated. I'm sure, though, that I looked generally unamused...which was far from the truth.

"Did I ever tell you anything about myself? Anything personal?"

Jeremy shook his head. "Not beyond what you were thinking during a game, I guess. I mean, we chatted about current events and philosophy and what we were going to do when we went home. You were quite reticent, but I liked that. Though, not without a personality..." His eyebrows rose, "...you were an acquired taste."

Jeremy took a good look at me, his eyes looked head to toe.

I was sure he knew something. How could I hide it? I knew nothing about the person I imitated...not much, anyway.

"You seemed unlike yourself, for the last month or so." Jeremy

sounded concerned.   "...and then you disappeared. Do you know
why?"

I probably had spent the time locked in my apartment, suffering
from depression, drug addiction, or some other form of breakdown –
perhaps the writings in my journal would shed more light. Truth of
the matter is I must have been taken to hell and back to have
changed to what I am now.

"I think I might have been having a bout with depression," I
suggested, not knowing any better.

Jeremy nodded.   "When the summer was starting, you
mentioned, in passing, that you had met a girl. Know anything
about that?"

"No."

"So, did you hit your head?" he asked.   "How did this all
happen?"

"I just...woke...and recalled nothing." I pondered how I would
even attempt to explain the truth, if I had wished to. "This was
yesterday, actually."

"Really? Well, I think you should see a doctor." Jeremy stole a
final glimpse of his watch. Jumping from his seat, he seemed to have
lost track of the time. "Oh man. I am late. I have really got to go, but
it is good to see that you are alive, Dante. Are you okay? Do you
have a place to stay?"

"Yes," I said. "I know where my apartment is." I was not sure
yet if I could or would ever return to that apartment, the place of my
waking.

"Great. You should come next week and play, I will be here.
Saturday at eight."

He walked to the door, turning to get another curious look at
me.

"I'll be curious to see how things are going? Bye Dante. Glad
you're okay."

He left, but I remained for a few moments, looking at my
picture on the wall, wondering about the stranger wearing my
corpse as a body.

Dante Fairchild. My name is Dante Fairchild, I thought the words
over and over. It did not seem right, to be associated with
something totally foreign to me, someone I could never draw a tear
for.

No! My name was *Dante Fairchild.*

I was denied that past, having been reborn into a new, grim
world. I would have to start over from scratch, form a new identity,
else everything would be meaningless.

I could not go on in search of someone who did not exist anymore.   I was forever independent of Dante Fairchild, born through him.

My new name was Child.

Chapter 6 – Southey's Secret Weapon

A young woman slowly opened her eyes, staring into utter darkness, her cheek pressed against a cold, hard floor. Lifting her heavy head off of the concrete took much effort; she needed both hands. Her elbows buckled from her lack of strength; it was the hardest pushup of her life. She groaned – a nasty headache. Her head hurt merely from being conscious; she heard the throbbing of her own temples in the dead silence.

She sat upright, not knowing which direction she should face.

Something was pressed against her skin; she peeled sticky globs from her face and hands. The floor felt mucky, covered in a mysteriously wretched matter.

What's that smell? She wondered, inhaling. A nauseating emanation filled the dank, still air, not the foulness of human waste, but equally as disturbing.

Listening to the darkness, the only sounds were her slow and steady gasps. She waited for her head to stop spinning, but it would not cease; her temples throbbed loudly.

"What's wrong with me," she uttered lowly, just to hear her own voice.

Massaging her skull hardly lessened the pain. The ache did not appear to be the result of a bludgeoning; her shaky hands examined her head, but there was no lump or cuts. She struggled to recall what had happened, where she was…but her mind felt intoxicated, and she couldn't think straight.

When her pupils were fully dilated, she was still scarcely able to distinguish a thing in the dark.

I'm definitely indoors, she thought.

Slowly, she rose to her achy, bare feet, staggering briefly. Sticky filth from the floor was wedged between her toes, and finding a clean place to step was guesswork.

Rubbing her arms, she attempted to ward off the cold that seeped through to her bones, but her hands were clammy, and the friction of skin on skin was less than ample.

She did not have much clothing on. Her cotton short-sleeve shirt exposed her midsection to the damp air. Her extremely high-cut denim skirt did not protect her from the rough, rocky texture of the floor; and the skin on her legs was covered with sores, not to mention more of that putrid matter lying about.

She began to examine each of her fingers. *My rings.* She felt her wrists, neck, and then her earlobes. *My…my jewelry. Who took it?*

"Echo?" She blurted; her utterance speedily returned to her, telling her of the close confinement of her surroundings.

When she raised her arms, her hands slapped against a rugged cement ceiling.

Then, a glint of light caught her eye, sparkling like a lone star.

Tiptoeing cautiously across the room, her arms swept the air in front of her, lest an unseen protuberance strike her face.

When she neared the wall, only a few feet from where she had been lying, she aligned her eye to the ray of light – a desperate attempt to escape the darkness. A small boarded-up window sat high on the wall, almost on the ceiling; a crevice between two rotted panels allowed the sun to seep through.

Tracing the edges of the small window with her fingers, she searched for a hold on one of the planks, but they were secure, fitting tightly inside the narrow frame of rock. Even if she had managed to undo the blockade, the opening was not wide enough for anyone to crawl through.

Standing on her toes, she peered through the tiny crack in the wood. There was nothing visible within the narrow view allotted by the tiny gap, just the dipping sun, hanging over the horizon from its swirling, fiery perch.

Where am I? Her palms stroked the wall, curiously, suspecting the room's cylindrical shape. *There has to be a door somewhere*, she thought, her hope lingering.

With her left hand pressed to the concrete wall, she followed the curve around the room. Her right hand extended outward to warn her of hidden obstructions. Tapping with her foot to make sure there were no holes or hazardous objects, each step was carefully placed on the chilly floor. The floor was free of the gummy, chunky filth around the perimeter of the room.

A noise echoed in the dark; the distinct sound of a tinny metallic clink, lasting only a split second, sent her heart on a rampage. She halted, listening for what she thought she imagined, hearing only her own frenzied heartbeat.

Inhaling deeply, she tried to decipher that retched smell.

Is it an animal? I bet it is rats! She squirmed at the idea of being in a dark cell with smelly, filthy rats. *I hate rats, oh please not those.*

Remaining still, she anxiously listened for anything.

It was just my imagination, she thought, hopelessly studying the darkness for any sign of motion.

She could not decipher the layers of shadow clouding her vision. But the golden ray that breeched the boarded window fell upon the floor's center, and a fine wisp of light, almost totally absorbed by the surrounding darkness, lit a fist-sized area. The small, faded spotlight illuminated an area where a metal pole rose up from the floor. Links of a chain hung from the pole, ran across the floor, and quickly disappeared into the darkness.

Please God. Don't let there be an animal in here with me. Please God please.

Careful to remain silent, her clammy palms pressed against the wall. Her fingers felt for anything – a door, a light switch.

Her breaths were deep and heavy. She struggled not to gasp aloud, but her head felt light, dizzy. Just when she felt as if she would fall unconscious to the floor, overcome with anxiety, the cool, stony wall gave way to a rough, dry texture.

"A door!" she exclaimed, too excited to contain herself.

Her heart filled with hope, and she felt the wood with both hands, just to make sure it was real. To her dismay, there was no handle, knob or opening of any sort, only metal reinforcements running horizontally across the splintery surface.

"Come on!" She pounded her palms against the wood until her skin seared from the friction. "I have to get out of here!" Determined to alert somebody of her presence, she continued striking the door, instead, with her fists.

The door did not even shake on its hinges.

When her wrists were cramped and tender from the pounding of her fists, she threw her shoulder into the wood with all her weight. The door shook, but her small frame and light body reeled back from the force.

When it became clear to her that she was helpless, she sobbed into her sore, bleeding hands. The echoes of her tears filled the room, and when her cries reverberated in the small cell, it sounded like her own voice mocked her.

What do I remember last? She rubbed her head, frustrated at her lack of recollection. *How did I get here? I was out…in a car…Who was with me? I drank something. I was lightheaded…I remember that.*

Her mind scrambled to recall the events leading her there, but something interrupted her thoughts – the sound of something stirring in the dark – likely the chain, scraping on the floor. But the rattle stopped almost as soon as it started.

Her eyes scanned the room, but all was dark, except where the fading daylight had breeched the cell.

"Hello," a male's voice called from the dark.

"Ahhh!" She screamed, falling back against the wall.

When the unseen lurker shuffled, the chain jangled, clinking off both the floor, and the pole.

Again, she slammed her fists into the door, but could not ignore the pain in her hands, and soon had to stop; her fingers were so limp, she could hardly curl them to strike it.

"Nobody is out there right now," the voice told her.

Desperate to be heard, to make a noise, she clawed at the door; but splinters found their way deep underneath her nails, and she halted.

Nausea—she breathed in deep, heavy gasps to resist vomiting. Too weak to stand, she lowered to the floor.

"Yes...Relax for a minute," the stranger coaxed.

As benign as his words were, something about his tone frightened her. Each syllable sent a chill up and down her spine, and in her heightened emotion, she mistook the beating of her own heart for a languished knocking at the door – a hallucinatory salvation.

"I'm in here," she cried out, even after she had realized her optimistic delusion.

The voice spoke to her, either oblivious or apathetic to her fear of it.

"Please," it said softly, and very unthreateningly, "...do not be afraid." His tone possessed a dreamy quality; the walls did not repeat his utterances, his speech devoid of even the slightest reverberation. "You are not here by my bidding."

His words defied her understanding of his location; for it seemed that they moved about, yet she did not hear the scuffing of chain, or flesh, upon the concrete floor.

Adrenaline coursed through her veins, urging her to move, to react, and she was unable to shed a tear in self-pity.

"What is your name?" Its call seemed to precipitate down on her.

She did not reply at first, still attempting to understand the nature of the speech directed at her. It seemed to linger somewhere between thoughts, and spoken words.

"Your name...," it repeated.

"Mana...Ustinova," she stuttered, her nerves shaking.

"That is a beautiful name. Russian?"

"Uh-huh." She whimpered.

"I thought so," it spoke, sounding intrigued.

The chain rattled loudly; links clanking off of each other echoed fiercely.

Mana, with arms wrapped around her legs, rocked nervously on the floor. Her eyes shut tightly, her mind raced frantically; she tried to convince herself she was dreaming.

The rattling drew nearer; metal scratched across the concrete with each slow step the figure took.

Mana stood up, shrieking and pressed her back against the door as hard as she could.

The figure was only a few feet from her, and emitted a foul aroma, which was more than unbearable. His shape was almost discernable up close; she might have imagined it, though, but the contrast of his pale skin seemed to glow in the dark, like fallen snow on a winter's night.

I have to find a way out! I have to find a way out! I have to find a way out! She repeated in her head.

The desire to turn and struggle with the door returned, as futile and painful as it seemed. But she did not dare to turn her back to the stranger.

"How long have I been in here?" she uttered, scared and confused, and willing to humor the unlikely notion that she was actually safe with him.

"I don't know. I was asleep when you arrived. Maybe a couple hours." His lack of fear unnerved Mana, who wanted to hear some distress in her acquaintance's voice, if only to verify that he was on her side.

The figure loomed an arm's reach away. She could feel the presence, cold and still; it rendered her frozen with fear. The air seemed cooler around the figure.

"But I have been in here over a week now, maybe more. I can't be too sure."

Mana's stressed imagination painted many horrid faces on the darkened figure, perpetuating her fear. "What do they want with us?"

"Us? They want nothing from you. Your role in this ordeal is tertiary, at best. I am jealous."

The figure extended his left arm toward Mana; the bones in his hand crunched and creaked as he combed the air inches from her face. The chain let a final jingle as the remainder of its slack was absorbed into its tightly drawn links.

"Get away from me!" she screamed, her voice filled with rage. With a wild swing in the dark, a blind shot, she slapped his arm away, but he did not react.

Keeping close to the wall, she rounded her way back to the sealed window; the faded ray of dusk was totally negated by the surrounding gloom, and soon, there wouldn't even be a twinkle to grace her with a sense of direction.

The chain fell to the floor as the figure turned and slowly followed her to the other side.

"Help me!" Her lips were inches from the miniscule slit between the boards. "Someone...please...!"

Mana pounded the blocked window's boards with her swollen

hands; she gripped the thick planks with her fingertips, already sore from splinters, and pulled with all the strength her pained fingers allowed. Fingernails tore free from her fingers, and she cried out, losing her grip, falling violently down on the floor with a blood curdling cry of pain, which lingered long in the cell.

The shackled figure had almost reached the restraint's limits, but stopping shy, granting her more space. "Don't hurt yourself needlessly," his voice whispered.

"Shut up! Please, stay away from me! Just stay away!" Her hands were cupped, pressed to her chest as she nursed the pain in her bloody, swollen fingertips; it was unlike anything she had ever felt. Sickened at the thought of hearing her own pained echoes, she struggled not to scream again.

Mana scurried back to her feet, and propped against the wall.

"You were brought here *for* me." He took a large stride forward. "But don't let that fact deceive you into thinking I'm happy things turned out this way. Mine is a despicable lot too." His voice developed into a deep growl which seemed inhuman. "*He* put me here."

"Who?"

"Southeeeey!" The figure in the dark screamed the name as if he attempted to summon him with a demented war cry. But his voice was not static; the tormented howl breezed around the room, from above and below Mana. The terrible, supernatural cry chilled the air, the chain jangled fiercely, filling the room with the ear-piercing clatter of many dancing links. And the wooden door creaked, like some unimaginable force pressed against it.

Mana, shut her eyes, covered her ears, and tried to escape, even if to the recesses of her mind. Her knees buckled and she stumbled, falling to the floor.

She remained there, huddled against the wall, her teeth clenched painfully tight with fear. She knew now that the creature could not quite reach her, and that she was safe by the wall.

"I apologize. It was not my intent to frighten you." His voice returned to the peculiarly reserved tone he originally presented.

"Why am I here?" Her weakened voice was hardly audible – barely above her breath.

"You... are my *food*...."

A brief silence followed as the words were slowly digested by Mana's frazzled mind. But when the chain moved again, it drove her to rise to her feet, fearful of what the figure intended to do.

"Southey, in his love of pain, would never allow me to merely reach out and take..." His outstretched hand wriggled inches from Mana's face.

She heard, again, the creaks from the bones of his fingers; the sound disturbed her deeply.

He continued, "...nor would he grant you the mercy of a swift and easy passing...," he lowered his arm, unable to reach her on his own, "...which is why he took away your things. Your *decorations*."

Mana wept, wondering, *How did he know I wasn't wearing my jewelry? How could he see?*

She traced the walls around the room, running her hands high and low against the concrete, hoping to find a grate, a tunnel, anything. It was so frustratingly dark.

The voice continued to speak, though she ignored his words. "Southey has suffered, and only feels better when others feel worse than him. He wants us both to suffer to his ends." A low growl teetered on the threshold of hearing. "There is no way out, Mana. Come to me."

"Shut up!"

"You are the second one he has sent here. Do not allow yourself to go insane... like the first one did."

"Shut up! I am not going to let you near me!" She hurried to the door, kicking it with all her might. The thud was easily absorbed by the hard wood. After a few devastating slams with her bare foot, there was a disgusting crack; her toes bent awkwardly – the bones had split in their joints.

Yelping in pain, she dropped to her knees, chaffing them on the concrete, and held her beaten foot with her bloody hands, painfully twisting her toes back into a somewhat normal alignment.

"For hours, that poor girl ran and ran like a trapped rat," the echoless voice spoke. "I tried to calm her, but every inhuman word I spoke sickened her with fear. She screamed until she coughed up blood, her voice reduced to scratches...and I, driven mad by hunger...and fear...watched her circle around and around in the dark, like an animal. I wanted to ease her suffering...and mine."

Mana leaned against the wall, tending her crunched foot.

The figure continued to iterate the grisly tale. "Soon, I became the devil. I relentlessly beckoned her toward me, and cursed her...never letting my guard down. My wickedness drove her to bang on the door, and even the stone walls, until every useful bone was broken from the repeated pounding! I could not grab her to end her misery, and even in utmost pain, she would not come to me to be freed from it."

"Stop talking!" Mana spit into the darkness – an insult with little sincerity, an emotional whim from a traumatized mind.

"She finally passed out, hours after using her skull to beat at the door. I told her I would have been swift, merciful...but she did not listen."

"Someone will come back to check on me!" Mana yelled, though not believing her own words.

"Yes, they will. They came back for her. They found her bruised and broken body paralyzed at the foot of the door. She hardly batted an eye when the light from the hall spilled onto her face. I wonder if she was even aware when he kicked her within my grasp."

Mana keeled over, vomiting onto the floor.

"It has been less than an hour, and look at you. How much are you suffering already...self-inflicted, death-fearing masochism? You are going to die, accept it with grace."

"What the hell *are* you?" Mana cried.

"A vampire, and I have not fed in many days."

"Please just stay away....please...stay..."

"Mana, in time, I will become ravenous and monstrous. You will find yourself caught in a horrific storm. I implore you, come to me now and see it end in peace. I will not tear you apart like some ani..."

"I am not going near you!" She interrupted, and was shocked that she had almost considered settling.

"Mana...if you think you are afraid now, wait until I am at the command of my true nature. The first woman hammered her body against the walls in a suicidal mania. I do not want to witness such sickening agony, such pointless despair again. I do not enjoy your misery!"

Mana rose to her feet to scream at him, to attack him, to do anything but sit there and listen to his despicable suggestion. But when she stood, her fractured toes crunched gruesomely, and she tumbled forward in the dark, knocking the wind from her lungs.

The vampire lunged at her with a wake of rattling chain behind it. His frigid hand clasped her wrist.

Mana writhed as he pulled her across the floor, toward the center of the cell.

Her remaining fingernails dug deep into his flesh with a nasty crunch, but failed to loosen his grip. She cried out, but hadn't the energy to do much else.

"Mana..." He called her name over and over as she cried and pleaded. "Mana...Mana...what a beautiful name. What beautiful eyes."

Mana could hardly squirm under the heavy weight of the corpse upon her. A sharp pinch against her throat halted any chance she had to scream. She beat her fists into the creature's head with no avail.

As her stressed heart thumped rapidly, trying to replenish her head with the blood that was siphoned from her veins, her hands fell to the floor in resignation, moments before she fell from consciousness…finally escaping the dark hell.

The vampire dismounted and sat still against the pole in the floor's center. There was no reason for it to move anymore.

The vampire stared at the new corpse; from under Mana's long, black lashes, mascara streaked down her creamy cheeks. Her heavy red lipstick hid the paled lips, emptied of blood. Her clothes were scanty and tight, a compliment to her slim figure.

The vampire returned to rest, at peace from the feeding.

Hours later, from behind the cell door, the click of a padlock sounded, then the sliding of a heavy latch, and with a groaning creak, the door swung inward sending a light pillaring across the bloody, gorily splattered floor.

Maida stood at the entrance; the short woman had on loose-fitting silky wrappings which exposed her thin arms. Her long, grey hair fell free across her tiny shoulders, lacking the usual string of beads and stones to tie it back.

She cast a mistrustful eye upon the motionless vampire corpse that sat lifeless on the floor, and then, holding a small, brown satchel in her left hand, she took a step inward, leering down at the deceased girl.

When the wrinkled woman whistled through her thin lips, the click clack of nails echoed in the small hallway, and two German shepherds entered. Without a collar or leash, the large hunting dogs demonstrated their obedience, and stood at her feet, awaiting her command.

Her hand pressed to her chest, "Guard me…," she squeaked, her voice high and eerie, like a child's. She then pointed at the vampire, looking at the dogs' eyes, "…ready."

Their posture tensed up, ready to pounce, flashing their teeth with lips that twitched up and down. Their growls echoed through the tiny cell like an engine.

The vampire, who had shown no signs of being other than a corpse, stirred at the threat.

Cain and Abel circled around, closer to the prisoner, spewing droolish snarls at him.

Reacting to the very real threat of being torn limb from limb, the vampire lifted to its feet with an impossible jump, hitting its back to the low ceiling with a dull thud.

Cain and Abel barked at the sudden maneuver, but did not

approach the vampire.

"Be still, leech." Maida's eyes widened and she held out the small bag in her hand.

Her palm, extended toward the frantic dogs, kept them at bay, but did not silence them. The dogs salivated at the rotten meat standing in the cell; it had graced their tongues before.

The vampire stood motionless, facing the two dogs.

Much of its donned apparel was now tattered rags, the fabric having been torn away. The creature's skin was riddled with bite marks and tears in the flesh, reminiscent of previous encounters with Cain and Abel. However, a graver token of the vampire's captivity was its right arm; half of the limb was missing. Nerve, tendons, muscle and skin hung from below the elbow, where a fractured bone jetted from the gnarled stump. The stub had seeped a thick ooze of coagulated, deadened blood.

Though appearing prepared to defend itself, the vampire was virtually helpless. A metal ring around its neck was so tight, a mortal would have suffocated. Hanging from the steel cuff, aside from a small padlock, was a rusty chain, which stretched toward the center of the cylindrical cell, where a small pole ran from ceiling to floor. The length of the chain disallowed the captive to reach the encircling wall.

Boot steps sounded in the hall, clopping with a slow and steady pace. With his shadow preceding him into the cell, Southey stood and stared at the mangled vampire from the safety of the door.

The many cuts on the left side of Southey's face and neck had become thick scabs, many of which had already been picked, leaving the skin pink and irritated. Southey seemed a bit more tired than usual; dark rings around his eyes rendered his already-thin face skeletal, and he repeatedly widened his eyes, as if he were trying desperately hard to stay awake. "Try anything," he scowled, "...and you will suffer for as long as I can arrange it."

As he picked bits of tobacco from the cracks of his teeth, Southey glanced at the dead woman on the floor, her face already pale.

"Follow your own advice leech," Maida motioned for the vampire to approach her, but the creature did not move. She said, "You are going to die, accept it with grace..."

The vampire's wispy, haunting voice hissed at them, "You don't want to kill me...," the creature's mouth, fresh with blood, opened wide, and its black, shriveled tongue hardly wriggled as the words formed in the air before him, "...you want to torture me."

"It doesn't have to last *forever!*" Southey snapped back. He rubbed his temples, squinting in pain, and groaned softly.

Maida whistled, and the two dogs stepped closer to the vampire, their heads low to the ground, their eyes peering up at their enemy.

"*Final* warning," she squeaked. "Or we could remove that block in the window. Let the sun in. I hear that the slow-rotting brought on by daylight is a much more terrible fate than this."

Southey nodded. "Oh, it's a *blast*," he said, his voice was lacking enthusiasm. "They cry out so loud that it scares my tenants."

Maida held up the small brown satchel, jiggling it. "I would love to see that."

Gazing with a cold stare, the vampire walked towards Maida as the two dogs followed, growling each step of the way.

Maida smiled.

When the creature neared the chain's limit, it extended the stubby arm toward her. Maida reached out from the safety of the cell's perimeter, and grabbed hold of the gruesome limb. "This is what happens when you resist me." Reaching into the small brown satchel, she scooped out a squirming fistful of maggots. "If you would just let me in, let me see everything, then there would be no need to punish." She then slapped a wriggling mass of whitish-crawlers on the damaged arm, saying, "Maggots are such wonderful purifiers." She laughed. "...they never eat *living* tissue."

She continued to hold his arm, watching the critters burrow into their host.

"There you go," Southey laughed wickedly; a sinister grin was on his face. "Now you're making yourself useful." Through his semi-toothless grin, he spit on the vampire, with saliva darkened from a recent cigar.

The vampire, showed no pained facial contortions, or spasms of discomfort of any kind – a reflex innate more toward living things; instead, the cell filled with a low wail, and a haunting growl, which sent the two dogs into a barking fit.

Maida released the vampire's arm from her grip, and wiping away the remaining larvae from her hand, she stepped back.

The vampire slid to the back of the cell, out from the light and into the shadow. Desperately shaking its mangled stub, maggots fell free to the floor, landing in puddles of blood. But many of them had chewed deep into his arm and could not be shaken off.

Southey lowered his head, as not to scrape it on the low ceiling, and entered the cell. "I know you supposedly can't feel pain, but..." He pointed at the tormented vampire. "There has got to be something *really* unpleasant about that. Every one of you cursed leeches reacts the same way."

The vampire used its only hand to dig the burrowed flesh eaters free. When scooping with its fingers failed to remove any more, it tore the very skin and muscle off of the bone and threw the flesh to the floor, already laden with gory remains.

"You'd better hope they don't lay any eggs," Southey chuckled. "I've seen that happen. It's like leprosy, but much quicker."

The dogs lowered their heads and sniffed the treat that fell before them, but Southey stomped his foot and they ignored the rancid snack.

Maida crept toward the center of the cell, and grabbed hold of the deceased Mana's ankle, dragging the corpse out from the room.

"Thank you Maida." Southey's voice was raspy and tired and he seemed generally displeased.

Southey whistled. Cain and Abel heeled beside him, still on guard, tails low and teeth exposed.

"We found that witch fairly easily, thanks to you. We buried her right next to her little cabin. She was an ugly one...that's for sure."

"You could never destroy her!" From across the cell, the vampire boomed its voice at Southey, as if standing directly by him.

Southey flinched, but otherwise seemed unphased. "Before she was *killed*," he stressed, "...she said that I was sent to her." He stepped closer to the vampire, avoiding, as best as he could, the flesh and blood on the cement. "Did she know that I was coming? I had no idea leeches could communicate far away from each other, though, perhaps I should have."

Southey narrowed his eyes. The heavy loss he had suffered on his pseudo-successful hunt for the witch angered him deeply. Not only had he lost his last-remaining son Jacob, but Sam had been bitten by the witch's foul mouth, putting him out of commission for a while – a pain Southey knew all to well, from a close call many months back. And with Sam seriously ill, bedridden for a week, and with no one to aid Southey until his return, he was unable to do anything but wait. And he was not a patient man.

Southey pointed at the vampire. "If you think that you are in control of this, you are *sadly* mistaken!" He laughed to himself, but he was not in high spirits. "Eventually you will tell us everything you know."

On the night Sam was taken to the hospital, the night of their terrifying ordeal in the mountains, he had suggested to Southey that he too take a few days off and rest. But it did little good; the past week had been disastrously tiresome. Southey was haunted by his experiences in those woods, unable to forget, to disregard the nightmare and move on.

Nearing the end of his patience, Southey wanted desperately to slaughter the shackled demon before him, convinced that the vampire was aiding his nightmarish antagonism from his dark cell. However, tempted by the benefits of keeping it alive, and relatively unharmed, Southey exploited the monster with the help of his personal medium, Maida – a self-proclaimed spiritualist.

Maida returned to the cell, and stood at the entrance, looking in at Southey. Her fingers clenched tightly a few sheets of blank paper and a small pencil.

They watched the vampire struggle to eradicate its body of the few remaining maggots.

The vampire raised its eyes to Maida, and with words that Southey did not hear, directed thoughts to her.

Stay out of my mind!

Maida grinned, and returned her thoughts to the creature. *I will sooner see you killed, devil.*

"Then do it!" a ghostly voice screamed, booming throughout the cramped cell, but producing not one echo.

The wooden door began to swing shut, as if the vampire's words had pushed it.

Southey turned to catch the heavy door with his boot, before it sealed them inside. Struggling with the ghostly force pushing it shut, he wrestled the door back open.

Cain and Abel lunged at the vampire, sinking their teeth deep into its legs.

Maida laughed, unphased by the event. She whistled to the dogs, ending their attack. The canines returned to her.

You do not frighten me, evil one. Maida spoke into the vampire's mind. *Resist me further, and I will have your other arm eaten too, then you will be helpless to dig the maggots out.*

Southey, having the door under his control, opted to remain in the hall with Maida.

"This isn't going to work as I hoped," Southey exclaimed to her. "How so?"

Southey kicked the door with his steel-toed boot, hardly denting the wood. "She *knew* we were coming! I almost got killed! Sam is out sick from a bite! The point was to make this easier, not *deadlier!*" Southey gripped his long, yellow hair and pulled. "Things better go smoothly next time or this whole scheme is over!"

"It's easier than your old methods...walking the streets and alleys, scrutinizing everyone who passes you." She stared wildly at Southey. "You haven't found any leeches on your own in half a year, so you said. Perhaps they're getting too smart for old methods." She pointed into the cell. "I got results right away. Maybe not exactly what you wanted, but it was only my first try. I can see into its mind...tell you where others are...and eventually, where *he* is!"

Southey nodded.

Maida smiled. "This is a powerful weapon we have."

"I just can't afford another hit like last week." Southey, standing in the narrow hall outside the cell, shut the heavy wooden door, and locked it. "That hurt."

Maida, with her eerie voice, reassured Southey as best as she could. "That festering witch was strong... different, somehow." Her brow lifted, and her eyes were full of concern. "That witch put a spell on you, Southey." Her voice was troubled, her eyes widened slightly.

Southey's head reeled back in disbelief. "She wasn't really a witch!"

"There is an ill-omened fog around you. I can see it...a dark and faded cloud...a curse! It will consume you, if you allow it." Maida placed her wrinkled hand on his sweaty forehead. "How are your dreams of late?"

"My dreams..." Southey had not mentioned to anyone, except Sam, of the recent night terrors which tore him from sleep.

The witch in the woods haunted his dreams, awakening him in a breathless fear. The first night, shaken from the terrifying encounter in the woods, and grieving his losses, he expected something. But night after night, she persisted, staring at him in his dreams, reaching silently through the darkness. Her white hair branched upward like the warped and knotted limbs of an ancient tree. The bones in her feet, buried loosely in the soil, snaked along the earth around her like roots. With shadowy, eye sockets and a blackened mouth, the witch gaped at him – and when Southey walked around the rooted figure to escape her hideous gaze, a loud wail pierced the air – the witch turned her severed head toward him, slowly, on its slanted stump-of-a-neck.

Southey would try to close his eyes, cover them, but her gleaming, ghostly image passed through his flesh; helpless to deny the frightful apparition, he stared at her in terror.

The witch never spoke to him in those terrible visions, but when Southey woke, freed from the cold, sweaty nightmare, his bedroom was often beset by fell voices whispering his name at the border of his imagination. Relentlessly, they pursued their ghostly disturbance, even when he lay still, pretending to be asleep.

"Don't let her deter you." Maida waved her finger like an

angry mother. "We are at a turning point. This creature will break. Soon, I will know where they all have been hiding. They cannot make a fool of you any longer!"

Southey nodded...agreeing merely due to his exhaustion. "Okay."

Maida nodded. "Now go see about Sam. We'll need him soon. I promise."

Southey turned and left Maida to her work.

Chapter 7 - The Church

Night after night, I lingered about the streets, tracing quiet roads and alleyways across the city and back, searching for others, and trying to make sense of the madness. Did the question 'who was I' even apply anymore? For with each night that passed, the horrific things I had seen and done since my waking filled the amnesia stifling my mind. Any attempts to recall memories of whom I once was only served to remind me of what I was now.

First thing upon rising each night, I would return to Bayview Park — the only place I suspected I might ever find Arthur again. There, between the trees and the ocean, I waited for his presence to announce itself. I played chess amongst a clique of humans too passionate about the game to notice of the many peculiarities about me — or to care. So long as I didn't open my blackened mouth too wide, or forget to play the ventriloquist when engaging in what few words were rarely exchanged, I found myself growing comfortable in that scene, and quickly learned the vampire art of guising.

There, in Bayview, I spent hours submersing my mind into chess, listening to the delightful melodies of the flutist's practicing against the crashing of ocean waves, and with luck, I forgot about the world outside of that small checkered board. However, that soothing medicine would only carry me so far. The crowds always left mid-evening, as the park filled with homeless sleepers and criminal folk — and I would follow suit, continuing to roam. Arthur never came to save me from my restless wandering, and each dawn, for most of one week, I returned alone and in despair to that crypt in the cemetery.

I read a few journal entries each night, hoping but not believing that they might shed some light on who I used to be...and why I became what I am now. Unfortunately, most logs were just vented rage, frustration or loneliness.

One entry was odder than most:

May 18 - 5:10am
Something weird just happened. I was sleeping when a terrible noise woke me up. It sounded like a scream, but it was unlike any scream I had ever heard. It didn't soften or slow down like someone who'd run out of breath. It just kept going. At first, it came from another apartment, and I assumed it was that annoying fat neighbor of mine. But then the voice grew louder as the

*cry seemed to float through the wall, and suddenly I
heard it as if someone screamed in my room. I was so
scared I covered my sheets over my head like I was a kid
again. After a minute, it finally stopped. When I moved
in, almost a year ago, one of my neighbors warned me
that this place was haunted. The landlord is supposed to
be a real nut too. Lots of rumors about this place.
Maybe that's why it was so cheap. Man, the sun is
bright this morning...I don't think I can go back to sleep
now.*

Rumors about my apartment complex? I wondered, and pondered
the notion of returning to Redbank Apartments sometime.

I stopped reading when an impending sunrise reared beyond
the eastern horizon, shrieking its siren – a warning I knew too well. I
returned to my resting spot in the cemetery only to find an omen
urging me to move on: empty beer cans, cigarette butts and other
litter were left lying around; a private celebration with no respect to
the host. Even the name Blavatsky, carved on the stone tome, had
been defaced. I needed to find a new location immediately, else risk
being discovered. I slept there one last time.

The following night, I rose at dusk with a dismal familiarity – a
reminder of what I had almost managed to forget. A dull throbbing
pain, a mounting hunger – I had not taken blood in six nights. I had
desired to lunge out at passers-by, on several occasions; it was not
from hunger, but from a longing for that warmth following the kill –
warmth that seemed to breathe life into my hardened corpse, even if
just for a few moments. Both times I had indulged in that want,
dealing death with a fatal bite, the numbness innate to me ended,
and I felt connected to something...something undeniably powerful,
terrifying and real. But until I knew more, I resisted my urges to kill,
not wanting to yield to desires of which I did not understand fully
their nature or their purpose. If I did take a life, it would not be
avidity, but necessity – a right to be free from pain.

Six nights after my previous kill, the desire to strike again
welled up inside me. Though I knew I could resist the urge, deep
changes inside me lessened what few inhibitions I had. When I
passed people, their heartbeats and breath were loud and clear to
me, and the warmth of their auras begged me to draw near, to follow
them. Their bodies delicately vibrated with life – a life I wanted to
absorb into me.

But there was one thing even harder to resist than those lively
rhythms, something which amplified as my vampire hunger grew.

Whereas neither the air, nor my tongue, brought flavor to my experiences, emotions replaced my sense of smell and taste. My receptivity to the essences of different mental states, or different moods, sharpened as I familiarized myself to their effects. When a passer-by grew uneasy about my appearance, I felt a change in them, physiologically and psychologically. When a child cried, or when somebody laughed, or cursed in anger, it was accompanied by a unique aroma, one that could not be concealed by a steady breeze.

Fear, and its entire kin of emotion, invoked an especially delectable sensation – one which I had relished on a few occasions, one that stirred my thoughts, riling me to lash out. How grand it felt to be feared. Perhaps it was their rapid heart, with its taunting rhythm, sending blood coursing through their veins, or maybe I enjoyed the power I felt over those who feared my presence. The more I walked the city, the more I realized I had an affinity for phobia; it reeled me in like a moth to a flame.

At some point in my scouring for a new place to spend my days, I detected fear's savory nuance stronger than I yet had experienced. I was too intrigued to ignore the intense signal. But as I honed in on it, a familiar awareness stirred inside…a vampire was close. How did I know? – I can never be sure. I had stopped trying to understand everything.

My unholy eyes, looking in all directions, searched faster than my corpse could ever have moved, flying through the air like an excited ghost, and abandoning my corpse by the street. When my gaze drifted towards a nearby parking garage, the lure strengthened, and on the fourth level, I saw a dark, green car, parked alone.

I looked closer, unseen…a spying phantom.

Inside the vehicle, a middle-aged man repeatedly turned the key in the ignition, but the car only choked. His heart pounded, his breaths were fast and tedious, his brow sweaty. Frantically, he struggled to open the door, but there was something holding it shut. His fingers scratched at the locks, but they did not release. The terrified man, with wide eyes ready to jump free from their sockets, halted from his flailing to glance out the windshield.

A tall, large framed woman, with pale skin and fierce yellow eyes, was walking slowly towards his door. A daunting sight, lingering somewhere between lively beauty and hideous death, her red lips contrasted her sickly fair skin, as did her black, gaping mouth which flashed lengthy, stained canines. Short, lifelike red hair curled up under her ears with elegant wings. Her brawny physique endowed a commanding presence; perhaps she had been athletic when living. Now, as a vampire, her softened muscles were just for show. She wore what appeared to be light armor; a heavy black vest seemed to be the type used to stop bullets.

When the vampire neared the driver's door, she lifted her arm, motioning with her long finger for him to come closer; and before he could react, the windshield on the car shattered, but did not cave in.

The trapped man lunged across to the passenger seat. He pulled on the door handle with no avail, and desperately, he heaved his weight against the door, rocking the car on its tires.

With her fiery yellow eyes fixated on the trapped man, she stared at him inside, unmoving, her hands pressed to the window, leaving a grimy smudge.

Her voice emanated from within the car – a raspy whisper which tormented the driver inside.

"I know what you did…," she said over and over.

Covering his ears with his hands, the terrified man shook his head as if he disbelieved what he saw and heard.

The air seethed with that irresistible emotion; I was hypnotized at horror's pungent bouquet, and almost forgot what I had been seeking for so many nights. Wanting to meet that vampire before she killed and ran, I returned my attention back to my corpse, where it had stood-by like an out-of-place mannequin.

Hurrying to the garage, I circled up the stairwell, heading to the fourth level, where the luxury sedan was still parked.

The scene was over. The driver side door was opened, and the man's upper body protruded the shattered passenger door's window. His arms dangled lifeless against the exterior of the door, inches from the pavement. A fresh bite on the back of his neck dripped blood, as thin red streams branched along the contours of his pasty death mask, falling into a thick, crimson puddle. His eyes were so wide, it is a wonder they didn't fall free from their sockets.

"You're young. I can tell." Her soft, feminine voice spoke.

She stood by in the shadows, waiting for me, it seemed, with yellow irises gleaming in the dark…surely a similar breed as the pair I had. Fresh blood stained the rim of her mouth and chin. The sight would have sent any living man running, but I was relieved to find her there.

She raised her right hand and squeezed a smile through the tight skin of her face.

"Who are you? Where did you come from?" I asked.

"Where did I come from?" She blurted, laughing with a still and unmoving mouth; her amused snicker dissipating into the air. Her face had a look neither content nor disproving, simply a relaxed expression. "You came to me." Her lips trembled slightly as she mouthed along to her words, "I remember the feeling…the realization that you are not dead anymore...and then the realization that you aren't alive either...staggering into a world so familiar, yet so terrifying."

From a pocket, she pulled out a small rag, which she used to wipe clean her mouth. As she removed the blood from her face, her soft, feminine voice shifted into my mind.

I saw you watching me just then. She sounded amused. *We can share thoughts...you did not need to come all the way up here to talk to me. What did you really want, besides talking?*

I returned the gesture, joining in a telepathic chat. *I was beginning to wonder if I was alone. I came to find out about you.*

Her arm lifted, pointing toward the dead man leaning from the window. *Maybe you could not resist his fear. We all desire it, among other things.*

Who was he? I asked, looking back at the dead man, but my head remained fixed on her.

The victim was unlike the greasy and foul drunkard I first killed, and even more unlike the mumbling, sickly cripple I took later on; the man she had killed in that expensive-looking car was a clean shaven, nicely dressed, business-type man. I wondered what motivated her to end his life, among other possibilities.

Mr. Polidori was a very bad man...and karma just caught up with him.

And who are you?

"Mira," she whispered aloud. "That's who I am now."

"I'm Child, now," I replied. "Since my waking, I have roamed for days to find another vampire."

"It appears, from your tidy appearance, that you have already found...or rather, that he has found you, as is usually the case."

"Arthur?" I asked.

Mira lifted her shirt up, and I saw the heavy stitching climbing from her navel to her sternum. "He took me to Lucia too, gave me a clean slate to work with. But that is all he will give you. I promise."

"Do you know of other vampires?"

Mira nodded her head, resuming her telepathic talk. *There aren't many anymore. Not here. Most of us remain inland, on the west end. It is safer there. I only came here for him.* Mira pointed toward the dead man who had grown paler as that crimson puddle beneath him widened.

There was something mischievous about Mira and the nature in which she engaged in thought – something which dissuaded me from joining in. As her thoughts spoke to me, her voice danced around, seeming close, then distant...all while in my mind. While this happened, my memories, of Arthur, of the tomb and of Bayview

Park, stirred inside me. At first, I thought it was I who recalled the events, but in a moment of intimacy, I saw thoughts that were not my own – her memories. The images flashed like a daydream and I observed them passively, it seemed.

I saw the rusty fossils of a playground drowning in a thriving sea of grass. Behind them, an abandoned school of brick with boarded up windows stood in sheer darkness, without a single nearby light to cut the shadow. I did not recognize the place.

Another image flashed. A gangly old man, with bright blonde hair, stood in a hallway amongst a group of men; they stepped over dead, bloodless limbs, and fired shotguns into doors and walls, as flames climbed the wood panels.

I then saw a dark and dusty, cluttered cellar, with a wooden floor, and bodies draped over each other, like a group suicide – Mira was among them.

I snapped out of the trance.

"What is going on? Stop that!" I blurted thunderously. The familiarity of her experiences seemed all too real. The borders of my identity skewed as if I remembered having been there, having seen those places through her eyes…and I assumed she had shared in what of my experiences she had seen.

"What are you seeking, Child? If you want to play games, go back to the park. If you are looking for other vampires, then follow me. You don't have to be alone."

"I want answers, and if they can be found in your company, or others', than so be it. What I don't want is to travel far just to find that my inquiries are futile, and that there are no answers to be had. I can do that on my own. So if there is anything you can tell me now, I'd appreciate it."

Mira stepped closer to me, and I felt the warmth of her kill lingering inside her…riling my own hunger. "My, you're feisty. Your effort in coming with me will not be wasted. The others and I can teach you about the new world…a changing world. The old ways of vampires have been antiquated, and are dangerous. Don't become left behind, like others…like Arthur. Join me, and see what the future offers for the damned."

Mira brushed her hand across her head, removing a red wig; in that one, simple motion she seemed to transform into a darker creature.

Like Arthur, she was bald, except where thinned patches of sickly blond hair hung from her flaking scalp. Numerous cuts in the flesh, and chips in the skull, covered the top of her head, but she appeared to have avoided serious disfiguration.

"Come. Help us, Child. Help yourself." Mira turned and walked down the stairwell, carrying the fiery red wig in her hand.

I followed her out from the garage, prepared to let her lead me to others, but an uneasy feeling left me with inhibitions, and I questioned the soundness of following her so blindly.

"How can you help me?" I asked.

"I can offer you a purpose….isn't that what we all want?"

I thought back to Arthur, whom I still wanted to meet, to hear his opinions; and before I uttered my disproval, Mira answered me with her thoughts.

If you don't want to come yet, you don't have to. Go and find your friend, and when you see that the fool will not take you into his company, you will come looking for us. We are the future of vampires…and he is the past.

Behind the parking garage, there was a grassy hill which we followed down to railroad tracks that stretched east to west. Without trying to persuade me to follow, Mira departed west along the tracks, speaking to me with confidence, or perhaps arrogance, but either way it was intriguing.

Follow these tracks west when you change your mind. We're at the other end. Good luck, Child.

Mira left, and I turned east along the tracks, back toward the city, hoping I had not erred in my decision.

* * * * *

While I headed back along the tracks, I opened my journal and flipped through it. At first, the same ramblings filled each page. Then came a new variable…

May 30 – 11:45pm

I met someone today. Well maybe 'met' isn't the right word. I paid for her company, but that's not to say we didn't get to know each other better. I've seen those Taxxxi Cabs around the city. I've heard the gossip. I'd never have the gall to call one up, but this young lady was walking through my lobby as I came in. The way she smiled at me…maybe I was over-receptive, but I thought she liked me. It wasn't until we got back to my room that I found out what she did for a living. What was I to do? I'm so lonely.

I immediately thought of the photo in my pocket – of me, and that girl with the golden locks and black dress. *Was she whom I wrote*

about? I thought. *We look happy, like a real couple.*
   I kept reading entries.

   June 5 - 3:05pm
   I can't shake Olyvia from my mind. Her blonde curls are burnt into my eyes like a flashbulb. I know it's just me overreacting to social stimuli. I never spend time with people, so it figures I'd get attached. Am I wrong to like her? She's a person under all that pain....At least I know how to reach her if I want to see her again.

   Olyvia? Is that her name? I removed the photo of the young blonde and me; written on the back with a marker was 'D&O'. *Dante and Olyvia.*

   June 25 - 11:30pm
   When Olyvia showed up tonight, I gave her some flowers I stole from a cemetery. Real nice ones. She really seemed to appreciate it. She didn't even charge me. I still offered the money, but she said she would lie to her pimp...say I wasn't home. She likes me.

   Pimp? I thought. *What was the late Dante Fairchild getting involved with?*
   There were many 'meetings' over the next dozen pages, and they grew increasingly alarming in their nature, signifying a potentially dangerous sneaking-around type of relationship – perhaps leading to his demise, and thusly my waking. I kept reading, hoping for an answer as to what had happened to the old, dead me, on that fateful night.

   July 5 - 5:55pm
   This is an odd relationship Olyvia and I have. Is it me, or my money she is here for? Sometimes I pay, sometimes I don't, but we always have a good time. I hope her generosity isn't putting her at risk. She only needs my money so that her pimp doesn't get suspicious. She told me she has a secret e-mail address. Sometimes she can sneak to a neighbor's apartment, or check her mail on clients' computers. She says that's the only way we can talk when not together. I'm finding it harder to let her leave, knowing what she does when not with me. I've asked her why she does it, and she just shrugs and

changes the subject. Next time I see her, I will ask her to quit, and maybe her and I can leave this city together. I want out. I hate it here. But I can't go alone.

A mile down the railroad tracks, I entered into a quaint neighborhood. Rapt in the pages of that small, mawkish journal, trying to find some semblance of who I was before my waking, I detected a familiar ambiance...of death...knowing very well who I would find when I followed the scent; Arthur's presence felt distinctly different than Mira's.

Finally, our paths had crossed again. On a quiet street, Arthur stood outside a small church, peering up at a steeple, as if he had waited for me to discover him there. He was wearing the same black raincoat from a week before.

I was not within one hundred feet of Arthur when his voice carried through the air, whispering to me, "Do you know *why* humans *need* fear?" he asked.

I did not reply, but kept walking closer.

Arthur continued, "It makes them feel more alive. Fear is the only thing that *truly* motivates anyone to do anything. Fear of losing...fear of pain...fear of death." Arthur turned to face me. "Without fear, there would be no heroes, no monsters...without it, there would be chaos."

A mural climbed the church's stony tower. At the base, just over the main doors, was depicted the devil in a murky precipice, awash with the souls of the fallen; his hooves were buried in a tangled mound of thin and naked bodies. With pained expressions, those beneath Satan reached up to him with bony, tortured hands, clawing at the thighs of the horned master of sin and darkness. The steeple lightened in color and theme as it ascended. In the center of the sacred depiction, a purgatory was swarming with youthful angels, robed in white, lit from above by a precipitating radiance. At the pinnacle of the steeple, rolling white clouds kept the sun from sharing its light with those trapped below; and the bust of the Lord Jesus, crowned in thorns, had been carved in such a manner as to extend out from the flat, stone wall, giving his upper-half dimension. Clenched in his right hand, held high by his head, a massive cross soared in the grey, night sky.

Arthur stared at the picture; speaking softly, "Long I existed in shadow, embracing my purported nature, accepting it with open arms. For a lifetime, I was a solitary creature in the dark, emerging from shadow only to kill. That was my purpose...it seemed...to dwell in abandoned buildings...forgotten places...a beast among the insane indigents of the cities of the world. Over the years, I fed only from what fell through the cracks of society." Arthur paused, "...or folks unwise enough to venture needlessly into society's neglected and abandoned environs. When homeless drifters saw my corpse laying in filth, they presumed me to be just another victim of poverty. Over the decades, I had grown devious and strong, knowing how to exploit fear to my advantage...using devilish tricks to steer wandering eyes from my physical self. Those misfortunate enough to sneak a glimpse of me trudging about spent their final moments in terror. When my presence would be discovered, I would move on to a new city."

Arthur walked up the steps of the church, and the wide, wooden doors swung outward to greet him.

I followed him in, and we walked a red carpeted aisle, between two clusters of pews.

A gallery of stained glass, with seven windows on each side, darkened from the night sky seeping through them; long, red tapestries fell from the ceiling, draping the walls separating the mosaics.

Sitting in the front row, an old woman hung her head silently in prayer, unheeding our presence. Candles by the altar remained lit, their light flickering off the marble walls.

Arthur's words shifted into thought, perhaps to avert the attention of the lone attendant.

I grew tired of it. Like you, I wanted to find answers...purpose. Unlike you, I was not fortunate enough to waken in such a manner as to discover a single shred of truth concerning my past life. You see, after my waking, I had nothing to compare myself to. My actions were based solely on what I perceived...that I was a creature to be feared, a creature that exists only to destroy life. Thusly, I had no reason to believe I was anything other than a vampire, which is, perhaps, why I walked that road so far.

Are you something other? I asked him, silently, when his words had stopped for more than a few seconds.

Only by choice.

Arthur sidled into one of the lanes and sat. He called for me to join him, and I rested with him in the silence of the church.

He continued his stream of thoughts. *In time, I found the need to seek out different prey, but in a modern city, in this city especially, a vampire cannot mindlessly stroll about. This isn't some medieval farming village, or some gullible colonial town. Technology makes it harder for us to hide amongst the living, and humans are slowly being reminded of something strange and ancient lurking in the shadows. The age of vampires living peripherally in the safe Eden of mythology is ending. What once had been thought of us as fact is quickly being revealed as superstition. The stories always exaggerated the truth.*

Arthur paused for a while, perhaps awaiting me to ask one of the hundred questions floating through my head...and then continued his narration.

Bands of hunters are surfacing throughout the city...many of them ill-informed thrill seekers of no real threat, but they know what to look for. One man, known as Robert Southey, has taken it upon himself to organize many of the interested parties within the city into a dangerous network of spies. The further into the populous we drift, the greater the need to remain hidden.

Is that why you befriended Lucia? I thought to him.

No. I met her many years before the surge in hunters. One evening, over two decades ago, I felt the mourning of a young woman...lured to her troubled mind, caught in a tumult of sadness, hatred and pain. Her torment was so sincere that I felt it deep within me. I saw her thoughts. A young boy, murdered by his own father, lay cold on a slab. Though she wanted to, the woman could not physically bear a child of her own, and seeing a precious gift mercilessly wasted, she longed for justice, rightfully so. She wanted to carry out that justice herself, but was in no position to do so. Her genuineness moved me and I whispered to her from afar, offering her a release from the sadistic fantasy polluting her every thought. I made Lucia an offer.

I recognized the story; Lucia had left much unsaid – things which Arthur put to light.

I found the boy's father through his own guilt, through his paranoia...his fear of getting caught. He was hiding in a motel, waiting for night to make his escape. I awaited him in the trunk of his car, and when he took to the road, he soon heard a pounding from inside the vehicle. When he pulled over to investigate, he opened the trunk to his death. I lunged at him with a ferocity I had not yet released in all my years. I felt immaculate, tearing his tainted soul from its undeserved body. I tasted something, finally, after all those years – something to end the bland existence I had settled for.

What did you taste?

Evil! There was something hidden deep within that murderous father's soul, something that changed the flavor of the kill, something I longed to absorb. Through the consumption of evil, I had bettered the world...I had helped Lucia. She kept her promise, crafting my corpse into a presentable appearance.

Arthur's mouth began moving, and his whisper breeched the silence in which I had found comfort.

"When Lucia was done, she named me Arthur...after the dead boy. She said I would live on *for* him, in his name. I still visit Lucia from time to time."

Arthur and I sat in silence; the whispers of the prayers coming from the front of the church were as soft as the burning candles.

His words rang in my mind once more.

Armed with the guise necessary to walk among the living, I no longer had to settle for what prey presented itself. I sought out those who harmed others, greedily, sadistically...for Lucia...for Arthur. Slowly, the monster inside me disappeared, and in its stead, a soldier of providence rose up...an unlikely purifier. Now, I follow evil's pungent scents of guilt, self-hatred and fear, ending the reprehensible and wicked lives when I track them down, often catching them in their selfish acts. I have learned the pleasure of justifying my existence, because while vampires have the right to be here, we also owe to be here. I have continued this path because there is a harmony to it. I become more than just a monster. I become part of something greater.

Arthur's words made sense; he spoke of a purpose, a reason to be. Before, I had seen my numb, lifeless corpse as retribution, perhaps of some former sin – one I was not granted the luxury of recalling, nor able to beg forgiveness for. I saw only that I was a taker of life. Arthur showed me I could be also a shaper of fate...I could be something else...of value. Perhaps I was not cursed. Perhaps I teetered on the edge of good and evil, in a hell parallel to and overlapping the world of the living, aptly placed to keep the balance. I would need to appease both the light and the dark.

"Is that why you led me to Lucia? Is that why you prevented me from attacking that man in the park?" I inquired, curiously.

"Yes," Arthur smiled, and he let his voice carry into the air. "It only takes a few thoughtless choices to change the world entirely. I learned this some years ago...during a weakness of my own will."

The woman in the front of the church stood from the pew, genuflected at the altar, turning toward the rear. She glanced at Arthur and me, in our cold silence. I turned my head to smile, keeping my fangs at bay behind my lips, but she seemed unnerved. Without returning the friendly gesture, she exited the church and left us alone.

When the boom of heavy church doors closing filled the room, Arthur's deep voice continued, "My past imprudence planted the seed of a future storm – one that, to this day, still rains down upon this city. I have tried to rectify that by finding new vampires, and pointing them in this direction."

"Like Mira?" I asked. Mira's eyes were clean, like mine, and Arthur's, and she and I bore the same disemboweling scar.

"Yes, and one of her older, surviving acquaintances...an old familiar of mine whom I had a falling out with many years ago. And others whom have long-since been destroyed. I brought them all to Lucia in hopes they would take her gift as an opportunity to embody the finger of God...to be a silent force working to purify this world...to defy their own deathly physical perversions."

"What happened?"

"They all have veered from that path. They have become involved directly with the world of the living, which will only corrupt them further. They intentionally expose themselves to what they think is to their advantage. But the world of men is treacherous and uncompromising. Vampires were created to live quiet shadowed existences. We are *meant* to be myths. There can be no true coexistence on a large scale. It is only a matter of time before those vampires suffer for their arrogance. Southey's hunters have decimated that clan over the years, and he seeks to finish the job...among others. He is a vengeful man. That is why I remain alone. I do not allow others' mistakes to be my consequences, and I do not expose myself unless absolutely necessary. I am inexistent in the hunters' minds and I aim to keep it that way...until my undoing."

Arthur paused, standing up. "I risked discovery when I intercepted you. Some of Southey's hunters were near Bayview Park that night I found you...but I distracted them."

"You saved me? Thank you."

"Death would have been a pleasure compared to what sinful vice Southey would have exacted upon you. At the cost of men's lives, he has captured vampires before, studying them...figuring out our real weaknesses from mythological ones. He seeks out facts within fiction."

Arthur descended the long aisle, toward the altar. The gates of heaven were painted inside a cupola in the ceiling high above his head. He stood underneath in silence.

I remained seated. My divine eyes were next to Arthur – my words pierced the air beside him, asking him to continue sharing his wisdom.

"How can I remain hidden, like you?"

Our bodies one hundred feet apart, we conversed as if I stood next to him at the altar, or as if he sat next to me.

"You can walk successfully among humans if you bear in mind your true nature. You are primarily a spirit and are not contained within your flesh, as humans are. You, your spirit, exists around it – occupying a much wider space than the boundaries of your corpse. Your virtually-unbounded spiritual vision allows you to perceive everything within its range, but nothing outside of it."

I thought of the grim, grey overcast sky that plagued the city ever since I started walking the streets as a vampire. *Was that grey wall not cloud, but the limits of my own eyes?*

Arthur sensed my pondering, and said, "You shall never gaze upon the stars or moon as long as you remain a vampire. Neither shall you gaze upon distant mountains on the horizon, or their reflections in the lakes. For it is not light hitting your eyes which causes you to see; it is that which your spirit eclipses that is to your awareness. And since souls pass through solid objects, you therefore are able to see through any wall."

"Then I can manipulate anything I can see, since those things would be within my influence?"

"Not entirely. On earth, life rules over death. Thus, as a spirit, you cannot directly affect anything living – neither man, animal or plant. You can see them, hear them, but never feel them or move them to your liking. If you wish to harm a human, you must do so with your corpse, physically, or through other non-living matter."

I thought back to the thug who had tried to stab me a few nights ago. I had halted his knife effortlessly, yet when he punched me, his fist was uninhibited by my will; I could not stop his flesh. It made sense now.

Arthur spoke, "When you are face to face with an aggressor, it would be wise to acknowledge that humans are physically stronger than you. Your corpse is weak, breakable and you will carry the burden of every injury as long as you shall be. If you wish to last through time, you must minimize direct exposure to your aggressors. You must become a ghost in the mind of your prey – a noise in the dark – a paranoid thought in their mind. If you must confront them, you can take hold of their weapons or tug at their clothing and jewelry."

"By this logic, I would be near helpless to stop a naked man?"

"Yes, a naked man is free from your influence, and you would need to resort to trickery. You can lay waiting in one spot, and project your voice somewhere else, or rattle distant objects for distraction, making it impossible for people to track you down. When you learn how people react to fear, you can draw them to you or send them running."

I stood, and as I approached the front of the church, Arthur's words followed in the air beside me.

"These tricks – projecting noises, moving objects, and most of all, suspending your corpse as you are now, will drain you of strength, weakening you to the point of uselessness. If you push yourself too hard, you will collapse into sleep."

"And if I fail to drink blood, I shall decompose?"

Arthur turned to face me.

"It is the life in the blood that sustains you – a force released when the victim dies. You see, Child...you must kill to live. It is of no benefit for you to leave a victim alive...blood is just a means to attain the energy that drives you. You can wait days and days between feedings...and it is wiser to do so, since few deaths will go unnoticed. But as the nights roll by, you will begin to grow hungry and dangerous. If you wait long enough, you shall act out of desperation, and not reason."

I felt that horrible feeling once before – when I wakened. I was in near-torturous agony and lashed out, killing my first victim without foreknowledge of my nature, or my intentions. The discomfort had risen up in me again, and I would not resist it too much longer.

"Just as humans often forget that they have a soul, you can easily forget that you have a corpse. To survive in this world, you must incorporate both mind and body. While Lucia's work has been a great enhancement to your appearance, you will not passively fool everyone whom you cross paths with – especially hunters! Every living creature can sense deviations in the mannerisms of their own kind. From a distance, you shall be safe as long as your skin remains painted and uncut...but up close, they will notice the lack of expression on your face, and the stillness of your breathless torso. With practice, you can learn the part, but even your best efforts will fall shy of perfection."

"You appear to do well," I said, and meant in. For if it was not for the presence I felt when near him, I might overlook Arthur as a potential corpse. Though, beneath that clothing, and the makeup painted upon his hands, neck and face, he was as pale as I.

"This is also very important, Child." Arthur's voice grew stern, and foreboding. "You have spent nights in the cemetery...just be careful not to sleep on or in the bare earth, outdoors. There are many creatures that savor that taste of dead flesh...worms, crows, maggots. No one is without predators...death eats life eats death."

"If you knew I was in that cemetery, why didn't I see you earlier? You let me wander for days! You could have saved me from much self torment!"

"I do not rise every night anymore. It is needless. Only a few times in a month do I venture out from this church."

"This is where you rest in the day?" I was shocked.

"Yes, for almost ten years now. Here, in the dark corners underneath this church, I hear the prayers of humans who come to beg God for help, mercy and justice. For some people...I can answer their prayers. For others...time will tell."

Arthur did not embellish on that, and I did not ask.

He continued, "I have lasted almost a century because I am careful, and remain alone. And you can not stay with me. It is safer for both of us. Besides, I'm sure you do not want to get caught up in the unfortunate details of *my* situation."

Mira had prophesized this.

Arthur turned, walking toward a small door in the rear corner of the church.

"I suggest you take advantage of the night's youth and seek a safe haven to remain in the day. If you desire to speak with me, feel free to return anytime."

"Is that all there is to say?" I asked, a bit disappointed.

"All I know comes from what I have seen, and done. The same will be true of you, no matter how much I teach you. My only advice to you is…don't become a slave to things not of your own, and don't go seeking out those vampires in the west."

Arthur disappeared behind the doors, to rest in his sanctuary, without waiting for a possible objection by me. Without any idea of where I would go, I left the church, and commenced my wandering.

Chapter 8 – A Dishonest Man

Commissioner Paul sat at his antique oak desk, his throne in his office at the city's police station, downtown. A box on the floor, meant for files, had the majority of its contents clumsily organized into two piles of folders upon the large desk. A briefcase on the floor was shut, and the gold letters A.P upon the lid were gleaming from the overhead light. Arnold had forgotten about the dark blue ceramic mug, filled to the rim with cold, black coffee, still awaiting his taste buds' approval.

Arnold Paul rubbed his hands to his eyes and groaned; turning his attention from the computer monitor, he looked to the cracks on the ceiling, trying to decide if it was time to have a janitor re-plaster it.

A thought entered his mind. *Oh yeah. Before I forget again…*

Sitting up in his chair, Arnold grabbed hold of the mouse and moved the onscreen cursor toward a program, double-clicked, and was immediately prompted to enter a password, to which he input:

N-i-e-t-z-s-c-h-e

A catalog of names, along with related personal information, appeared on the screen.

Arnold shuffled through papers scattered on his desk, and when he found what he was looking for, he clicked the cursor on a blank search bar, and entered:

Preston, Charles

Within a few seconds a message appeared:

Unable to find name(s) on list

He wasn't one of mine. Arnold cupped his chin with his left hand, licking his teeth in a nervous manner. *Who would have knowingly entered one of Robert Southey's buildings? Who killed you…Charles? What really happened in there?*

Arnold began to think back to his visit with Southey a week prior, when a knock at the door startled him; he jumped in his chair, hitting his knees off the underside of his desk.

"Who is it?" he asked, as he quickly turned off the computer monitor and adjusted the mess of papers on his desktop.

A man in his forties opened the office door, poking his head in for Arnold to see.

Leaning back in his chair, stretching his arms back, he smiled and said, "Detective Calmet, how are you tonight?"

"Not bad, Commissioner." The visitor walked in, shutting the door behind him. His white shirt was damp with sweat; the fall night was unusually warm, and the breeze through the opened windows was a relief. "I have got some information for you," he gestured at the papers on Arnold's desk, and walked over to the window, looking down. "...if you have a moment, that is."

"Absolutely." Arnold sat up with his elbows on his desk; his fingers were interlocked, and he rested his chin on them. "What can I do for you?"

The commissioner had assigned Detective Calmet to investigate the murder at the Redbank Apartments – the death of Charles Preston. Given the nature of the murder and his familiarity with Robert Southey's sensitivity to these types of events, Arnold had requested to be kept personally updated on any developments, as soon as they happened.

"There's news." Detective Calmet scratched his slightly balding head.

"Tell me we found Lance!"

"No...but you were right. He was connected to it." Calmet walked up to the desk and sat sideways on its edge, with one leg on the floor.

Arnold reached for the mug and took a sip. He snapped his fingers impatiently, with a mouth full of chilly black coffee.

"If you recall, Charles's step-daughter, Miss Preston, was the only witness. She claimed that she saw two dead bodies that night...the freshly murdered Charles, and some other body. As you know, when we arrived, we found only one, though she stuck with her story."

"Uh-huh." Arnold reached into a side drawer of his desk, removing a packet of biscotti cookies and placing them beside the mug.

"When we first talked to her, Miss Preston had said she didn't get a good look at the corpse's face, you know, with Lance waving a gun around."

"Of course." Arnold locked his fingers behind his neck, stretching his arms outward like wings. He moaned as the bones in his joints cracked.

"Well," the detective continued, "...we did a door to door but nobody we talked to had any information. We were left with no description on a body that wasn't there. Not useful. Naturally we followed other leads. Just a few days ago, when we were getting desperate, we talked to Miss Preston again."

"And...?" Arnold asked, impatiently.

"Having had a few weeks to cope with what she went through, she now says she remembers who the other dead guy is...a neighbor from her building, who she had seen around in the halls...when he was alive, that is." Detective Calmet pulled a small notebook from his front pocket of his tan suit coat; he flipped through the small pages, mumbling to himself.

"The mystery corpse lived on their floor?" Arnold paused, furrowing his brow, and waiting for the detective to continue. "So when you did a door to door, you didn't talk to everyone." He removed a biscotti cookie, dipping it into the cool, stale coffee. He took a bite.

"No. It was real late...a few people didn't answer, or weren't home. We went back and checked the doors we missed after Miss Preston's revelation. We narrowed it down to one apartment at the end of the hall." Detective Calmet paused, nodding, "We have ourselves a double homicide."

"You found *another* body?" Arnold was surprised. He glanced up at the clock on the wall. This would be a late night.

"No," the detective replied. "There was nobody there. The room was a disaster, but what do you expect in a place in *that* part of town. We searched and found a coiled copper wire with traces of skin and blood, and there were more blood stains on the bed sheets...not matching Charles Preston's."

"Who lived there?" Arnold mumbled through a mouth of soggy cookie.

"One Dante Fairchild. There was no form of ID in the room. We ended up finding the useful stuff on his computer...and did some searches on it."

"*How* useful?"

"Well, Dante moved here from Syracuse, New York over a year ago. He has no criminal record there or here. He did have a job as a grocery picker at one of the nearby warehouses, but that was only for a short while." The detective paused, realizing he was heading on a tangent. "Anyway, the point is that there were a series of messages on his computer. One of them said - I'm on my way over. It was sent the night of September 6th, by the screen name Olyvia138. Then, three days later, on the 9th, not half an hour after the Preston murder, a message was sent back to Olyvia138 from his room. It said 'See you soon.' "

"Ok. What's your point?" Arnold hadn't any idea where the detective was going.

"The lab results on the skin and blood suggest that, if they are indeed Dante Fairchild's, he was murdered on the 6th, not the 9th."

"That's weird. If that is true, who sent the message on the 9th?"

"Perhaps the same guy who killed Charles Preston," the detective suggested. "Maybe they are connected somehow. If Miss Preston is accurately recalling her incident, then Mr. Fairchild's body was taken from its deathbed, and into the other apartment, sometime between the two murders...between September 6th and 9th."

Arnold tried to digest what he was hearing. "And then where did it go? No, there's still something missing." He glanced around the room, as if the answer was hidden among the many clippings covering the two corkboards on the walls.

The detective nodded. "When we searched his computer further, by stroke of luck, we stumbled onto saved e-mails sent between Mr. Fairchild and one Miss Olyvia Cross. Very descriptive e-mails." The Detective paused. "You are not going to believe this."

"Keep talking."

"It seems that Miss Cross was a call girl whom Mr. Fairchild had grown particularly fond of. Their relationship had developed beyond business, and Dante wanted her to quit prostitution and run off with him."

"Classic love story," Arnold mumbled, sarcastically.

"Apparently her boss," the detective stressed the word heavily, "...had grown knowledgeable of their courtship, and he insisted she stop seeing him." Detective Calmet then pulled a small, square piece of plastic from his pant pocket – a computer disk. "There were a number of such letters; some of them were pretty tender at points, I must say. It's too bad." He held the diskette out in front of him. "I have physical copies if you wish to see them."

"This will do."

The detective tossed the disk onto Arnold's desk then continued speaking. "After a few days, we managed to track Olyvia Cross down. We approached her with our concerns, and she broke down immediately, sobbing up a storm. She basically admitted to having killed Dante Fairchild on the 6th! We have her in custody now. But the real twist is this..."

"Yeah?" Arnold was on the edge of his seat. He suspected where this was going.

"Ms. Olyvia Cross was a call girl for Taxxxi cabs!"

"That's Lance's racket! I knew he had to be tied into all this!" Arnold slammed his fist off the desk.

Lance DuPrey, was a self-employed criminal entrepreneur, who had a record of soliciting women, and narcotics-related felonies.

Though outwardly a crooked man, he managed to keep his trail fairly clean. The cops had failed for a long time to pin him down to something substantial. Taxxxi Cabs was a sketchy transportation and escort service that had been under the watchful eye of authorities; but with a legit taxi service as a front, there was little that could be done. With Lance tied to Taxxxi Cabs and the murders, certainly police would easily bring down the prostitution ring.

The detective loosened his beige necktie, taking a deep breath. "Olyvia claimed that Lance was going to kill her if she didn't kill Mr. Fairchild. I definitely believe her. I guess she had given the deceased a few freebies, and Lance was furious. Apparently, Lance has been abusive enough to some of the girls to send some of them running. Olyvia said that some of her colleagues have disappeared too, and that Lance has been acting real funny lately. He is currently in the process of scouting for more assets, I guess."

Arnold was nodding, putting the pieces together in his head. "Yeah. That's why he was at the Preston's apartment, right? Purchasing the step-daughter?"

"Perhaps...but Charles Preston had taken advantage of the Taxxxi Cab service in the past. Apparently Lance and he were already acquaintances."

"How do you know that?"

"Olyvia met Mr. Fairchild in the lobby quite a few months ago...," he hesitated, and continued, "...apparently, after she had already visited with Charles Preston."

"Sick," Arnold sneered.

"It was love at first sight."

"That's sick man," Arnold repeated. "It's just one big, happy family over there."

The detective continued. "So all that remains is to figure out who sent those messages from Mr. Fairchild's room...after he died. Why was his corpse moved from murder scene A to murder scene B? And of course, where the hell did it go after that? It'll be tough to prosecute without a body. We'll need to dig up some of Mr. Fairchild's medical history to tie him to the murder weapon and blood stains. Hopefully, though, his body will surface somewhere."

With shifty eyes, Arnold stared into space; he had just put together a piece of the puzzle that Detective Calmet couldn't ever have on his own. Arnold reflected on the two tooth-like scars found on Charles Preston's neck, and on the mysteriously moving corpse – not to mention how foolish a vampire would have to be to knowingly enter the very site of the craziest known hunter.

Could a vampire have been born in one of Southey's own buildings..., Arnold thought to himself. *...killing Charles Preston and sending that* *message?* He took a deep breath, which caught Detective Calmet's attention.

Arnold Paul was no stranger to vampires. For the sake of his career, and knowing how such issues had ruined Robert Southey's career, the commissioner kept his true opinions of those dark creatures to himself – even lying and hiding things from Southey, whom Arnold knew was legit. The wild-eyed hunter saw through his façade; Arnold was sure of it, but maintained his denial. To deal with vampires, and those killed from them, took special consideration, and Arnold only shared his knowledge and concerns with those he trusted 110%. Detective Calmet was not one of those people, but was the better of lesser men to send to such an anomalous crime scene. Arnold had enough help in place to keep loose ends tied, and to make this murder seem like just that...a simple murder by a simple criminal.

The detective interrupted Arnold's deep thought, "I suspect that on the 9th, Lance made a stop over to Mr. Fairchild's apartment to check on his lady's kill. Then he removed Dante's body to hide it, perhaps next stopping in to kill Mr. Preston. But why wouldn't Lance remove Mr. Preston's corpse too? Something just doesn't add up. And then there's always that other question."

"What's that?" asked Arnold; he was only half-listening.

"What exactly happened to Mr. Preston?" The detective scratched his head, nervously. "The forensics team has mixed suggestions."

"*Vampires*?" Arnold blurted.

The detective looked embarrassed. "Yeah, well...they see a lot of unexplained stuff. They need to fill the gaps with theories, or else leave everything open ended. I wouldn't put it past Lance to have bitten him – that dog!"

Arnold chuckled perfunctorily. "Yeah...hey, you didn't tell Mr. Southey about this *other* murder, did you?"

"Not yet...but he knows we've been back to investigate and..."

"Don't," he snapped. "You know how wild and unpredictable Southey is. We don't want to encourage his delusions."

"Yes sir."

"We'll try to keep this as quiet as we can...and then when we have real answers to tell him, I will be the one to tell that nut."

The detective raised an eyebrow suspiciously. "So...how do you plan on finding Lance?"

Arnold smiled, almost maliciously. "Don't worry, detective. That's *already* taken care of."

Chapter 9 – The Western Clan

I went against Arthur's advice, chasing Mira west along the tracks. A few more nights walking the alleys and avenues of the downtown seemed a drab idea. I disliked the streaming mechanical drone of the busy streets, and the intense humming of electricity from all around – streetlights, headlights, sirens, cell phones, power lines and the patter of crowds' feet – they all resided at the threshold of my tolerance, overwhelming my senses and clouding my thought. I needed to escape. Besides, I was too curious about Mira and what answers she might reveal to me. What harm could there be in seeing another perspective?

Determined to learn something more about my past, even if it be irrelevant, I removed the small journal from my coat's front pocket. Only a few entries remained; many of the last pages had been torn out, or scratched-over with a pen. However, the final entries were of the most relevance to me.

July 15 - 6:30pm
I had it all worked out. What to say to Olyvia. How could she refuse? I offered her a way to be free, someone she could trust, and she looked at me like I was insane! Does she really think she owes anything to her pimp? I got mad when she showed no faith in my plan, and I yelled at her...called her naïve and brainwashed, among the kinder things. She ran out on me. I'd like to see this pimp, and tell him off.

August 5 - 4:20am
I haven't seen her in so long. I can't call her, except to call Taxxxi Cabs, and one of the drivers usually answers the phone. Olyvia must have told them that I had tried to talk her into leaving. They now refuse their services to me. The last time I called, some guy named Lance answered the phone...sounded real angry. I think it might have been her pimp. He threatened me, saying if I ever called again, he'd send somebody over to see me...from Lance's tone, I assumed he didn't mean a call girl.

I read that entry again and again, focusing on that unpleasantly familiar name – Lance. He was the man who put that bullet in my corpse on my first night, the man with that fancy, silver-headed octopus cane I had taken with me. Apparently, Lance also ran Taxxxi Cabs. It was a wonder that the cab driver picked me up that first night, being that I suspiciously held his boss's prized cane. He might have easily beaten it from my cold, dead body. Certainly Lance's anger at Dante's courting of Olyvia was a factor in his demise...and consequently in my waking. It seemed I had scared off Lance when perhaps I should have killed him. I had missed my chance at the man responsible for the wire mark on my throat, but how was I to know – without a sense of who I used to be.

August 25 - 2:20pm
Just when I had given up hope, after many unreturned e-mails, I finally received an e-mail back from her. I can hear Olyvia's voice through her typed words. I know she wants out, but she is too scared...scared of change, scared of Lance. Why can't she just take a chance? What has she got to lose? She somehow has found comfort in the familiarity of that lifestyle. She's better than that. I have to help her. It's the right thing to do.

Sept 6 - 8:20pm
Finally! I spoke to her again, just briefly though. She sent me a short message on my computer saying she would come over. I don't know how she plans on sneaking away, but it doesn't matter. Once she is here, she is not going back. I won't screw it up this time. I won't yell. I know just what I am going to say...and then we'll leave this town ASAP. I know things are going to change, I can feel it. Soon, a whole new life will open up for me. Man, my room is such a mess, and she'll probably be here any minute.

Dante's final entry was optimism wrapped in irony. A new life was soon to open up. Just three days after that excited log, I would rise up as a vampire...born from his murdered body.

Did Olyvia do it, did Lance, or someone else? Why does this unfamiliar life seem so intriguing? The more I thought about it, the more improbable it seemed I would discover the truth, for those answers lay in a world I could no longer be a part of.

Moving west along the tracks, I had fallen into deep thought pondering the nature of my becoming, and disregarding any need to maintain a presentable posture or stride, I resembled a gliding zombie. Sauntering in a limp and lifeless manner, I had let my head tilt back, gaping the mouth, and my arms hung stiff and still by my sides. My corpse, being suspended by spirit, not muscle or bone, listlessly swung its feet from my languid attempt to fool others into thinking I actually walked. Only the toes of my sneakers struck the earth, pushing pebbles with each slow pendulum-motion; and moving at a steady pace, without the normal rise-and-fall innate to walking, my corpse drifted along, like a specter in the dark. It was easy to forget about that dead body, that puppet of flesh which I toted around; and doing so resulted in a limp, lifeless presentation which would surely bear dangerous penalties in view of humans. Once I realized my lack of effort, I recommenced control, bringing each foot flat onto the earth with each false step, swinging my arms, and keeping my head upright.

Half an hour into my traveling west, the railroad skewed from the shoulder of the city and cut through a small region of dense trees; the surroundings darkened to an almost flawless silence. At once, I reveled in the lush night air, heeding every creature's presence far around me with uninhibited clarity. Soon after, the trees spread out around a clearing. At the mouth of a wide field, I passed by what was once a small farm. A heavily dilapidated silo seemed ready to topple with the next push of wind, supported only by an adjoining barn, with rotted black wood. In the farm's untended field, loose fabrics hanging from a stake might have once been a scarecrow.

Across from the grassland, a secluded hamlet, decrepit and bereft of all liveliness, sprawled on either side of the tracks. The railroad ran intrudingly close past the ruins of small wooden buildings, which were scattered all around the clearing. In its day, the town might have boasted five or six dozen residents at best; now, it was uninhabitable. Toppled chimneys and rotten wood fell into old, cracked foundations which had become thriving gardens. Only a few single-floored homes remained standing; but heavily deteriorated, their opened roofs breathed the fresh night air, and the absence of doors welcomed critters from porches overlain with grass and shrub.

Below the crest of tall grass covering much of the land, old roads, reduced to a network of gravelly trails, clearly demarcated their old routes. Protruding the waving canopy of grass were relics of picket fences – slanted stakes, weathered and eaten away to look like sticks again – which traced forgotten land divisions. Dozens of small wooden crosses, and thin slates of rock, eroded beyond readability, gathered in one corner of the village. The petite graveyard, which offered a fleeting tribute to perished and forgotten lives, appeared to have died as well.

What turned that quaint nest into a tragic fossil – a wisp of a shadow of its former self? We were both once favored by time – filled with an empty optimism, a delusion of immortality. Now, we are both hollow on the inside – yet, not entirely without purpose! To exist is to have a purpose; after all, how could it be any other way?

Though I still had no guess as to what my purpose was, upon second glance, I saw that the antiquated hamlet was not dead...just changed. That vestige of a former century served a new and humbler master now. Many animals dwelt within the shabby walls of those shack-like houses. Scores of crows gathered on spotty roof tops to clamor in the night. Thousands of insects crawled within the softened wood, feeding, and breeding more life. Dozens of saplings grew inside the vacant lots, thriving on the debris-turned-compost. The grass and shrubs, no longer oppressed by man's desire to shape his surroundings, grew tall, wide, thick and tangled, providing shelter to many different things. I doubted any former residents, if they could look now at their old yards and fields, would recognize the land they thought they had known.

Could that decayed hamlet rightfully be called dead? It may have died, but everything dies, only to be reborn as something new.

Everyone dies...This thought somehow comforted me.

Laying on the tracks, on the far side of the ghost town, I saw Mira's red wig and picked it up.

Perhaps this is to encourage me to keep going, I thought. The area seemed familiar. *Or perhaps I am to stop here. Have I been here before?*

One final forgotten building was just ahead. The small structure of tarnished red brick had tall, narrow windows. It looked like an old school. On one side of the lot, rusty remnants of a playground poked out from the overwhelming sea of grass. I had seen this place... in Mira's thoughts. It was one of the images her and I shared in a moment of intimate conversation.

Without needing to move from my path along the rails, I looked into the building and beheld a twisted heap of burnt wood and brick. The roof had caved inward, burying almost all evidence of anything inside; but the burnt legs of old wooden chairs and desks poked from the wreckage, and chalkboards still clinging to the walls, were covered in layers of ash. I knew there was nobody inside those ashen walls, or anywhere else in the ghost town, or I would have felt a presence.

With no reason to linger, I continued out from that place of abandoned memories, and followed the railroad over a narrow river, where the earth was level far and around me. A human would have been able to see for miles, but my vampire eyes could not. A bleak horizon of dark grey circled far around and overhead, obscuring all things beyond its border. Buildings, trees and other objects entered through into my awareness hundreds of yards ahead, as if a thick fog receded, revealing the world to me. Conversely, things which fell far behind me were consumed by that same innocuous grey void. I had not noticed this limitation among the cramped buildings of the city, except when I failed to see the stars. In the wider, open spaces, I realized how vulnerable I was – from a distance.

The tracks bent back towards the city, to an unfamiliar area. The darkness I enjoyed was tainted by the dim glow of a lower-class area. A wide road, seldom without a passing car, veered alongside the tracks, and I found myself scrutinizing my stiff mannerisms whenever a vehicle cast its lights upon me. With each step into the populated area, it became more and more important that I guide each gesture with care.

On one side of the tracks, duplexes and small apartments formed small neighborhoods. Many loiterers occupied porches and stairs in front of the homes, observing activity, shouting and laughing merrily, and enjoying the warm autumn night. The other side of the tracks was lined with old mills and factories, few of which seemed to be operational.

Wanting to keep out of direct light, I kept my course on the railroad. I often caught the attention of people chatting on street corners and sidewalks. Most glances cast in my direction seemed merely curious about the stranger walking along the railroad alone and in darkness. Two men seemed particularly intrigued by my presence, and when I turned my face to glare at them, to show some presence, the taller, muscular man nudged his shorter, friend, and spoke into his ear. Despite their quieted voices, and my being many yards away, I picked up their words clearly.

"Check it out. Who's he?"

"I don't know. I don't recognize him from around here."

My vampire eyes monitored the keen denizens, even as my body continued on its course. Their heartbeats stirred, their breath halted, and I felt a shift in emotion, not fear per se, but a curious excitement – it was more attention than I wanted.

"What's he carrying there?" asked one of the suspicious men. "A wig?"

"I think so."

I hardly had a moment to make a decision, when my interest was diverted in another direction; I felt the rousing of a vampire. Had I finally reached my destination?

Where are you? I demanded. I sent my thoughts out to the presence, but continued walking.

Figure it out...and do it fast. You may have been spotted, a brutish male voice asserted.

A vampire's vision may be limited greatly in distance, but that limitation is more than outweighed by the ability to see in multiple directions and around or through objects. With moderate effort, I scrutinized the two men far behind me, while at the same time honing in on the vampire's presence among the wall of factories and mills.

I detected the vampire skulking in the shadows, in an alley between two buildings. As I drew closer to my undead kin, I knew there were more of them nearby. It is hard to describe my knowledge of other vampires' positions; I sense their company instantly – like when you suddenly remember where an object is that you were looking for. Its image flashes in your mind, and at once you know where to go.

I finally made my way across an empty parking lot, where stood a three-storey brick mill, with a large smokestack towering on top. Many of its large, multi-paneled windows were limited to the second and third floors; and upon one windowless brick wall, arched in near-indiscernible faded white lettering, were the words 'Myers,' something else, 'Textiles.'

I stepped into the shadows, where the creature waited. The one who spoke out to me was a large, barbaric-looking vampire wearing a dirty red blindfold tied over his eyes, and a heavy black vest, some type of armor, tattered from use. His corpse suffered many brutal injuries, and rather than hiding his wounds aesthetically, he wrapped his limbs, hands, neck and torso in layers of heavy-duty industrial tape; little skin was exposed, and what was showing had been coated in thick, black paint. Every part of him was covered over – from his face, to his boots, even the tape. This served well to hold him together, and to camouflage the grisly gashes and other lesions plaguing his unhealing corpse. However, I doubted the creature oft ventured out where a person could look upon him, and fall to the ground, terrified at the mangled black beast.

I heard his heavy words spoken into my mind again. *You look as if you just stepped out of a beauty parlor...savor that. It'll be useful.*

Who are you?

I'm Bruce...the problem solver around here.

Are these the same problems that rendered you a rag doll?

The very same ones. Bruce wore some kind of large knife; a curved blade was fastened to the top of his right arm by a series of straps. The weapon was crude, but sinister looking, and covered in dried blood. *I like practical solutions, not playing dress up and pretend, sneaking among the sheep. I know what I am. I am the wolf.*

Bruce smiled, flashing a grin of silvery metal; an artificial palette of teeth installed in his mouth gave him razor thin canines; but his were longer than the natural teeth borne to vampires, and with two additional fangs protruding right besides them.

Bruce was a mascot of fear and brutality.

"Were you waiting for me?" I asked him.

His heavy voice spoke aloud, "I was looking out for any malicious snoopers, like the two men you passed by."

I glanced back, and far – past the lot, over the tracks, across the street, and to the other side – where those two men who had seen me were once standing. They had moved on.

Bruce spoke up. "I was told you might walk this way tonight. And she'll want her wig back." He turned and walked to the back of the mill, deeper into a dark alley, scraping the armblade along the building's wall. "It's a good thing you came. We could use the help. A mild slaughtering six months ago killed half of us off."

A heavy metal, door in the back had no handle on the outside. A metal lock unhinged inside, and then, at Bruce's bidding, it swung inward, greeting us as we reached the entrance.

"Hunters?" I thought of the name I had been warned about. "Southey?"

"Yeah," Bruce cursed. "A monster in his own right. Almost died too. Lee bit him, but didn't have time to finish the job."

"Lee?"

"Yeah. Follow me. He wants to meet you."

I followed Bruce inside, where an enormously wide room, with a very high ceiling, spread out over much of the ground floor. Not an ounce of light pierced the dark. Six doors lined the furthest wall, and a broken staircase by the rear door offered passage to upper levels, should one manage to cross a collapsed section. Small holes and metal bolts, protruding from the cracked wooden floor, seemed to be the shadow of long-since removed machinery. Scattered crates and timber occupied little of the overwhelming empty space.

Bruce crossed diagonally through the pitch blackness of the windowless room, making his way to the sixth door. Not needing to guise his gestures, Bruce slid through the dark like some frightful apparition; and I followed suit.

Two cats greeted us. Bruce halted and lowered his arm.

A large and lanky, silvery cat, and another with brown and black fur, nudged their heads against his hand, and then against my ankles.

"Your pets?" I asked, noting the strange affection I was receiving.

"Cats have an affinity to vampires. I don't know why, but wherever we settle, in time, stray cats will gather." Bruce continued across the room, toward the sixth door on the far side. "They eat the rodents and other creatures which would normally gnaw at us as we rest, protecting us. It's a good relationship."

Beyond the main room was a smaller area with only one window, through which the city's artificial light entered. Beneath a large wooden hatch, which lifted open at our arrival, a wooden stairway led into a deep cellar. Hidden beneath the ground floor, in the darkness of that cellar, was an assembly of old machinery, still fastened to the floor.

"Welcome, Child." Mira's voice called through the dark. Her bald corpse was lying limp over two other bodies, huddled together in a corner of the cellar. More cats were resting with the corpses, curled up in their clammy arms and legs. "Are you finished with your friend now?"

"For now," I replied.

Like an idle marionette summoned by her master's hand, Mira's corpse arose from the pile, falling up on her feet. Her sudden lift startled the cats that had been sleeping beside the pile of cold flesh, and they scampered off when the other two corpses levitated to their feet, standing beside Mira.

A short, slender young man, appearing to have died in his late teens said to me, "I am Lee. Welcome to my clan."

Lee's voice was youthful and not innately intimidating like Bruce's; though there seemed to be a tone that spoke the pain of many decades. His light blue eyes looked like the clear sky of a summer's day, and I knew they were false like mine, perhaps gifts of Lucia. His face and neck were touched up sloppily with makeup, perhaps ample at a distance, but awkward close up. Some flesh on his arms was singed and colored like a burnt marshmallow, and bite marks perforated his hands and arms. Though suffering a moderately tattered body, his head and face remained rather unscathed. The dark brown hair still clung to his head, though injuries to his skull had left the covering thin and spotty; he had enough hair remaining to tie back into a tail.

Something about his aura, his presence, unnerved me. Like Mira and Bruce, Lee also wore a black vest, full of tears and holes from bullets.

Lee extended his clammy hand, on which were mangled stubs for fingers; the tips were cauterized – the closest thing to healing a vampire was allowed.

"Call me Child." I reluctantly shook his hand; it seemed an awkward gesture for our type.

Lee snickered at my name, and then gestured to the slightly taller, but more grotesque woman beside him. "This is whom we call, Elspeth. She is a newborn, like you…," he paused, "…and not as fortunate as you to have visited Lucia so rapidly."

Elspeth was a naked death, not made-up to look otherwise, appearing as she had been the day of her waking. Her sunken sockets housed her original pair of eyes, darkened to a sickly green, and fallen back into her skull. Unhealthily thin in life, now in death, her tight skin accentuated her skeletal frame. Her upper teeth pressed into her concave cheeks, and blackened spots covered her face where bruises never had time to heal. Her awkward fingers bent unnaturally, victims of untreated rigor mortis. Both of her wrists were cut deep, stained with blood, and devoid of any healing. The wound was self-inflicted. Jet-black hair, still lush upon her head, hung to her shoulders in a tangled, knotted mess. She, more than anyone in that cellar, appeared like a corpse one might find at a crime scene, a few days after the crime – Elspeth was hideous.

Lee thought his words. *I have tried to reach you, Child. But you have risen each night since your waking.*

Standing in a small circle in the darkness, the five of us conversed silently. Our voices echoed in each others' minds – a communal telepathy.

When we sleep, Lee explained with a ghostly whisper, *our thoughts are one. We can speak to each other from afar during rest…*

But only at night, Mira interrupted. *Daylight severs contact and isolates us. If you would only have slept through just one night, you would have heard us calling you. But I remember how it was…restless searching, staying awake until dawn, only to be chased into hiding by the light. Nothing makes sense.*

It is dangerous to be alone. Elspeth's voice called out. *I heard Lee calling and I went to him.*

We need to be together! Only together will we find our place. Lee laughed in a jovial manner, but unconvincingly sincere, like a madman. *But you are here, now. We need all the help we can get these nights. We were spotted by lowly hunters, one evening a few months back. They relayed our whereabouts to Southey who came with guns and fire, destroying our hideout. I almost killed Southey that night…I let my arms burn so I could get next to him, but time was not on my side, and I had to flee.*

I left my wig there for you to find. Mira held out her hand; the red wig flew from my hand to hers, and she placed it on her bald head.

We lost three that night… We're lucky that you and Elspeth both came when you did.

Bruce joined in, thinking, *Sometimes it is years between new wakings, and often we need to travel far to find other vampires. They can rise anywhere, at any night…wherever a dead body lies.*

Mira's voice called out, *I have heard that for each vampire killed, another is born. So we can't really be killed off…we're meant to be here.*

Lee's voice was groaning. *That sounds like something Arthur said. Take his words with a grain of salt.*

Was my vampirism a random occurrence? It seemed independent of contact with other vampires; after all, I hadn't any bite marks to justify it. Was I chosen by something not of the physical world…or did I simply just happen?

You see, Child, Lee whispered into our group, *the nature of our manifestation is a double-edged sword. Humans, because of their tales, fear our bite for the wrong reasons. Vampires are not in control of their reproduction… that belongs to the realm of living things. However, we can never be exterminated…not as a species. Death cannot be killed. As long as people die, there will be potential hosts for vampires. The only thing no one can be certain of is where and when a new child of death will be born, and rise up.*

Mira seemed more comforted by her own words. *Luckily, most people still believe vampire lore, which has little validity.* Her optimism faded, as she continued. *But Southey has tried to change that for years.*

Bruce growled. *Southey is fighting a battle he can never win. He must know that by now. I think he enjoys the pain.*

Lee raised his arm, speaking aloud. "Bruce, Elspeth, I'd like you both to stay and guard our quarters, while we venture out."

Without a word, Bruce and Elspeth turned and exited up the stairs, leaving Mira, Lee and I standing in the dark cellar, with a few cats swirling around our ankles.

"So," I asked Lee, carefully forming my lips to the words, "Where are we going that they will not be following?"

"You, and Mira and I are going on an errand." Lee replied with his mouth synchronized almost flawlessly, as if to show me he could do it better.

"…an errand?"

"Just grabbing a few things on my grocery list," Lee chuckled, as he climbed the cellar stairs. His toes knocked against each step as he rose to the next floor. "Are you two coming?"

Mira turned, and I followed her out of the cellar and back into the large room upstairs. Lee started his way across the spacious dark, following close to the long wall with six doors on its face.

"Why don't they come with us? Wouldn't they be of help?"

Lee's snotty tone snapped back at me, "They'll be more of a help guarding this place. Someone needs to make sure no snoopers come by. If we get discovered here, we will have no choice but to move on!" He did not acknowledge the two cats that had crossed the room to greet him. "Besides, look at them, they'd stand out violently where we are going. Elspeth will need some work before I stand by her side..."

"and...," Mira added with a slight laugh. "...we can't take Bruce anywhere. He has abandoned any desire to blend in among humans. He prefers to stay in shadow."

Lee sounded annoyed. "Bruce also has a knack for violence which draws more attention to us than I intend to."

"What kind of attention do you seek?" I asked, thinking of what Arthur had said to me – warning me of the danger there.

"We have our allies," Lee snapped quickly.

"Allies like Lucia?"

"Lucia did me, Mira, and few others a favor. I am grateful for that, don't get me wrong. But she is not my ally, else I'd go back to her again to fix all my damages."

The third of the six doors lining the wall swung open with a hearty creak of old, swollen wood. Lee passed through to the adjacent room, into a multi-car garage with a wide door.

A small, black car with one hubcap was parked on a greasy, cracked concrete floor in the center. Numerous holes had rusted through the body, and there were many scratches in the paint, but otherwise the vehicle remained in fair-looking condition.

Before I had time to wonder if the car functioned, its doors swung open, and the rising garage door on the facing wall illuminated when the car engine roared to life – the key in the ignition turning, seemingly on its own.

Lee moved toward the vehicle; his posture was limp, like a dead man hanging from a noose, and his arms hung behind him as he swiftly glided toward the car.

"I have my sights set on a bigger prize than merely trying to look alive and hide forever in the gutters like some damned creature. I am sure if you stay with us, you will appreciate what I have created. Those that stay with me are protected."

Mira's mannerisms were similar, floating low to the ground in an eerie manner. In the pitch darkness, with no worries of being seen by humans who might act out in violence, it made little sense to waste effort or energy with superfluous gestures; and a vampire is much swifter when free of the need to curb his movements with the incorporation of steps and rhythm.

"Where did you get the car?" I asked.

"Allies." Lee smiled, but it did not bless his cold face; it seemed forced through his tight, dry skin. He fell into the driver's seat and said, "You will know more soon enough. Stop asking so many questions! All you need to worry about is surviving, which is what we are doing now. You are hungry, aren't you?"

"A bit."

"Well, I haven't fed in almost two weeks," Lee snapped. "I cannot wait anymore."

I sat beside Lee in the front, as Mira had already placed herself across the backseat. Lee motioned the car's three doors shut; and with his hands resting at his sides, and his feet far from the pedal, the car rolled forward and out of the garage, with a ghostly manipulation of the controls.

On the main road, there were frequent passing cars, yet our presence among the living went virtually unheeded inside our vehicle. Only when we stopped at a crossing, and pedestrians on street corners would curiously glance in, was there a sense of suspicion; but we never lingered long enough to stir trouble.

Mira said, "Make sure to look alive up there, Child," and she laughed from her cold, still corpse laying in the backseat.

Lee drove the car less than a mile, and turned on to one of many dead-end roads branching off of the main street. At the far end of that road, as we were driving closer to it, a street light suddenly shattered, dropping glass shards upon the sidewalk. The light flickered for a second, and then died.

"Thank you, Mira," said Lee as he parked the car in the newly formed shadow.

We stopped just outside of a small one-floored home, layered with light green siding. The petit house had but five windows total, and a tiny back porch hardly had ample room for the gas grill. A fair number of small trees, dividing the properties, helped shield us from neighbors; but the houses were cramped close together, and there were always many directions from which someone might look out and see us.

Lee explained, "There are two people inside this house, see?"

I peered through the walls of the home, my gaze floating through the small rooms inside. Just beyond the front door, in a cluttered living room, an older man in shorts and sandals with gold chains buried in his bushy chest hair was reclined in a leather armchair. As he stared, almost hypnotized, at the television, a plume of smoke rose up from the lit cigarette idle in his mouth.

In the next room over, behind a wall that divided the kitchen from the living room, a strung-out looking woman with a perm of dark grey hair, scrubbed pots and pans in a filthy sink. Dropping a grimy sponge on the counter, she stormed around the corner, and into the living room. "Will you shut that off?!" She slapped his head with her wet hand. "You've been at it for six hours. Do something useful!"

"Eh, beat it, will you?" The man hardly flinched at the aggression, and didn't turn his glossy eyes away from the screen, nor did he even blink on impact. "I'm not bugging you. Leave me alone!" He waved his hand at her, shouting an obscenity.

The woman went back to her cleaning in the kitchen.

When I had returned my focus back, Mira said to me, "This is Rodney and Julie Gallop. They make a living selling kidnapped infants and children.

"How do you know that?" I questioned Mira. "Do you know them?"

Lee stepped from the car. "I have read a few things about them. Nowadays, it is unwise to kill without some discretion. One must be more...*selective*."

I thought back to Arthur, and his choice to feed exclusively off the ethically deviant. He tracked criminals with their own heightened emotions. Failing to pick up on any sense of reason, I asked, "And how did you find these people?"

"We looked them up," Mira said, as she left the car and walked up to Lee. They stood on the darkened walk and waited for me. "We'll show you how after."

Lee impatiently called out to me with his thoughts, *Hurry Child! We must be quick about this. This is a populated area.*

With large strides, and swinging arms, Lee swiftly darted across a small lawn of dead grass and patchy clay, toward the side of the house. *Always assume someone is watching you.*

Mira followed behind Lee, moving just as lively, and yet making hardly a noise when her foot struck the grass. They pressed against the outer wall, as not to be seen through one of two windows at head level.

I followed, standing alongside them in the margin of shadow created from the broken streetlight.

You and Mira will go through the back door, Lee commanded with his thoughts. He pointed toward the small porch leading around the back of the house. *I will go in through the front...follow my signal.*

Mira crouched, moving swiftly below the windows, and I trailed behind her, silently climbing over a railing and onto the back porch. A sliding screen door, ripped in many places, led into the kitchen. We stood out of sight, watching the woman inside. Her back was to the screen door as she washed dishes, but often she turned around to grab a quick puff of a cigarette in an ashtray upon a small card table. Her heart raced, perhaps from the residual anger of her spat with her husband, and though there was no hint of fear in her to drive me, the beating of her heart taunted my waxing hunger, calling to my bloodlust.

Mira's soft voice spoke inside me. *This will be easy. Watch me distract her and open the door.*

From within a cupboard came a slight rattling of plates and dishes. Mrs. Gallop jumped at the sudden sound, and wiped her soapy hands on her greasy, pink blouse. She looked up to where the sound came from, but did not see a cause, and stood with her hands on her hips. Slowly, the screen door slid open in its track, but the scratchy metallic noise was covered up by the rattling of plates.

As Mrs. Gallop pulled open the cabinet door to inspect, the rattling of plates ended. She stood motionless, contemplating what had happened, unaware that the screen door had slid open.

Did you see that? Mira seemed amused. *It's that easy to keep them distracted. Just reach out with your ghostly touch.*

Mrs. Gallop, confused, turned around to grab the cigarette, and as she sucked the smoke down, she noticed the screen door was opened. She could not see Mira and me just behind the outer wall. Before she took a step toward the door, I took a turn in the haunting. Almost effortlessly, I reached my ghostly hands into the refrigerator and broke a jar inside; its contents seeped out the fridge's broken seal, and onto the floor.

"What the hell is going on in here?!" Mrs. Gallop yelled, stomping over to the fridge to investigate.

Rodney Gallop barked from behind the kitchen wall. "What are you breaking in there?"

"Nothing!" She yelled as she witnessed the broken pickle jar inside. "I thought we were done with our rat problem!"

All lights in the house shut off at the same moment, and I knew it was Lee's doing.

Mr. Gallop screamed from his chair when his precious television had silenced. "Ugh! What the hell is happening now? Did you blow another fuse?"

As she walked over to the counter, fumbling in the dark to grab paper towels, Mrs. Gallop yelled back, "It was probably that stupid TV being on all day. Get off your butt and fix it!" Her voice crackled from the anger.

Mira glided across the linoleum floor with a swift push. I followed her, creeping up inches behind the soon-to-be victim.

Mrs. Gallop turned around, perhaps feeling the cold presence of our corpses, but certainly not hearing our approach. She stared into the dark at what she might have though she imagined, and as her pupils enlarged in the fresh darkness, her mouth fell open, realizing that two people stood inches from her.

Mira reached out and covered Mrs. Gallop's mouth with one hand, to prevent her from calling out. But then a terrible cry came from the other room. Mr. Gallop had a run-in with Lee.

Upon hearing her husband's blood curdling cry, Mrs. Gallop turned her head. Mira quickly gripped her short grey hair, and yanked her head back so her throat faced upward. Then, Mira opened her mouth and pressed her fangs through the soft flesh of her neck. Mira's hand could not keep the frightened woman from screaming through the clammy fingers over her lips.

Join me, Child. I know you're hungry.

I took hold of the other side of Mrs. Gallop's neck. Her warm blood surged from out of her body and into my icy corpse. The sudden attack on the veins in her neck sent blood spraying from Mrs. Gallop's mouth with a gurgling cough, through Mira's suffocating hand.

Mrs. Gallop tried to free herself, but there were four clammy hands keeping her pinned by the counter, and it only took her a moment to resign her efforts and accept fate.

Mira and I were eye to eye, and as we siphoned out the life, the world around darkened. At the instance of Mrs. Gallop's demise, when death nestled inside her, that indescribable energy I had lusted for, that potent life force, filled both Mira and I. Together with Mira, in that intimate moment, I felt a shared burden, a brief end to my loneliness – an emotion I hadn't been graced with since my waking.

The world came back into focus and we released Mrs. Gallop from our jaws. Her corpse fell limp onto the kitchen floor.

Lee walked into the kitchen with a blood-stained grin, and with Rodney Gallop's ankle clenched in his hand, dragged the dead body over to the pale, lifeless woman. "It is important that we try to eliminate any *obvious* evidence of our activity." Lee said, lifting a cutting knife from the sink water. The two dead bodies stared up at us with terrified expressions, frozen in place for the police. Walking over to the ex-couple, Lee used the knife to stab their necks where each set of our fangs had penetrated the skin. "Let them find another crook to blame it on. We don't need rumors." He then placed the knife into the dead man's hand, and using a dishtowel, wiped the blood from his face, chin and neck.

Mira took the rag and cleaned herself as well, and handed it to me. "Rumors spread fast in this part of town," she said as she turned to follow Lee out toward the living room. "...and they eventually bring hunters."

Like a band of undead assassins, we waltzed in and out in a matter of a few minutes. With the power to see and touch from a distance, there was hardly a reason to doubt we were capable of taking any life we chose, reaching anyone in any building. We were demigods.

Outside, however, our luck changed. A group of four men stood in the driveway of a neighboring house, watching the three of us as we walked back toward the car. Perhaps they came to investigate the busted street light, or maybe they had heard the final screams of the Gallops. Either way, it was clear from their tense posture, and focused attention, that we were of the highest suspicion to them.

One of the men stepped forward and called out to us with a voice that wavered from nervousness, "Who are *you*? You know Rod? Hold up one second...Hey!"

Get inside the car! We have to leave now! Mira thought, as not to alert the four men.

Lee started the car, still a few steps from it. *Why didn't I take Bruce along? He'd make them think twice about interfering.*

When it became clear we had no intention of stopping to chat, the other men began to walk quickly toward us, reaching for the guns concealed beneath their jackets.

Lee and Mira, quicker to act than I, reflexively inhibited the men's approach. As the men took their first steps, the two vampires' meddling hands lingered around the unsuspecting aggressors like a spiritual fog. The four men staggered backwards, their shirts and jeans tugged upon with enough force to tear strips of fabric free, and those men with necklaces found the chains and wires pressing into their own throats. Their arms flailed, they dropped their weapons, and the four jostled men fell to the grass, cursing as their heads crashed to the hard earth.

In the few seconds bought from Lee and Mira's intervention, I jumped into the backseat, and we took off in a wake of screeching tires. We were not so swift as to prevent the car from a few hastily fired, but shockingly accurate, gun shots from the irate men.

Unfortunately, it did not end there. The four toppled men climbed into a car of their own and gave chase.

"Stay low and out of sight," Lee told me as he steered back onto the main road. He kept the headlights off. He did not need them to see clearly, and it helped conceal us. "You'll not want to risk getting shot up. You don't have armor like us. Damn, why didn't I invite

Bruce? He'd have taught them a lesson."

Lee and Mira both fell lifeless on the front seats, and I mimicked them in the back, falling limp and out of sight of the windows. The car appeared to onlookers that it drove by itself.

"Are these hunters?" I asked.

"It seems so," Mira said, "but I don't believe they are Southey's men. I don't recognize any of their faces!"

"No matter," Lee grunted, "It's awfully suspicious that they happened to be next to our target. If I find out this was a set up..."

"...A set up? By who?"

"Enough questions, Child!" Lee screamed. "Concentrate on the problem at hand!"

The hunters gained on us rapidly. One of the men stood through the sun roof of the small, sporty vehicle with a semi-automatic pistol held firmly with both hands. He fired bullet after bullet, ripping holes in the trunk and rear windshield with every sloppy shot he fired. In the back seat of the rapidly accelerating vehicle, two other men leaned out the window with similar guns, firing at our car as Lee swerved erratically down the street, trying to keep our car from traveling in a straight line.

Most people on the sidewalks ran for cover in advance, hearing the slews of gunfire. A few individuals, unphased by the shots, stared awkwardly at our seemingly empty car being chased down the street.

When the rear windshield shattered, raining down broken glass on me, the head rests of the front seats burst into chunks of fabric and wispy padding as bullets tore through them.

Mira, focusing her phantom energies at the pursuing vehicle, manipulated the guns of the three firing men, trying to twist the handles from their sweaty palms, and throwing their aim off.

"I can't disarm them," she said, frustrated. "They are holding on to their guns too tightly."

"Help her Child, I have to pay attention to the road!" Lee ordered. "We cannot return with them following us, and we'd better lose them fast because we are attracting attention!"

"Break for a moment!" I yelled at Lee.

"What?"

"Just do it!"

Lee slowed down, and the enemy car, having suddenly caught up with us, slammed into our rear bumper. The three gunners, leaning from the windows and sunroof, shook from their perches. In that moment, I concentrated on one gunner's weapon, pulling it from his loosened grip at the moment of our cars' impact. The gun darted through the air, through the rear windshield, and into my awaiting grasp in the back seat.

I sat up and aimed the gun out the rear windshield. Attempting to pull the trigger, I struggled with dead, numb fingers, failing to utilize the weapon adequately. However, when my mind focused only on the narrow, metal trigger, as opposed to pulling back on my corpse's finger to shoot the gun, I managed to successfully return fire. I found it difficult to aim the pistol; my vampire vision, being in no way binocular, was not suited for a gun's sights. My aim was poor, hardly striking their windshield, which cracked and sent the driver swerving across the road in surprise.

The other two armed men wrestled against Mira's trickery as if a strong magnetic force pushed and pulled their guns around. When they eventually managed to aim in the proper direction, their shots were far from accurate. Mira had her hands full keeping the hunters from busting our tires with bullets.

"Forget shooting at them!" Mira sounded a tad annoyed. "Go after the driver."

Our car passed by the abandoned mill, but Lee did not dare to pull into the lot. He turned left at the next intersection, looping around the block.

The hunters' car slowly climbed beside us – soon, the two gunners would have easy shots of us lying upon the seats. Though their guns shook in their hands, the haunted hunters did not seem afraid. Instead, their annoyed faces told of the many times they had struggled against the power of vampires. None of the men kept on any of the accessories or jewelry they were wearing before the chase ensued, not even their shirts – a preventative measure against our phantasmal manipulation. These men weren't totally devoid of experience.

Focusing into the enemy car, I pestered the driver who prepared to ram our vehicle into the oncoming lane. I cursed into his ears, calling for him to stop, and sweat beaded upon his brow as my voice darkened to a demonic tone. Clasping the sweaty steering wheel with my ghostly grip, I jerked it, to his unexpectedness, and his car veered for a moment, before he regained control. The driver's face became cold and stern, followed by a subtle smile as he realized what I tried to do. He sat up, wrapping his arms around the rim of the wheel for extra support; his muscular arms overpowered my underdeveloped influence and I found myself unable to jostle the wheel from him.

Then, as soon as the obvious answer to the problem occurred to me, I looked to the impending car's brake, and with all my force, I pressed it to the floor. Its tires wailed loudly, leaving smoking black strips across the pavement as it fishtailed, spinning to a halt. The gunner atop the sunroof slid out of the car and fell painfully onto the asphalt.

As we sped away, turning corner after corner to avoid any chances of another chase, the three of us sat upright and Lee placed his hands near the wheel, ending the illusion of an autonomous car.

"This car is a wreck!" Lee cursed. "We are lucky those men did not catch us during the kill or we would not have left there in such fine condition!"

Lee rounded cautiously back to the old mill, careful so that no one would see our car enter back into the garage.

Mira said, "We'd better rest. It is nearly morning, and we have stirred up enough commotion that it won't be safe for us outside for a while."

"It better settle down quick," Lee said to her. "I have a meeting in a few days."

Chapter 10 – Southey's Promise

All was quiet in the basement headquarters of Redbank Apartment #1. Alone at his desk, Southey slumped over in his chair, using a rolled-up newspaper as a pillow. His arms reached across the hard metallic surface, hanging over the far edge, and a cigar had fallen from his grasp when he fell from consciousness, burning away on the cement floor. Southey was physically and emotionally drained; he had spent much of the last week awake and afraid.

The witch in the woods did not die with that stroke of Sam's blade. Though her decapitated corpse lay two feet beneath the earth, her restless spirit persisted, lingering at the boundary of Southey's sanity. Each night since the excursion in the mountain, the same horrendous vision taunted him in his slumber.

In the pitch blackness of the woods, the witch's pale skin emits a soft and iridescent glow that lights the surrounding emptiness. With a saddened, gaping mouth, she stares odiously at him through hollowed, blackened cavities, her orifices teeming with beetles, spiders and night crawlers. Her feet rooted in the earth, she is unable to walk to him, but reaches out with cracked and dry wriggling fingers, beckoning him to come closer. Her flowing white hair branches upward, unnaturally, and slowly sways as if underwater. Unable to avert the frightful image by turning his head, or closing his eyes, he is forced to watch as the skin near her ankles becomes dark and ridged, like bark. Slowly, a transformation seeps up her naked body, covering every inch, until all that remains of her is the likeness of a tree. When her pale glow finally succumbs to the encompassing shell of bark, and her arms and hair become stiffened like branches, three deep openings in the trunk linger where her saddened face rests its final gaze.

Usually, Southey would wake up, panting and mumbling; and if he managed to fall back asleep, she would be there waiting, glowing in the dark recesses of his subconscious. However, when he was awake, ghostly whispers persisted during his conscious state – shadowy voices so soft that a head full of his own thoughts would often suffice to bury them.

Occasionally, when Southey's recurrent nightmare ended and the ghostly image of the witch-tree faded, he was graced with a few moments of peaceful sleep – in which he recovered little but much needed strength.

It was during that peaceful calm when Southey had a woeful dream – a vision of his two late sons. Standing before him in bleak silence, the boys would not raise their heads to meet their father's saddened eyes. Though their mouths moved, Southey could not hear their words. Colin was covered with deep gashes and bloody shards of glass that jetted from his body – a reminder of his final moments in life. Jacob stood beside his diced and reddened older brother, with his ankles buried inches below the earth, trying but unable to pull himself free; slowly, Jacob's ankles turned black and hard, and the woody shell climbed up his body, covering all. As Southey was turning away from his two boys, disheartened by the sad dream, another figure faded into his sight. A fair skinned young woman with long auburn hair and bright hazel eyes stood behind the two boys, and with a hand on each son's shoulder, she smiled at Southey. A long time ago, her dimples warmed Southey's soul; now, her rosy cheeks crushed his heart and his hopes, like the fond childhood memories of a man on his deathbed, pining for one escaping moment of those carefree days.

The images faded, leaving Southey alone in a dream of black.

"Hey," a familiar male voice pierced into his dream. "Hey, it's me."

A prodding at Southey's shoulder woke him up. His heart raced, refusing to forget the nightmare.

With a hand cupped over Southey's shoulder, Sam gently shook him, saying, "Hey, how's it going?" A gauze on Sam's neck bulged out from the swelling of the wound beneath.

Southey lifted his head from the desk. He moaned and pressed his hands to his lower back, arching backwards – cracks followed. Feeling surprisingly revitalized, he was still in no mood to cast a smile at his old friend, Sam, whom had been absent for well over a week now.

"Eh," Southey grunted. "I feel like crap." Southey rubbed his hands across his sweaty face, combing his bright blonde hair with shaky fingers. "I thought for a while that you weren't going to make it. What did the doctor say?"

"Septicemia..." Sam gently patted the white bandage with his fingers. Two large abscesses had formed where the witch's putrid teeth punctured the skin. When Sam turned his neck to one side, the tender sores pressed together, stinging sharply. "That filthy leech infected me with five strains of bacteria. They administered antibiotics in time or I'd be dead already." Sam shuddered, coughing nastily. "After a couple nights' rest, my fever went away steadily. I still got some symptoms, but I figured we've wasted enough time already."

"Hurts like hell, don't it?" Southey rubbed the bulbous scar on the side of his neck. Reaching across the desk to a swirled grey-and-white marble ashtray, Southey grabbed a half cigar; with a flick of his silver butane lighter, the ashy, black end lit a deep red, pluming smoke into the air. "Did they ask you about *how* you got it?"

"Yeah," Sam chuckled, "...at first I told the truth."

Southey's brow lowered, finally turning his head to see Sam. "Why would you do *that*? Now you're going to have a 'jackass' on your medical record." With his eyes closed, Southey rubbed his temples, sucking in a deep breath of smoke.

"No offense," Sam responded respectfully, "but most people already associate me with you...and that carries connotations of its own." Sam's smile was almost buried by his mustache. "When the silence got too awkward for the good doctor, I said a diseased monkey bit me and we're all going to die."

Sam reached onto the desk and picked up a sheet of paper with several names and addresses scribbled on it. Most of the names had been marked with an X, indicating that they had serious criminal records – a near-flawless consistency among most victims of vampire attacks over the last fifteen months.

Sam read them to himself, "Briggs, Aaron; Gallop, Rodney; Gallop, Judy; Polidori, John...," his voice trailed off, "This it?"

Southey let loose a cloud of smoke from his lips, watching it swirl and settle on his desktop. "Yeah...spanning the last few weeks. Most of those weren't in the obits, as usual. I had to call a few of your friends to find out about them."

Sam walked to the massive satellite image of the city hanging on the wall behind the desk. Examining the placement of small circular stickers on the city map, Sam checked to see if the names on the new list had been added. "What the heck is going on out there?" Keeping track of where vampire victims were found was one way to know which areas to keep an eye on.

Rising in his chair, Southey walked around to the front of the desk and pulled the cigar from his mouth to speak clearer. "Attacks are...fixed...somehow. Look at the caliber of victims."

Sam took a deep breath, before the air filled with cigar smoke. "So what? Leeches usually keep their kills among the lower classes and the socially delinquent. It's safer."

"I know, but in the last year, it seems that these victims are more consistently felons...rapists, murderers." Southey paced about noisily, trying to cover the whispering voices in his head. "I know leeches aren't researching their victims, so how do they do it?" Southey perched the cigar in the gap of his broken teeth, mumbling below his breath.

He turned and hurried over to Sam, snatched the list from his hands, and held it in the air, continuing his rant, "I know these crooks aren't all just *stabbing* each other in the necks…it is a decoy. Leeches are trying to cover their own tracks…but it would take more than that to remain secreted this long. Why is it so hard to find them, now, after all these years…? What has changed?" Southey's voice trailed off to a halt, yet his lips continued to move.

Southey did not appear to notice when Sam reached out and gently plucked the paper from his grasp. "There really aren't many left around here anymore," Sam reminded him. "We've done a good job."

Southey's voice rose to clarity from a low murmur. "Yeah. It'll be near impossible to find these leeches soon…" His teeth clenched tightly. "And I still haven't found *him*. Where *is* he?"

"Well that's why you hired Maida, right? She seems to be doing her part." Sam tossed the paper back on the desk. "One of her visions is bound to lead us to the one that killed Ellen." Sam nodded, as if he were trying to raise his friend's spirits.

Southey ceased his ranting when he heard her name – Ellen. He stared at Sam as if a revelation befell him. How long had it been since he heard her name? Aside from his most recent dream, he had not even thought of her in years, except on the anniversaries of her death.

Sam broke the silence. "When you finally get him, you can come back here and punish this pitiful bastard… for Colin's sake." Sam pointed his thumb over his shoulder – at the arched wooden door in the corner.

Southey did not hear Sam's words; he had fallen deep into a painful, yet fond memory – one that fueled his hunt and drove him forward, even when he managed to suppress it – which was most of the time.

"Ellen suffered in silence for days before she let me know." Southey's voice cracked. "I thought she had the flu at first." He sat atop the desk and sighed. "She was just sick…no big deal. But she was acting different, distancing. Then her body broke out with cysts. The skin on her neck turned black and swollen. The doctors had to keep her drugged just to keep her heart rate down. Her neck and face swelled so much…" Southey closed his eyes, turning his head from Sam in shame. "…I was too disgusted to even kiss her goodbye when her heart was failing, even though I knew that I only had seconds left with her."

Southey's eyes welled with tears, his face gleamed with hatred. "What she must have thought of me." His brow lowered over his narrowed eyes, wrinkling the skin on the bridge of his nose. By repressing that memory, that other life which seemed foreign in retrospect, he had nearly forgotten how his life had taken its current and cruel tangent.

"Damn their filthy venomousness...God! They're a cancer to the world!" Southey hollered, hopping from the desk, awakening the dogs across the room; Cain and Abel watched their master break down.

Southey clasped his ears with his hands as if he tried to muffle some bothersome sound. Shaking his head, his phlegmy voice grumbled. "Why didn't she tell me when it happened? Why did she hide it? We could have stopped the infection...prevented full-blown septicemia."

Sam reached out to pat his tormented friend on the shoulder, but Southey stepped back in refusal. Sam tugged at his mustache and said, "Would you have honestly *believed* her?"

Southey took a deep breath and with his hands still covering his ears, he continued, "At first I didn't...when Ellen finally told me in the hospital. I had been yelling at her, grilling her because I knew she was lying about something. She was a bad liar...a *horrible* liar. A good girl. I remember looking at those blackened holes on her neck and wondering what really happened. Who'd ever heard of such a thing?" Southey said the word slowly and clearly, "...*Vampire*. She whispered those words, and had I not been looking right into her bright, hazel eyes, I'd have never believed her." Southey shook his head. "She was afraid to tell me because she thought...thought she was going to...to turn *into* one."

"I can see how that legend got started," Sam rubbed his neck and recalled how horrible it felt when his immune system reacted to the bite – the blood poisoning. His body grew cold, his heart pounded in his chest. A horrible headache persisted, making him short tempered. He grew lethargic and incoherent, seeming very unlike himself. Then the antibiotics began to work their magic. If Southey hadn't taken Sam to the hospital as fast as he had, Sam's old body would have suffered much more.

Sam hadn't seen Southey openly talk of Ellen in many years. Southey tended to bottle up her memory, especially in the latter half of the decade since. This led Sam to wonder, from time to time, if Southey even remembered what started all of this. Sam was a bit refreshed to see that, even in this tough time, Southey hadn't lost semblance of his former self.

"I promised her...I *promised* her! I swore on her deathbed that I would find him, *find* it." Southey pointed down and behind his shoulders. "Two scars. She stabbed him twice in the back with the knife I gave her when we moved here. I have checked every ruined leech's corpse for those scars, hoping to see that demon defeated.

But I will find him."

Reaching into the side of his boot, Southey removed a small, silver poniard from a sheath between his leg and the inner-cuff. "If Ellen hadn't been brave enough to fight back, she would have died there, and I would never have gotten to say goodbye, or given the chance for vengeance." He clenched the blue, ceramic hilt tightly. "This knife *will* finish the job." The short, narrow blade no longer glimmered as it once had years ago, but remained sharp through disuse.

Southey made a fist, biting intensely on his index finger. His eyes darted to and fro. "Sam! Do you hear it?" He walked closer to Sam, leaning towards him. His voice sounded frustrated. "Do you hear those voices? What are they saying? Damn it!"

Sam's face filled with concern. "You're *still* hearing them?"

"Yeah." Southey pressed the palms of his hands to his face, twisting them against his eyes. "But I think that I am so used to them that I barely hear them anymore…but they are there. That is what really makes me sick."

Sam shook his head. "I heard them for a few hours after the woods, but I think that was just shock."

Southey paused and listened with his hand to his ear. "Are they saying my name? I don't know if…" He gnashed his teeth together; the squeaking of bone on bone made Sam squirm. "…if they're condemning me, or calling me."

Sam cocked his head toward the arched wooden door in the corner. "You're sure it's not just him?"

"Of course I'm sure. Leech captives have messed with me before, but this is different. These voices follow me everywhere!"

Southey threw his cigar at the large, satellite image hanging on the wall behind his desk. The smoldering hunk struck the cracked glass covering, and the butt burst into dozens of glittering pieces.

"For the love of God, shut up!" Southey screamed, his voice squeaking from the strain on his larynx.

Sam walked over to the map and brushed away any remaining fiery specks. Taking a deep breath, he anticipated the additional stress his next words would add to Southey's already overworked mind. "We'll need more men if we are to go out again." Sam glanced down at a stack of sketches lying on the desk, and picking them up to inspect them, he said, "I got your message the other day. Are these the new ones?"

"Yeah… Maida managed to find where the remaining horde fled to." Southey smiled; his grin was hollow and unconvincing. He rubbed the lump on his neck, thinking back to his last encounter with those vampires. "We can finish them off, hopefully. I doubt their numbers have climbed significantly."

"I'll contact some of the other hunters." Sam nodded.

"Everyone else is a joke," Southey spat on the floor. "We *had* the best team...the only ones with an edge." Southey burst a single laugh, as if he wavered on the brink of a breakdown. "Now *that's* all over."

"Well," Sam rubbed his chin. "Bad options are better than no options. We still have a couple trustworthy sources. There's that one Jamaican guy who used to hunt with us a few years ago."

Southey placed his beloved dagger back into its sheath. He removed his damp, sweaty shirt, tossing it to the floor. After kicking off his booths, he slid his pants down.

Sam interrupted. "What are you doing? You're not going in there *again* are you?"

"I have to release some built-up aggression. I don't want to worry about him using any devil tricks on me. I know what I'm doing."

"I know you know what you're doing. I just don't think this is going to help in any way." Sam consoled.

Southey removed his socks and underwear. "It's not about helping me. It's about hurting him...hurting them!" His laughter mutated into a smoker's cough. "I'm beyond help!" He spit on the floor. Cracking his knuckles against his cheeks, he then reached to the desk, picking up a ring with many keys on it.

Southey walked to the arched wooden door in the corner.

Sam whistled at Cain and Abel, who watched curiously at their raving naked master. The two German shepherds trotted across the cellar to Sam, who removed his long, grey coat, draping it on the desk.

"You can't hurt them...not like this." Sam walked towards the door.

Southey held his finger up in the air, and said, "Just because they don't feel it, doesn't mean they don't *not* appreciate it!"

With trembling hands, Southey pushed the key towards the lock – but when it neared the keyhole, the entire set jingled violently, as if the keys tried to break free from the metal ring. His clenched hand quivered as if he arm-wrestled an invisible opponent who pulled at the ring of keys from inside the cell, beyond the door.

Struggling to align the key properly when thrusting for the lock, Southey missed the keyhole and struck the door, dropping the keys to the floor. He immediately stepped on them with his bare foot.

"He's trying to stop me." He laughed insanely. "He knows I am coming and he *thinks* he can stop me!" Southey lowered his voice and grinned. "You're only making me hurt you more, leech! I'm going to..."

A metallic groan slowly filled the basement. Cain and Abel turned from the door, bursting out into a violent barking fit. The heavy metal desk, which weighed hundreds of pounds, slowly tilted forward, spilling its contents onto the cement floor.

Sam ran over to pull the desk back, but it had leaned too far and was too heavy, crashing onto the cement with an ear shattering thud. For only a moment, the frenzied dogs ceased barking, humbled by the metallic clamor; they resumed as soon as the echoing clang faded.

Before Sam could raise his arm to calm the canines, the two riled dogs hushed. Their ears pivoted, picking up a sound the two men could not. The dogs' growls became a light whining. Turning around and around where they stood, their heads whipped back and forth as if attempting to see something at the back of their heads.

"Heel," Sam yelled a couple of times, and when the two dogs responded, he scorned, "You know better than that!"

Southey lifted his foot, careful not to expose the key until his hands were positioned to snatch it, lest the devilish spirit of the vampire drag it to the furthest corner of the room. With both hands tight around the key, Southey lifted it without interference, pushed it into the lock successfully, twisting it with a click.

Pushing the arched wooden door with all his weight, expecting some type of resistance, Southey stumbled into the narrow hallway beyond, his naked body tumbling onto the cold, downward-sloped concrete floor.

The skin on his right arm burned painfully, turning red and sore from striking the abrasive floor.

With the two dogs behind him, Sam followed into the short hall, keeping a small distance from his disturbed colleague.

For a moment Southey laid there naked on his back. With his left hand rubbing his bloody arm, he stared up at the ceiling with its many stone blocks arching from wall to wall. Set inside a small nook in the ceiling, a single light flickered, dimly lighting the tiny passageway.

When Southey rolled over onto his stomach, lying with his ribs painfully pressed to the floor, he stared at the wide, heavy oak door at the end of the hall. The narrow slit between the floor and wood let the nauseating odor of death seep through to his nostrils. The foul-smell was not the result of imprisoning one vampire, but many over the last few years.

Southey pondered how familiar he had become with the scent of death, and how, through that tiny underground cell, he had become a monster *to* the monsters – to vampires.

Years into Southey's personal mission, it proved evident that almost everything he thought he knew about vampires was false – or at least skewed from the truth. Relying mainly on the testimonies of others to base his strategies, Southey's earliest attempts at hunting vampires went poorly. In those days, Southey, a respected commissioner with the power of the police at his disposal, sent men into ghettos and rundown areas, to search forsaken and abandoned lots - popular areas for vampires. The police claimed to be attacked from all sides by the 'invisible' aggressors – claiming their fellow officers went mad, acting irrationally, and turning their firearms on each other. Many officers died in a short period of time, and it did not take long for Southey's position as police commissioner to be at risk; yet driven by the loss of his love, Ellen, he continued as long as he could, until he was without a job and even thirstier for revenge.

His desperation to continue the search for vampires soon paid off. Whereas irrational and outdated hunters, using antiquated techniques, searched coffins and cemeteries armed with wooden stakes and crosses, Southey quickly learned the correlation between rumors of ghosts and vampire presences. In time, he began to find them more easily.

"Are you okay, Southey?" Sam stepped toward his friend who had lain still for an uncomfortably long time.

"Yeah," Southey gurgled.

With both arms, Southey lifted from the floor, rising to his bare feet. He faced the thick, wooden door at the end of the hall.

Southey had his underground shelter constructed with the idea of being able to stand safely in the presence of a vampire – to study its strengths and weaknesses, and to develop his hunting techniques. Keeping the cell concealed with earth not only muffled the loud noises he sometimes made when he experimented on them, but it also seemed to suppress the creatures' powers.

The first vampire Southey caught lasted only a few days before it starved and began to rot; but not before a maddening display of its lust for blood – acting animalistic, asserting its spiritual prowess with desperate cries and yells that left some of his nearby tenants frightened and curious. It had never seemed desirable to Southey to keep a vampire alive through a slow and steady regimen of victims, until recent months, when he met one of his newer and more eccentric tenants – Maida Mordane.

Maida approached Southey with what he thought would be a growing complaint – one he had learned to ignore. Maida had experienced a haunting in her apartment. Unlike the other tenants who griped about moving objects, or whispers and yells awakening them from slumber, Maida claimed to have had related and often terrifying visions accompanying the strange occurrences.

Before Southey could turn away from the purported psychic, she handed him drawings she had done when influenced by the presence in her apartment. There was a picture of a dark cell with a solitary wooden door and a figure, chained to its center. There were sketches of desolate inner-city areas Southey knew were frequented by vampires. But one drawing that chilled Southey most was a portrait of him. In that grim sketch, his furrowed brow pressed down on his bulging, white eyes; his toothy, punctured grin ran ear to ear from behind the barrel of a shotgun. When he realized what the drawings really were – things as seen through vampires' eyes – he told her his hobby, beseeching her to act as his psychic informer in exchange for paying her rent indefinitely. Maida accepted. Southey's latest prisoner was their first test subject.

Southey's naked body was growing cold in the damp underground hall. On the thick oak door leading into the cell, a large padlock, requiring a separate key on the ring, held a heavy metal bar in place, which in turn prevented the door from 'accidentally' opening. When Southey found the proper key, he released the padlock with no interference, and tossed it to the floor. He then lifted the horizontal bar up from the supports holding it to the door. The wood creaked on its hinges, as the door swung violently inward without a push from Southey. Slamming into the inner wall of the chamber, the door's thunderous boom dwindled long before the walls absorbed the echoes.

"Inviting me in now, are we?" Southey twisted his neck side to side, cracking the bones. He sighed in relief. Being naked, he had nothing to fear from the vampire inside, as long as he remained out of reach – which he had no intentions of doing.

Southey stared into the dark cell; his silhouette reached across the blood-splattered floor, over the vampire's corpse.

The corpse was positioned upright against a pole in the center of the cell. It did not stir at the arrival. A splintered bone jetted from the center of the blackened stub on its right arm – mangled above the elbow. A slew of punctures and gashes covered much of its legs and torso, and the clothing that remained wrapped around the corpse was tattered, and bloodstained from the two victims it had been fed. A chain ran from a metal cuff around its neck to a thick pole embedded in the cell's center.

Southey stood in the doorway and looked to his side where Sam waited with the dogs. "I don't know how much longer we're going to need to keep this leech alive, so you might want to give what's-his-name a call. We may need to cash in on that last girl...to buy us enough time to do the job. I don't want to risk this thing dying on me...not until I kill it myself."

Sam shook his head. "We've got time, don't worry."

"Better safe than sorry."

Slouching so his head would not graze the ceiling, Southey cautiously stepped into the shallow, cylindrical cell. Heel to toe, he inched towards the seemingly lifeless prisoner, and said "You can play dead...I'm still going to beat you for what you did to my boy!"

With a shrill cry that jarred Southey, the creature lunged from its sitting position; the chain rattled as it rose from the floor without warning. The vampire's outstretched arm swiped the air inches from Southey, who laughed and hopped back into the shadow along the edge of the room.

Southey snatched the extended arm, grabbing the clammy, pasty wrist of the creature that stood two feet away. The grisly vampire stood motionless, but stared ravenously at him with its green eyes.

"What are you going to do?" Southey's taunt echoed as he twisted the arm clockwise.

The vampire hunched, not from pain but to reduce the cracking of its bones, trying to keep its only arm intact.

Southey pulled his foot back and kicked the legs from beneath the creature – but it did not fall, wavering in the air for a moment as its legs quickly dropped back to their natural positions.

Southey let go of the sickly, wounded arm and snorted, "Freak."

Sam stood in the doorway; at his sides, Cain and Abel held their heads low, growling at the undead prisoner. Their hind legs tensed, quivering from the anticipation of either Sam or Southey's command, when they would pounce on the helpless creature, tearing him apart with ease.

"We don't have time for this Southey, come on!" Sam yelled into the cell.

Independent of the ghostly words whispering from behind Southey's head, the vampire slowly opened and shut its black and bloody mouth, "Your days are over Southey. She'll have your soul in the end..."

Southey knew who the creature meant by 'she' – the witch, the nightmare that poisoned his mind ever since he ventured into those woods.

With a bellowing cry and outstretched arms, Southey ran forward, shoving the corpse backwards. The vampire turned its head to bite its captor's arm, but Southey avoided the gory poisonous fangs with a quick hook punch to the vampire's head, and after slapping its only usable arm away before the creature could sink its fingers into Southey's neck, he forcefully pushed the vampire back into the darkness on the opposite side of the cell.

"I'll *never* show you what you want," the vampire taunted, knowing why it had been taken. "You'll have seen your sons die in vain!"

Southey had taken a step back, pondering the words. He then ran at the creature again, but failed to get close. Without bending its knees, or pushing off of the floor, the vampire lunged to the other side of the cell, gliding on air, and filling the cell with muffled, ghostly laughter.

"Watch out!" Sam yelled at Southey, who had barely had enough time to duck the chain which nearly met his throat.

Southey turned around, but the creature was fast and silent. Before he could orient himself, he heard a metallic rattle, and his head was painfully met by the slack of the iron chain – summoned to whip through the air by the angered vampire.

Southey wailed in agony, like a madman. His eyes filled with tears from the crushing sensation of the links against his forehead. He stumbled backwards, grabbing hold of the chain before it fell back to the floor. Pulling on the chain with all his strength, he reeled the vampire toward him, like a dog on a leash.

When the two enemies made contact, they wrestled to the ground, and Cain and Abel immediately ran over to them. Southey over-powered the creature, and knelt on top of it. The chain rattled wildly, cracking its links together in the air by Southey's head, but did not reach far enough to strike him. The dogs snapped their jaws inches from the creature's head.

Southey stared into the vampire's gaping, black mouth which turned to bite the hands that pinned its neck to the concrete floor. The steel cuff that the creature wore around its neck prevented it from tilting its mouth downward, toward Southey's oppressive hand.

A low and terrifying wail circled around the room, igniting the two encroaching dogs into a frenzied howl; they backed away, distracted at the deep moaning. Southey's hair danced in his face as cool gusts of wind blew erratically within the cell, carrying with them, the tormented cry of the shackled vampire.

Near-blinded by his own hair, Southey raised a fist and struck the creature in the face. He pulled his hand high over his head again, hoping to break the vampire's face with one more crushing blow to its skull; however, when Southey's fist fell, the vampire's body slid suddenly to the side. Being on top of the corpse, Southey lost his balance, and his angered fist crashed into the cement. He yelled out as the searing tinge shot into his wrist; the damaged bone filled him with throbbing pain. Clenching his arm, Southey forgot about the vampire beneath him and almost fell victim to its bite as it lunged upwards.

Sam darted into the room to help, but not before the dogs pounced, sinking their teeth into the vampire's corpse. Sam pulled Southey back toward the door, and when Southey was safely in the hallway, he yelled, "Cain, Abel...heel!"

The dogs released the writhing corpse and returned to the hall.

Sam shut the large oak door, and locked it.

"You senile son-of...," Sam started to say, his hand covering his face, stressed from the near loss of Southey.

"Shut up! I don't want to hear it," Southey blurted, nursing his wrist. His forehead was already bruised from where the chain had hit him.

"Are you even going to be ok to go out later? You look like you haven't slept in days."

"Yeah, I haven't, remember? Whatever...what's a little pain anyway...Sometimes it is all that reminds me I'm even alive anymore." Southey walked out of the hall, following Sam and the dogs into the main room.

Sam walked to the desk and knelt, picking up the papers, folders and other scattered objects that had fallen when the desk toppled. Southey walked toward the mess and reached down, picking up his pants and one of his cigars that had spilled on the floor.

"Don't worry about that mess," Southey snarled. "We'll fix it later. But thanks anyway." After he had pants on, Southey was happy to see that his shaky, sore hand could successfully flick his silver, butane lighter. Passionately, he sucked the sweet smoke from a new cigar. When he was full of the thick, savory smoke, he held his swollen, shaking hand in front of him in laughed. "At least I can heal you worthless freak!"

Sam stood up, annoyed with the recent events. Though he was not convinced that Southey was healthy enough to pursue their mission, he knew he would not be able to talk him into resting longer. Among the scattered papers on the floor, was one picture of an old mill, on the other side of town. Sam picked it up, and asked, "So, this is where we need to go next?"

"Yeah. The sooner the better, too. They likely suspect we're coming."

"Well, help me load the van and I'll make some phone calls. I'm *sure* we can find someone to help us do this." Sam headed out of the basement.

Southey followed him, and said, "We're going, one way or the other."

Chapter 11 – The List

Lee, Mira and I returned safely to the garage, though we left a wake of commotion in the streets. Anyone who witnessed the car chase gathered for police, and thankfully no one had seen when our car looped back to the mill. Just to be safe, we waited behind the garage doors to see if anyone would wander in our direction. When it became certain to Lee that we had slipped away successfully, he walked closer to the shot-up, riddled car.

"Look at this wreck," Lee said, observing the damages.

Most of the vehicle's windows were shattered, the body marked by dozens of bullet holes, and the rear bumper hung loose, ready to fall.

Lee cursed and said, "It's not like I can just buy a new car! This thing is useless to us! It'll only draw attention."

Lee's angered cry shook the walls of the garage, rattling the garage door, and filling the air with a pained howl. The small black car started rocking on its tires, side to side, and any remaining windows burst into fragments, as did the headlights and dashboard display. One by one, large dents formed in the exterior, as Lee used his powers to pound the body of the car; heavy groans and crunches followed each jagged bending of metal. A few seconds after he unleashed his frustration, the car appeared as if it had been beat up by an angry mob; but not so badly that it seemed incapable of ever running again. It was just more useless to him now.

Lee collapsed to the ground, exhausted from his exertion. "Ugh," he groaned. "Sometimes...I forget our...limitations." Lee passed out, his corpse limp and lifeless. "...must rest."

Mira lifted her comrade from the floor, hoisting his body over her shoulder. "This happens a lot."

"What does?" I asked.

"Lee loses his temper, throws a tantrum, and then passes out. Sometimes I'll find him somewhere in the city, worn out and being nibbled on by rats or birds. It is how his fingers got so mangled! Once, after one of his fits, the police found his idle corpse and put it in a body bag."

"What happened?"

"Me and Bruce created some distractions, luring the cops away long enough for us to free Lee." Mira turned, with Lee over her shoulder, and walked out from the garage, into the mill.

"Will he be ok?" I followed her into the large, windowless room on the ground floor, where we were welcomed by a few of the accompanying felines.

"Yes. A bit of rest and he'll be fine. But in less than an hour the sun will rise, so we might as well call it a night. We've stirred enough trouble to last a while."

I followed Mira through the furthest door, into the small one-windowed room where shaky wooden stairs led beneath the mill.

She said, as she descended below, "Be careful Child, not to overexert your powers, should you ever become so enraged, or desperate. Our powers, even amongst the strongest vampires, are highly limited."

Down in the pitch dark basement, Bruce and Elspeth lay huddled, lifelessly upon each other.

Bruce's voice grumbled in the air, though his corpse remained still. "Lee should learn to control his temper, instead of causing us trouble by ruining what little we have!" Faded grunts and curses wisped in the darkness as Bruce expressed his frustration in a haunting way. "I never got a chance to use that car! Do you know how impossible it is for me to travel through a perpetually lit city looking like this?"

"What happened?" Elspeth called out. "What went wrong?"

"We were spotted by some hunters...not Southey." Mira dropped Lee on top of Bruce and Elspeth's corpses with a hollow thud. "They chased us, shot up our car, but we lost them."

Mira stood over the three stacked corpses and draped her body on top. After her limbs had fallen still, she lifted her arm, motioning to me with her finger.

"Child, come and rest."

I walked over to the heap of flesh, a bit hesitant to join such a morbid bed. I collapsed, falling into a deathly sleep, succumbing to the dark, calm – to the still and serene emptiness which my sprit occupied when released from its anchorage in the physical world – a realm hidden between dreaming and death. Their voices rang out in the darkness around me, and when we were not speaking directly to one another, our private thoughts were audible as if we all existed in one mind – an endless void of varying cries and whispers.

"What is happening?" I asked. It had been a week since I had heard voices at rest, and I was still unfamiliar with what I was experiencing. "What is this place?"

"There is nothing physical about this realm," Lee responded. "...in limbo, there is nothing to see. Here, we are of a collective consciousness, sharing our thoughts and memories."

Lee's voice shifted from merely being beside me in the darkness, to inside my mind – into my definitive core. *If you wish to see something, all you need is to focus on someone. What have you got to show me, Child?*

Images from my earliest hours after waking flashed in my mind, like a dream but much clearer. I saw the abusive tenant from my apartment, overweight, out of breath, in his sweaty white shirt, and Lance, with his burgundy suit and fedora, holding his bizarre octopus cane. They stood in the hallway of my old apartment, arguing over what to do with my corpse.

Nothing here, Lee whispered, observing the first people I ran into. *What else?*

The image jumped forward. My teeth clenched the neck of the puggish man – my first victim. His gurgling death rattle marked the moment I first knew what I was.

You will never forget your first, Lee laughed.

The images raced by, and I saw myself outside the apartment, stiff and awkward, like an old man suffering from arthritis. I walked along the sidewalk, hidden beneath my sunglasses and long coat, cloaked in shadow. I passed a small parking lot, in which a large, black utility van sat idle. I remembered the man who sat in the passenger seat, his face aglow from the smoldering red cigar in his mouth.

Ah, Lee seemed content. *Now there is something worth remembering. That is our most despised Southey.*

Bruce's low, burly voice cut into my thoughts. *You walked right past him, Child.*

That is where I wakened,. I told them.

Bruce seemed uplifted by the news. *That's an omen of Southey's end, if I do say so myself.*

Is that where he operates from? Lee seemed especially interested. *If I could only tell exactly where it is – then we could pay him a visit.*

Mira's voice joined in. *We have tried for years to discover his base.*

Lee's voice burrowed deep into my mind, crawling around in a most uncomfortable and intruding manner. Against my will, he stirred more thoughts, and directed them to his viewing. *Show me how you got here, Child! Show us! Where did you come from? Where is Southey?*

Stop it now! I yelled, frustrated from my lack of control. *My thoughts are not for your scrutiny.* The memories ceased, my mind grew dark again, and their voices expelled and returned to the void around me.

"If we are to work together," Lee seemed amused at my discomfort. "...we need to pool our resources. If you happened past the hive of Southey, I should like to know it. I almost got him once, you know. Look for yourself." Lee paused. "Look into me, Child!"

With the amount of effort it takes to drift in or out of a

daydream, I focused on Lee's words, on his essence – daring to peer into his mind.

Memories flashed. I saw a small brick building near a set of train tracks – a school with boarded-up windows near the edge of a ghost town. Largely intact, the interior was not yet charred and crumbled. Inside an empty classroom, standing against a chalkboard, were Lee, Bruce, Mira, and three other vampires I did not recognize, each of whom were as sickly-looking as Elspeth, with natural death masks, and pasty uncovered flesh. Thunderous gunshots rang out, breaking the walls, and then the vampires spread out to adjacent rooms.

I had dwelt in the walls of that old school for years, Lee informed me as the images raced by. *When we were discovered, hunters destroyed it.*

The memory flashed forward, showing a half dozen near-naked men walking the school's only hallway, with curved blades fastened to their arms, and shotguns blasting swarms of bullets through the walls. The man in the lead was tall and lanky, with a cruel stare and long fiery, yellow hair; he menacingly toted his shot gun, which he gripped tightly with both hands. He was who I had seen sitting in the black van my first night.

That's Southey, Mira's soft voice commented.

This is when they slaughtered us, months back, Bruce rumbled, angered by the memory. *But I killed one of them, and that's when I managed to snag me one of these fancy arm blades.*

The image jumped ahead again. Fire blazed up the walls and along the floor. Two of the vampires were in pieces, their chunks scattered among fiery debris. The hunters wrestled to shake free the remaining vampires who used their limbs to cling to the violent intruders. Unable to safely shoot them off of each other, the desperate hunters pressed up to the flaming walls, screaming in pain as they tried to ignite the vampires. Lee had managed to cling onto the king himself – Southey. Ignoring his own arms and back, which were slowly burning, Lee fought with the riled hunter, refusing to let go. They toppled to the floor and Lee sank his teeth into the screaming hunter's neck.

I pulled from the memory, returning to the darkness of limbo.

"Time was not on my side that night," Lee said. "But there will be another chance. We will repay Southey for that intrusion."

Bruce snarled. "Perhaps you will lead us to where you were born, and help us end his meddling."

Distracted by the sound of many budding voices, I did not answer Bruce. A change befell the dark, empty void – something I had experienced before. We had rested through the day, the sun outside had set, and when the final rays of light fell to the veil of night, swarming voices filled the darkness – the same eerie banter that greeted me when I first wakened. There was no daylight to divide distant vampires and me. I knew then that the layer of almost indiscernible chatter was the thoughts and cries of others like me, resting in the night, up to half the world away – from the west, where the sun had fallen behind the horizon, to the east where the sun warned of its arrival.

Most of the voices were too far, too faint to understand. Indeed, it seemed that few vampires remained in or around the city, but it was *their* voices and thoughts which spoke out the clearest.

In the distance, amongst the mesh of thoughts and whispers, a female wailed, her voice rising above the others. Her torturous cry frightened me intensely. Occasionally, other pained cries would shrill in the distance.

"What is that?" I yelled. "Answer me!"

"That was someone's waking, Child," Mira said. "Vampiric birth is painful. You cried out when you woke, as did I."

I could have woken up, rising from that mound of corpses and escaping into the night. I wanted to, but I was hypnotized by the strange place. Knowing better what it was, I listened to the thoughts and cries of others far away – a realm filled solely with voice, memories and emotion. I honed in on one familiar voice through the dark – a voice not too far away.

Arthur's words reached into me. *Why did you go there? You are only closer to danger now.*

I wanted to learn more, and I wished not to be alone. Where was I to go?

Loneliness comes from lack of purpose…detachment from what you are. If you truly desire to find your place, you must do it on your own.

You left me with many questions…too many to make a wise decision, I replied, defending my choice.

Many things will remain unanswered, no matter how much I tell you. But… if you need an example…one soul can point you in the right direction. She is the one who mentored me…many many years ago.

Where can I find her? I was interested.

Head north, to the mountains beyond the city. Leave tonight. Without a car, you may not make it back before sunrise.

Images spilled into my mind as Arthur spoke – a highway surrounded by trees, a path by the side of the road, leading beneath a green canopy into deep woodland.

Search for this entrance into the woods, his thoughts narrated the imagery. *It can be seen from the road. If she still roams her kingdom, she will find you…you can be sure of that.*

Who is she? I asked, but the image faded, and Arthur's voice receded back into the whispering waves of voice. *Arthur? Hello?*

I relaxed and I fell into a deep trance, listening to the virtually indecipherable sea of calls and cries until I was summoned awake.

Lee stood over my corpse.

"Child...come, I have something to show you. Tonight is a special night."

I was the last remaining vampire to rise, laying face down on the floor. The cats were still gathered to keep me company. When I rose to my feet, the felines scampered away into the darkness, and Lee turned and climbed the wooden stairs out of the cellar.

I followed him across the wide, empty room on the first floor, to the heavy, metal door in the opposite corner, by the collapsed staircase. Outside the mill, Lee turned right and walked to the rear of the large brick building. An old paved lot, bumpy and covered in cracks and holes, stretched the width of the old factory, devoid of all cars, but claiming a few shopping carts. Beyond the lot, past the rusted, chain link fence surrounding it, a steep hill fell to the edge of a stream.

"How do you feel...," I asked Lee, "...after your little outbreak?"

Lee stopped in the middle of the dark lot. "I take great care not to be seen by hunters. Meek as those ones were, a little motivation goes a long way with them. We've managed to stay below the radar for months, but now there will be talking amongst the wrong people. I don't want to be chased from here."

"What did you want to show me?"

"You'll see soon enough. We're meeting someone important."

"Someone alive?"

"Yes. Any more questions?"

Lee appeared annoyed at my inquiries, but I was not about to be dragged into any situations I felt uncomfortable with. I might have objected to meeting a human if my experience with Lucia hadn't been so helpful. Perhaps there would be something to be gained from this experience as well.

Yet, there was always an underlying tone of deviance with Lee. I sensed that there were deeper motivations which he kept hidden. I wanted to learn about him.

"Do you know anything of your prior life, Lee?"

"Quite. I was more fortunate than some vampires that way. I was not thrust into immediate danger as many of us are." Lee stood face to face with me, with light blue eyes livelier than the rest of his body. "My waking was far from here, in the safety of a bed, locked in my own room. I spent many of my first nights pouring over old newspaper clippings saved in a personal scrapbook, and even a diary."

"I found a journal, too." I said, trying to relate to him, but he was unimpressed.

"I'm happy for you. As I was saying, I came from a wealthy family. It seemed my parents died in a plane crash when I was only thirteen. Being the only child, I inherited their fortune and lived at home with an uncle until I turned eighteen. Then he left, and I stayed in my parents' estate for the next year or so. Apparently, I was quite the paranoid eccentric after that...and a major insomniac. I read about all my crazy plans of protection in the diary I had written in for years. All the ground floor windows of my mansion were reinforced, impossible to open or break. I had all phone lines uninstalled because I feared being spied on. Even the exit doors had been sealed up, except for one which had a special lock that could only be opened from the inside, using a particular key."

I listened to the strange account of Lee's past life, but without judgment, since I knew he was without memory of it. "I take it you lived alone?"

"No." Lee smirked. "I had live-in help. But I gave only one set of keys to be shared among the entire staff – three maids, a cook and a gardener. The only other set of keys was kept with me."

"How did you die?"

"When I was nineteen, I binged on sleeping pills. It took me many nights of searching to get all the information I just told you. At first, when I wakened, I knew nothing except pain and hunger..."

"...and cold," I interrupted.

"...and cold. I did not wander far to find the answer to the riddle – what have I become? I had been locked in that room for days, unresponsive to the knocks of the house staff. When the head maid came knocking that last time, after my change, I was unable to resist. I took her life, desperate to end my suffering. When I finished, I stared down at her dead body and knew what I was." Lee paused, his voice became humbled. "And then I took her set of house keys, hid her corpse, and began the search for who I used to be."

"Perhaps you are the same person," I suggested.

"I doubt that! If I had but an inch of my former self in me, I'd have wept for my own demise, or the loss of my parents. When I found out what I was, I rejected that forgotten life. I am emotionally severed from it and claim no responsibility ...just as you are not the person who died in that body, and you are not responsible for whatever it was that created your new form." Lee paused, perhaps doubting his own words.

I stared up at the lifeless, solid grey sky and listened to his story.

Lee continued, "I survived in that house for almost a month before I found it necessary to leave. I had taken away the only means of escape for the servants, and thus, for a while, I had the means to survive...locked within the walls of my reinforced mansion. I practiced stalking them, haunting them. The trapped staff was terrified at the disappearance of the head maid." Lee laughed, amused at his story. "I wandered the halls at night, rarely heard, seldom seen. I did not answer their yells when they happened to catch sight of me leering at them from far down the darkened halls, nor did I answer their knocks on the doors of the rooms in which I locked myself during the daytime."

Lee's tone slowly grew disturbingly wicked and amused as he told of his monstrous presence in that mansion. "They demanded freedom, but I was having too much fun to let them go. Why it is that my soul soured and rendered me a child of the night, I shall never know. But I accepted it with open arms. I was the devil, and that house was my hellish playground. In their final moments, those helpless humans must have thought the gates of hell opened up. I reveled in pure horror. What I wouldn't give for another chance like that..."

"Then why did you leave?"

"Every week, I'd succumb to the escalating pains of hunger and take another servant's life, preying upon them until the last one remained, almost a month after my waking. When it was all over, I found myself alone, knowing I would need to leave...but at least I had developed some clever tricks to aid me."

"Was Lee your name in life?" I inquired.

"No. I was called Jonathan. But Southey calls us leeches so often that I adopted 'Lee' as a nickname when he yelled it at me, but coughed and fell short of completion!"

The conversation ended when a large, silver Cadillac with tinted windows pulled around the corner on the far side of the barren lot. Slowly rolling across the bumpy pavement, its headlights shone on the two of us – the only source of adequate light for the three men inside to see Lee and I.

"Lovely," Lee halted his story at the arrival.

The car parked, facing us, and the back doors opened. Two men stood from the vehicle. A large, muscular man, with no hair and a handlebar mustache, stood up first. Appearing as a bodyguard, he wore jeans and a black tee-shirt; his sleeves were rolled up far past his elbows, allowing his large tattooed biceps the freedom to flex when his arms crossed at his chest. The second man, much shorter, less built, and wearing a dark grey suit, exited the vehicle, holding a briefcase in his left hand. He was a younger man, perhaps in his early thirties.

Together, the two men walked around to the front of the car where Lee and I stood waiting. The burly guard stood at the well-dressed man's side, and with a cold hard stare, he glanced around defensively.

"Who is this...another one?" The suited man glanced at me, pointing with the hand holding his briefcase. A ruby ring on his finger was as red as blood.

Lee laughed at his guest. "It's not like I create them...so don't get on my case, commissioner." Lee's mouth did not move when he spoke, though his blackened teeth glared at the men.

"Don't do that freaky ghost-talk crap with me. You know I hate that. Just keep him in line, like the others..." The commissioner glanced at me, perhaps curious as to my rather lively appearance – at least compared to Lee's battered body. "...in accordance with our agreement."

The commissioner opened his briefcase, on which, large gold initials A.P., were set onto the top. He pulled out a small black binder, handing it to Lee, and said, "I'm sorry it has been so long, but I figured you had your mouths full with the last list I brought."

Lee held the binder and flipped through without the use of his hands. "Lovely. This should last us a long time..." Though he motioned his mouth accordingly, Lee's voice yelled ghoulishly through the air, some distance away from his pale lips – behind the two men. "...now that there are so *few* of us!"

The guard's biceps bulged in reaction to the sudden, random burst of voice, but otherwise, he remained still and watched in silence.

"Well, be more careful then!" The commissioner yelled at Lee. "I heard about the *incident* the other night. Guns were fired in public, causing quite a stir. That wouldn't happen to have been your doing, would it?" His voice grew tense, and he talked low, as if he feared to be overheard.

"You know we don't use guns, Arnold...that's so dishonorable." Lee turned his back to the two humans. "And by the way, I could use another car...mine's been shot to hell."

The commissioner grabbed the lapel of his suit coat with his right hand and laughed. "I gave you a car so we could expand our range, not so you could get into battles with your enemies."

"When are you going to do something about all these punk

hunters? They are getting annoyingly abundant." Lee walked across the lot, out of the headlights and into the darkness, leaving me standing alone with the two men.

The commissioner squinted as he tried to track Lee strolling in the shadows. He yelled into the dark, "As long as they aren't shooting at any *real* people, I'm powerless to do much. All I can do is control police investigation when you take from the list. I can keep certain events below radar...keep Southey and all the others in the dark...," his voice was almost screaming, a lot of ferocity for such a physically unintimidating man. "...granted that you keep your activities *off* of the public streets!"

Lee whispered into Arnold's ear from far across the lot. "You don't have to *yell*, Mr. Paul, I'm right here."

Arnold jumped from the surprise. Lee's laugh filled the air.

Lee's voice brimmed with annoyance and anger. "When are you going to scratch my Southey itch? Why do you let him walk the streets, and turn angry men into hunters?" He paused, "I will tell you why, because you hope he will kill me! I know you dislike the way I work...I can smell your hatred at every meeting."

The commissioner handed his briefcase to the guard and stepped out of the headlights toward Lee. "I don't even know where Robert Southey works from...or I would gladly take him in myself for all the damage he has caused," he yelled, angered at the accusation. "He moves around a lot, and..."

"You aren't being totally honest with me!" Lee interrupted, in disbelief.

"Southey is *your* problem, not mine!" the commissioner blared. "When he starts killing humans, then he will be *my* problem, and on *your* list!" The commissioner turned his back to Lee and walked back toward the light. "If it weren't for me, you would not even have a menu! You'd have no one to steer attention away from you, and you'd soon be discovered and killed by a raving madman."

Lee replied, "If we did not agree to curb our prey, you could end up with quite a public fiasco." Lee growled, "If I wanted to, I could summon others to mercilessly slaughter anyone I felt was cherished by you..."

"You'd better calm down." The commissioner leaned towards Lee, with his finger pointing inches from his pale face.

"...your wife?" Lee threatened. "...your daughter."

"Stop it!"

Lee continued, "Remember, I can get to you. I know things about you."

"I've got more power at my disposal than you do, you sick stiff."

"Maybe, but I've got nothing to lose! I've already died, and gotten old since then...your death threats are asinine. If I ever find out you helped Southey, or set us up for a fall, you will be one sad story just like him!"

"Your run-in with those four armed men last night was a coincidence...and they have been arrested for their part in the destruction. And don't accuse me ever again."

The commissioner turned and walked back to the silver car, and turned to face Lee when his hand gripped the door handle.

"Just take it easy. I *can't* keep you secreted if you cause public scenes like the other day. This deal can be beneficial to the both of us. The people on these lists do more harm to society than vampires do. Our jails and prisons are overcrowded. We're wasting tax dollars babysitting felons who'll never straighten up. Vampires are like the surgical maggots used to eat away dead flesh so a wound can heal quicker. We can clean up this city, one crook at a time." He snapped his fingers, "Come on, Gus. Let's get out of here."

"Sure thing, Mr. Paul." The bodyguard turned at his boss's command and entered the silver Cadillac.

They left us standing in the dark parking lot.

I took the binder from Lee's hand and glanced at its pages, pondering what I had overheard. Lee and the others were being given a list of people to prey on...a list of criminals. Each page consisted of three names, each with a photograph and a brief description.

I glanced at the first name:

Eugene Perkins.
White male. Age 59. 5' 5'' 160lbs. No known scars. May have a thick moustache and a receding hairline.
Former butcher, vending machine repairman. Perkins was the president of a gun club in Boston, MA. Perkins has ties to, or may have traveled to, New Hampshire, Maine, or Massachusetts. He is reportedly seen living with his brother at 1011 East Fayette St.
Perkins is considered a career criminal and a master of assumed identities, specializing in the burglary of jewelry stores. Recently released from prison after serving four years for the kidnapping and assault of his thirteen year old son.

I flipped through the pages of the black binder; there were about thirty names altogether.

"Were those two we killed...?" I didn't finish before Lee interrupted.

"...yes. They were on a different list...the second list, which is now exhausted. Every few months, the commissioner will bring us another. If we stick to it, we will be protected."

I looked back at the roster of expendable lives. I flipped through the many pages of names, reading the lists of criminal records. One man's photograph caught my attention:

Lance Willard DuPrey.
Black male. Age 41; 5' 11''180lbs. Tattoo of tiger on back. Known to dress expensively and carries rare, customized canes in a variety of animal shapes.

A former bookie, and drug dealer, DuPrey has a long history of sex offenses and is responsible for the pandering, prostitution and suspected murders of young women.

Lance...Lance... I said the name over and over in my head. I thought of my journal; because of the vaguely documented events leading up to my waking, I was now certain Lance knew something about Dante's demise. Had I known before, I'd not have scared him off that first night. If Lance and I crossed paths again, I would ask him...and then, perhaps, exercise death upon his miserable existence.

Lee grabbed the binder from me, sending it flying through the air into his waiting grasp. "I am glad to see you're interested. This *is* a group effort, after all."

"Why are you doing this? Is it to ensure that your victims are unworthy to live ...to prevent killing innocent people?" I asked Lee sarcastically.

Lee snickered, "On the commissioner's end, perhaps. Fact of the matter, the world is a much different place than it was just twenty years ago. It is much harder for vampires to survive in a world of dying superstition." Lee raised the binder in the air. "This *list* gives us a place...an active role in shaping the world to include us in it."

"We were born into darkness for a reason."

Lee snapped at me, insulted that I should question him. "What do you know, Child? You've got as little experience as Elspeth does. Only she's smart enough not to doubt me! I have been around for a while, and trust me…we hardly have a chance otherwise. We're outnumbered *millions* to one. As long as humans fear death, we will be hated and unwelcome. When you inevitably have run-ins with hunters, and you start wearing down, looking hideously out of place, like Bruce, you'll see how hard it is to find peace here. You'll do anything to get a moment of serenity. But right now, everything is fresh and new to you, and you are under the delusion that you have some sort of control over it all. Well you *don't!*"

Lee drifted silently across the lot, back towards the mill.

I followed him through the shadows. "Do you think that a police commissioner is really afraid to cross you if it serves his best interests? If you threaten him enough he'll prob…"

"He'll do nothing!" Lee screamed back at me. "I have a few tricks up my own sleeve, and he knows it. Besides, he realizes the potential there is with hired death. I have heard of similar negotiations forming in other cities. Vampires are the perfect assassins. No one is out of our sight, or touch." Lee stopped outside the heavy, metal door leading into the mill.

"Can you be sure that these lists are even valid? Who is to stop the commissioner from putting anybody on this list?"

Lee laughed. "Are you suggesting a difference between right and wrong?" His tone grew amused. "At first I thought you were concerned about getting caught. The particularities of those on the list are unimportant. What is important is that we do not draw attention to ourselves from the mass population." Lee paused. "With the public looking the other way, we can rule the shadows with impunity. Then, with time, we'll gather together enough of us to rise and take our place among the living."

"That seems like a foolish quest."

"*Foolish* is to continue on a course that leads to your own destruction. It is through adaptation that anything stands a chance. Long ago, mankind was much less capable of finding and killing vampires, but today we are not so fortunate. Did you or did you not receive Lucia's aid? Without it, you would not have graced the streets this last week as you had. Without it, you would have been chased back where you belong, into the shadows by your own prey. Keep one thing in mind when you acknowledge the rights of those who would kill you with no regret…of *men* – their laws were not made with vampires in mind, so you'd be a *fool* to honor them."

"I don't plan on being a law-abiding citizen, but the idea that to kill is wrong is not man's law."

"But what choice do we as vampires have? It is a natural law that everything has the right to its own survival. People will die, one way or the other, Child. You need to embrace the beast inside you. You see, back in my old mansion, I experienced the pleasure of uninhibited destruction, having a free rein over life and death behind those reinforced walls. It felt so good to be a god to the fearful, to be the most terrible moment of someone's life…and I will do what I can to be that god once more…to have some sense of control."

I repeated Arthur's words to me: "We have the right to be here, but we also owe to be here."

"Ugh!" Lee moaned, sounding disgusted. "You're already quoting him! Let me make one thing clear," he turned around to face me. "If you think your angelic daemon friend, *Arthur*," Lee slurred the name, "does what he does because he is honestly concerned with the well-being of humans, you are naïve. His actions, and mine, achieve the same end result…so what does it matter what path takes us there? Arthur knows just as well as I do, that humans value life differently at a variety of levels. Nobody really cares when a *murderer* or a *rapist* or a *pedophile* is killed, so long as the crime is not overly heinous. As long as we don't kill the rich and the well-to-do, or the socially significant, we will have a place in the gutters of society…but with my help, we shall rise up and take an active roll. You were right about one thing, Child. We have the right to be here…and I have all intentions of staying!"

"You and Arthur are nothing alike. If he finds peace, he earned it. You allow yourself to be exploited. You are not the glorified monster you think you are. You are just a tool!"

Lee gripped my dead flesh with his spiritual hands, and with a sudden rush of cold energy, my corpse was thrown far backwards. Before I hit the pavement, I managed to twist my corpse in the air, lessening my fall by landing on my feet.

Lee stood a few yards away and laughed. "You need to learn to be humbler. You don't know enough about our state to pass judgment onto me, let alone to put Arthur on a pedestal! Do you know *why* he chooses to live the way he does? Do you know *why* he wants to remain hidden away?"

I walked back toward Lee, angered but unwilling to start a fight. I sensed Bruce, Mira and Elspeth nearby. If my antipathy riled them in a similar manner, I doubted I would be capable of fighting off four angered vampires. Instead, I accepted my humiliating moment and listened to Lee try to justify his position.

"I knew your friend Arthur well many years ago. He found me, like you. Before he adopted his piety, he was like any other vampire…a monster at heart. One fateful evening, he sunk his fangs into a young woman, some social worker who drifted into the range

of a ravenous vampire. By a stroke of luck, she managed to stab
Arthur in the back, nearly severing his spine. She escaped. As you
may or may not know, a vampire's bite is nearly fatal if not treated
immediately...and she did not. As it turned out, that lady was the
fiancée of then-commissioner Robert Southey. It is because of
Arthur killing Southey's beloved that he became aware of our
existence, and thusly hell-bent on destroying vampires. It is because
of Southey's insatiable lust for vengeance that he has so tirelessly
pursued our destruction. It is because of his perseverance that we
need a list...outside help. As long as your coward friend hides from
what's coming to him, the rest of us will suffer in the wake."

Could Arthur have caused all this? I wondered why he would
have withheld such a serious detail. I recalled something he had
said – 'my imprudence planted the seed of a future storm.' Arthur
withheld what that seed was, but now I knew. *Should I still trust him
and seek out his old mentor?* I wondered.

Lee had been snooping in on my thoughts – an intrusion I could
hardly prevent.

"You realize, now, the vagueness between good and evil? What
man or creature can rightly cast such a judgment? I do not think you
wrong for what you believe...just less wise. But how were you to
know, right?" Lee extended his hand as if to invite me to join him.
"You do not need to seek anyone else out...the front of the vampire
revolution is here, with us. Together, we are strong. Alone, we are
hunted."

I reached out and shook Lee's hand. "If I am truly unwise, then
you will not question why I am to leave tonight. I am not ready to
accept this, to settle for something I am unsure of. If I find nothing
out there for me, then perhaps I will return in defeat."

"You may be stupid, Child, but you're a strong one. I can tell."
The metal hinge behind the door lifted and it swung open into the
large, dark room inside the mill. "If you are to make this journey
north, you'll need a car. Take it. I don't want to be seen in that
wreck. I can get another one out of commissioner Paul."

"Will it even work?"

"You worry too much for a dead man, you know that? We'll be
here waiting when you come back."

"Thank you, Lee."

Chapter 12 – A Small Victory

The night was warm and breezy, with a patchy fog hovering over the city; each whim of the wind shifted the visibility as swirling clouds danced on the street. Sam steered the black van down a quiet avenue on a poorer side of town. Sheets of paper were rolled up in his hand as he gripped the wheel. He glanced over at Southey, who sat beside him, and Sam observed what he believed were the signs of an eventual mental breakdown – spasms, low mumbling, a clenching jaw, irregular breathing, and shifting eyes, all told Sam about the suffering of his friend. In the long week Sam had been away in recovery, Southey changed for the worse.

On one side of the road, small apartments and duplexes were built so close together that someone could walk a block by hopping from rooftop to rooftop. Some homes' lawns seemed like small junkyards; sidewalks were littered from opened trash bags piled on the grass, waiting to be picked up. Groups of people sat together on porches to escape the dank humidity of their stuffy houses.

On the other side of the wide road, beyond the driver's window, railroad tracks ran parallel to the street; and not far beyond them, a strip of factories, mills and plants loomed in decay at the small, lower-class suburb's feet. Few industries there were still operational. Many of them had shut down when a surge of cleaner, high-tech industry sprouted all over the city years ago. Many of those forgotten places remained sealed up, condemned and awaiting to be demolished.

Southey leaned out the passenger window, biting down on a half-smoked cigar. He stared at darkened and clouded street signs passing by, failing to read many of them. Frustrated, he slammed his fist off of the dashboard.

"Which one of these streets is Cleveland Drive?" he asked Sam. Southey strained to read the crooked, shadowed signs at the intersections. The poor visibility, coupled with his aging eyes, made the remedial task quite a chore. "God, I hate bad directions!" he shouted and shook his head. "I can't believe these are the only guys who'll come with us…"

Sam was not paying attention to the streets on Southey's side; instead, he searched for a particular building on the industrial side of the road. Maida, their seer, had sketched some images while tuning in to the mind of the imprisoned vampire – images that confirmed Southey's suspicions regarding vampire presences on the western side of the city.

"Well, we're lucky we found anyone," Sam said, defending his selection of backup hunters. "Nobody wants to hunt with you because of your recent streak of bad luck."

"Bad luck...," Southey blurted. "Things may not go perfectly, but I find these damned leeches...and I kill them." He held out his stubby cigar and turned it to see how much he had left before biting back down. "Everyone else just chases shadows like idiots, but I..."

"There is *another* reason," Sam cut him off. "You have pursued these devils so long now that you have become..." He paused, speaking a bit faster than he was thinking.

Southey turned to glare at Sam. "*What* have I become?"

"You have become...what they hate." Sam paused again. "Especially the older leeches, which for the most part seem to be the ones we just can't kill."

"Is that so bad? That they hate me?" Southey sniveled and laughed to himself. "...they hate me because they fear me." He flicked the stubby cigar out into the street, in the path of a passer-by. Southey pointed down a dead end road with a half dozen tiny wooden houses. "There! Cleveland Drive. For the love of...how the heck did we drive past it the first time?"

Sam turned right, down the small street, and looked out his window to read the addresses of the homes. "What number is it?"

"Eleven. It's the last one, I think." Southey opened up the glove box and removed a small phone. "I'm going to call them. I'm not getting out of the van."

"My point earlier," Sam continued the abandoned conversation, "...about why you can't find help anymore, is that you have seen a bunch of your men die in the last two years, including both of your sons. No other hunters ever report any casualties."

Southey raised his voice. "That's because no other hunters ever *really* find any leeches...at least, not *intentionally*, so they're always unprepared. Their stories are exaggerated too. All they are good for is giving me some idea where to look during a dry spell."

"I think what these wary hunters are wondering is...," Sam leaned back in the seat and cracked his knuckles, "...how many more of your men will die before you join them?"

Southey digested Sam's comment through a long pause, and then asked, "What does *that* mean?" Southey scowled at him.

"If there is one person who can stir up a hornet's nest of trouble, it's you."

Southey pointed at a tiny, brown house on the right, snapping his fingers to direct Sam's attention. "Trouble means results in this business, you know that! It's a simple fact."

Southey dialed a number into the cell-phone.

Sam pulled over by a gravel driveway and parked the van. "But you always walk away. Some think that you have let others die to save yourself, basically."

"*You're* still here." Southey thought of saying more, but the phone rang.

Sam smirked, "Barely. A man of my age, getting sick like that, is hard on the body. If we had gone back for the bodies, or equipment, I might have not made it."

Southey turned to look at the bandage on Sam's neck; his mind raced back to that night in the woods. When he had been beleaguered by the dark, and the voices, and the fear of the witch, he ran. Southey ran, screaming, leaving Sam alone to be bitten.

He was breathless, wondering if maybe he had actually betrayed Sam's trust. Sam had been by Southey's side, offering his full support, even in the earliest days – the days when even Southey was doubtful as to the existence of the vampires walking among them.

I turned around, Southey's mind stirred with guilt. *I went back for him. I acted emotionally, not logically…but I didn't abandon him…or my sons.*

"I do what I have to do…" Southey said below his breath.

Sam changed the subject, not wanting to make Southey feel worse than he already did. "I find Arnold Paul's relative apathy a bit suspicious, especially with all your public incidences in the last year alone. I mean, we're not exactly *discreet* anymore."

Southey turned his head from Sam when there was an answer on the phone.

"We're outside. Come on out." Southey shut the phone and replied to Sam, "Mr. Commissioner hasn't done anything because he knows deep down that I'm legit. He knows something's up in this city. He has to have seen something by now. He saw what tackling this problem did for my career, and he needs me because he's a coward. I'm supposed to keep things under control while he prances around in his Italian tailored suits. But that's okay…I'm not in this game for my reputation, or my image."

Sam reached for the brim of his grey mustache, tugging on the hairs. "I heard from a few of my guys that Mr. Paul has been nosing around this here part of town recently…not in the company of street cops or detectives. You know," Sam paused, "…off-duty type of business."

Southey perked up. "His silver Cadillac?"

"The plates matched, apparently."

Southey murmured to himself, "What is he up to? Is he finally looking into this stuff? I was hesitant last time he visited, but if he really needs proof, I should just show him what I've got back in the cell."

"No, no, no." Sam raised his hands in refusal. "You had the chance *last* time, before we crossed the point of no return. We've got too much of a mess in that cell now to take the risk."

"Okay...okay." Southey pointed out his window at two heavy men strolling down a gravel driveway towards the van. "Here they come."

Bill, the taller man in front, was Jamaican. A black tank top fit tightly over his muscular body, and the dark, tanned skin of his broad arms were covered in tattoos. Thick black hair hung loose against his back. When he smiled at Sam and Southey, his grin stretched wide against his large jawbone.

"Hey hey! Mr. Southey." Bill pointed to the heavier, less-fit, fair skinned man behind him. "This is Blair."

Blair was a bit shorter than Bill and a bit heavier as well. He was mostly bald, but had enough red hair behind his ears and on the back of his head to grow out and tie into a ponytail. He waved at Southey and Sam; it was his first time ever meeting them.

Southey pointed over his shoulder, to the back of the van. "It's unlocked."

The two men climbed in back of the van. Sam turned back to the two men and nodded.

"Thanks for coming, Bill...Blair. We shouldn't be too long. This isn't a search." Sam put the van into drive.

"What's the plan, then?" Bill asked with a heavy voice, so awkwardly loud he almost sounded angry. "You know where some vamps are?"

Southey yanked the rolled up papers free from Sam's hand. "Leeches!" After finding one sketch in particular, he handed it back to the men.

Blair reached out and grabbed it first, curiously. "Hey, I have seen this place. It is around here somewhere."

Bill grabbed the picture from his friend to inspect it. "Yeah, turn left at the end of our road. It's about a mile away, down on the right." He rubbed his thumb against the sketch's pencil markings, smudging the lines. "So, what does *this* have to do with anything?" Bill asked. "This is just a drawing."

The hurriedly–drawn sketch depicted a series of fairly large factory-like buildings. The rundown brick building in the center seemed to be the focus. It was three stories high, with a narrow smokestack rising from the roof. One of its walls hadn't a single window on its entire face, and written in an arch near the top of the wall, were some indistinguishable letters, crudely sketched in pencil by Maida. At the base of that wall, in an alley formed by a neighboring building, was drawn a blackened figure; it was too dark to make out any details, but there was something attached to its right arm – a blade.

Bill squinted in the dim light to see the figure on the paper. "Is this one of them?"

Southey grunted, "Yeah. I have reason to believe that a few others have also nestled in that place for the past few ·months, or longer."

"Really?" Bill sounded surprised.

"So, you lost a few men? Both of your...," Blair thoughtlessly blurted, but was stopped mid-sentence when Bill's elbow struck his rib.

Bill interrupted, "Blair knew Dario. They were both bouncers at Fatty's Bar."

"He was a good kid." Blair said.

Southey reached into the inside pocket of his coat and removed another cigar; he rubbed the cool, leafy surface under his nostrils and whiffed deeply. "Yeah, he was alright." Removing his silver, butane lighter, Southey sparked up his smoke. "We got what we went for, that night. Dario did not die in vain."

"Blair has never been in a hunt," Bill said. "But I saw some action with Colin over two years ago...before things quieted down."

Sam tossed in the words, "I remember that."

Bill smiled and said, "So, I've told him a bit what to expect."

"Yeah," Blair said and chuckled, "...over a few pints of beer. Or I'd have never agreed to come."

Southey sighed, and looked back at the stout man in the rear of the van, eyeballing him. He would have preferred people with experience for a task like this. Blair looked as if he should be repairing computers, but if he was capable of being any bit physical, he was of some value.

"Why did you stop hunting, Bill?" Southey turned to face who he felt was the better of the two men. "Colin liked you, I recall."

"It's too slow for me...the searching, anyway. Now, I'm too busy customizing bikes at my shop to really hunt anymore. I hadn't really heard of any incidences for a long time now...except for some kind of a car chase...on this very street, in fact. Anyway, I figured you killed them all." Bill laughed.

"No," Sam looked over to meet Southey's stare. "Not all of them."

When the fog shrouding the road receded, and the men were suddenly within eyeshot of the destination, Blair pointed out the windshield. "It's that one down there, with those garage doors on the facing side."

Southey gestured for Sam to pull immediately over to one of the many available parking spots along the road; he then held up the sketch to compare with the actual building.

"Why are we parking so far away?" Blair asked. "Why don't we park in the parking lot up ahead?"

Southey snapped, "I know what I am doing, you dumb...!" He halted, not wanting to insult the only help he managed to scrape up. "Don't question me, for God's sake! It is to my understanding you are new at this."

"Yup," said Blair, not realizing how much the fact annoyed Southey.

"Well, I won't leave you in the dark about why we do things..." Southey took a lengthy puff of his cigar, and with a lungful of savory smoke, coughed his last words, "...the way we do them." Southey grinned, exposing his few missing teeth to Blair; he blew the smoke at him through the holes.

Blair turned his head to the side. He saw the wide eyed sneer in his periphery and flipped Southey off – who laughed, unphased.

The van pulled to the side of the road. Sam and Southey exited and rounded back to open the rear doors for Blair and Bill. When they hopped out, the van squeaked, lifting from the release of their weight.

Sam leaned in to the back of the van and pulled a duffel bag toward him. When he was certain no pedestrians would soon walk by, and feeling shielded from traffic by the thick atmosphere, he dropped the heavy bag to the ground with a heavy clank of metal.

Southey knelt and unzipped it, reaching inside. He removed a pair of thermal vision goggles, handing them to Sam, and then he removed two heavy flashlights, placing them on the sidewalk.

"Our mission is to burn the place down," Southey said as he reached back into the bag. He pulled out two metal canisters which looked like large flasks. "Sam and I will do that task with these fancy cocktails he concocted. We will go inside to set the fire. I want you two outside preventing any escape attempts through any of the potential exits."

Blair scuffed his sneakers against the sidewalk. "You're going to burn it down? In public? Are you nuts?"

"You didn't mention this on the phone." Bill was displeased, his voice loud and intimidating. "This might be more than we had in mind."

Southey removed four pump-action shotguns from the bag and

propped them, barrel up, against the rear bumper. "Don't worry." He handed Sam a box of shells to load the guns. "We aren't going to stay to watch it burn to the ground, though it'd be reassuring. We'll be gone before anyone knows there's a fire. Besides, we have the cover of night and fog. No one will see us run back to the van, and no one will see the smoke until we are on our way."

"I still say we should park closer," Blair threw in the comment after a brief pause.

Southey reached into the duffel bag and said with his head turned back to Blair, "I have been chasing a few of these particular leeches for years. They know my van...half this town knows my van. Parking away from the scene is a precaution."

Southey handed an armblade to Sam, and then took the only other for himself. They removed their coats and shirts, tossing them into the back of the van. Sam and Southey put the contoured base of the curved metal blade on the top of their arms; they tightly fastened the straps underneath, starting by the wrist, and ending at the shoulder.

"Don't *we* get one of those things?" Bill asked, looking down into the empty duffel.

"No can do. I'm low on supplies." Southey finished tightening the weapon to his arm, making a right hook motion to test it out.

Bill took a step toward Southey. "What?! I helped Colin make the prototype in my shop with my welding tools! I should *own* one."

Southey didn't turn to look at the aggressive step, though he was intimated. "I lost some equipment in the woods a couple weeks ago...and my son. I haven't gone back yet." Southey closed his eyes; as soon as his residual vision faded and darkness settled in, a pale glow appeared. Within seconds of shutting his eyes, Southey was facing the same inescapable vision that haunted his dreams. "I don't know if I can *ever* go back." Southey stood up, facing Bill with a stern expression. "You guys are just getting shotguns. Sam and I are going into a potentially close-quartered area. We need the armblades more."

Southey clipped a flashlight to a strap on his armblade so that it needn't be held.

"Remove all unnecessary accessories," Sam instructed to Bill and Blair, as he copied Southey and fastened the other flashlight to one of the straps on his right arm.

Bill reached into the pocket of his jeans, cursing lowly, not happy with how things were going. He removed a switchblade, a lighter, and a set of keys, tossing them into the emptied duffel bag.

Blair appeared confused. "Why are we doing this?"

Southey gave a questioned look to Bill whom supposedly had

---

told Blair much prior to his agreement to come. Bill shrugged.

Southey turned to Blair and said, "Leeches aren't the sculpted, young-looking, action-heroes your Dungeon and Dragons buddies told you about. Okay? They're basically zombies. They break easily, and they don't heal. Thus, they will usually do whatever they can to avoid a direct confrontation...like devilry...." Southey reached out and grabbed a small necklace which Blair wore, continuing, "...like strangling you with this lame gold chain, or tearing out that tongue ring I just noticed you have."

Southey held out his hand, awaiting Blair to remove his add-ons, and continued, "Leeches are first and foremost, ghosts. They're malevolent poltergeists...a force you can't ever touch. It is that aspect of them which you must be concerned with."

Blair removed his gold chain, tongue stud, plus an earring and a wrist watch. After he tossed them into the bag, he shook his head, saying, "That's all I have."

Southey continued his brief lecture, "If leeches really want to hurt you, but have nothing worth grabbing on to, either on your person, or in your surroundings, then they have to come out and fight physically. That's when you shoot them...or burn their nest down."

Southey zipped the bag and stood up; starting with Sam, he handed each hunter a freshly loaded shotgun.

"Never use a pistol, or any other one-handed gun. It'll get bitch-slapped out of your grip before you can get a clear shot off. That's why we use shotties. Just hold on tightly with both hands...all the time!" Southey opened his eyes wide and smiled a tobacco-stained smile as he clenched his shotgun.

Sam explained to Blair, "You see, their ghosts can't *physically* harm you. They can't grab your limbs or strike you...only their *corpses* can. I'd suggest you remove your shirt too. Anything that isn't your own flesh and bone is a potential handle for them."

Bill and Blair tossed their shirts into the van. Blair removed the tie holding his thin red hair into the small ponytail.

"Hunting leeches in the winter is a real pain in the ass." Southey spit on the ground. "You have to learn to deal with the cold...you can't bundle-up with heavy clothes. Dogs are a necessity."

"Why?" Blair asked.

Southey shut the back of the van. "Normally, we bring dogs along. Since they are free to be naked in public, they're always invulnerable to the ghosts. Plus they are much faster, and they can easily catch and tear those fetid corpses apart. I like the irony when I see a leech running from a pair of fangs, but not so much that I will send my beloved dogs into a burning building. Sometimes they get stunned or confused by the ghosts. They aren't perfect."

The four men were armed and ready. Wearing only shoes and pants, they walked along the sidewalk, toward the mill, holding their shotguns to their sides as not to alert anyone who might walk close enough to see them.

Less than one hundred yards from the destination was an intersection with one road leading past an empty lot toward the mill.

Southey stopped to look around. The fog had closed in around the area, and the clouded mill appeared almost invisible – a darkened wall of grey on grey. Headlights on the passing cars, just yards away, appeared as pairs of dull glowing orbs moving through the fog.

"How's it look, Sam?" Southey kept his eye on the mill.

Sam panned the thermal goggles over the misty neighborhoods in the area. "We should move in now, before the fog clears and we lose cover. There are a few people around."

Southey led the men away from the street, over a set of railroad tracks, and through an empty parking lot toward their destination.

Blair pointed to the thermal goggles that Sam held. "Do those help you find vampires?"

Bill spoke up first, "No! I told you yesterday. Vampires don't show up on thermals. That is how we used to find them in a crowd."

Southey took over the teaching of esoteric vampire hunting tactics. "There are plenty of other ways...not using thermal goggles."

"Like what?" Blair asked.

Southey pointed to his face. "A leech's facial expression is normally blank and lifeless, like someone who is totally cracked-out. They don't blink, and they don't ever sweat, either. When they walk, their bodies do not shake with the impact of each step. In fact, their stride is usually smooth and consistent, and when they swing their legs, it sometimes seems out of rhythm with their pace."

"Why?" Blair asked. "That doesn't make sense."

Southey responded, "Yeah it does. Leeches are dead bodies suspended upward. They just try to look like they are walking. Don't try and trip one, it won't work."

"What else?" Blair was getting interested fast.

"Well...," Southey thought for a moment. "...Leeches can not breathe...and they can't fake it either. In winter, it can be a useful tactic to single them out from a crowd of steam-blowing pedestrians."

Southey turned from Blair, wanting to move on with the hunt. "Because leeches have ghost-like senses, you can't be sure if they are seeing you or hearing you at any given moment. These bastards could be eavesdropping at this very second, taking note of what we brought and counteracting us." Southey looked ahead to the mill. "But maybe not. They sleep for many nights in a row, sometimes."

"How do we know for sure they are in there?" Bill asked.

"We don't...until we see a corpse," Southey said. "Just because they are pestering you with tricks, doesn't mean you're directly upon them. They have a fairly wide range of influence. That's why it's important to undress as much as possible. Once you get within that range, it doesn't matter if they are on the roof of the next building over, or inches away on the other side of a thick concrete wall...they *will* sense you. Once we get over there, we're practically announcing our presence, so keep it down."

"Let's hope we can get in," Sam said, failing to see a door which hadn't been sealed in some way. "It will be impossible to set this place on fire from the outside."

"We're doing this tonight, one way or the other," Southey snapped. "If what I suspect is true, then these leeches knew we were coming when Maida drew that picture."

"What makes you think that?" Sam asked, unsure of what Southey meant.

"The witch knew we were coming...," Southey sighed. "That thing in the cell somehow warned her...and I assume it warned these leeches too. They will probably not hang around long knowing I mean to finish what should have been finished months ago."

Southey rubbed the lumpish scar on the side of his neck. Blair made a face at the nasty, little discolored lump.

"You were bit?"

Southey nodded.

"What did you do...pour holy water on it?" Blair scratched his head.

Southey started to roll his eyes, but noticed that Blair had carelessly allowed his shotgun barrel to point towards Sam. Quickly, he reached out and grabbed the barrel, violently steering its aim toward the ground.

"You idiot," Southey mumbled, trying to muffle his anger. "Have you not heard anything I've said? If one of those things had been present, it'd have pulled that trigger!" Southey grabbed Blair's thick neck with the long fingers of his left hand, and glared at him, saying, "Always hold your gun tightly, as if your life depended on it! And never aim at your comrades! That's a *universal* rule!"

Blair immediately squeezed Southey's wrist, ceasing the clammy grip upon his neck. Southey made a pained face. "Sorry...but keep your hands off of me!" Blair's voice grew threatening for only a moment; he realized how stupid his mistake was and let Southey's intrusion slide.

Bill laughed to himself. "Blair has personal issues with being touched...and being a bouncer, it makes for very amusing stories."

"I don't care! Don't laugh. It's not funny!" Southey pulled his arm free and turned away. He continued walking. "God, I thought you told me on the phone that he wasn't *useless*!"

The fog seemed to dissipate, and with each approaching step the mill appeared clearer, more detailed. When they stood just a few yards away, the rest of the world around them was swallowed in a thick, milky fog.

Sam pointed to a potential entrance on one side, near the back of the brick building, beyond an alley. "That door might lead in."

Southey gripped his gun tightly and pointed to the other side of the mill. "You two go around that way and look for any openings...windows, hatches, vents. Take note of anything a person could fit through, and add that to your list of things to guard. Sam and I will be trying to get inside through that rear door."

"Don't we get a flashlight?" Bill asked as he glanced behind him into the dim, fog. "Man, you are really skimping on us here."

"We only have two," Southey snapped. "I didn't get a chance to buy more."

"You are a mean old man," Blair said.

"It is going to be very dark inside," Southey justified. "You at least have some secondary city lighting to help you. Besides, flashlights are bad in the fog. And you don't want to draw attention to yourself...from pedestrians."

Bill and Blair walked away, annoyed at Southey. They disappeared around the front-right corner of the mill.

Sam and Southey walked along the left side of the mill, through a narrow alley. It was very quiet, and when the stillness of the night set in, Southey heard the whispers in his head rising into his awareness – the voices he could only hope to ignore. He began making a low growl, just loud enough to cover up the whispers only he could hear.

Sam was a bit confused, but accepted it as Southey losing his mind.

At the back corner of the mill, a large parking lot spread behind the building. But the men stopped before that, at the mill's back corner. A heavy metal door, rusty, without a knob or handle, stood between them and the inside.

Southey extended his arm. Still growling lowly, he shifted the murmur into words, "Damn it, there is no way this door will be op…"

With just a meek push, the door widened a few inches, creaking deeply from rusty hinges.

Southey immediately held his gun up to the entrance. "Well, what do you know?"

The two old men looked at each other, wondering what to make of it. Neither had turned on their flashlights yet; pitch blackness awaited them beyond. Southey pushed the metal door the rest of the way open with his boot, again, with a deep groaning of old hinges. The dusty, worn, wooden floor inside the mill disappeared into the thick dark, only a few feet from where they stood.

"Do you hear that?" Sam asked, pointing his ear to the darkness inside.

Southey heard only the raspy, tormented whispers in his head. "No…what do you think you…"

Unexpectedly, a string of twelve cats scurried out past the men's feet, whining with deep, sorrowful meows, one after the other. Years of hunting had taught Southey and Sam that cats were a sure sign they were close to their targets. There existed a connection between felines and vampires which he did not understand. On occasion, Southey would find strays gathered behind his apartment complex, sitting on the very earth where just a couple feet below, was the cell with an imprisoned vampire. He would often allow Cain and Abel the opportunity to remind the felines that there were no visitors allowed.

Southey smiled as he watched the dozen cats scatter into the night fog.

"How many do you think are in there? Did Maida say anything?" Sam asked as he flicked on his flashlight.

"She saw four of them…definitely some of the leeches from that last fiasco back in the spring."

The men shone their lights into the dark, pointing their extended arms, and the spotlights, across a large, dusty, windowless room – virtually empty. Only a few crates and boxes, and chunks of plaster and wood, were left about the spacious floor; the worn, cracked planks were strewn with wooden bits and other crumbly matter from the damaged walls and ceiling. Six shut doors lined the furthest wall. Far above their heads, a tall ceiling was strewn with old lead pipes and wires. Tangled cobwebs coated everything. A staircase, adjacent to the back door, climbed to another floor;

however, halfway up, the rotted wood had collapsed, leaving a large gap to jump if one wished to explore the upper levels.

Southey reached over to a switch on the wall and flicked it on and off with no effect.

"Here we go," Sam whispered, as he walked across the dark, towards the first of the six doors that lined the opposing wall.

Bill and Blair walked alongside the mill, along a narrow, eroded paved way once meant for cars to drive around to the back. Hardly anything seemed unusual or of interest. The first and most obvious of things to guard were rusty garage doors on that side. Both men strained hard, trying to lift them, but the doors did not budge. All other ground-level doors and windows were blockaded with concrete and brick built to keep people from gaining access into the old building's various sections.

The two men followed the long side of the building to a much larger, empty parking lot in the back. Lit only by the surrounding lights of distant buildings and streets, the wide open area was not only heavily shadowed, but foggy.

"Hey, check that out." Bill pointed to the backside of the mill after he turned around to look at it.

Three wooden doors were built vertically into the wall. The first was about fifteen feet up, and each other door was one level higher than the one below it. Some type of stairway had existed once, but now, a few holes and bolts spanning a demarcation in the wall's texture were all that remained.

Blair stood at the base of the wall's center, and looked up at the first door. "I guess someone could escape through this bottom door...but I wouldn't want to jump."

"You'd be ok," Bill started laughing. "You'd bounce."

Blair turned around and looked across the parking lot, where an old rusty fence lined the edge of a descending hill. "I'm getting bored already. I thought we were going to be hunting vampires, not obeying the orders of some testy pyromaniac."

"Don't worry about Southey," Bill said. "Just go along with him and he's cool. He may be crazy, but he is not insane. This stuff is real, man, and Southey doesn't give bad advice." Bill pointed across the lot to the side of the mill that Southey and Sam had walked. "Stand down there and I'll stay here. This way, we can see on three sides."

"Whatever." Blair turned and headed through the fog, to the other corner, grumbling to himself. "They'd better not take too long in there or I'm leaving."

When Blair reached the other side of the lot, he glanced into an alley, to an opened door on the corner. Seeing the dim light from Sam and Southey's flashlights, he ignored it and turned to face Bill across the lot. With features heavily obscured by the fog, Blair would not have recognized Bill had he not know his identity ahead of time.

Bill whistled to himself. His view of Blair was almost blocked entirely in the grey cloudy murk. His fingers clenched the barrel of the shotgun tightly, which he kept pointed to his left, toward the narrow road he had walked down.

"Hey, you alright?" he yelled to Blair, realizing only after that he probably should have remained quiet.

"I'm fine," Blair's voice called back through the fog. He then asked, with a cheap Stallone imitation, "How you doin'?"

Bill heard the muffled laughter and joined in. But when he glanced up at the three doors high on the mill's rear wall, to his curiosity, he noticed that the top door was slightly ajar. At first, he doubted his senses, but it seemed that with passing seconds, the darkened gap grew wider, ever so slowly.

"Pssst," he hissed at Blair, who did not hear his friend's whispers over his own joviality. "Hey, Blair," he raised his voice, still keeping an eye up at the door.

"How you doin'?" Blair asked comically, oblivious to Bill's growing concerns. However, in a moment when the fog thinned, he saw clearly that Bill's gaze was fixated on the wall, and he glanced up. When he saw that the top door had opened about halfway, his smile dropped. "That wasn't like that. Was that like that? Bill!"

Blair walked forward to see better into the gaping doorway almost thirty feet up.

Bill pointed his gun up at the door and walked forward to meet Blair. "I think we should be concerned about this. Maybe that's where they are...and they are planning on escaping."

Blair gawked up at the door, holding his shotgun loosely with one hand. "Are they going to turn into bats and fly away?" He sounded worried. "How can we possibly stop *that*?"

Bill punched Blair in the shoulder and said, "Don't be stupid. They can't do that. And hold your gun like you mean to use it!"

Blair lifted his weapon up to the door, staring at the widening entrance through the sights of the shotgun. In that moment, with their attention focused above, both men hushed and it became obvious, if only from their mutual response, that there indeed was a sound coming from the opened door above – a slow and heavy scratching.

"It sounds like something is being dragged around...like a wooden chair, maybe," Blair suggested, tilting his ear toward the doorway to better hear the noise.

A low sound, like wood on wood, was getting slightly louder. The door was fully opened now, and it seemed to them that at any moment something would appear before them in the doorway above.

Bill, being more experienced, was more paranoid from the onset of strange activity. He glanced around, turning from the opened door; staring into the dark fog far at the edges of the parking lot, he wondered where their attention should really be. "One of us should be keeping an eye out." The fog wasn't as bad as it has been a few minutes earlier, but his visibility was still limited to about fifty feet. "I've hunted before, and you never know what to…"

"Watch out!" Blair yelled aloud. He ran towards Bill, pushing him in the back with all his weight.

Unprepared for the sudden shove, Bill stumbled forward and fell onto the asphalt; before he could curse at Blair for the intrusion, a massive crash of wood exploded in the otherwise still night. A heavy table had fallen from the opened door above, breaking into many shards and splinters which danced across the parking lot before falling still.

"Man," Blair was short of breath. "You just missed it! This table came flying out when you turned around!" Blair lightly kicked at the heap of fractured wood in disbelief. "Wow, I can't believe it didn't hit us!"

Bill lifted himself off of the ground and rubbed his chaffed palms against his pant leg. "I don't know whether to thank you or hit you." He walked toward the wreckage, which had landed in the very spot he had been standing. "Something just tried to take me out."

"Should we go find Southey?" Blair asked.

"That's what the vamps want us to do. There's something up there." Bill looked back up to the door, listening. A new noise rose above the silence. "Do you hear that?"

Blair looked to the door and listened intently. "Yeah, it's a voice…right? Is it crying?"

"I think so. We have to stay here…" Bill's voice trailed off as small pebbles fell from the edge of the opened door. When Bill heard the tiny rocks clacking off of the ground inches in front of him, he leaned in closer to make sure he wasn't imagining it. "I wonder how Southey is doing."

Southey and Sam had opened the first two of the six doors, behind which, they found only empty rooms with no obvious signs of vampires. Both men doused the floors and walls of each room with the odorous liquid from their metal canisters, leading a zigzagging trail from one room into the next.

The next few doors led into a wide garage. Junk, covered in old blue tarps, and scraps of wood and metal lined the walls of the empty room. A quick peek revealed nothing of concern. Southey panned his lights across the concrete floor; a glitter caught his eye.

"What's this?" Southey walked to the center of the garage and kneeled down. Broken glass scattered across the floor. Though the floor had numerous old oil stains, one seemed a bit fresher than the others. Southey rubbed his finger against a shiny stain on the cement. "A car was here within the last couple weeks or so."

Sam asked, "The commissioner's?"

"No. Not with an oil leak."

The hunters exited the garage, trailing the flammable substance behind them.

As they reentered the large dark, windowless room, turning to see what lay behind the sixth door, Sam noticed something on the dusty wooden floor he had overlooked. Cats' paw prints dotted the floor, but more importantly, solid narrow trails traced across the dusty surface. He pointed and said, "Leech tracks."

It was known to both Sam and Southey that, unless they were in guising, vampires hardly touched the ground. When vampires moved about, especially in the dark, often they did not take steps; this resulted in their toes dragging across the earth as they moved.

Most of the vampire tracks in the mill led in and out of the sixth door, in which, Sam and Southey found the smallest room. A lone window high on the wall had not been fully sealed, allowing a miniscule amount of faded city light to enter. Near the center of the floor was an opened hatch, and a steep wooden stairway led down into a dark pit – a basement of some sort.

Southey held his shotgun tightly, the barrel pointing into the ominous dark. The armblade strapped to his right arm naturally hooked forward with his aiming posture, and the flashlight clipped to the straps illuminated the old, distorted wooden floor below.

"I know you're down there somewhere," Southey taunted, pumping his shotgun in preparation. He kept one finger behind the trigger, lest a clever vampire waste one of his shots. "You can never hide from me again! I have found a window into your world and I will finally crush each one of you." Southey paused, awaiting a reply that did not come. "You can come up and kiss my gun, or you can stay down there and be buried in fiery wreckage!"

Sam turned to glance back out into the large room from where they came, shining his light to verify his safety, but preparing for anything.

Southey let go of the shotgun with one hand, to grab the metal flask wedged between his hip and pant waist. As he shook its contents over the wooden stairs, the canister shot out from his hand, clanking violently onto the cellar floor, and seeping its contents below.

Southey grinned when his suspicions were finally confirmed. Then, a young, male's angry voice lifted into the air from the shadowy pit. "Release him, Southey...." It seemed to hover slowly up the stairs, but was wide, filling the air around him, almost disorienting him. "You can't control what you don't understand. Release him..." When the voice neared Southey's face, he felt a chill in the air and menacingly, the voice continued, "...or die."

Southey reached into his pocket and removed a wad of wooden matches. He leaned down and struck the match heads against the wooden floor. As they burst into flames, he replied, "I can't do that yet," and tossed them down below.

The basement lit up as the floor and the stairs glowed blue and yellow from the low flames enveloping the wood.

"Burn in h..." Southey barely spat the words out when his shotgun tugged down toward the flaming stairs by their powerful, ghost hands. Southey had only one hand upon it at that moment, and refusing to let the gun go, almost tumbled down the stairs. He squatted low to hold his position and attempted to pull his gun back from their influence with both hands.

"Just let go of it!" Sam yelled. Let's ignite the rest and get out of here!" Sam reached into his pocket and pulled out some of his matches to set the rest of the place ablaze.

Southey struggled with his shotgun. The moment he removed his finger from behind the trigger, it fired against his bidding, splitting the top steps and exposing more of the surface to be consumed by the growing fire.

"Damn!" Southey yelled. Without warning, the gun was released from the troubling force, and Southey, at the peak of his effort to hold on to it, stumbled backwards, off-balance, smacking his head off of the wall. He dropped his gun and fell to the floor.

Southey's shotgun lay still to his left – out of reach. As he leaned over to grasp it, he caught sight of something lunging from the depths of the fiery basement, high into the air – a leap impossible for any human.

Both hunters recognized the creature from years of hunting – a lean and tattered vampire the size of a teenager, with brown hair pulled into a short tail. It reached down to Southey with arms charred from their last encounter – the skin colored like burnt charcoal. Its pale-blue artificial eyes glimmered from the fire below. The airborne vampire gazed downward as Southey scrambled for his gun.

Southey rolled out of the way as the vampire passed a few inches overhead, pushing off of the wall behind the frazzled hunter, and launching itself back over Southey to the other side of the small room.   Something then caught Southey's eye; the creature was wearing a black vest, some type of armor, it seemed.

Southey cursed, gripping his shotgun.

Sam, reacting to the sudden attack, fired a poorly-aimed shot, chipping the vampire's legs. Before retrying, Sam struck his matches and lit the trail of fluid that spanned all over the first floor. A blue flame stretched out the door and forked in many directions across the large, empty room, heading into each of the other doors; within moments, fiery fingers climbed the walls and the crackling of burning wood grew loud.

"Get up!" Sam yelled, backing into the main room, seeing it clearly in the brightening fire.

As he stood up, Southey put his finger to the trigger and fired a quick and clumsy shot. The black, bullet-proof vest on the vampire frayed, and the creature was pushed forcefully into the facing wall.

The vampire laughed in a bratty manner, and said, "Think you can survive another bite? I don't!"

Southey, heeding Sam's anxious pleas of retreat, turned toward the door.   But another vampire leapt up from the depths of the burning cellar, with a foreboding and pained scream so wide in effect, it seemed that the walls themselves were cursing. Just as Southey stood at the doorway, he turned to see the hefty, blackened creature falling down from its leap above.

The second vampire was much more threatening in appearance than the scrawny, boyish one. The large creature was so thick with black paint that its details could hardly be seen, even with the growing light of fire. A red blindfold covered its eyes, and like the other vampire, it was equipped with a heavy, black vest.   To Southey's shock, on its right arm was one of his fallen comrade's armblades. The crusty blade cut downward at Southey's head as the vampire fell onto its feet inches behind him.

Southey quickly raised his shotgun to repel the strike; the shotgun barrel bent, creasing from the force of the blade, and Southey fell backwards, out into the larger, fiery room.

Sam watched Southey tumble by his feet. He wrestled with his shotgun, trying to aim at the impending, blackened creature that stood in the doorway, but one or both of the creatures slapped the

barrel of his shotgun around, making the task nearly impossible –
even with both his hands firmly on the weapon.

Frustrated and desperate, Sam pulled the trigger at his first
opportunity. It was a fine shot, but the barbarous blackened
vampire reacted quickly, and without need to push off of the floor
with its legs, the creature scooted behind the wall with a swift
motion.

The shot bought Southey a moment to act. He dropped his
useless, bent gun and stood up. Running ahead of Sam, across the
growing blaze in the next room, Southey hurried for the heavy metal
door across the long, burning floor. Sam followed, both men
knowing very well that behind them, the two vampires were in
wrathful pursuit. Southey was not surprised when his escape
swung shut before he was even offered a glimpse of freedom on the
other side. He was surprised, however, when the thousands of tiny
bits of wood and rock lifted from the floor as if the debris' own
personal gravity had been reversed. The fragments hit both men in
the face, blinding them for a moment as their eyes met the dust and
sand.

"You're not getting away this time," a voice hissed into
Southey's ear.

Southey glanced over his shoulder at Sam. The two vampires
were close behind him, gliding across the room with their feet just
inches above the wooden floor. Determined to catch the hunters, the
vampires were ambivalent to the rising flames that could so easily
consume their dry dead bodies.

"Sam!" Southey screamed and turned to face the situation,
realizing how direly close the creatures were. "Look out!"

Sam, knowing very well what he would see if he turned, also
knew he would not have time to fire a shot. He tossed his shotgun
ahead to Southey, and with a motion extremely agile for an old man,
Sam spun around, with his right arm extended – the blade cutting
through the air.

The smaller vampire was swift, and leapt high over Sam, almost
totally vertical, missing the sharp blade, and kicking its feet into
Sam's face as it lifted toward the ceiling.

Sam winced from the kick to his head, but managed to keep his
eyes focused on the grizzly, blindfolded creature next in line. The
black, monstrous corpse flashed a metal grin at Sam from behind
cracked and tattered lips; at the same time, the creature lashed out
with its armblade – the two enemies engaged in battle.

As soon as Southey's sweaty hands gripped the shotgun tossed
to him, he lifted up the barrel at the bratty vampire falling down
from the ceiling. Chillingly, with what sounded like two of the same

voice, the vampire laughed and screamed at Southey simultaneously, with a mouth gaping black and still.

Southey's adrenaline surged. His hatred for the creature gave him the strength to overcome what resistance he felt in the gun barrel – like a heavy weight was tied to it, making it harder to lift. As the creature fell upon the shaken hunter, with its stubby, mangled fingers inches from Southey's face, the shotgun barrel sunk into its gut. Southey pulled the trigger; the swarm of bullets severed the vampire's torso almost completely in half – only one hip was partially intact. And though the corpse ripped open, no bowels fell from its torso. Only a small, lightly bloodied pillow of some sort, which had been inside the creature, remained among the bits of flesh and bone. The finished vampire fell to the fiery floor with a gory thud, and without hesitation, Southey cocked his gun, pointing the barrel at the creature's head and pulled the trigger. The vampire was finally defeated.

Sam's heart pounded hard, and the heat in the room grew rapidly. He staggered backwards, intimidated by the larger vampire's use of an armblade. Reflexively, he held up his armblade in defense. Metal clashed, and before Sam could react, he was pushed back with the creature's frigid hand. He fell to the floor, landing painfully on fire, and rolling away. The vampire lunged at Sam, but Southey had destroyed its ally and ran over to play the defender.

When the creature saw it was outnumbered, and with the flames growing, he orbited swiftly around the hunters, keeping his face at them, and was grazed by the many semi-accurate shots fired by Southey's shaking gun. The vampire jumped up the collapsed staircase, disappearing into the smoke that spilled up onto the second floor.

The pebbles continued to fall. Bill and Blair listened to the eerie cries that came from the opened door high on the third floor; at first, it had sounded like a child crying, but soon they agreed it was a woman laughing slowly and softly.

"I don't think we should stand here," Blair suggested. "It's just a matter of time before something else comes crashing down from..."

Before he could finish his words, the middle door opened quickly.

"What the...?"

The bottom door opened thirdly, and with a stream of creaks and thuds, the three doors opened and shut over and over.

"I'm shooting one of them," Blair said as he lifted his shotgun.

Bill, breaking his attention from the dumbfounding display, turned his head to the side; in his periphery, he caught sight of two figures coming at him through the fog.

One of them, a sickly thin, pale woman came into clarity fifteen feet away. Skeletal features pushed against her skin as if at any moment, a shard of bone would tear through. Her tight skin gave her face an awkward stare; deathly eyes, sunken and green, were twisted inside her sockets and her cheeks dipped far into the sides of her mouth. Horrid bruises covered her face, neck, and arms. Her hair, hanging in a twisted, tangled mess, was blacker than any he had ever seen.

The other vampire was taller, with more meat on her bones; and unlike the skinny one, she was not as obviously a corpse. Short, red hair was neatly styled upon her head, and her yellow eyes seemed alive, not festered and shriveled. Her skin was not as pale, and her lips were painted red. As they both glided through the fog, with their feet hardly touching the pavement, the vampires opened their blackened mouths.

Before Bill could warn Blair what was happening, the scattered scraps of wood and splinters from the broken table swarmed upward at him. He screamed as the hard bits of wood struck his body all over.

Blair sprung around at the wailing of his friend, but was too late blocking with his hands to prevent the debris from striking his face. A wood fragment met with his eye and he welled up with tears, covering his face, screaming, "Oh my God! I can't see! Help!"

The shotgun was pulled magically – it seemed to Blair – from his loosened grip. It slid far across the parking lot, scraping away into the fog.

Bill tried to keep his eyes on the vampires, but the chunks of wood swirled around like a swarm of angry birds, crashing into his head, and cutting his exposed skin. Though he repeatedly batted pieces down, in a few seconds, they would fall upward at him and continue as if the storm was focused on him alone.

"Look out!" he yelled at Blair, between grunts of pain. Blair had staggered away from the swirling wreckage with his hand on his face and his back to the vampires. "She's coming toward you!"

The thin, nasty vampire moved hastily toward Blair, but Bill quickly reacted; he turned and fired at the creature honing in on his friend. The pellets struck its left side, shattering the boney arm free from its shoulder. The vampire fell, but before it settled, it immediately bounced back up and continued at Blair.

Though he could hardly see, Blair lunged at the creature,

screaming his own personal war-cry. With his hands firmly around the vampire's only remaining arm, he easily wrestled it down to the pavement.

Bill's body was sore from dozens of hits by the whirling wooden wreckage, and the resulting splinters reaching deep into his skin. He cocked his shotgun, but did not have the experience to think of keeping his finger behind the trigger; it immediately fired off, shooting the bullets into the ground. He cursed, annoyed at the vampire's intervention.

A nefarious laughter came at him from all sides; it was her voice, he assumed. The pain, coupled with her mockery, drove him wild. Unfortunately, his gun writhed and he struggled to gain control of it – all the while, her presence grew closer, just on the other side of the spinning wake of wood fragments. He swiftly kicked out at the vampire. His foot struck her chest, but she only slid backward a few feet, not falling over.

Blair had easily positioned himself on top of the boney black-haired corpse. With his fingers deeply rooted in her loose hair, he pulled her head back, slamming it down into the ground over and over.

"You are one nasty little lady!" he screamed. Blair reached for a stake-like fragment of wood lying idle on the ground. He stabbed the back of the creature's neck repeatedly, ignoring the ear-piercing, haunting scream that circled in the air. His heart pounded, adrenaline ran through him, and in a moment of animalistic fury, with his hands gripping the ragged black mane, he tore the head free from the neck once it had been mostly severed. Blair threw the decapitated head at the remaining vampire, yelling, "You want some, too?!"

Bill was now swinging his shotgun like a club at the wood fragments, batting them far in different directions. He kept moving, to avoid the debris, but also to keep focused on the red-haired vampire who darted around him in total silence, watching him struggle to keep from being hit by the stakes and splinters.

When the severed head of her partner smacked the ground, the remaining vampire fled across the parking lot, moving backwards into the fog, with her yellow eyes facing Bill until the fiery stare was swallow by the grey night.

The scraps of wood fell to the earth, and free to aim as he pleased, Bill ran across the lot after her, firing into the clouds until his last shot was used.

"Are *you* ok?" Bill yelled to Blair as he returned from his futile chase.

Blair's eyes were red, tears ran down his face. "Yeah, that was totally wild!" He huffed deep and hunched over to regain his strength. "Are you ok?" Blair looked at the many small cuts and bruises on Bill's face, arms and torso.

"Yeah," Bill gently patted his sores with his finger.

The two men saw smoke pouring from the three opened doors on the mill's rear wall.

"Looks like they did it!" Bill pointed. "Come on, let's get out of here."

The two men ran to the side alley where Sam and Southey had entered, finding the metal door shut. Without hesitation, Blair threw his weight against the door several times. It soon opened up and smoke poured out, mixing with fog.

Southey was hoisting Sam up from the fiery floor near where a fragmented corpse's flesh bubbled in the fire.

"Hurry!" Southey yelled. His tense face told of their respective encounter. "Let's get out of here before the police show!"

The four hunters made haste to the black van. Because of all the sealed windows, the mill was not yet visibly aflame from the outside, and they escaped well before the wails of fire engines raised high into the night.

Chapter 13 – Confrontations

I left the four vampires early that evening. With Lee's permission, I took the damaged car which he no longer desired. Though the body of the vehicle had been riddled with bullets and was dented all over, it functioned. I steered the rattling, windowless car toward the highway, and north from the city.

The only drawback, the very reason Lee no longer wished to utilize the vehicle, was the attention it brought from passers-by who slowed down, or stopped entirely to stare at the unsightly wreck with its busted exterior, and the strangely sullen driver sitting limply upright in the driver's seat.

When I traveled by car, I was free from my puppetry – the need to suspend and move my corpse was minimal, necessitating only that I press a pedal and turn a wheel, as opposed to heeding to the vast and subtle motions I was required to mimic if I were to walk past suspicious eyes safely. I enjoyed the virtually effortless mode of transportation.

I followed north on the highway for a few miles until the buildings, lights, and much of the accompanying traffic receded with the borders of the city. The grassy clearing in the surrounding area filled with trees. Before long, the road climbed higher through an area of dense foliage. The highway rose along the base of what was either a large hill or a small mountain. The road narrowed as it ascended, the surroundings grew darker, and with its shattered headlights, my car cruised virtually invisible to the few travelers passing in the night.

Not long after I questioned the foolishness of my decision to drive so blindly into the unknown, the way leveled off and continued on through the forest. Moments after, I saw beside the road, down a shallow embankment, two empty pickup trucks parked adjacent in a clearing of short grass. Lured by a strange familiarity with the surroundings, I pulled the car over to the shoulder of the road. I had been shown this place in a thought – from Arthur. I parked the car.

I listened to the mountainside, and the forest lingering beyond a thick wall of leafy trees. The darkness in the air, the stillness from the lack of electricity and mechanical commotion, endowed me with a miraculous sensitivity, an incredulous understanding of my surroundings, allowing me to detect a dizzying range of sounds, and see everything as it happened around me. I could detect things much further away, as opposed to when I was in the city.

Trees swayed to each push of the wind, filling the air with the sound of dancing leaves, as the clatter of branches scraped together. Countless ferns, shrubs and tall grass, dancing at the mercy of the sky's breath above, mimicked the soft hush of ocean waves.

But there were things even more subtle, yet perfectly evident to my vampire senses – so clear, no human could ever understand.

The piercing squeaks and scratching scampers of dozens of rodents, snakes and other nocturnal creatures called out clearly; I saw each one scattered below the swaying swells of shrub and grass. Though I could not see stars in the grey mass above me, thousands of clamoring crickets and grasshoppers swarming about the verdant hillside were all individually present to me. Torrential clouds of mosquitoes filled the air with the sharp buzz of uncountable wings, humbled only by a veritable plague of bats scouring the sky; their high-pitched wails rang out all around me.

When I absorbed this vast spectrum of life, present far and around me, the synergy of all the voices of all the living things, both plant and animal, produced a symphony of the night which performed throughout the darkness of the mountain. I felt alive in a way I had not yet experienced since my waking.

I could have stood there for hours, listening to the vivacious hum of the mountainside, but something off-key caught my senses, something differentiated from the rest of the sounds. A low rumble rattled far off into the woods – an engine.

I followed the sound, towards a well-trodden path which sloped downward, deep into the dark woodland realm. Soon, I wandered into a darkness transcending the endless shadows that choked every step of the journey.

As I wandered further, the distant rumbling grew louder. The hard, clay path was wide and clear, winding around knolls, forking again and again – a testament of the numerous outdoorsmen, over the years, who explored the mazes of trails woven deep throughout the wooded labyrinth.

Soon I came within range of two men riding off-road bikes around the looping trails of the dark, hilly mountainside. Only the lights on the front of each bike kept them from the ominous darkness around them. They cheered and laughed; they looped around the many trails, their excited voices almost totally buried by the intrusive sound of their engines.

I remained safe in the lightless void around them. Even when they inadvertently veered close to me and their headlights passed over my wandering corpse, I remained unnoticed against the endless, dancing shadows of the forest. The two men posed no threat to me, nor was hunger driving me to act, and lacking any reason to become involved with them, I wandered away, deeper into the woods – lest the distasteful roar of their bikes, robbing me of night's euphoria, drive me mad enough to silence them forcefully.

The path narrowed; patches of grass thrived where footsteps had long been absent. Hard, dry clay became thick with mud – but my feet did not sink into the muck. A deep silence in the air was flawed only by the creaking of trees' bark, when their trunks bent in the wind, and by the raspy scrapes of tangled tree branches in the canopy. The surroundings grew much denser and colder as the plethoric forest of predominantly evergreen trees deepened. Many branches reached across the trail at head level, but many, higher up, kept the sky from ever peeking down through their net. Chokingly large amounts of thick, gnarled roots bent and broke the surface of the earth; their knotted fingers tangled across the forest floor like bulbous veins. So many saplings and young trees grew in the space between older trees' trunks, that one could have hardly walked ten steps in any direction off of the path.

My thoughts and focus drifted from my corpse, wandering free among the trees, soaring through the cramped forest where people could not easily venture; and with immaculate vision, I beheld the forest from all sides – crystal clear to me in seamless shadows of the night.

It was then that I first noticed something horrible and tragic hiding within the forest. There was something different about these trees; their trunks and limbs were slightly distorted, appearing bulbous where branches forked into new growth, and though they seemed healthy, their postures were hunched over slightly. Yet it wasn't as much their odd form which alerted me; I felt something beneath their bark, a feeling of tension and of terror.

I sensed I was being watched from all sides; a presence lingered – many presences. At first, I thought I had found her, the elder vampire who had guided Arthur long ago.

Come out. I came to see you, I thought. But she was not receptive.

Then, I heard many voices all around me. A ghostly chatter lifted above the silence; many utterances resounded over the forest floor. They were not the voices of vampires, but of something else altogether. It was the trees...warning me with whispers, cries, pleads and screams. Their ravings were incomplete phrases, making them difficult to understand, but they spoke with undeniable fear. I felt it in the air as real as I did in humans. How was this possible? Surely, it was a devious trick by a powerful vampire. I listened carefully to the eerie voices rising up from every inch of the woods.

"I see...is it her?"

"...the witch ..."

"…shouldn't be here…leave."

"…a witch…she's real?"

"…in the woods!"

"Lost…the woods…she's…!"

"she's there…!"

"…get my gun…now!"

The forest grew vibrant with voices each passing second. I could hardly decipher words when the murmurs climaxed, but one thing was certain – they all were warning me…of the witch in the woods.

I halted, overwhelmed. I was afraid – afraid of something unknown.

As with every other vampire to have crossed my path, I unmistakably sensed her presence. Even if I hadn't, a sudden outcry among the voices would have warned me, for her approach stirred the mysterious voices into a terrified babble, producing a wake of terrified cries that was maddeningly ominous.

Her ghostly presence lingered before me, inexplicably distinguishable from the pitch black forest air. I halted there among the towers of wood and bark, waiting for her to speak to me. With her transcending vampire eyes, she examined me; her corpse remained hidden somewhere, deeper in the woods. As she studied my corpse in silence, the voices screamed with terror among the closest trees, some firing phantom gunshots into the night.

I spoke into her mind. *You are the one that roams these woods? The elder vampire?*

A raspy, old woman's voice responded. *I am.*

Are you too, the witch in the woods?

I am, first and foremost. Her ghostly presence fell back into the woods, yet her words were just as clear in my mind. *Come to me,* her voice whispered as she receded deeper into the dark. *I have not had a visitor in many years.*

Turning from the path, into the thick woods, I followed after her presence, where her corpse awaited over a small hill. Not far into the dense trees, I came to a mossy hillock. Bulging from atop the green mound, a wide, dead tree stump, sitting four feet high, perched proudly. The stump's old, gnarled roots kicked out from its base like massive legs and dove beneath the ground, warping the forest floor for many yards around.

Small shrubs, wild flowers and other vegetation thrived in the damp, softened wood on the stump's flattened top. Roots from the greenery above had burrowed into the stump's thick, rigid bark, following crevices down to the soil. Vines, climbing up from the fertile plateau, took hostage the neighboring trees' low-hanging branches, and a web of green vines reached in all directions, connecting the surrounding trees to this one wooden mound.

On one side of the rotted stump, a wide fracture in the wood stretched from the base to the top, creating a hollowed shelter contained within it. I stood at the split in the stump. She was inside.

An old, frail, womanly figure, with long, white hair, exited the dank shelter and stood before me. Her pasty corpse was weathered into a thin, almost skeletal figure. Her body was naked, yet dressed in swirling patches of moss which had found shelter, growing upon the dead flesh. Vacant eye sockets and a gaping mouth with cracked and shriveled lips rendered her face like a skull; however, the pale skin of her face was deep with wrinkles, and a thin ridge of cartilage remained where her nose once rested. Wisps of spiders' webs hung from her face. Virtually all semblance of her former self had rotted away; her ghoulish appearance, coupled with the maddening voices, would drive any man insane.

Her jaw lowered and her mouth remained open and still. "Welcome Child," her voice spoke softly, sounding young and welcoming. From inside her fanged, black pit, spiders crawled onto her lips, and then scurried across her face. The arachnids made use of every orifice in her head as a shelter. "What brings you to my home?"

"I came to talk to you."

"Then walk beside me and we shall get to know each other a bit." Her skullish, lifeless stare wavered into a faint smile – a reminder that I had nothing to fear.

The witch led the way back to the narrow path; her graceful movements left each plant and tree virtually undisturbed, as if she harnessed the winds to carry her feet. Bits of bark and twig hung from her matted, white hair, and nesting inside her tangled locks were larger spiders whose legs were exposed when the witch's hair swayed; they scampered up her back, deeper into the hair.

I had pondered the infestation of her skull for only a moment when she spoke up.

"For my protection," she said. "The spiders eat creatures that would otherwise ruin what relic of a body I have left. I could not exist in these woods long without them. There is no existence without coexistence."

With her arms extended, she caressed the branches and trunks of trees as she passed them, whispering words to them I did not understand. Throughout the woods around us, the ghostly voices hushed at her command, and the fear I felt throughout the forest waned, as serenity returned.

I began pondering many things to ask her, but she spoke while my mind raced to find the words.

"What is it you sought by coming out here to see me? An answer? A friend? Hopefully, not a place in my realm, for it is my realm only."

"I hoped you could tell me what we are, what I wakened into."

"I could say it in one word, but you already know that answer. Otherwise, you'd not have come for my advice." The witch's mouth gawked widely; her gums had all but receded entirely, making her nasty, soiled fangs seem longer.

"But what is it all *for*? What purpose could there be to it other than punishment?"

"Perhaps because you haven't given it a purpose yet, you feel punished," the witch replied. "Self reward in lieu of self pity. Only you can give yourself the greatest of all gifts, or take them all away."

"What are you saying? Tell me what I can become, beyond being a foul creature...or is this all there is? Am I fated to this, *doomed* to wander in darkness like you and every other vampire?"

Her ghostly gait halted and quickly she turned to me; her words summoned a gust of wind, and each syllable rattled the branches of nearby trees.

"I am not doomed!" she hollered; her voice wailed high in the canopy. Her flowing white hair whipped in the air like the flailing arms of a madman. "I am a creator, the mother of this new forest...the protector of its inhabitants! It is what I chose." The wind settled down and the bugs and spiders that had been blown free scampered back to her tiny, muddy feet and climbed the moss shrouding her legs. "You look around and see a prison of wood, perhaps...but I see creation. This place is my will and my reward. As long as we have our will, we cannot be doomed."

"How do you do that? The wind?" I watched, with avid curiosity, as the final breeze settled and the rasping of branches fell silent.

The witch in the woods held her hand out to her side and spread her thin, soiled fingers apart. A cloud of fine dirt rose off of the ground and lingered beneath her hand.

"You can move any matter which has no will of its own. Just heed your limits until you more intimately learn them." The dusty cloud spun like a small tornado and burst free, scattering grains of sand around us in the night. "That is what makes vampires so powerful. We are not limited to our body...It is dead and therefore we are free from it."

The witch continued along the path, until the dense woodland suddenly opened up at the edge of a large clearing. I saw, on the other side, a small dilapidated cabin standing all alone beneath an open sky.

She led the way to the wooden shelter and said, "I would have been doomed well over a century ago if, at my waking, I wallowed in pity and did not take it upon myself to realize what power I had inside me...taking my throne here."

"Your throne?" I asked, "Are the trees your subjects?"

"And I am theirs. You see, before my waking, this area was dying. Few areas brimmed like you see now. The land had been raped, and the shaded earth had become dry and lifeless all over the mountain. Trees were scarce, and lazy hunters came to shoot the bucks and bears and other creatures who mourned when they found their homes destroyed. The ease of the hunting made men greedy and there was much wasted life and meaningless death. I felt that waste, and I ended it."

"What did you do?"

"I took the offenders' lives whenever it was in my power to do so. Did you not hear the hunters and loggers and heathens calling to you...warning you to turn back? They tried to save you from their fate."

"The trees?   Those are the souls of ...?"   I did not fully understand yet the depth of her solution.

"...they're the souls of the trees, now," she clarified. "I gave the trees their voices – their blood."

"How?"

"I reaped life, not selfishly for me, but for my woods. Every single body I have fed on, for a century, is buried here, beneath earth and root, spawning new life each day. I turned those who came to destroy the land into a force that made it flourish."

"The trees are graves?"

"No! A grave is where you remember a life that once was. It is where coffins keep from the earth what it should rightfully reclaim. There are no *graves* in these woods. Here, I channel life and death into something new and greater...something immortal."

I looked back to the woods, and its trees, with their distorted limbs, massive roots, and cries of fear. The fertile forest had grown fat off of the corpses of men – of men who came to claim a piece of the forest – instead becoming a piece themselves. A world within a world existed – a legacy she began over a century ago.

We stood outside the tiny, empty cabin; it was raised a few inches off the earth. A spider hung from one corner of a missing window, laying the foundations of its future web.

"This is the place of my waking." The witch pointed her thin finger at the missing door.

"You lived out here? Alone?"

The inside of the cabin was cramped, too small for two people to live comfortably.

"So it seemed," she said. "I had...things, back then. A bed, tools I had crafted, clothes I had made, and trinkets I had collected from the forest – even poems I had written. But everything was taken by curious hikers who came to see the witch's cabin."

"Did you learn why you were out here? What reason?"

"I wanted to be with nature. I wanted to be with me." She said.

"How did you die?"

The witch pointed her skeletally-thin hand at a hole below her left breast. "I think I was shot...but I will never know the reason why."

She breezed away from the cabin, out into the center of the clearing, with her dirty toes skimming the grass; her hair trailed behind her like a cloud, its form slowly shifting.

The witch spoke with a distant voice, "One of the things I had found inside the cabin, from my living days, was a dream I had described on paper. I read it over and over." She paused for a moment, as if trying to recall. "I had dreamt, once, in another life, of an awful forest where there were no trees shading the earth. Instead, endless rows and columns of tall, narrow, metal cones were built into they ground. They spread across the hills and by the streams as far as could be seen, blindly reflecting the sun. An incessant humming of generators replaced the soothing sound of wind. They were devices built to convert the air into oxygen, and as I wandered along the brown earth, lost in a grid, I saw scores of animals, starving and gasping their final breaths."

The witch halted her description, lifting her pale, skeletal hands up. "At the time these hands wrote that dream, the forest was at a decline. It was her greatest fear, to see such purity so heavily devastated. And when I read her nightmare, early into my waking, I knew what she would have wanted to do, but never had the power as a human...as an old woman."

"Why can't vampires remember anything from before they rose up?"

"You can't remember because that was not you...and if you could remember, would you want to resume that role?"

I thought of the few things I had read in that journal – of the frustrated, depressed words written by a young man named Dante Fairchild, who seemed lonely, and cut off from the world, or at least wholly dissatisfied with it. I thought of the gritty part of town and the dirty apartment he had lived in, and the impoverished neighbors who seemed no better off than he was. I thought of how little I would gain from resuming that life.

"No," I said. "Not anymore."

"Then why do you try to be something you are not meant to be? Dressing like humans, talking like them, walking like them...*fearing* them, even."

"I assumed my other life was..."

"You are not your past. You are not your name. You are your purpose. I am no longer defined by what lived and died inside that cabin, but what now lives in and is feared by this forest...defined by the very forest itself. I believe that *she* died so that I could be here to carry out her dream. If you wish to know better what you are, you must first stop fearing what you are, and embrace your true nature."

"My nature seems to be only to destroy. Of what importance is that? People would die with or without my help."

"Not the *same* ones." She laughed. "The mere fact you exist suggests your necessity...your importance."

"But how is it that we became vampires? There seems to be no cause for it all. Things like this don't just happen. There *has* to be a reason." I wanted just one simple question answered – 'why?'

"Reason is independent of its being discovered. The most powerful forces in the universe are invisible. Sometimes it suffices to know simply that those forces are there and working, and not to try and understand them."

The witch raised her arms, summoning a gust to shake the limbs of the trees bordering the clearing. Beneath the soft crunching of branch and needle, the murmur of men's souls grew louder.

She said, "Vampires linger between dreams and death...two powerful forces capable of many things." She lowered her arms and turned to me. "None of my prey truly died. With every sapling that surfaces in spring, with every creature that returns to the safety of my kingdom, I grow...I live vicariously through them. If it were not for my cause, my will, I would merely be a corpse in a cabin, a shadow of something that is no more. But here...I live forever."

"You could still be killed. We are not immortal, after all."

"That is irrelevant. Even gods die when believers stop believing. It would be foolish to think I would ever find immortality within myself *alone*. You must be a host to something greater than yourself if you wish to live forever. That is what I have done."

I looked around at the vast mountainside, and the security in which she reveled. I said, "Here, it is easier. You have freedom. Your have no neighbors to hunt you."

"You will *always* be perceived as a monster in humans' eyes.

Do not make it your task to change that, or you will lose. Perceptions should only be used as a means to a goal – never a goal itself. What you need to do is find a way to expose the vampire in a way that pleases you, not shames you...and if you truly find some purpose in it all, then you have succeeded."

The witch turned and walked across the clearing, back to the darkened path. I followed her, observing the trees closely. Emotions stirred beneath the bark when we walked past them; the forest was a collective consciousness of all the lives taken.

"How long will you continue to tend to these woods?" I asked her.

"My days are soon to end. Few dare enter these woods with ill-intentions anymore, and I will not kill innocent wanderers who come to respectfully admire my work. I *am* these woods now, and I refuse to leave them to find prey; thus, I often go many weeks without taking a life...and it weakens me."

"Many weeks? I feel I could hardly last one."

"That will change with age," she informed. The witch turned and walked silently off of the path and back into the woods.

"Is that it?" I asked. "Is that all one hundred years has taught you?"

"No," she said, "It has taught me much more, and I hope you too will experience the pleasure of those discoveries. Take some time away from the city to escape your repression. Then, you will more clearly see yourself as you want to be. I have no better advice than that."

Will we cross paths again? I spoke into her thoughts, hesitant to see her leave.

In your moment of utter darkness...think of me and I will save you. Until that time, farewell.

The witch wandered back to the stump, to her mossy throne amidst the viny trees. Though I asked her about this 'utter darkness,' she did not reply.

I followed the path back, through the almost silent woods, listening to the lowly whispers of the forest, and thinking of the words the witch had spoken.

When I returned to my car off the side of the highway, the two pickup trucks were gone. I drove the car back up the grassy incline, onto the road, and returned south along the highway. I decided I would heed her advice and leave the smothering confines of the city. Before I left for good, however, I wanted to talk with Arthur once more.

* * * * *

It was well after midnight, and though there were hardly any people up at that later hour, I opted to abandon the unsightly vehicle on the highway, just outside the city. I would not take the car with me when I finally left. I wanted only my own cunning and craft to guide me on my eventual journey.

Back beneath the artificial lights and mechanical clamor of the city skyline, the night air lacked the euphoric stillness, the clarity the mountains claimed. I strolled silently along the sidewalks of the downtown, through man-made canyons of glass, steel and brick. I longed for the faultless shadows I had walked through in the mountains, but had to settle for dark alleys and lots.

When I entered a familiar part of the city, I heard a sound I had not savored in many nights – one of the few sounds on the streets which defied the grimy, artificial setting. Beyond the black cast iron fence surrounding Bayview Park, from beneath its modest canopy of trees, the jubilant melody of a flute lifted above the bland, ambiance of the city.

I followed the luring song through the black gates of Bayview Park, and toward the bubbling fountain in its center. The fingers of the tall, thin man danced across the top of his flute; with his eyes closed, bobbing his head up and down to the rhythm, the soft song fell from his lips into the air as he paced among the shadows of scattered trees. I listened for a few moments, and when he noticed my presence, perhaps sensing my appreciation, he nodded.

I walked toward the far end of the park, where I saw a lone man hunching over one of the many chessboards. He stared at an arrangement of the pieces beneath the dim lighting of not-so-nearby streetlights. His mind was rapt in the moment, seeing poetry and meaning hidden among the wooden armies.

The fair skinned young man looked up from the board when I neared him. His eyes widened, but he was not afraid. In the shadowy park, with Lucia's makeup still aptly in effect, I appeared like anyone else.

The young man ran his fingers through his dark hair, stretching his arms, saying, "I was about to leave, but if you're up for a game, I am too." He gestured to the opposing seat, unaware of the nature of his deadly guest; his heart beat slow and steady, and I sensed his delight…not one ounce of fear or apprehension tainted his mood.

"Nothing would please me more than to play a game with you," I mouthed, forcing a smile, and then sat across from him.

My numb hands clumsily picked up the pieces to set them into position, but my stiff fingers slipped, dropping them back to the board. He noticed my poor hand control, and perhaps thinking I had some ailment, reached over and finished the task for me.

"It's ok. I can get that for you." He looked up at my face, a bit curious. "My name is Drew. You are?"

"Child."

"Haven't heard that one before," Drew seemed to enjoy the news. "I usually don't play here...," he said as he accurately centered the pieces on their squares, "...but I'm growing to like this place. That flute player is here almost every night and I find myself staying until he leaves. Is that weird?"

"Not a bit. It is nice to listen to." I nodded. "He lured me here tonight, and other times as well."

"Nothing stirs the mind like music." Drew finished aligning the thirty-two black and white pieces, giving me control of white.

"I agree. Do you play anything?" I asked.

He gestured down to the table, and chuckled. "Only this. Ready?"

For an hour, Drew and I played under the serenade of the flutist, the gurgle of the fountain, and the sound of ocean waves from the bay behind us. I lost my troubled mind in the silent beauty of the game, recalling, with each move, what the witch had said to me, and how I could embrace her example. It was then that I realized the parallels between her teaching and the chessboard...and between the chessboard and life. Things were much deeper and more meaningful when you looked below the surface. The power of the pieces came not from within, but outside, from their function – contingent to everything around them. Even the most insignificant gesture by a weaker piece can render the most powerful pieces ineffective. And more often than not, the gains and losses in chess were invisible to the inexperienced eye. Yet, as invisible as they were, they drove the game forward, defining it. To stand a chance, each move I made had to have purpose, had to work for some goal; otherwise, each move spiraled to chaos. Everything affected everything, thus aimlessness led to quick defeat. When I began to look beyond the physical aspects and see these underlying patterns, these truths woven into the fabric of the game, I saw purpose, I saw reason, and I won.

"Checkmate," I stated after having heard it from his lips twice already.

Drew nodded his head and smiled. "I didn't see that coming. Good one." He stood and gathered his pieces, dropping them loosely into a backpack by his side. "Hey, if I see you around, I may want a rematch."

"Of course."

He waved, walking out through one of the gated entrances along Bayview's perimeter. "Goodnight!"

I watched Drew out of the park; I don't know why – perhaps benign curiosity. I watched him cross the street, my eyes beside him. Then, only by chance, I noticed two men who stood on an opposing block from the park's gate. They appeared to be staring into the park – staring at me.

One of the men looked strikingly familiar. He was tall and gangly, with bright blonde hair, thin, but hanging loose upon his shoulders. His face was angry, his grin was yellow. It was him – Southey – the man I walked past on my first night, the man I saw in Lee's thoughts, the man who searched endlessly for vengeance against Arthur.

Southey had spotted me with some type of device; he held something up to his eyes – some type of electronic binocular. How did he know? From that distance, he should not be able to see past the makeup, even with binoculars. Had they followed me there?

The younger man next to Southey was much shorter, and more muscular, with dark hair and tan skin; he held a phone to his ear. On the ground, by his feet, was a large bag; I easily saw the shotguns, and the two curved blades with straps, hidden inside.

They did not seem to know I lingered in the air around them, watching them watch me. I was invisible, staring into their eyes, listening to their hearts' tempos rise when they suspected something of me. I listened to them speak.

"He's just *sitting* there Southey. We should go in." The younger one whispered, awaiting a reply. "Shouldn't we?"

Southey spit at the ground and his face shriveled with annoyance. "There are too many people in the park, Dario. We'll need help, too. When he moves, we'll follow him to a less crowded spot and take him out. Any word from the others?"

"Yeah," the young man listened intently to the phone. "Sam said he and the boys will be in position on the other side of the park soon. We got this leech, man. No problem."

Southey smiled, but the contented look seethed with anger and hate. I felt it in the air around him. "Good. This leech is mine!"

When the danger became apparent to me, I lashed out, tearing the strange binoculars from Southey's hands without physically moving an arm. As Southey lunged out to catch his device before it met the concrete, many yards away, my corpse rose from the metal chair and darted across the park.

Weaving through the trees to break the hunters' line of sight, I crossed to the park's side, opposite to where Southey stalked.

Somewhere beyond the iron fence, I knew other hunters were honing in, alerted to my presence. I did not know who to look out for among the dozen pedestrians walking the surrounding area – they all seemed rather clueless to the hunt unfolding among them, but I maintained a lively gait, stepping, swinging the arms, looking alive to blend in. I picked one gate at random, taking a chance – but chance found me.

Across the street from me, two different men hurried past the park, and had it not been for one thing, I would have overlooked them in that tense moment: One of the men held a unique cane in his left hand – with a silver head shaped like an octopus. It was Lance!

I assumed the filthy lout would be able to shed some light on what had happened to Dante, what led to his murder, and my waking. It was still unclear to me who really murdered Dante. Perhaps it was Lance. Be that the case, I would unleash hell upon him, and even if not, I could splurge and take his life. I did not need a conspirator's death list to tell me that Lance was expendable. I would be doing the world a favor by scraping his filth from the street, and I would get to pay back the man who put a bullet in my corpse…even if it didn't matter.

Lance twirled his fancy cane, strutting along the sidewalk, occasionally glancing over his shoulders, but never seeming too concerned with my presence walking thirty feet behind him. The man beside him, keeping Lance's attention averted, was short and nervous in his mannerisms. But Lance would not turn to face the guy, and seemed to want to shake him off of his tail with a hasty pace.

I followed dangerously close behind, wanting to defensively blend among them and escape the area which would soon be searched by ambitious hunters. I eavesdropped on their perverted conversation.

"What did I tell you about this?" Lance seemed annoyed. "You know how I feel about doing this in person."

"Sorry, man. I've been needing some company. And I thought maybe you could lend me a hand?"

"All of my ladies are out. My boys are driving them to their high-paying appointments. Why don't you just go to a strip club or something?"

"Aw!" he groaned. "No way. I liked the one girl with that Russian accent! Oh man, she is nice."

"Yeah, well, Mana's out making me some money."

"Lance! I have been hanging around here for hours looking for you. Help me out!" The short man grabbed Lance's arm desperately.

Lance flailed his arm outward, slapping the man in the forehead. "Ok, just shut up. I do have a new dame waiting at my place, but she is a little picky...not exactly into squirrelly coke-heads like you."

"I don't care who she is, really!" The shady man bounced with excitement.

"I'm not promising you anything. Follow me."

I followed Lance and his client for just a few blocks, beyond the commercial section, to a serene neighborhood; two rows of small but clean-looking apartments lined a quiet, empty street. Beyond the backyards of some of the homes was the perimeter of the old, large cemetery I had spent my first few days hiding in. Unless the sun caught me off guard that upcoming dawn, I had no reason to go in there again.

Lance stood outside the steps leading to his ground floor apartment. He removed a set of keys from his pocket and turned to his acquaintance to speak.

"You'd better be quick. I got a lot left to do tonight." Lance jingled the keys as he searched for the one which would open the door.

I stood across the street, hidden in shadows, watching him, waiting to strike. There were many things within my power, but I wanted, most of all, to get high off of his fear, and to make Lance suffer for the misery he no doubt has caused others.

Being there were no pedestrians around in the earliest hours of the morning, and no signs of the hunters, I was free to do anything. When Lance motioned the key to unlock his door, my vampire hands rushed in like a breeze. I sent the set of keys careening into the air; they fell to the grass, obscured by the shrubs lining the apartment.

"How the...?" Lance turned to see where the keys landed, and the other man joined in the search.

I walked closer, until I stood a few feet behind the distracted goons.

"Lance..." My ghostly voice whispered across to him, almost inside his ear cavity. I extended my hand, and the set of keys launched from their hiding spot, rattling to and past Lance's head, then finally into my grasp.

Lance cursed in frightful surprise. Both men turned around, to see me, the strange figure luring intimidating close – wearing a long coat on a warm night, staring with the greenest of eyes, whose liveliness defied the bland expression of my cold face. I threw the keys over my shoulder, and across the street.

"Who the hell are...*you*?" Lance stood from the grass and studied me closely. "You...look familiar." He held his cane at his side, and his hand scurried to grip it tightly, I assumed, to prepare for a strike.

"You remember," I said in the most inhuman way. With my arms spread outward, my shirt lifted up, seemingly on its own. "You were so scared, you forgot your cane." When my chest was exposed, with thick and grisly surgical stitches clear against my pale skin, I pointed to the bullet hole in my chest. "I'm glad you got it back."

Lance looked down at the bulbous, silver octopus perched atop the dark, wooden staff. Although outwardly calm, his heart pounded in his chest when he realized where he had seen me before.

Despite the false, green eyes which sparkled in my sockets, despite the paint, crèmes and powders which covered my white, veiny skin, despite the lack of bloating and odor from the fluids that once collected, distending my dead flesh, and despite the covering-up of the strangulation markings on my neck, I knew Lance saw through to the foul corpse he once encountered.

The customer, having seen enough, ran down the sidewalk without saying a word. It did not even occur to me to stop him; I had my focus on the tense, riled pimp in the dark green suit.

Lance reached into his pocket and held out a photograph in front of him, comparing the image to my likeness. I did not need to physically move to see what it depicted – it was the picture the Taxxxi Cab driver had taken of me after I handed over Lance's cane. Though I wore sunglasses in that picture, my other deathly features, untouched by Lucia, were highlighted from the flash – and even the scar on my neck was visible behind a gap in the jacket's collar. That cab driver must have shown Lance the photo later when he returned the beloved trinket to him – what Lance must have thought when he saw that photo the first time.

"I don't believe it," Lance whispered. His blood raced through his veins at the command of his panicked heart; I became aroused from the taste of his fear in the air and struggled not to lash out at him.

"Y...you. Not a...again!" Lance stuttered. "What the hell are you? Stay back!"

I slid closer to him, without a leg moving to warn him of a first step. "I'm a vampire now."

"No. You're...dead. You *have* to be!" Lance groaned, distraught at my sight. He debated the validity of my presence; his face swelled with tension. "She *killed* you."

"*She*...killed me?" I asked him, finding the answer suddenly exposing itself to me.

Without a physical gesture to warn Lance of what was to come, I used my powers to attack, and gripped the sturdiest thing he wore. Lance hollered in surprise when, to his total confusion, his thick leather belt became like a lasso for me to manipulate. My spiritual force pulled fiercely upon it, and thusly jerked his hip outward. Unprepared for such an act, he stumbled and fell hard, onto the sidewalk.

"Why would she kill me?" I hollered at Lance, hanging my blackened mouth wide open so he could stare up and inside from below. "Speak up!" My voice rattled in the air like concentrated thunder.

Too terrified to take his eyes off of me, he reached blindly for a small black gun hidden in his coat pocket. Before his trembling hand could grasp the gun's handle, I noticed the chain he wore under his shirt, and tightly closed it around his neck, creasing the skin of his throat. Lance released the gun and reached to his neck with both hands, clawing at the chain.

"This is what she did to me!" I cursed at him, and allowed the putrid muck within my dead mouth to ooze past my lips, splattering on the ground beside him.

Lance writhed on his back, his tongue pushing past his lips. He attempted to roll over, but with ease, I held that loop of gold as if it were fastened to the pavement. Lance was helplessly pinned.

While Lance's spasms slowed down, and he appeared to have accepted his fate, I knelt by his head, gazing down at him. My lips moved, but not offset to my words. I flashed my teeth, clenching them tightly so he could see the dried blood that coated them.

"Tell me…" I removed the picture from my pocket – the one of me, Dante Fairchild, and that cute, young woman, with the blonde curls and a huge smile, together on a sidewalk with a Taxxxi Cab in the backdrop. We looked so happy. I held it out for him to see. "…Is this her?" I asked, and released the chain before Lance passed out.

His wheezing and coughing delighted me. I waited for him to gain control of his frantic lungs.

"Answer me!"

"Yes," Lance coughed and sat up, his hand outstretched at me in some desperate attempt at defending himself. "…that's her. You thought you could sweet talk her into giving it to you for free. You thought she *loved* you? Idiot! That's what my ladies *do*…they make you feel good. But no one takes things from me…especially my favorite cane!"

"I don't believe you…" There was not enough written in the

tiny journal to argue what really happened, but from the little I had read, it seemed that Dante had perhaps found something. "Why would Olyvia do that?" I asked. "Why would she betray me?"

Lance turned to face me, still sitting up and rubbing his irritated neck. Though still very much afraid, groveling like a dog in the face of death, Lance lashed out. "She killed you because I told her to – like the obedient *bitch* she is!"

Lance swiftly swung his cane, but with a mere whim of my mind, I set it off-course and it missed me completely; the dense, silver head atop the cane struck the pavement, breaking one of the eight arms of the octopus.

"No!" Lance yelled, annoyed. "Why won't you die?"

"You knew who I was on that first night! When I killed your friend...Charles?! Didn't you?" I asked.

"...yea." Lance mumbled, his voice quivering in disbelief.

I was finally ready to end his life when there was a horrible twist of fate. Dogs barked from far away; I detected the sounds of their sharp nails striking the pavement with each frantic but distant step. Half a dozen men ran hastily in my direction; though still over a block away, they were soon to be directly in my line of sight.

Southey and his men were armed and in my pursuit. Lance's scummy friend must have alerted them. I shouldn't have let him go so easily – his feared expression pointed them right to me, and those two large dogs probably smelled my rotten flesh a mile away.

The canines were dangerously close before any of the men; being free from their collars, I had no way to stop the vicious beasts without sacrificing my body. When the roused dogs saw what their keen noses had promised them, they picked up speed and snarled with gnashing, white teeth.

To my utter disappointment, I ran in the opposite direction, leaving Lance behind. I fled behind one of the buildings, and across a wide, grassy field, which stretched a short distance toward one side of the massive graveyard.

To move so smoothly with such speed took an effort I had not yet summoned. I knew I would not be able to carry on at that rate for too long. Luckily, the ivy-covered fence of the cemetery was near, because the dogs closed in quickly.

The tall, Victorian gate reached almost six feet into the air, and there were no openings wide enough in the bars to pass through. When I got within a few feet of the perimeter, I propelled myself over the top – a leap beyond the reach of muscle alone. Iron points lining the top of the fence snagged my long jacket's tail, and I crashed to my knees in the wide, row of shrubbery that lined the inner perimeter of the fence. My torn garment hung from the top of the fence like a flag to alert hunters, but no more giving of my presence than the dogs that arrived and immediately poked their faces between the bars. To my relief, there was not a gap to allow the snarling canines in.

An old greenhouse resided on that edge of the cemetery. Long and narrow, with a slanted roof, large panels of steamy glass were supported by a wooden frame. One side of its exterior had been swallowed by ivy, and its interior brimmed with an abundance of flowers and plants. It likely spawned many of the greenery decorating the plots in the cemetery. An outer garden flourished on one side of the structure, and on the other side, a trail led deeper into the cemetery.

I fled past the greenhouse, along the path; its weak, transparent walls could not hide me, nor could it withstand the force of angered hunters. The cemetery was heavily shaded, thick with night; the canopy of trees and uneven terrain gave me a chance to stay out of sight. I prayed I would find somewhere to hide, but I had not been to that section, and did not know where to find an accessible tomb. Even if I barricaded myself in a crypt or tomb, holding the door shut with all the force I could muster, those men would not leave me until I was torn apart. Their voices grew louder as they gathered against the gate to hoist each other over the top.

I had not run far into the graveyard when I found a tomb built deep in the side of a descending hill. The steel door rattled violently, groaning as I attempted to will it open, but an age of rust and swelling hinges had sealed it in place.

I glanced back at the gate, where three of the hunters had already made it inside. The man in the front was Southey. The two younger men by his sides, whom I assumed were his sons, looked very much like him. They had fiery yellow hair like their father; however, the younger son had tight curls, unlike the straight, long hair of his older brother – who seemed to be the spitting image of his dad.

When I saw Southey turn to help the other hunters pass the dogs over the fence, I knew I would not have enough time to find safe haven. Within seconds of those clawed paws landing on the earth, I would have only seconds longer before I was wrestling with them. I had to act immediately.

When the dogs were inside, the three Southeys turned to the path and ran into the cemetery, as their canine colleagues darted far ahead of them, beyond the greenhouse. With a shotgun clenched tightly in each of their hands, a sharp curved blade attached to each of their right arms, and maddened, determined expressions, they marched into the cemetery, passing alongside the long, antique-looking greenhouse.

The lush, dense life that grew within the walls of glass reminded me of her...of the witch in the woods. I heard her voice in my head; her words echoed – 'embrace your true nature.'

My spirit lingered at the greenhouse, pervading throughout the air like a flood of psychic energy. Focusing intently on the surroundings with meticulous precision, I saw the hunters from all sides as if I were the air which they passed through; I heard their trio of heartbeats dancing together like wild drumming. I became intimately aware of the greenhouse, of its walls of glass and wood. My mind detected every nail embedded inside, every pane of warm, foggy glass, and each pot and jar beneath the thick, humid air. With the same transcending force that moved my corpse like the vampiric puppet it was, I released all my anger and fear with a shattering supernatural force. A fierce gust pushed through the greenhouse, shaking the plants inside like a hurricane. The wooden frame cracked violently, its walls skewed toward the three Southeys. Every pane of glass burst, sending thousands of shards swarming in the wind, toward the three startled men.

Because of a seemingly faultless prophylactic strategy against my influences, much of the men's bodies were undressed, exposed to the air. This only aided my brutal attack. As it were, neither hunter was in any position to avert, or block the mass of razor-sharp fragments. The man closest to the greenhouse, the older-looking son, stood between the glass storm and his kin; he took it worst. His body was pierced with glass shards and splinters which tore the flesh from his bones. He choked on his own blood as he fell to the earth, pushing the shards deeper with every finalizing spasm.

"Colin!" Southey cried out in horror, even with many bits of glass sticking into the skin of his left cheek, chin and neck. Overall, his injuries were much less severe, only a scratch here and there on his body. "Jacob!" Southey yelled at his panicked son. "Are you ok?"

Jacob, who stood furthest away from the greenhouse, suffered major cuts across his bare arms, when he instinctively blocked the mass of debris; however, he took a jagged piece of wood in his right eye. His hands reached to his face, but he screamed when he bent his arms, the protruding razors of glass cutting him more.

I was pleased I had stopped those hunters and I was more than content to watch them squirm torturously in the dark. However, the other two hunters had finally cleared the cemetery's fence, and worse yet, the two dogs were just a few yards away from me.

Southey hunched over his dead son, his hand cupping Colin's

slit throat, trying to keep the blood at bay, but it was futile – Colin's eyes said enough – he was dead.

When the backup hunters ran to help their captain, Southey screamed at them, "Sam, Dario, go get him! Hurry! Don't let that damned leech get away!"

The two dogs lunged from atop the hill, flying toward me with gaping jaws and killer-eyes. I understood why Southey had chosen dogs. I was helpless to stop them, to divert them as I had done with guns and knives. With no better option, I held out my right arm to physically deter the raving beasts. One of the dogs ensnared my right hand in its powerful jaws; the other canine quickly joined in, biting a few inches higher, puncturing and tearing the flesh on my wrist.

I tried to shake the creatures free, but they pulled ferociously, keeping me from escaping Sam and Dario, who looked down at the scene from atop the hill.

The first dog fell back with the sound of breaking bone when my right hand detached, my fingers now hanging from the animal's mouth. With only the weight of one dog holding me down, I spun around with all the energy I could muster – but I was tired, having spent a great amount of energy on my lethal stunt. The dog accepted the challenge and tightened its bite as the spinning lifted him off of the ground, slipping only when its teeth scraped down the bone, toward the stump.

The two men atop the hill, an old man with a bushy mustache, and a young, tanned muscular youth, raised their shotguns. But, likely fearing to injure their dogs, they hesitated to pull their triggers, as I spun around and around, with one of the animals hanging from my damaged limb. The canines were doing just fine without bullets for backup.

Seeing my immediate doom when the other dog returned to take another piece, and when Southey staggered to his comrades' sides atop the hill, I made a final, desperate effort, to save myself. Scattered around the cemetery were many obelisks, pillars and other stony protrusions. In a similar fashion as before, I focused in on the heavy, towers of rock, and with the last ounce of strength I had, I pushed them with a force that sent a cold wind at the hunters. Few of the stone structures toppled, but they weighed so much, and fell so close to the frightened men, that when the cemetery filled with their dull thunderous boom, shaking the earth at the hunters' feet, all the men's attention was temporarily diverted.

The last thing I recall before I blacked out from exhaustion, my corpse falling to the earth at the mercy of the dogs, was watching the hunters dive in all directions, nearly being crushed by the crashing of rocky towers.

With all my energy spent, and when the men rushed in with their guns leading the way, I heard Southey's gritty voice yell through the darkness, "Hold fire! I want this leech *alive!*"

Chapter 14 – A Deadly Deal

After the successful attack on the vampire layer in the mill, with fog still swaddling the earth, and distant sirens echoing more and more silently each escaping mile, the black van headed back to the small parking lot of the Redbank Apartments. Southey insisted that Bill and Blair come with them, until things settled down.

Though Sam and Southey were unscathed, the other two cohorts were less fortunate. Blair suffered cuts to his face, a scratched cornea, and a few minor scrapes to his arms and head. However, Bill had been the focus of the attack; the storm of wood had been centered primarily around him. He was bruised all over; numerous cuts and scrapes ripped his skin, and large splinters stuck out in many places. Bill also received a sprained wrist from having been pushed by Blair to evade the falling table.

Luckily for the two battered men, Sam was more than capable of patching up minor scuffs and cuts; a moderate supply of medical aid was available at the base. As soon as the four men returned back to their headquarters in that basement, any wounds would be cleansed and treated.

Southey knelt down on the concrete floor to greet Cain and Abel, who wagged their tails excitedly when their master first entered the basement. When Blair had descended the metal stairs, he passed by the two canines. The dogs immediately started barking at him, intruding the space by his feet.

"What did I do?" cried Blair, as he stumbled backwards in surprise, with one hand on his watery, irritated eye. He defensively held out his free arm, between his midsection and the dogs' snapping mouths. "Get them to stop! Back off!"

After a moment of amusement, Southey called the dogs back and silenced them. He then turned to Blair. "What else have you got on you?"

"N...nothing, really," Blair stuttered as his hand pressed to his pant leg.

"These are ex-cop dogs," Sam informed. He motioned the two wounded men over to a corner, behind the stairs. "Once, they were used to seize drugs and find dead bodies," he laughed, reaching for a large medical kit on the wall. "Now, they just find dead bodies."

"That means...," Southey walked up behind Blair, "...either you are a leech, or you are high."

Blair nervously pulled at the small red ponytail hanging from the back of his nearly-bald head. "I'm not *either*...yet." He and Bill chuckled. Southey was not amused.

Sam opened the white case and removed rubbing alcohol and cotton swabs, bandages, tweezers, and for the fortunately few gaping cuts, a needle and thread.

"I think we should sit tight for tonight." Sam handed them each swabs, moistened with alcohol. "There are some vacant rooms upstairs." He glanced up at Southey, who was whispering something and plugging his ears with his fingers. "Feel free to stay for your troubles."

Bill pulled a large, sliver free from his left arm. "Do you think we got away with it?" He dabbed the puffy, red cut with the cotton.

Sam offered Blair a tube of cream for his red, swollen eye. "You may need to go to the hospital tomorrow." Sam turned to Bill, answering his question, "I'm sure you two will be fine, but we left some evidence behind...like Southey's gun, and that container he used to start the fire, both with his prints."

Southey had already resigned to his nervous pacing; though physically exhausted, having lost many nights' sleep over the last couple weeks, he was in no mood to rest...and face that horrifying image in the dark.

With his shaky hands gripping his thin, yellow hair, he spoke, "The commissioner won't let this slide. Why did I do it? I had to do it! But if we get caught, they'll come and find him." Southey pointed far across the dim room to the small, arched, wooden door by his desk. "They'll see what we've been doing and arson may end up being the least of our problems."

"Who is *him*?" Bill inquired, nodding toward the back of the room.

Southey hesitated for only a moment. "I have one captured alive."

"One *what*?"

"A leech, a vampire!" He blurted, impatiently, walking up to Bill. "In there! I may never get another chance like this, I can't have interference now."

"What for?" Bill could hardly believe his ears. "What good is it alive?"

Southey scornfully replied, "Ever wonder why I know so much about them? This isn't the first one I have captured." He turned his back to the men, and stomped away, across the room, yelling loudly so the men would not miss a single word, "When I first became aware that these soul-sucking things existed, there were well over a dozen...just in this city alone."

Southey walked to the large satellite image of the city hanging in its cracked frame, behind his desk. He continued "...but over the last couple years, there have never been more than a few."

Southey turned to the desk where a small wooden box rested on top, and removed a fresh cigar, holding it beneath his nose and inhaling deeply. He put it in his mouth.

"The ones that remain, for the most part, have been around for many years, some longer than Sam and I. I killed one tonight." Southey removed his silver, butane lighter and fired up his cigar. "They are smarter than the brainless zombies I normally exterminate. They hide better, make up their faces, feed less often and my old tactics of hunting are becoming less effective...but now there is a solution!" He held his finger up in the air. "In case you haven't noticed...," Southey reached onto his desk and grabbed a handful of sketches piled in one corner, "...leeches are incredibly psychic beings, using telekinesis and telepathy as tools." He walked around the desk, across the basement and faced the men, with the sketches clenched in his hand, and the glowing cigar perched in his lips. He spoke, "To defeat your enemy, you must know your enemy. But more importantly, you must know *where* your enemy is."

Southey offered the drawings to Bill, who reached out to receive them.

He continued, "A while back, I met a woman who, for all her ridiculous eccentricity, has a very useful and exploitable skill."

Bill examined the papers. "These look similar in style to the one you showed us earlier." He flipped through them while Blair looked on.

"They should. Maida, my spiritualist, drew all of them. When she is close to one of these creatures, she can connect, somehow, to their minds and see things...images, which she draws on paper...for me."

Bill could barely decipher a few of the drawings. Not every picture was something obvious; many were abstract, and could not be summed up as a person, place or thing. However, a number of the sketches were quite clear – places the men recognized from all over the city.

One drawing was of a fountain in a popular park downtown – a statue of three children seeking shelter from rain beneath a large mushroom; each child held the stalk with one hand while reaching out into the rain with the other. Another picture depicted a church steeple know for its dreary mural – the devil stood at the bottom, his feet upon a pile of banished souls; far above his head, angels in white light filled the sky. At the peak, a bust of Jesus clenched a large cross in its right hand, high in the air. Yet another drawing appeared to be the inside of a crypt. Dark and without much detail, a pillar held upon it an opened book, carved from stone; a name, written across its pages was unclear, except for the fancy capital 'B' at its heading.

Southey grabbed the drawings from Bill. "These are places he has been," Southey explained. "What is really interesting is that early at night, when the leech hasn't yet risen, Maida can hear other voices through him, talking to each other...but only at night, for some reason."

"Voices of other leeches?" Bill suggested, interested at the story.

"Yeah, we think so," said Sam.

"That is...wow." Blair got very excited, smiling with a squinty, gelled eye. "I wonder if she hears *hell*...tortured souls and stuff! That would be so...*neat*, to hear all those screams! Man! Hearing something like that could *really* straighten a man out, I reckon."

"Or not...," Southey whispered below his breath, turning away. Puffing nervously on his cigar, his eyes darted around the room. As he calmed down from all the earlier excitement, the voices, the plague of shadowy whispers haunting his almost every waking moment, grew more and more evident. He twitched every few seconds, inadvertently reacting to their intruding nature. Though he was sure they were only in his head, if only due to others' lack of reaction, it seemed sometimes that the ghostly calls were on all sides – just like in those woods.

Ever since Southey buried that witch's corpse, they called his name, warning him of her. The witch in the woods waited for him in the black pit of his dreams, and of his subconscious, hardly granting him a moment's peace. His absolute dread at the thought of facing her ghastly expression gave him the will to stay awake, to push his efforts and extinguish what vampires he could find before her incessant and woeful staring drove him mad.

"If you have a vampire hidden behind that door," Bill inquired, "...what is stopping it from getting at you through the wall with its powers?"

"Oh it tried at first," Sam replied. "They *all* did."

Southey interrupted, "But a few visits with the dogs, among other things," he smiled, flashing his holey grin at the two men, "...and he learned, like the rest of them. He settled down. I am in control!" Southey turned toward the wooden door across the room, taking a few steps and stopping in the center of the cellar. "Right?" He laughed madly, throwing his cigar across the room, striking the door with a fiery burst. "Isn't that right!" His voice echoed in the cellar. There was no reply from behind the wall, and the other men stared silently, until Southey snapped out of his intense staring.

"I want to see," Blair walked toward him.

"Not a chance," Southey held out his arm to block Blair from passing. He looked down at the stout man and stared for a moment, awkwardly.

A ringing came from Sam's pocket. He removed a phone and turned his back on Bill and Blair. "Hello? Yeah...never mind that. What...why not? ...Unlikely, just come on over and we'll discuss it. Fine, meet us outside then." He hung up, and turned to Southey, shaking his head.

Southey, who stared down at Blair as he listened to half the phone conversation, said to him, "It is time you two go settle down for the night. Sam and I have some business to attend to before we rest." Southey walked to the desk, opened a drawer, and removed a key from inside.

Blair had walked up to the arched wooden door, looking in through a small round window. "There's *another* door in there?"

Southey hurried over to Blair, who had already tried pulling on the locked door. He handed him a key and said, "Take this, go out and around the front door of this building – second floor, apartment 210." Southey squeezed himself between the door and Blair. "Go!" He yelled so loud that the dogs barked and ran over.

Blair took the key and walked away, wiping Southey's spit from his face.

When Sam finished helping Bill with his hard-to-reach cuts, the two younger men headed up the stairs.

"Room 210," Sam reminded. "There's food in there...enjoy. We'll be in touch tomorrow morning to take you home or to the hospital or whatever you need." He waved, as the men exited through the heavy metal door, talking lowly to themselves with a hint of dissatisfaction.

Southey rubbed his temples with his fingers; his eyes were closed and his expression told of the discomfort he was in. When Sam stood by him, Southey smiled and said, "At least I finally got that filthy leech back for biting me."

"Yeah," Sam added.

Southey faced him and opened his eyes, "They were wearing bullet-proof vests of some kind."

"Yes." Sam nodded and tugged at his mustache. "Bill mentioned that one of the leeches they encountered had some armor too. Where do you suppose they would have gotten something like that?" Sam's tone was more suggestive than inquisitive.

"Leeches don't kill *cops*." Southey bit his lip, continuing, "We'd hear about it every time...It'd be suicide in the long run. Besides...that type of armor is outdated now." He thought for a moment. "You said Arnold Paul has been nosing around there recently?"

"That's the word on the street." Sam raised an eyebrow, hoping that Southey was honing in on his theory.

"I always assumed he believed me a little, at least...but...," Southey walked back across the room, and ascended the stairs, stomping loudly. "...there's no way he is *helping* them, is he?" Southey pulled on his hair, "Whatever is going on has been for at least a year," Southey grumbled. "Maybe more! Leeches' trails are harder to follow. You can't get any good leads from the obituaries, or watching the news anymore."

Southey climbed the stairs and exited the basement.

"I know," Sam said, following upstairs and outdoors into the small parking lot. "...you have to ask a lot of people a lot of questions to get any useful information."

The tired men walked to the black van. The fog was burning away, and the brightest of stars were popping into view in the sky.

"Somebody's keeping a lid on things...containing it." Southey kicked the side of the van. "The police are keeping things from the public, and cutting me off from valuable information." Southey clenched his hands angrily.

Sam opened the rear doors of the van. "I think there might be more to it than that."

Southey paced around the parking lot, mumbling incoherencies under his breath. Every few steps, he would stop and look at his buildings, occasionally meeting eyes with tenants in the windows who looked down at their maniacal landlord.

Southey owned the three, small brick apartments surrounding the parking lot. A self-storage facility once stood on the site, but was demolished to make room for Redbank Apartments, named such after Southey's late love, Ellen Redbank, whose life insurance paid for the project.

Southey chose to build in the gritty, industrial area for two reasons: he had learned early on that vampires naturally averted artificial light when possible, and to walk or drive to his apartments necessitated traversing through an industrial area that remained will-lit throughout the night. Also, there were few pedestrians for miles around, making it unlikely that a vampire would brave the intense lights and the labyrinth of barbed fences, stumbling on Southey's place of operations. The actual hideout was located in the basement beneath Redbank #1, the building where Sam, Southey and Maida resided.

Redbank #2 and #3 were directly across the lot. A few weeks earlier, a tenant was murdered in Redbank #2 – Charles Preston. The handling of the situation by police was very strange, and

Southey was not allowed near the scene. Then, not too long after that incident, police returned for more clues. Southey got a message from authorities informing him of another tenant's disappearance and possible murder – Dante Fairchild. He lived on the same floor of the same building as Charles Preston, only, unlike the first incident, Dante's body never turned up. In both cases, police refused to disclose the details of the murders with anyone, claiming that to do so might impede progress in the case. Southey always remained very suspicious of those incidents.

After pacing around the parking lot, deep in thought, Southey walked over to the van and leaned against it, taking a deep breath. He tried to ignore the frustratingly persistent voices haunting him, which was easier to do with the buzzing of high-powered lights and generators that were heavily scattered among the surrounding warehouses, trucking stations and factories.

Sam peered into the back of the van and tugged out one of the duffel bags, letting it fall to the ground. As he hauled it back into the basement, he pointed through a clearing of buildings, at an approaching car. "Here he comes."

A deep red coupe, with a spoiler and tinted windows, turned onto the dead-end road and pulled into the lot and beside the black van. When the door opened, a man in a black shirt and emerald green jacket slid out of the leather seat; in his right hand, he held a cane fashioned with a silver octopus atop the staff – one of the eight arms spiraling vertically along the cane was missing.

"Lance," Southey called out to the arriver from behind the van, "I was hoping you would have had something for me." Southey flicked the fiery stub into the street and walked around to meet his guest. "I'm a bit disappointed."

Lance stood near the back of the van and gazed inside. "I'm done," he said, shaking his head, curiously poking at one of the large bags with his cane.

Rather than ask Lance not to touch his things, Southey pushed one of the van's rear doors shut, knocking the cane out of its path.

"We agreed on three, didn't we?" Southey reminded him. "I'm sure a man with *your* reputation can find me one more."

Lance held his cane up, pointing the large, silver head at Southey. "Of course I can find *more*, but my ladies aren't stupid, and when a couple of them go missing, they act up. So I am through." Lance shouted, turning his back on Southey. "I did you your favor, as sick as it was…," Lance mumbled, "…giving you bait to catch and kill other vampires!"

Southey turned to face his guest. "It is working! Don't think their lives were *wasted*!" he reassured. "With those girls' generous pledge, I have killed three more of these things! Do you know how long it has been since I killed three so quickly? I just need a little more time to get the rest of them."

Lance shook his head. "It just sounds too crazy, even after what happened to me. I have real problems now, anyway."

"Do tell," Southey replied to Lance, intentionally sounding uninterested.

"I'm hiding out because the cops are looking for me. Because of that, I can't use my cabs. This isn't even my car! I have to send my ladies around on foot, which slows down my business. The last thing I need to do is lose what girls I have left."

"What happened to your desire for revenge?" Southey slammed the van's other backdoor shut, and stood with his hands to his hips, glaring at Lance. "It seems that just a couple weeks ago, you were willing to do anything to help me exterminate these things. Has your ego healed from your near-death experience?"

"I got over it," Lance walked forward, brushing his right shoulder against Southey as he passed him. "I feel more guilty than angry, now. Besides, this isn't *really* revenge anyway, since you killed and burned the one that attacked me…correct?" Lance cringed at the thought of seeing that ex-client of his one more time.

"Yeah, yeah," Southey rolled his eyes, grinning while his back was still turned; he had not been totally honest with Lance. "But that is beside the point!"

On the night Lance and Southey officially met, the hunters were doing a routine sweep of the city, ending what had been a long, dry spell. Splitting up into groups, Southey, Sam, and the late Colin, Jacob and Dario, plus the dogs, Cain and Abel, with their keen noses, scanned areas where they suspected a vampire had been frequenting. Using thermal goggles, Southey and Dario happened to notice that one of two chess players in Bayview Park was cold as death. They were baffled, never having seen a vampire so bold as to sit in the presence of a human being.

They contacted the other hunters, but before the trap was set, the vampire fled through the cover of the park's trees. Southey chased after, but as it was near-impossible for any less-than-fit man to catch a vampire on foot, they lost track of it.

When Southey had lost all hope at finding that vampire, he saw a man running as hard as he could, with a look of terror gleaming in his eyes. The frightened man pointed them to where he had encountered 'a zombie.' Southey and his men found that zombie standing over Lance, who cowered on his knees.

Cain and Abel ran ahead of the hunters, chasing the vampire away from its would-be prey, inadvertently saving Lance's life. The men followed the sound of the riled dogs into a nearby cemetery, and within those iron gates, Southey suffered a terrible blow. His oldest son, Colin, died when a nearby greenhouse shattered by vampiric trickery. His other son, Jacob, was blinded in one eye and cut all over his arms. Southey himself suffered many cuts to his face and neck. In the end, the dogs pinned the vampire until it collapsed from exhaustion and was captured. They secretly transported it to their van.

Lance, having been left in the street without answers, and emotional from his terrible encounter, had opted to follow after the hunters. It wasn't hard for him to follow their excited voices in the still of night, and when he finally found them gathered by a black van, Lance waved them down, demanding an explanation to his strange experience. Having lived in the city for years, they recognized each other, and though Southey had never spoke to Lance before, he knew what he did for a living. Many times, Southey had seen Taxxxi Cabs dropping off ladies at Redbank Apartments, but he never acted against it. He focused on matters more important to him.

At first, Southey had tried to rudely brush Lance off, overwhelmed with his injuries and the loss of his son – but Lance had been persistent, so Southey exploited the situation to his advantage. Southey had assumed that it might take Maida weeks to dig through his captured vampire's psyche to find the vampire he wanted most; this meant he needed to feed it a few times, but he had no running theory how. Until the moment Lance approached him that fateful night, Southey had assumed the solution would fall on his lap – he was right. Southey cunningly provoked Lance into swapping a few girls for cash and assurance that what happened to Lance would not happen again once the final few vampires were killed. Lance, shaken and angered, accepted.

Southey had made sure to keep the prisoner a secret from Lance. He had told him, on that night, that the creature had been killed, and that the hunters were going to burn the corpse. Southey figured if Lance had known he wanted to keep the creature that attacked him alive by feeding it his own donated ladies, then Lance would not likely have gone along with the insanity. So Southey lied, telling Lance that the women were used as bait to lure other vampires.

"Good," Lance believed Southey's lie. "They all should burn."

Lance stood motionless in the small parking lot; he looked up at the orange-colored sky, tinted from the bright city lights reflecting off of the scattered clouds. He tried to come up with a better reason why he wanted to back out; apparently, guilt was not a good enough reason for Southey's cruel determination.

Lance shook his head. "I was just overreacting that night, and for weeks after. I was paranoid." Lance paused, his curiosity had by the heavy, metal basement door on the side of Redbank Apartment #1. "What goes on down there, anyway...in your *infamous* little cellar?" He walked across the lot, past Southey, saying, "I've heard a ton of crazy rumors."

Southey turned around and followed Lance, yelling at his back, "I *did* pay you three-thousand up front! That is a lot of money for an old man going broke, like me."

"Here," Lance turned around and held out a wad of one-hundred dollar bills in his right hand. "This is one-thousand, since I failed to deliver on one of the three girls."

Southey remained calm on the outside, but struggled not to lose his cool. He grabbed the cash, shaking it in the air. "That was three-thousand for the *entire* job, not one-thousand per head. Bring me either one more girl, or give me two-thousand more dollars!"

"No! We're even!" Lance turned from Southey, waving his silver-headed cane as he continued to the basement door. "Do not piss me off old man."

Southey narrowed his eyes, angered at Lance's dissent. "The cops have seen you around here, Lance. The commissioner has asked me about you. He thinks you murdered my tenant, Mr. Preston."

"Well I didn't!"

"What did you see that night, Lance? I've been curious. A vampire, perhaps? I would like to know more. The cops all lied to me."

"I wasn't even *there* when it happened!" Lance lied. "It's all circumstantial evidence. I know nothing!"

"Well...either way, he wants to talk to you, and I have kept my mouth shut, so far."

"Are you threatening me?" Lance turned his head back to Southey. "If I get caught, I will tell them about our deal. What have I got to lose at that point?" He tapped at the basement door with his cane.

Southey laughed, "You'd be just as responsible, and besides, they'd laugh at you as they have at me for years. No one is going to believe a story like that, especially coming from a lout like you."

"There *must* be some evidence in here!" Lance reached out and pulled on the handle of the heavy door, but it was locked. "What is down there anyway?"

The door opened from the inside, and Sam stood between Lance and the basement. He looked at Southey, asking, "Did you knock?"

"No," Southey grinned at Sam while Lance's back was turned. "Lance did."

Lance was trying to peer over Sam's shoulder to get a glimpse of what was down the metal stairs. He looked into Sam's eyes, "I want to know what you do down there. There are a lot of rumors about what goes on, and I am sick of being left in the dark! I deserve an explanation for my part in all of this!"

"Ok," Southey agreed. "But I want your word that you will not tell anyone what you see." He stood behind Lance and extended his slender hand.

Lance reached over and shook it, "You got it."

Sam turned and led the way down the stairs, and into the underground room. Lance, noticing immediately the shelves against the wall to his left, walked over and examined the weapons.

"What is it with all the shotguns?" Lance asked.

"You need something you can hold with both hands. Accuracy is not as important as power." Southey walked to his desk on the opposite end of the cellar.

"Look at this!" Noticing the long, curved blades fastened to straps, Lance laughed, rubbing his hand against the dark, blood stained arc. "I saw you guys wearing these things on your arms that night. This is killer!"

"That was my son's invention. Armblades come in handy when you get up close." Southey opened a drawer of his desk and removed a ring with many keys on it. "You can't drop it." He put the set of keys in his pocket and reached for a cigar.

Lance thought back to his first encounter and the gun that was thrown mysteriously from his hand – from the vampire he didn't know was there...and then he recalled how the keys to his apartment were tossed from his hand, the night he almost died.

Lance examined the buckled straps holding the weapons to the shelf. "Why is everything fastened down like this?"

Sam, who kept a close eye on Lance, responded, "...to prevent any *accidents*."

Lance saw the thermal goggles, night vision goggles and heavy duty flashlights lying inside an opened box. "Don't you guys use holy water and silver bullets too?" He laughed, shaking his head. "This isn't what I expected to see." He tapped his cane against one of many, damaged wooden crates and boxes. "What happened to these things? Lose your temper?"

Neither man replied.

"What are in these boxes?" Lance asked as he tried to peer through the damaged opening of a crate.

"Ammunition, very minor explosives, chemicals…" Sam started to say, when Lance was suddenly distracted by the large satellite image of the city hung on the back wall by the desk.

"It looks more like you are running a SWAT Team, Southey." Lance walked up to the large, incredibly detailed map on the far end of the room; he rubbed his finger against the tiny round stickers stuck to it. "What do these markers mean?"

"Some are murdered people. Most are missing people…the majority of which you'd never have read about in the paper." Southey smoked passionately on his cigar, spilling smoke down from his nostrils. "Any other questions?" Southey made no attempt to sound complacent with Lance's curiosities.

Lance pointed to the left side of the map, to the large web of damaged glass where it seemed to have been struck. "You got anger management issues, Southey?" He turned to observe some of the damaged and flickering lights hanging from the basement's ceiling. When he saw the box of cigars on Southey's desk, he asked, "May I?"

Southey nodded, reaching into his pocket to toss Lance a book of matches. Lance took a few puffs on the cigar and turned around, gazing at the basement in all its blandness and generally empty space. Then he inquired about the seemingly misplaced arched wooden door in the corner.

"What is in there? A wine cellar?" Lance walked over to the entrance, and he peered through the tiny window near the top of the door.

Southey laughed. "No, though when I am done with it, I think that could be an *excellent* idea." He held up the set of keys in his hand, shaking them; he had already prepared them for this anticipated moment. "What I have in there is a *secret* weapon…a little too *extreme* to keep sitting out here in plain view for everyone to see."

Lance raised his eyebrows, interested, and smiled. "Really? Heavy artillery, eh?"

Southey walked past Lance and unlocked the door. "Something like that." He pushed the creaky door open, revealing the dim, short, sloped and narrow hall of stone, with an arched ceiling.

Cain and Abel, aroused by the activity, walked over to the entrance. Usually, opening the door meant they were to guard

Southey, or attack the creature.

"Stay." Southey held out his hand to the dogs. He motioned Lance with his finger. "Come on. I think *you'll* dig this especially."

Lance followed Southey into the dim, arched passage, taking deep breaths with his nose. "What is that smell? I've been in some nasty places before but…"

Southey stood in front of a larger, heavy oak door at the end of the hall. "Don't mind the smell," he interrupted. "The dogs have used this place for a bathroom on several occasions."

Using another key on the ring, he unlocked and removed a padlock from a horizontal bar, and then lifted the beam up, allowing the door to be opened freely. Southey pushed the door open halfway, intentionally using his shadow to eclipse the vampire in the floor's center, hiding it from Lance.

"There it is!" Southey proclaimed, gesturing Lance to step closer and look inside.

"There is what?" Lance poked his head into the dark room, "What's this? Stop messing around and turn on the light so…"

When Lance turned his head from Southey to look around the odorous, black room, Southey snatched the cigar from Lance's mouth and pressed it into his left eye, twisting it.

"Ahhh!" Lance screamed in pain, dropping his cane to the concrete as he reached up to grab his seared eyeball. "What the hell?"

Southey wasted no time, immediately pushing Lance's head into the solid rock of the door's frame. "The deal was three!" Southey screamed. "Three!"

When Lance buckled from the blow to his skull, Southey shoved him into the cell, slamming the door behind him. Southey quickly lowered the bar; he then fastened the padlock, but not before the wood shook with the ferocity of Lance trapped inside.

"Southey! Open up *now!*" Lance pounded on the door with the weight of his body. "People know I am here, they'll come looking!"

Southey reached down and picked up Lance's cracked cane, smiled to himself and said, "Sorry Lance, my resources are running low!"

Sam stood at the end of the short hall, listening to the frantic, heavily muffled yells.

Lance cried out, "Fine! I will give you another girl, just open up! I'll give you *two!*" The pounding of the door halted for a moment, and no longer loud with anger, Lance's voice quivered the words, as he realized his company. "Who's there?"

Southey exited the narrow hall with a grin, shutting the small, wooden door behind him, and locking it. The sound of Lance's cries could hardly be heard over the barking dogs, who often reacted to the stirring of the vampire.

"Well, that ends that." Sam shook his head.

"And I saved a thousand dollars!" Southey laughed, holding out the wad of cash. He walked over to the desk and laid the silver octopus cane upon it. "What a *deal*."

Chapter 15 – A Monster in the Cell

I was surprised when I regained consciousness, since I had assumed, in that second before I collapsed from exhaustion, with the dogs' teeth grappling at my bones, and the angered hunters circling around, that I was done for. But it seemed I was to become a tool of Southey's cruel and twisted will. When I realized this, I sprung hastily to my feet, only to discover a fate perhaps worse than death.

I was alone in a dark, round cell, made entirely of concrete, and immediately, I felt cramped and smothered. A single locked door of sturdy wood, reinforced with metal bars, was the only feasible escape. Across from it, on the other side of the small chamber, was a slim opening along the upper part of the wall. It was too small for any human body to fit through, and was tightly boarded up; it peeked up to the sky through a small tunnel dug in the earth above it. I fearfully wondered if its sole purpose was to allow sunlight in.

It appeared that I was underground, and I believed I had been sealed in some type of grave. I tried to peer past the cell's solid rock wall, but my vampire eyes obtrusively met the impermeable obstruction of solid earth behind the concrete; a barrier of dirt surrounded almost every inch of my prison's exterior, and it practically rendered me blind. Despite the improbability of my escape, I was not even allowed to grope at the circular wall in futile desperation. A shackle, so tight as to asphyxiate any living man, was bound firmly to my neck; the large, steel cuff pressed against my jaw and collar bone, and I could not open my mouth unless I tilted my head backwards. With little slack, a chain fell from the metal cuff, running to a pole embedded in the center of the floor. I was not going anywhere.

My only means of escape came from the freedom of my eyes, ears and hands – the ghostly ability for my mind to drift, passing through and beyond objects, beholding things some distance around me. I may have been physically bound, but my reach defied the boundaries of my corpse, and hopefully, that cell. As unlikely as it seemed that I alone would be able to change the course of actions unfolding against me, my will was strong, and I was determined to fight back, even if in vain.

The only section of the cell with a break in the encasing earth was beyond the chamber door, and therefore, I was free to glance through. I took the liberty of peering beyond, into a short and narrow hallway with walls formed of large stones, and a low-hanging, vaulted ceiling. The short hall was also underground, but sloped upward to a second wooden door; smaller than my chamber door, it arched along the contours of the hall's ceiling, and a tiny circular window was centered at its peak.

On the other side of the arched door was a wide basement – a place I did not recognize. Like a curious ghost, I breezed around the room, wondering where I had been imprisoned. The two dogs that had hunted me down, tearing meat off of my bones, rested peacefully in each other's company, awaiting the return of their master near the base of a metal stairway – but not without a sense of concern. They were attune to my rousing, and my unseen presence could not deceive them. The savvy animals, with suspicious eyes, and ears perked high in the air, turned their heads as I secretly floated about, growling and rising to their feet when my phantom presence neared them.

On one side of the grimy, dim and spacious cellar, was a heavy metal desk. It was cluttered with papers and notebooks, and a box of cigars sat on its surface. Suspended on the wall behind it was a large map of the city, and though I knew very little of the area, I recognized places – a lone patch of green near the east side was obviously Bayview Park, and I watched the highway run north, from the city and towards the mountains.

On the other side of the basement, boxes and crates were stacked on the floor. A large medical kit hung on the wall, covered in bloody handprints. In that corner, a set of shelves were built into a wall; shotguns, large curved blades designed for arm wear, electronic-looking binoculars, and other devices, were carefully fastened to the shelf's surface with straps and buckles.

I looked up and out through the walls of the basement. Immediately, I recognized the area. In the center of an unsightly industrial section, surrounded by webs of fence and rail, were three dilapidated brick buildings on a dead-end road – Redbank Apartments. Ironically, I had been taken one building over from the place of my waking.

Attempting to peer far away, I noticed something peculiar about my poor senses. Just as a candle's flame declines more and more as it is covered and kept from open air, being in that underground cell somehow muted my strength. The deep earth, which almost entirely surrounded my chamber, rendered my perceptions weak, decimating the range of my sight and influence. The bland grayness that defined my undead eyes' horizons, keeping stars and other distant objects from my awareness, lingered portentously close by. I could hardly see beyond my prison. Southey must have learned over the course of many years that it was to his advantage to keep vampires hidden beneath the earth. His fiendish cunning had left me wallowing in desolation, and I pondered what horrors he was capable of with both his knowledge of my weaknesses, and his hatred for my kind.

Not long after I had risen in my cell to discover the dire development, the sun's siren cry announced its reign over darkness. As dawn set in, I went from cursing the cell walls to thanking them, cowering inside, fearful of the vaporous fire filling the air outside. Powerless to do anything, I collapsed to the floor and fell into the peaceful darkness of my mind.

I dreamt of her, that first of many days in the cell – of the witch in the woods, and her petite, thin, raggedy body. She strolled through her pillared kingdom; her arms, like branches, graced against the surrounding trees, and the wooden subjects, with their knotted limbs, creaked and groaned, as if they attempted to genuflect as she passed by. The fabric of life in the forest rippled with every step she took, and with her every tending thought, the winds stirred the leaves and needles to sing to her. Her majesty beckoned me to question more deeply, the nature of what I was, of what defined me.

The witch in the woods had told me to think of her in my time of darkness. Why? Could she have known what was to come? And if so, why didn't she warn me? I could not imagine something more terrible than what had happened to me; just when I had realized how powerful and free I actually was, everything was taken away.

Who is she? someone's thoughts spoke into my mind. *...that foul thing in the woods?*

A friend, I answered. I should not have heard other voices; I was not near other vampires, and was separated from contact by miles of horridly golden, sunlight. Yet, someone joined me, sharing my private thoughts. *She is not foul*, I added, defending her goodness as I recalled the majesty of her realm.

She's the witch? the strange woman asked. *Isn't she? She lives in those woods.* Her voice was eerie, higher-pitched, like a young girl's, but burdened, tainted with the wisdom of pain and death and sin.

I recalled the long, narrow path, choked by the surrounding trees, leading to the clearing and the cabin where the witch once lived as an old woman. I saw the tiny shelter, alone in the open, with its rotted wood, and a spider making its web where a window once was.

She used to live in the woods, I whispered back, cautiously. *But now she is the woods.*

...and the cabin?

It is just a place, nearby. I grew suspicious of the string of questions, and wanting to know who I was speaking with, I asked

...Who are you?

There was no reply at first, yet I felt her present there. It was not entirely dissimilar to when I shared memories with other vampires – except I could not see into her mind – and somehow, I knew she was not a vampire.

She laughed softly, and her thoughts spoke clearly to me, saying, *...Someone who wants to know about you, where you've been, who you've seen. That's all.*

Memories rapidly stirred inside me. I thought of the tomb I had slept in those first few nights. I saw Bayview Park, and its central fountain. I visualized the gloomy mural of good and evil upon the steeple of the church I had visited. I was certain I had not recalled the memories intentionally. Had this mysterious voice summoned them? I cleared my mind of the images, and all went black and still for a while.

That was good, what else can you show me? Her voice and her thoughts grew unwelcome to me. I sensed her malice.

Cautious of the situation, I thought back to the witch, as she had instructed me to do. I thought of when she and I strolled along that seldom trodden, overgrown path in the forest. I recalled her frightful features, her ghastly, infested eye sockets, her white, spidery-hair, and her skeletal digits. Hoping the image would deter the foreign voice from looking further, I focused on the most ghoulish of the witch's details – her gaping black mouth, and fangs, soiled from a thousand deaths, embedded into her dried and decayed gums.

Many know of the legend of the witch, the voice said. *So she is vampire, and not a ghost...interesting. Where is she now? Show me more.*

More images danced in my mind, but I managed to cease the display.

Leave me! Get out of my mind! I screamed inside the black pit of my private thoughts.

The mysterious woman's mocking laughter faded, leaving me to silence. It was not long when I felt something horrid, a sensation worse than my deepest hunger's cold and throbbing ache – a new and terrible awareness.

An indescribable pain woke me when it was still daylight. I was lying on the floor as the sickening feeling persisted, its terrible sting cutting me, somehow – a non physical pain, yet wholly real. I sensed motion – the crawling and writhing of critters somewhere within the cell.

Where is it coming from? I wondered, in agony.

I looked to the mauled stump of my right wrist. Burrowing into the opening of my severed arm was a writhing glob of maggots, pushing deeper inside, pulsing the skin just below the surface, with a ravenous craving for dead meat. How long they had been at it, I did not know. A noticeable section of my arm had been eaten, and the cleaned bone jetted out from the stump by a few inches. Though I could feel nothing through my corpse, an utterly hellish feeling seeped through me, something deeper than anything I had yet experienced.

I used my only hand to claw at the stump of the damaged arm, frantically scraping the maggots out and onto the floor. I tore another inch of meat off of the bone just to ensure I removed all of them. When there was no more writhing within my arm, and the torturous sensation ended, I looked to the floor in horror as the horde of hungry critters devoured the splattered mess of discarded flesh.

I brooded over what I had been reduced to – the helplessness of my situation. Eventually, the night would return, and I would be withheld from its beautiful canopy. With no means to satiate my growing hunger, I would eventually feel the stirring of pain, that dull, cold throbbing – an inescapable discomfort, a constant reminder of what I need to do, what I need to be, to exist. How long would I have to wait until I starved, until death tore me free from those shackles?

Unwilling to resign, I looked past the cell door, past the short hall, and into the basement. The room was no longer empty. Southey sat at the wide desk, flipping through strangely familiar drawings. The fresh cuts on the left side of his face were a gruesome memento of our recent encounter, and surely, a reminder of the death of his son. Beside Southey, looking over his shoulders were two others. A man, appearing a few years older than Southey, and much less worn from injury, had a thick, grey mustache that buried his upper lip; he was at the hunt the night I was chased to my doom. The other companion was a short, grey-haired woman in a loose, flowing dress which hid her rounded figure. Her long grey hair was gathered in a thick tress with beads and stones woven in. When she spoke, I immediately identified her unusually high voice; she had permeated my thoughts moments earlier.

Flipping through the sketches, the three talked quietly to themselves.

"I thought that was just a ghost story," the older gent said as he tugged at his whiskers. "Are you sure?"

The eccentric woman nodded.

"Even if you are right, Maida, most of these are junk," Southey dropped the drawings onto the desk. "They're practically all trees! I can't find my way through a forest with some half-assed drawings as maps."

"That's all I saw this time." Maida's eerie voice was bizarrely youthful, defiant of her older face. She took the sheets from the desk, pulling one from the rest, and held it to Southey's face. "Look! There's a cabin somewhere with a path behind it. Find that! He was there with the witch. She cannot be far."

To my amazement, I recognized the doodles on the paper as vague illustrations of my dream – crude, yet strikingly accurate portrayals of my thoughts I had inadvertently shared with that mysteriously malignant woman.

Southey shook his head, "No! Go back and try again. As much as I hate all leeches, this would be a waste of my time. I'm looking for one I believe is still hiding in the city! I hunt in urban environments, not out in the middle of nowhere." He reached for a cigar that awaited him in an ashtray on the desk.

The woman put her hand on Southey's chin, turning his face toward hers. "This witch has been around longer than all of us. I knew someone who disappeared in those woods long ago, and I would like to see his memory honored. Surely you can empathize."

Maida grabbed the unlit cigar from Southey's perched lips and tossed it to the floor. "And I told you not to smoke around me!" Her yell was like a spoiled child. She stared deep into Southey's eyes and he seemed spellbound by her words, "Go into the woods, Robert Southey. Do what I ask. Kill this ancient scourge and take away a trophy worthy of the greatest vampire hunter. In time, I will have much more useful information extracted from your festering guest in the cell next door."

Maida released Southey's face, and closed her eyes, grinning, as if she knew already that Southey would obey her.

"Okay..." Southey thought to himself for a moment, and nodded, seeming still a bit unconvinced. "Sam, call our friend," he sneered, "Mr. Commissioner." See if he can pay us a visit tomorrow. Since we won't be rustling his feathers by firing guns within the city, maybe he'll finally help."

Sam nodded, "Doubtful, but I can call."

"Great." Southey leaned back in his chair.

"Kill the witch!" The woman laughed to herself, wringing her hands together.

I understood, at that moment, what I had become. Not just some monster in a cell, and not just some scapegoat for an angry man to exorcise his personal demons, I had become a tool against my own kind, against my will. I was being imprisoned, to be exploited, aiding Southey's quest for extermination. I would not have it!

Like an angered poltergeist, I struck the large map of the city hanging behind them, leaving a cracked web on one side. The sudden splitting of glass startled the three plotters, and they jerked their heads to see the damage.

The two dogs, already on their feet from my presence, were now barking wildly at the air. Before Southey had time to curse my obvious intrusion, I sent the objects upon his desk flying through the air with a clumsily executed breath of energy.

As the papers, pens, notebooks and newspapers scattered across the cement floor, Maida grinned at the display and poked Southey's arm, saying, "I think your leech needs to be reminded who is in charge here, hmm?"

Disgusted by her presence, her arrogance, I found the string of beads keeping her braid together, and pulled with intense force; Maida's mouth opened wide, and she squeaked in fear as her head snapped back violently. She staggered into a wall and flopped onto the floor, disoriented.

Southey snickered at her ordeal. He stood up, knocking his chair back onto the floor, and searched through his pockets, saying, "They *always* do this at first, Maida. I told you not to wear those stupid beads and things!"

My spirit raced around the dim, smoky basement, grabbing and striking everything I could. The dogs darted around the cellar with each violent gesture I unleashed. The crates and boxes slid and tumbled around the floor, their sides cracked and splintered. Lights hanging from the ceiling swung wildly with each phantom punch. The weapons on the shelves rattled when I tried to tug them free, but their straps were too tightly fastened. The complex binds eluded my blunt and unearthly hands, which seemed incapable of such intricate gestures. The triggers of the empty shotguns clicked when I pulled them, hoping for something, anything.

Hearing the rattling triggers from across the room, Southey laughed, looking over his shoulder at the wall, as if to acknowledge my corpse contained in the cell beyond. "I know better than *that*, leech!"

My anger carried my voice into an inhuman, faded scream, and I hollered at them from many directions, "I'll kill you all! Let me go!"

I pounded the cement walls of the basement; the dull thud echoed loudly, but the walls were much too strong to damage.

Southey walked towards the small, arched door with a ring of keys held tightly with both hands. His partner, Sam, seemed desensitized to the outburst, but the paranoid psychic, Maida, had her hand clenched to her braid to prevent a repeated incident, and appeared frazzled. They stood behind Southey as he fumbled with the keys at the door to the hallway.

I focused on the metal key ring malevolently, trying to bat it from Southey's fingers, but he easily overpowered me, unlocking the door. Trying to hold the three of them back, I pulled at their clothes, tugging at shirts, pants, and robe. Their arms and legs wavered from the interference as each annoyed person took their first steps, but when they used their strength to fight back against the possessed fabrics, they ripped, freeing my handle and rendering my efforts fairly useless. I ceased my storm of wrath.

In the cell, I prepared myself for retaliation. My corpse lifted from the floor, having been limp during my outburst. I then backed away from the door as far as the chain allotted. When the heavy, wooden door swung open with a mighty kick of Southey's boot, it slammed violently into the inner wall, like a gong.

Southey stood in the doorway, with a huge grin; the two dogs at his sides were squeezing their faces between his legs and the door frame, trying to get closer to me.

"Let's get one thing straight, leech..." He spit across the room, and as he glanced down at the strips of cloth ripped from his cotton shirt, he said, "...If you ever try anything like that again, I will pour a *heap* of filthy, crawly maggots over your sleeping corpse!"

Southey reached back to the angered woman, who held out a brown satchel. Reaching inside, and making a disgusted face, he pulled out a fistful of maggots, which sat passively on his hand. "These things *will* eat you down to the bone if you attack any of us again."

"Then kill me! I am not yours to command!" I growled at him, my still mouth flashed gritty teeth as my words poured into the air. "You will die as soon as chance allows me the opportunity!"

Southey snapped his fingers, and like bullets, the two dogs blazed into the cell. I skidded to the side, but I was no match for the amazing speed of the animals. The small environment was too restricting, and the dogs pivoted quickly, lunging back at me.

One dog clamped on to my leg, the other returned to my mangled stub, fiercely gnawing at the bone it had broken, as if it found its favorite chew toy. I was at the animals' mercy; no matter how hard I spun, or how violently I fought back, it only served to damage my corpse more, tearing the pale flesh, rendering my limbs riddled with teeth marks. I heard laughter from the onlookers in the hall, and knowing Southey was in full control, I lowered myself to the floor in defeat.

Southey yelled, "Cain! Abel! Back, now!" The dogs obediently returned to him, smacking their lips.

In tattered rags, with multiple gashes, holes and other injuries on my corpse that would never heal, I laid still, helpless, on a floor spotted with maggots and flesh.

Southey stepped into the cell. "Like I was saying...If you ever do anything like that again, if you make one noise, move one object, or say one word, I will spend a whole week finding ways to tear you apart." He smiled a holey grin and pointed across the cell. "And then I will take the boards off that window...let some light in here. I've seen what can happen to leeches in the sun, God bless it. It's a slow, sick and painful looking process, taking about an hour to turn whatever corpse you have left, into a rancid pile of meat. And your bones will make great treats for my dogs!"

Southey laughed, and patted the dogs' heads. Then he turned to look back at Sam, who nervously stroked his mustache. "Did he contact you yet? Is he going to deliver?"

"Yeah," Sam replied with a hint of shame in his voice. "He said he'll send one over for us tomorrow night."

Southey looked back into the cell; I had risen to my feet silently, and he had not expected to see me standing before him. His eye twitched, but he was not afraid. I did, however, sense his anger; he was disgusted with me and with each slow, deep breath, Southey's mind rattled with ill thoughts towards me.

"There's no reason to misbehave. I won't let you starve. So sit tight and shut up!"

The hunters shut the cell door and left; however, Maida lingered in the hall, behind the chamber door, with the two dogs at her sides, and with blank sheets of paper and a pencil. For most of that night, she persisted, trying to listen to my thoughts, to see what was my mind, and though, on occasion, her voice coaxed me into conversation, with much effort, I resisted her persuasions. Her presence was like a phantom itch I could not scratch – only ignore. I did all I could do. I did not reminisce of the places I had been, or recall the faces of the other vampires I had met, and those sheets of paper remained blank. I did not betray information to her, and after many hours, she left, frustrated.

Late into the next day, I awoke during sunlight hours when Maida returned to the hallway. She called out loud to me, through the door.

"You can't resist me forever," she spoke through the door, and laughed, waiting for a response while standing silently in the hallway beyond my chamber door. "We need you to behave now. Remember...try anything, and these will be only the start of your problems." In her hands, she stroked the small, throbbing satchel of flesh-eaters, as if she nefariously hoped to have the opportunity to implement it.

Curious as to the goings-on, I peered through the hall and into the basement, where more hunters occupied the room than before. Southey stood behind his desk, facing the large city map; leaning into the wall with his fists, he tongued a cigar in his mouth, while smoke fell from his nostrils. Far on the other side of the room, a small group of young men chatted with each other, playing cards, atop some of the crates and boxes. I recognized two of them; Southey's youngest son, with a scarred eye and both arms bandaged from the cuts he suffered the other night, sat next to the dark haired, muscular kid, who was also with Southey when he spotted me in Bayview Park.

To the arousal of the room, the heavy metal door atop the basement stairs opened. A familiar man entered and descended the stairs, wearing a dark, grey suit, and carrying a briefcase with the initials A.P. On his left hand, a ruby ring perched on his middle finger. It was the commissioner, the man who had met with Lee, providing us with the list of expendables.

What is he doing here? I wondered. I seemed to recall him telling Lee he did not know where Southey's operation was. I expected to see some sort of betrayal on his part, but to my surprise, he not only refused to help Southey, but he also denied any belief in vampires, hardly wavering in his skepticism, and consequently, infuriating Southey.

Arnold Paul knew about the scene in the cemetery the other night. He knew about Colin's death, and seemed to be getting short with Southey's public displays of violence. If anything, his visit wasn't about Southey's request for help, it was a warning. I could not understand, at first, why he did not arrest Southey. Given Arnold Paul's arrangement with Lee, it seemed that Southey's cunning antagonism would interfere, causing a heap of trouble for the commissioner. On the other hand, Arnold had told Lee he did not know where Southey was, yet there he stood. It then occurred to me that he was keeping both of his ends covered. The hunters were a great resource, and if Lee and his small following ever deviated from the list, or became too much of a burden, commissioner Paul could easily betray them over to Southey. On a similar note, if the hunters ever overstepped their bounds, Arnold could easily put an end to their little organization. Arnold kept both parties in the dark about his associations with their respective enemy; it was just a question of who would be double-crossed first.

By the time the brief visit ended, the commissioner had refused a plea of help from Southey, who angrily informed his men that they would go hunting for the witch in the woods alone.

Maida, no longer needing to threaten me into silence, exited the hall to speak with Southey, and reassured him that he could succeed if he just found the cabin, and the path beyond. The men gathered up their gear and left to kill the witch, and I was powerless to help her.

Night set in, and alone in misery, I went to rest, falling to the vociferous void of darkness, the overlapping thoughts of our collective minds which awaited unconscious vampires at night. I searched for the witch's voice among the sea of cries and whispers, trying to warn her of the impending hunt.

He's coming. Southey's coming for you with many other, I warned her, unsure if she heard me.

With thought, she whispered back, *And when he comes, I shall plant the seed of his doom, and of your freedom. I will curse him to his death. I will possess his mind.*

But what of you? There will be many of them, and with dogs.

I have many allies here. The witch did not sound worried. *I will not fail. I cannot fail. Here, I am forever! Stay strong Child...I have trees to feed tonight.*

That was the last I heard from her; she broke contact, and I assume, made preparation for what was to come. I called out to other voices, nearby and far away. I told them I had been captured, that I was to be used against them, by Southey, who found a way to see into our world, though me. My news stirred the anger of those who heard me, especially my acquaintances; I knew where they were, and this put them at higher risk.

We will find a way to help you, Child, Mira promised from across a sea of black. *Do not do anything to anger him.*

Lee cursed, his voice filled with ire. *What Southey is doing goes beyond good and evil. He must be stopped once and for all. We will reign the night again without fear.*

I am powerless to do anything. I thought of the maggots, and the horrible sensation they brought loomed in my memory. *I am below ground, chained in a cell. Unless he kills me soon, you may all be discovered.*

Then lead him to what he wants, Lee suggested. *Why suffer needlessly?*

I already have. He is off hunting one of us now. I thought of the witch.

Lee, seeing my thoughts, replied, *That is not what Southey really wants. You know who I mean. When the hunters return from those woods,*

Southey will continue to torture you until he finds Arthur.

Arthur's deep, aged voice rang out from the mesh of vocal ambiance. *Entering those woods carries a heavy price. Walking away with his life would not necessarily be victory.*

Lee snapped, annoyed at Arthur's voice, saying, *When are you going to atone for what you have created... and throw yourself at Southey?*

Soon enough, I expect, Arthur thought. *But as long as we continue to kill, we will have enemies in humans. Don't think your deal with the commissioner protects you from humans' wrath.*

The commissioner lied to us, I told Lee. *He has been here to see Southey, perhaps many times.*

What?! Lee cursed. *He has allowed us to be hunted needlessly, and for what? Does he not trust us?*

I was suddenly pulled from rest when a human voice cried out distractingly. I woke in my cell to find a young woman standing inside.

"Hello?" Shaken with emotion, her frightened, voice rattled the silence. "This isn't funny! Let me out! Answer me, somebody!" She rubbed her head as if in pain.

I did not move at first; she did not see me upon the floor beneath the pitch-blackness, and I observed her panic, indulging in the savory taste of fear. It was so close, and so strong, that I could not ignore it.

When nobody replied to her calls for help, she resigned her efforts and quieted, trying to get a sense of where she was. With her arms outstretched, she walked deeper into the cell, nearly treading on me. Unaware of the shape, or size of the room, and unable to see, the frightened lady crossed the floor, stepping over my passive corpse, oblivious to the monster beneath her feet. With her hands feeling the concrete, she followed the curved wall around the room.

I could have taken her life immediately, if I had desired. Yet I resisted, even though I knew she had been put there for that reason. I did not want to react like some animal, feeding off of what was thrown at me – there was no purpose, no dignity, in that.

Feeling the warmth of her presence, listening to the pounding of her heart and the short, rapid bursts of panicked breath screaming at me in the silence, I resisted the lure of her heightened emotions at first, but hunger would eventually creep up on me. I feared what I would become – would my true nature overpower my ability to choose the fate of myself and others?

Thus, a twisted game presented itself – a new layer to the madness. I would be driven to become what I desired least to be – a monster without a will of his own, meaningless in its existence and uninhibitedly evil.

I would have preferred to take a victimizer and not a victim, to become a monster to some other monster, like when I crossed paths with Lance that second time, and saw the fear in his eyes. Coupled with the knowledge of the terrible things Lance had done, I guiltlessly embraced my nature; I became the quintessence of a malicious karma, coming back around to smite him – a twisted justice turning evil back upon itself. However, I did not need some list crafted by an unhallowed hand to tell me whom to kill. I did not want the motives of others to corrupt what meaning I might find in the path I have chosen.

I watched the petrified lady stumble through the dark cell for a moment, and then I opted to try talking to her. "You are not alone." I could hardly get the words out before her yell covered them up.

Terrified of the sudden realization that she was in company, she screamed and ran along the wall, with her hands rubbing and clawing at the rough concrete. Finding the only door, she halted, feeling for a handle that wasn't there. She resorted to clawing and pounding against the wood relentlessly, desperate for aid that would not come.

I spoke to her softly, asking for her name, and pleading her to stop screaming, but my efforts only served to strengthen her fear. She would not heed my words when I told her it was not my intention to hurt her. Captivated by her horror, drawn to its sweet nuances, even I questioned the validity of my words.

I rose to my feet; the chains rattled against the concrete and her torment heightened to a new level. She crouched against the wall, curling up tightly. I walked closer, and with each soft clank of the metal links, she shrieked and spasmed.

With passing minutes, my temptations grew stronger; I was hypnotized by the frenzied beating coming from her chest. I watched her horrified eyes dart around the dark, trying to distinguish me from blackness, but it was hopeless for her.

When I neared the chain's limits, just a few feet from her, she stood up, and she cried out a long and terrible scream. Her overstressed voice dwindled to a rasp and she violently coughed, and reddened saliva fell from her lips onto the floor. She heaved, vomiting and nearly falling over, weakened from panic.

When I thought she had finally calmed down, she turned and pounded on the door, striking it so hard and so many times, the flesh quickly wore off of her hands. That did not stop her; resorting to using her arms, knees and feet instead, she thrashed herself against the solid wood until her bones began to break.

"Just stop for a moment. Talk to me. How did you get here?"

Every word I spoke seemed to rattle her emotions, driving her wilder. Limping from swollen joints and bruised flesh, she ran, around and around the room, like a maddened animal, trying to get away from me. Her desperation tempted me even more, and I could not shake the desire to lunge at her when she would sporadically stagger out from the wall.

When I tried to grab her, I found frustratingly few inches between her and my outstretched arm. She would not willingly move toward the center of the room. The chain ensured both of us would suffer as much as possible.

After hours of trying to talk her down, I had to end her suffering, for her sake or for mine. I became devilish; throwing my voice between her and the wall, I tried to get her to turn and run into the center of the room. I pulled at her clothes to get the fabric within reach of my fingers, but the tight clothing hardly lifted from her skin. She leaned into the wall to resist the ghostly tugging which she struggled to understand, beating her hands against her body in total confusion.

I grew frustrated, cursing her, tormenting her with my inhuman cries. I could not ignore her fear; her presence grew heavier on me. I had to kill her!

Both of us, at the mercy of our emotions, were trapped in this hell, perpetuating the situation to each other's torment. I became more and more demonic, which made her more scared, riling me further into madness. For hours, a sickening chase ensued. I was driven mad with desire, and refused her a single moment of peace. Beating herself raw against the walls and door, she ultimately collapsed by the door, out of reach, in a state of shock.

When the door opened later that morning, Southey and Maida stood in the hall and looked in to see what had become of her. I saw right away that something was different with Southey; his eyes were distant, his face almost without expression. His breathing was erratic and his posture tense. What had happened in the woods? Where was his mustached partner, his son? Southey's return made me fear for the witch, but from the sickened look upon his face, something spectacularly terrible had happened. Would this be what saves me, or would his heightened madness bring my torment to new levels?

Southey saw the tortured, incoherent girl lying still at the entrance to the cell, bruised and bloody, but still alive, and me, kneeling inches from her, held back only by a chain, with a gaping mouth of waiting fangs. With his boot, he kicked her within my range and shut the door, leaving me to ravenously finish her off.

I pounced on her, draining the life from her blood, feeling the warmth of her soul pass through me, invigorating my dead corpse with life's kiss. If I had the willpower to refuse taking her, I could have allowed myself to perish, but I was a vampire, and could not choose to be otherwise. The very fact I would devour whatever Southey tossed in the cell, meant he was in control of how long I would remain there.

Devastated at the prospects of liberation, but otherwise free from pain, from hunger and desire, I fell back into rest.

The witch was no more; her presence no longer in the murky realm of thoughts and memories. I called to her with no avail. The thought of her having been slaughtered by the likes of Southey riled my anger. I would make Southey pay for it, I just did not yet know how.

Many days passed; the wooden cell door didn't open again for what seemed to be at least a week's time. For a while, the only person I saw was Maida, who came each day with the dogs and the bag of maggots. She persisted at attempting to read my mind, and once in a while, tired at her tenaciousness, I would give in intentionally, revealing something utterly useless to her. Eventually, frustrated at my resistance to reveal to her those whom I had met, Maida opened the cell door and let the dogs have at me, or worse, with the dogs at bay, she forced me to endure being eaten by those small, writhing maggots. For a while, I held out, resting only in the daylight, as not to create a channel through which Maida would hear the other vampires.

At first, after he killed the witch, Southey hardly spent any time in the basement. I was unsure why, until he came to look over sketches Maida had drawn, I noticed his eyes were stale from exhaustion, and his skin paler. He mumbled like a madman, even when alone and unprovoked. Southey's fiery yellow hair suffered a few strands of white. Often I heard him cry his youngest son's name, Jacob, who never returned from the hunt. A raw and primal fear persisted in Southey; I sensed it intensely and had I not stood in those dark woods, heard those tormented cries, and seen the witch's corpse myself, I'd never have understood how one man could be so terrified. I knew she had cursed him, impairing his focus and keeping Southey away from me.

My pains of hunger grew steadily over that week, and I knew, when I woke to find a second young woman tossed into my cell, that I would not be able to resist her. Not wanting to witness again, that same degree of suffering, nor to experience the monster inside rise up and take over me, I carefully tried to talk to her. Unlike the first victim, I was able to get her to speak to me. I told her why she was there, and what happened to the first girl – of her needless pain. It was useless; she was horrified and quickly started down the same path as the first girl, breaking herself against the doors and walls. Eventually, she stumbled on a broken foot and fell mercifully into my range. Ours was a shorter agony than it might have been. Her name was Mana…what a beautiful name.

More days passed. From time to time, as he regained strength, or lost more of his sanity - it was hard to tell with Southey - he would storm into my cell, naked as birth, and free from my ghostly influences. With guard dogs as insurance, he beat me with his bare hands. He tried to extinguish the pain of the losses of his sons. He told me my plight would go on until he and Maida got what they wanted, and that he would feed me the entire city before he liberated me by taking my life. Sickened at what I had become, and just wanting it to end, the next time Maida came to my cell, I willingly gave up the location of Lee and the others at the abandoned mill. When Southey's partner, Sam, showed up for the first time since they had left for the woods, injured with a bandage on his neck, the two hunters wasted no time, using the newest sketches to lead them on a hunt for the four vampires.

My outlook grew even grimmer by the next day. Southey destroyed the mill, killing Lee and Elspeth. Mira and Bruce had managed to escape, luckily. I discovered this fortunate fact when I talked to them that night, in my resting state; they swore they would find a way to me. But I did not find out how. Our connection broke when I was stirred from rest, again, distracted by something present in the cell.

Under circumstances I did not understand, but openly welcomed, a third victim was put into the cell with me. I woke to find none other than Lance pounding against the cell door – just like the other girls had.

"Southey! Open up *now*!" Lance beat his fists into the door. A bloody wound on his head leaked down his face, and one eye was melted shut, with a chunk of smoking cigar welded to the eyelid. "People know I am here, they'll come looking!"

Lance found out the hard way of Southey's cruel and manipulative manners. Whatever deal the two men had arranged to provide Southey with lives to feed to me, it was broken at Lance's expense.

From behind the door, Southey grinned maliciously, holding Lance's damaged cane. "Sorry Lance, my resources are running low!"

"Fine! I will give you another girl, just open up! I'll give you *two*!"

I knew that I would enjoy eradicating Lance, but when I heard him say he had been the provider of the victims fed to me, I vowed to take my time with it.

"...Lance..." I dragged out his name into a long, dreary moan.

"Who's there?" He turned around, shaking his head back and forth, trying to make out the presence. It was much too dark to see, and he was down one eye. His mindset shifted from anger to fear; he did not yet know the ironic situation.

"It is funny how things have a way of working out, wouldn't you say?" I watched Lance's face go limp as he recognized the sound of my voice. Whatever forces kept bringing us together, in this life, and my previous, were about to end.

I made my way over toward him, making sure to drag the chain across the cement floor – being that the sound of it seemed to terrify the other two. "Perhaps karma is real after all, Lance. I mean, if it wasn't for your part in Dante's murder, I'd not be killing you now."

Lance screamed, swinging his arms around in the dark, with his back pressed to the wall. "You? How is...He said he *killed* you! No, this isn't happening!" Lance closely followed the wall around the room.

"He lied." I whispered, and from all over the cell my voice haunted him, repeating the words, "...he lied to you."

I was only a few feet from Lance, though he could not have possibly seen me in that sheer darkness. His pivoting head told me he had no real guess as to where I stood. I took notice of his layers of fancy linens, his jacket, leather belt, gold rings and chains. I felt their cool, smooth surfaces with my ghostly and manipulative hands, and with a quick but fierce heave, I had Lance stumbling into my range before he had time to realize what had happened.

"What the hell is going on?!" His limbs flailed as he flopped onto the hard floor, which was caked in blood, squashed maggots, and decaying flesh. Lance turned over onto his back, stunned and in submission, but he kept his head up.

"Where is Olyvia, Lance? Did you kill her, too?"

Lance stuttered and said, "That stupid little...She cried to the police...got herself arrested. Now they're after me..."

"...And they'll never find you...," I interrupted, rattling the chain against the floor, and continuing, "...not as you are *now*."

There was a long pause, a deep stillness, as Lance squirmed with the other maggots on the floor, pondering my threat, and waiting for the inevitable. Knowing I was hidden somewhere behind that curtain of black, and helpless to detect me, his nerves shook wildly.

I stood before him, invisible in that cell, trying my hardest to resist his sweet demise for as long as I could. Then, like a bolt of lightning, with the most foul and sinister howl I could summon, with the most intense decree of hatred as could be expressed, my hellish cry cut through the silence, blaring out behind Lance.

"Murderer!!"

Lance reflexively lunged away from my ear-piercing verdict, and when he did I immediately darted at him, kicking his face, and his head, back down onto the cement. There was a loud, hollow thud, and Lance's mouth filled with blood.

In the same terrible manner, I screamed, "You created me, and now you shall suffer for it!"

I listened to his incoherent mumblings, watching him attempt to crawl around the cell with limp limbs and eyes rolled back in their sockets, as he suffered a severe concussion.

"This is right...," I said to him, though I doubted his bruised brain heard my words. "...this is what I need to do. To kill you...and those *like* you. To hunt you like vermin!"

"I, uh. Stop it, wait. Pl...please. Uh, I didn't...I don't! ...S...Sou...South...Southey...?"

Lance's final words were a waste, as was his life.

Standing over him, I reached down and gripped his neck with my only hand, sinking my fingers deep beneath his flesh and tendons, and using them as a handle, I lifted him up, pressing him into the cell's low ceiling. My clenched fist squeezed his neck so hard that blood poured from his gaping mouth.

Burying my fangs deep into his jugular, tearing the flesh deep and wide, I was soon rewarded with Lance's death rattle, and that splendid warmth as his soul was ripped from his body. As soon as his heart fluttered its last, weakened beat, I dropped Lance to the floor and walked away from him.

I had finally done all I could do for Dante, and for me. That life could no longer have any relevance anymore.

That night I returned to rest, to that dark realm nestled between dreams and death, and tried to speak with Bruce and Mira again.

Arthur's voice found me first.

Southey hunts for me, Child. You know this. For years, I have been careful to remain hidden, and through my deeds, tried to achieve penance for the pain and trouble I have caused. If you lead Southey to me, you would not be at fault. You are a victim of the consequences of my actions, as were all the others he has slaughtered.

Arthur's passiveness to Southey puzzled me, and I inquired into the reasons of his inaction. *Why don't you leave the city? Why do you linger just to hide in guilt?*

As misguided as his actions are, Southey deserves his revenge, and if he finds me, I do not know if I would be right to keep it from him.

I don't want to lead him to you. My mind and Arthur's intertwined, and I showed him some of the horrible events that had unfolded in my underground chamber. *But I do not want to remain in this cell any longer.*

Then send him to me, Arthur offered, seeing the scenes of my nightmarish memories. *End your pain. I will accept whatever fate has chosen. Look at what I did to her, Child. Look at why Southey seeks me…*

Arthur showed me his thoughts, his memories from that fateful night, many years ago. I saw Southey's lost love, a woman with long, auburn hair and bright, hazel eyes, dressed in a wool skirt and white blouse, and carrying a leather briefcase with the initials E.R upon it. Walking along a sidewalk, in a dirty-looking part of town, she appeared to be in a hurry. When she glanced into a shadowed alley, something happened to catch her eye – an alley cat, a kitten, struggling to climb free from a filthy dumpster. Kind-hearted, she walked deeper into the grimy, littered alley, far into the shadows. Putting her briefcase down, she reached in and saved the trapped animal. When it was pulled free, she held it out before her, looking at it with a pitied smile, unaware of the tall, bald vampire, with a chiseled face inching close behind her. I watched Arthur sink his teeth deep into her shoulder. The woman flailed her arms, dropping the cat to the pavement, and with a free hand, she pulled from her pocket, a small, silver dagger with a blue, ceramic handle. With a swift and violent gesture, the short, narrow blade arced over her head, stabbing Arthur twice in the back. Freed from his bite, she ran out of the alley, clenching her bloody neck.

The memory faded, and blackness returned.

She was who Southey loved? I asked.

Yes. She perished a week later, and that thoughtless action of mine still shadows the city today, resulting in the harm of humans and vampires alike.

You could not have known what would come from it.

That is why it is so important to think about those you choose to kill. We may be capable of some good, but we are prone to much evil, and it takes effort to avoid chaos.

I thought back to the flutist, and how I had almost taken his life on that first night. His passionate song had soothed me in my confusion, as it did to all who fled beneath the canopy of Bayview Park. If I had taken his life, I would have robbed the city of something valuable, a purity of soul much too infrequent in the world. That was why Arthur was selective of his prey, not because it was a safer route, but because it made a better world, for him, for everyone.

Maida's presence began to grow heavy on my mind. I pondered fighting her, resisting her prying eyes in my moment of connection with Arthur, but seeing what I had, and recalling Arthur's approval of such a betrayal, I resigned to Maida's efforts. I let the memories flow for her. I thought of our meeting in the park. I thought of the church, with the dreary mural upon its face, the place I sat with Arthur, and talked. I thought of that woman Arthur killed years ago – Southey's love. I replayed her fateful encounter in my mind.

Having gotten what she wanted, what Southey had hoped for, Maida broke her connection and left with her prized sketches.

If it were truly my fate to perish in that cell, then who was I to change fate? Who was I to fight it? If it were meant that I should escape, I would deal with that when the time came. Until any further signs, I would have to put my trust in other forces.

Chapter 16 – The Long Awaited Moment

It was late in the afternoon, the day after burning the mill. Southey woke in a cheap motel room, alone. Sam had suggested that he hide out for the night, at least until it became evident whether or not the authorities would come asking questions. Southey had never attempted anything quite as destructive as setting an entire three-story building on fire, and he was unsure what to expect.

Better rested than he had been in weeks, Southey managed to get some scattered hours of sleep here and there, despite the stiff mattress and flat pillow. His utter exhaustion overcame him, and even her horrid face could not keep him from rest.

Staring at the plastered ceiling for what felt like an eternity, he wanted to get on his feet and leave, seeing that he had slept half the day away, but his achy back left him hesitant to sit up, and the thought of both his sons' deaths weighed him down.

Sam had left a few messages on his phone, the most recent one just an hour earlier, but Southey slept through them all; it was when he rolled to his side in order to scratch his back that he saw the blinking light on the phone and finally willed himself to sit up.

He listened to the most recent message, sent at 4:32 pm: 'Hey it's me. You okay? I'm starting to worry. Did you get the good news? Maida hit the jackpot, I think. Still no trouble, but there is something you should see. Turn on the TV. The news will be coming on. See you soon.'

Southey slid to the foot of the bed and tilted the small bolted-down motel television toward him. He turned it on to the local station. The previous night's adventure was on the five o'clock news. He leaned forward on the bed, watching intently.

A short, blonde female news reporter stood across from a smoldering heap of wreckage.

"Two people are dead and another injured when the old Myers, Wilson & Smith Textiles Mill burnt to the ground last night around 11:00 pm in what police are calling a blatant case of arson."

The news broadcast allowed Southey a first glimpse at his work. The fire appeared to have done its job well; one of the mill's outer walls had fallen into the parking lot, and the roof and floors had collapsed into the center, rendering the building a useless heap.

The camera showed a clip of a man receiving on-the-scene medical treatment; a bloody bandage was wrapped around his forehead; he said, excitedly, "...and we were watching the firemen put it out when the wall just fell on down and all this rock stuff flew threw the air, hitting us, and some cars...."

"Oh God," Southey shook his head. "Stupid bystanders, it serves them right for being so close to a burning building."

The reporter was back on camera, and said, "This and other long-deserted buildings have long been on the city's waiting list for demolition. Residents have complained for years of the dangerously eroded lots along this stretch of road, which have invited illegal activity for years, catering to the homeless and local gangs. To the frustration of many local residents, city officials have been procrastinating at getting this much needed demolition work done, and many of these buildings have been idle for well over a decade."

Southey knew he would not have a chance to grab breakfast. He lit a cigar and spaced out at the screen, listening for any red flags in the broadcast.

An officer on duty relayed information to the reporter, "Two homeless were killed. We found the remains of one victim buried inside, burnt beyond recognition. The other was a female. She was found outside, but seems to have jumped from the top floor, perhaps to escape the blaze. She severely broke her neck."

"Those weren't…" Southey gnashed his back teeth together; he knew there would be no mention of anything out of the ordinary with the deceased, not their identity, not the elongated canines in their mouth, not the armor they possessed when they perished, and especially not the strangely eroded nature of their corpses.

"It's already being covered up," he snorted.

The camera cut to footage taken just a few hours after the blaze was set. Parked in the back of the mill, almost obstructed by emergency vehicles, was a silver Cadillac with heavily tinted windows. Southey knew whose car it was; he had seen it pull into his parking lot many times over recent years.

"I'm speaking with Commissioner Paul," the reporter said as the camera cut to a young man's face. "Commissioner, was this a random crime, or is there some connection between this, and other destructive acts in the last few years?"

"We have been investigating these incidents for some time, and we have definite suspects. Fortunately, we have us a strong lead. Unfortunately, I cannot disclose that information at the moment."

"Were the two homeless victims responsible, in any way, for this?"

"No. Definitely not. They were in the wrong place at the wrong time. Many poverty-stricken folks take advantage of the accessibility of these places to sleep, which is what happened tonight. Unfortunately the two victims did not wake up in time to escape." Arnold looked right into the camera, as if he knew Southey was watching. "I can assure you that we will punish whoever is responsible. I will not allow this brand of random violence within my jurisdiction."

Arnold flashed a grin at the camera and when he turned away, Southey caught sight of a large red scratch, fresh-looking and about three inches long, on the back of the commissioner's neck.

"Hmm," Southey thought to himself, with some suspicions about the relatively fresh-looking abrasion.

Then, at the end of last night's footage, Southey caught a glimpse of the commissioner driving away from the scene; only, he left in a cop car, not in his silver Cadillac, which was no longer parked in the mill's rear parking lot.

"What...?" Southey did not know what to make of it.

The broadcast went live again, as the news reporter signed off. "We'll be sure to keep you updated as it develops. Until then, this is Becki O'Brian, channel three news."

Southey turned off the television. Suspicious, he pondered the situation. "What the heck is he...? Something is up! He'll come to see me. I know it!"

Southey puffed on his cigar; his eyes darted around the room as he concentrated on the problem at hand. His sense of severity heightened when he recalled Sam's good news, and how urgent it was that they act quickly, lest police intervene.

Anxiously, Southey grabbed his few belongings and left the motel. For safety's sake, he had not driven to the motel in his black van, rather, he made use of the sporty red car Lance no longer needed. The keys had been left in the ignition, to his luck. He would not have gone back into the cell to take them from his dead body.

When Southey returned to Redbank Apartments, pulling onto the dead end road and into the small lot among his buildings, he let out a sigh of relief – there were no police waiting for him. The idea of authorities coming for him was not the major concern to him; it was the possibility that they might interfere before he could do what he needed to do – get his coveted retribution. After succeeding, he would care less as to what crimes he was charged with, he would have kept his word to Ellen...that is what mattered most to him. However, it had been well over twelve hours since the fire was set, and Southey could not help but be suspicious of the police's delay – a sure sign that Arnold Paul had taken the helm in this investigation.

Sam and the two dogs were waiting out by the black van as Southey returned. Sam, loading a prepared bag of weapons into the back of the van, turned to nod at his friend whose face he could hardly see through the coupe's tinted windows.

Southey grinned at Sam, and then jumped from the car. He threw his half-smoked cigar into the street and hurried toward the building.

"Good morning...or afternoon, I could say. You got the message, I assume?" Sam sat on the back bumper, brushing his feet against the ground.

"Yeah, is Maida in there? I want to see what she's got." Southey blurted, as he walked swiftly past Sam. The dogs followed him, sniffing at his heels.

"Yes. What do you...?" Sam hardly got the words out before Southey unlocked the metal door and stomped hastily down into the basement.

"Maida!" Southey yelled, quickly growing impatient when he saw that she was not in the main room. He hurried across to the desk, where a fresh pile of sketches awaited his inspection.

With shaky hands, quivering from the idea that he might be holding the final clue, Southey turned the sketches upright.

As always, the drawings were crude, but effective. The first on the pile depicted a slender brunette with long hair, standing in an alley. She was reaching into a dumpster. A pale face loomed in the scribbled-blackness behind her.

"Ellen," Southey whispered, recognizing his love at once. The almost abstract lines on the paper had captured perfectly the essence of the curves in her body – which he remembered well. "...what are you doing?"

He looked at another of Maida's drawings; it portrayed the same woman reaching behind her, at a tall figure whose mouth was pressed to her shoulder. Her gaping mouth screamed in silence. Visible in her hand was the poniard given to her by Southey, used to knife the vampire twice in the back before escaping.

"Stab him, Elle. Get him..." Southey could hardly hear his own words, choked by emotion; his eyes welled with tears, yet his cheeks remained dry.

Southey flipped to the next one. The same deathly figure, the cause of Southey's ruined life, the target of his utmost and perverted hatred, sat at a pew in a familiar looking church. Next to his target sat the vampire now imprisoned in Southey's cell.

"You guys buddies?" he uttered.

Southey pressed the paper close to his tired eyes. He inspected curiously the vaguely-drawn features of his enemy. Ellen hadn't the energy to describe the vampire well to Southey, nor coherently, when she finally found the courage to, swollen and feverish on her deathbed.

"I'll kill both of you." His voice was weak.

Southey stared at the image closer and his heart skipped a beat when he recognized something about the church's interior. He reached for an older stack of papers, looking for a sketch Maida had drawn days ago. In that particular sketch was depicted a church steeple known for its dreary mural of good and evil. Although Maida's sketch did not capture the smaller details, Southey knew it well. The devil stood in darkness, at the bottom, perched upon the bodies of the damned; and far above his head, angels in white light soared in the heavens. At the peak of the steeple, a bust of Jesus emerged from the flat wall, clenching a large cross in His right hand.

"What kind of sick irony is this?" Southey mumbled to himself. Had the creature that he had searched for been hiding here for all these years? He did not want to believe it.

Southey clenched his fist, crumpling the paper into a wad. "That dirty leech! Ruining *her* memory with *his* festering filthy corpse!" Southey hollered as loud as he could.

The small arched wooden door opened, and Maida, concerned, exited the hallway beyond.

Curious as to his anger, she approached Southey. "What are you yelling about? Did I not find him for you?"

"Are you sure *this* is it, and not somewhere else?" Southey threw crumpled paper at her feet.

His doubt annoyed Maida. "I can't draw *all* that I see, and I saw *more* than this. That creature hides in the church's cellar...he killed her. I saw it with my own mind!"

Maida raised her hand in the air, as if she thought of striking Southey but decided against it when it became abundantly clear how irate he was over this development.

She glared at Southey. "Why?"

"This is the church where Ellen had her funeral. I go there every year...on the day." Southey closed his eyes and took a deep breath, and when it seemed he was calm and collected, he opened his eyes wide, and screamed, "He's practically spitting on her grave by being there! What a curse! What a ...a..."

Southey lunged at the large satellite map on the wall. He smashed a second web-like crack into the glass with his fist, tearing the skin from his knuckles.

"It is like God *Himself* is taunting me! Who am I, *Job*?" Southey kicked the frame again, this time with his boot. Glass shards rained onto the concrete; the map was torn.

"Then burn the church down with God *and* the devil inside." Maida's eyes widened. She enjoyed the sound of the idea and snickered, "Yes, let them work out their problems alone, *together*.

You've been in their crossfire *much* too long."

Southey pointed to the arched door, which Maida left ajar, letting malodorous air from the cell seep into the basement. "Is Lance still in there?"

"Yes. I was about to get rid of it."

Southey screamed at her, pounding his fist off of the desk, "You should have done that last night! What if the police came?" Southey searched through a desk drawer for something that was not there. "The keys! Maida, do you *have* them!?"

Maida hastily reached under her flowing dress; the jingle of metal was heard.

"They are safe. I wouldn't leave them lying around while you are gone."

"You had better keep those doors locked from the moment I am gone until I come back, and do not go anywhere, either, or I swear to God Maida...!"

Southey then reached into another drawer, removing the wide, short-bladed dagger, once owned by Ellen. Unsheathing it, he gripped its blue, ceramic hilt and held it high above his head.

Maida gasped, and staggered back with her arm in the air, defensively, as Southey stared up at the blade; it appeared to her that he was holding back laughter.

"Are you *afraid* of me, Maida? Do you think I am going to stab you?"

When he looked down, Southey unleashed a stare so foul upon Maida that she shuddered. His narrowed, watery eyes glistened red, like some hellish demon. Dark rings from exhaustion deepened the pits of his eyes like a skull, and he clenched his jaw so tightly, his temples bulged out. When he breathed deep, heavy breaths, his nostrils flared and his phlegmy trachea rattled like some growling creature. Though his fingers writhed nervously, like a dying spider, his posture remained tall and still.

He sheathed the blade, putting it between his boot and leg. "If all goes well, this will be black with filth tonight, not *red*...with yours."

Having witnessed how absolutely sinister Southey had become, and knowing how expendable everyone who stood between him and his goal was, Maida was humbled and her voice lost its sting.

"I will have the body gone long before you return, and then you can finish off the leech in there and call it a day."

"I'll call it a *life*," Southey grumbled.

"You're quitting?" Maida raised an eyebrow; the power she had tasted was too good for her to just walk away from. She had developed a growing lust for manipulating the forces of death.

Maida slowly walked closer to Southey. "Do you think you will just go on like it all never happened, dreaming dreams of victory until you die?" When she stood beside Southey, he turned his head to look down upon her, heeding her words. "There is *nothing* for you to go back to, not anymore…not with the things you've seen…not with the things we've done." She stood on her toes to bring her lips to Southey's ear, "…and not with the things you've *lost*."

Southey did not say a word, but continued to clench his jaw, and move his fingers nervously, staring ahead with a look as if he were not present at that moment.

Maida manipulatively attempted to channel his emotions into her command.

"The last ounce of Robert Southey, the widower still left inside you, will die tonight along with this foul leech!" She pointed to a sketch upon the desk. "With that transition, you shall become, and remain forever, *Southey*, the vampire hunter."

Southey uttered, almost incoherently, "No…I'll still be…the same. I'll still be *me*."

Maida interrupted him, "If you stop, their numbers will climb. What will become of the city? And those voices, those dreams…that damned witch's curse will haunt you forever. You must fight! Do not resign!"

Southey stared off for a moment, thinking, for the first time, of what use he would ever find for himself once he has achieved his goal. What if the police did not come for him? What if Arnold Paul continued to ignore his legal infractions? What would he do with his time? Could he possibly find serenity in everyday life, alone, without his sons, his love, his purpose, or his sanity? What was left to do but the only thing that seemed real to him – kill vampires.

Southey turned from Maida and walked back across the basement, toward the metal stairs leading up and out. Numb to the ghostly voices plaguing his mind, calling his name, he could no longer distinguish them from his own thoughts.

When his foot rested on the first step, he paused and said, "It's not my city anymore. It never was about the city to begin with. I need to get away from it…forever. As long as I am here, as long as I am me, I can never be free." Southey exited the basement in a daze of depression.

Waiting up in the lot, Sam was kneeling down, patting Cain and Abel, and when he glanced up at Southey, he saw the change in disposition. He hesitated before daring to speak.

"So, what did you think? It's him?" Sam stood, looking at Southey's face, concerned; he could not make eye contact with his troubled friend's shifting eyes.

Southey spoke with short breaths. "It's him. Definitely. We'll head out soon...Real soon. I'm famished. Weak. I just need a...a quick bite to eat. Drive through, or something. Okay? Where are Bill and Blair?"

"Are you going to be alright?" Sam asked, receiving an unconvincing nod from his friend. To him, Southey appeared as someone might if they knew there was a bomb attached to them which could go off at any moment. "I called Bill and Blair a cab, late this morning. Do you think we'll need them?" Sam hadn't ever seen Southey so distraught.

Southey rubbed his face with his hands, taking a deep breath and gaining a bit of control. "It couldn't hurt, but I don't want to risk the drive across town to get them. Maybe we'll just take the dogs instead...just once."

Sam looked down at Cain and Abel. "I imagine you are going against all reason, and plan on burning the place down."

"I'm not worried about the legal consequences." Southey mumbled to him, "I'm not planning on getting away with it."

"I don't want to see these dogs trapped inside, that's all."

"This leech could be a bit rowdy. We need a threat of our own." Southey looked down at Cain and Abel.

When the silence lingered beyond a few seconds, Sam gestured to Southey, "Well, I have the basics in the van. We can go whenever you want. I'd suggest soon, given the buzz we've generated, and the fact that it will be dusk in a few hours. We don't want him going anywhere. We can't afford a chase."

Southey looked up to the sky; in the west, the sun was trapped behind thick, cumulus clouds, tinted like fiery coals, while in the eastern sky, a crescent moon floated in a crystal clear sea of dark blue.

"Let's go get this bastard! I'm sure he's waiting for us."

The two men and dogs entered the van. With Sam behind the wheel, the four hunters followed the gritty roads up to the highway, and from there, around the small bay and into the downtown for quick drive-through food.

Sam parked in the restaurant's rear, and the hunters ate. Southey sunk his teeth into a greasy hamburger, and somehow, the food tasted better than ever, as if he tasted it for the first time.

Sam rustled through a paper bag for loose french fries. "You haven't said anything yet."

"About?" Southey inquired, his mouth full of beef.

"The church," Sam replied as he handed the dogs a couple plain hamburger patties. "I mean, how many times have you gone there...to pray...for this?"

"I don't remember. *How* many years has it been...? Anyway, the fact that this leech is in this church is not some gift from God... It is a slap in the face."

"It could be seen either way."

"Much too late." Southey tossed his trash out the window of the van and then reached for a fresh cigar. "*Way* too late." Before he lit it, he pulled it beneath his nostrils and inhaled, and it smelled so good, so fresh, it was like he was having the first cigar of his life.

Sam watched his friend's ritual, and the following pleasure as the first waft rolled off his tongue, striking the windshield.

Southey perched the cigar in his gapped teeth, and blurted, "How could he have been hidden from me for so long, and yet so close by? Damn it! Under my nose, even!"

"After we do this, I think you should just leave town."

"I planned on it." Southey snapped back.

"Don't worry about me," Sam shrugged. "I got places to go, people to visit."

For a short while, the two men sat silently in the van, listening to the dogs lick the remnants of food from the floor, and feeling the light wind blowing through the open windows.

Sam tugged at his mustache, deep in thought, while Southey sucked on his smoke, and when the dazed men became aware how much time had been wasted – almost forty minutes – Sam started the van. Before he could put it into drive, Southey reached over and put his hand on Sam's shoulder.

"Thanks." The worn out hunter said with a most faded, yet sincere smile.

Sam nodded and moved out from the parking lot, heading south of the main commercial sector. Less than two miles from where they ate, near the edge of a small, middle class neighborhood, the steeple of their destination loomed over the trees and telephone wire; the stone bust of Jesus Christ, holding a large white cross in his right hand, emerged into view.

Sam pulled the van into the lot beside the small church; there were a couple cars parked outside from an earlier mass. He parked in the back, to avoid detection by police who would likely travel the road at some point.

The men exited the van and stood still, looking around them cautiously.

"I will go in and send everyone out," Southey ordered. "You wait by the front door with the dogs until they storm out, upset at the angry man. Then come in."

He rounded to the back of the van and opened the doors; the dogs awaited permission to exit.

Sam stood next to Southey, "Okay. That might be good. I can keep an eye out for the time being."

Southey reached into the duffel bag and removed a small metal canister and some matches. "You hold onto my gun at first. I don't want to come off as some sort of serious threat, and have them call the cops on me. God knows they'd respond in a heartbeat."

"I don't think the gun is the only thing that'd scare them." Sam smiled. "No arm blade?" he questioned, as he attached one to his right arm.

"Nah. If he gets close enough, I will hold on to him until this baby gets her turn..." Southey reached down, patting the blue-hilted dagger from his boot cuff. "...or until the flames consume both of us."

Southey walked from the van, and around to the front of the church where he halted on the first step. He looked up at the mural and pondered the irony that his enemy was here, in a church depicting both God and the devil on its wall.

When he had first seen Maida's drawing of the church's steeple, he figured a vampire had merely passed it by; it seemed wholly unnatural to him that a vampire would want to enter a church, let alone live in one.

He climbed the short stairway, and when he placed his hand upon the door, a deep and unthreatening ghostly voice called in the air around him.

"I have heard your prayers over the years, on those lonely anniversaries. I have felt your mourning, your rage, and your want." The voice spoke softly, not opting for demonic yells and shrieks, as Southey had been accustomed to. "I *am* sorry," the voice continued.

Southey grinded his teeth together; hearing that killer's voice apologize to him almost numbed his hate – and the accompanying hesitation to proceed angered Southey.

With his shaking hand on the door's large metal handle, Southey waited and then grumpily responded, "...your *point*?"

"I am here *because* of that terrible night...to hide from you, the crazed hunter, in the *only* place you never went...in this church to mourn your lover. In here, you were never the monster you've now become. You were human, softened, and vulnerable. But when you left the sanctity of this church, your mind became rapt with hate."

"I plan to bring that hate inside, this evening." Southey pulled on the door, but it was resisting his efforts, by will of the vampire. Southey raised his foot to kick it in anger, but before he struck his boot against the thick wood, the voice spoke out.

"Killing me won't end your pain, Southey."

"Killing you is the only thing that keeps me going. I want revenge."

Southey was frozen; he was torn between storming into the church with fiery wrath, and asking the creature about Ellen – why he chose her? What was the vampire's obsession with Ellen's death that brought him to nest there? He could not believe that the creature possessed guilt; how could a monster, a born-killer, and guilt, co-exist?

"If your quest was to kill me, then why am I the last, of so *many*, to die?" The voice grew ominous, and bellowed, "Have you finally become that which you hate? What really dictates your life, and your choices?"

Southey thought back to the dozens of slain vampires, his two sons, and the hunters whom had fallen for him over the years. "Nothing can stand in my way...I swore on her deathbed! On her *deathbed*!! I promised her vengeance as I watched her eyes fade away from me! You could never understand what that means, never! And you can no longer hide from me you putrid, filthy, cursed leech!"

Southey pulled open the door mightily, and with no resistance, it swung open and slammed into the church's outer wall with a sharp crack of wood. He stepped into the rear of the church. Seven people sat among the pews, either looking down in prayer, or up above the altar, at a domed ceiling, painted with an image of heaven and its saints.

The fourteen stained-glass windows on the walls were still illuminated by the fading sun, and their prismatic light softly lit the fourteen rows of pews, which were divided by a wide, red carpet stretching to the altar. Matching red tapestries hung between the windows, reaching to the floor.

Southey marched slowly down the carpeted aisle, looking side to side at the faces of the faithful; most of them were elderly folk who had lingered long after mass, clenching rosary beads in their wrinkled prayer hands. No heads turned to see the crazed man strolling into the church, and Southey heard the soft murmur of scattered prayers, and then among them, the vampire's voice softly beckoned him.

"Go back, before it is too late for you," it warned him.

No sooner did Southey smirk at the suggestion did he notice a young, vibrant head of hair in the furthest pew up at the front. A police radio crackled, dominating the silent atmosphere. The police commissioner, Arnold Paul, stood up from the bench and turned to face Southey. He gestured the confused hunter to sit beside him.

Southey took a few more steps, but stood at the end of the bench, leering maliciously at the commissioner.

"What are *you* doing here?" Southey's harsh whisper was loud, unable to suppress his anger. "How did you know to come *here*?"

"I know a lot of different people, living *and* dead," Arnold nodded, sitting back down.

"I didn't see your fancy car outside."

"I was dropped off by some of my men under the assumption you'd come. I'm glad you did. I've been here for most of the day." Arnold tapped his police radio and said, "Backup is on the way now, so sit and pray things go smoothly." He stared forward, seeming unconcerned about Southey.

"I will not let you stop me from doing this, you backstabbing son of a...!" Southey screamed, kicking the bench hard.

The gasps of the concerned attendees could hardly be heard over the echo of his boot.

Arnold turned to face him, "Backstabbing? No...I was never on *your* side. But I'm not really on *theirs* either. I'm on my side and what is best for the city."

"What are you talking about?" Southey stepped closer to the commissioner, a lot confused. "How in any way does helping a leech help a city?"

"Vampires *have* to kill, Robert. There's no fighting it. You have been fighting it for years, and look at you. You're *ruined*." Arnold chuckled. "Maybe we should just learn to accept them. Anything can be a resource if you figure out how to tap into it properly."

Arnold slid along the bench, closer to Southey, and whispered up at him, "I'm told that you have found your *own* use for them." Arnold laughed and shook his head. "I never did ask you what was behind that little wooden door, but don't think I didn't wonder."

Seeing that Southey had no intention of sitting, or calming down, Arnold stood, glancing at the onlookers before continuing.

"When you control *who* they kill, you can get a lot done. The crime rate has dropped considerably in the last year, for instance."

"But...?" Southey was stunned. "How..."

"Every few months, for more than a year now, I have given groups of vampires a list of names. Think of it as...a diet. And they stick to it....well, *some* do. Not all vampires are within these isolated groups, and those are the ones who aren't protected."

"Protected? The armor?" Southey mumbled.

"Yeah, but that's only the start, though. I was referring to a public blanket to keep their presence unknown, specifically from you...and anyone else who would bear the public humility of being a vampire hunter." Arnold laughed. "If enough people believed in vampires, they would all be dug from their holes and destroyed in a day...and you'd be the hero, and not the crazy codger...which would make me a big bad liar. I hope you can see how your repeated requests for help have put me in a really awkward situation."

Almost choking on anger, Southey asked, "Is the leech in here one of *yours*?"

"No, I actually had no idea about him, until recently. Anyway, I didn't come here because of that...You killed two of my pets last night. Sure, you've done it before, but this was more serious, and now I am pressured to react. So I came here...to stop you...forever."

Southey, noticing Arnold's right hand moving toward his holstered gun, quickly interjected, "Is that why you have that nasty scratch on your neck? Pressure?"

Arnold lifted his right hand to rub the wound, "Yeah, they..."

Southey lunged forward in a mad rush of fury; he grabbed Arnold's head, pulling it downward, violently striking his forehead with a rising knee.

The commissioner was unconscious before he fell, lying limp between the benches.

Southey turned to face the concerned occupants of the small church, many of which were already rushing for the doors.

"Everyone get the hell out of here before I kill each and every one of you! Go, go, and go!" Southey screamed, pointing at random folks. While running up and down the aisle, he squirted the vaporous liquid from the canister around the church – on the altar, over the pews, on the tapestries hanging down from the ceiling, and then he threw the canister at the altar.

When he was satisfied, Southey removed the book of matches from his pocket. Before he could drop the flaming book to the floor, Sam entered the church, with Cain and Abel barking at the air wildly.

"I hear sirens! How did they know?" Sam yelled, confused.

Southey dropped the flaming book to the ground and the fires branched out across the room, up the tapestries, climbing to the ceiling, and down the aisle, reaching among the pews. He knew time was already running low.

"Because Arnold Paul is here! He's passed out for the moment, too much *excitement*."

Sam handed Southey a shotgun, and the angered hunter gripped his weapon and stormed to the front of the church, yelling to the presence he knew was watching over the event.

"Come on out and let's have it! I will *not* leave you to rest until I see you burn!" Southey fired a shot into the ceiling, sending plaster raining down.

A heavy, cool breeze lifted through the church; it put out all the candles on the altar, shook the lights hanging on long cords from the ceiling, and blew the flaming red drapes like fiery whips. The room howled in fury.

A booming voice cracked like the first note of thundering storm, "Then let's have it done with."

In a wave of clatter and clanking, the kneelers under the benches all fell from their up and idle position, rattling the church from front to back; when the clamor reached the back of the church, near the entrance, the doors swung open with a menacing force.

Southey saw the flashing of blue lights outside, from an approaching police car. Before he could worry about someone coming in, there was a tremendous thud of rock and stone from above them. The arm and cross from the bust of Jesus fell free from the steeple, crashing in front of the door; blocking the exit was a heap of rubble and wood.

Southey turned back to face the front of the church. He hesitated on his first step when, to his surprise, he saw a figure standing on the furthest end of the church. He recognized him from the sketches. Old in appearance, but not at all thin or weak looking, the tall, bald vampire had a chiseled face and the semblance of a statue, but was not so pale you'd immediately identify him as a corpse. He loomed motionless at the altar, in plain dark-colored clothes, with deep blue eyes gleaming from the flames.

"There he is!" Southey yelled.

He ordered the dogs to attack, but they were hesitant to move. Not only did the fire deter them from progressing, but they whined, shaking their heads, as if something pestered their ears, driving them back. The fire had spread far across the floor, and the room was filling fast with black smoke; he could hardly find anger at his dogs' disobedience.

Though the vampire hadn't moved an inch, Southey was losing sight of his target. He lifted his shotgun, taking steps slowly down the aisle, his gun's barrel leading each step. Sam was only a few feet behind.

A shot rang out, and instinctively, Southey turned toward the sound. Arnold Paul was standing upright. His nose was bleeding badly, which he held with one hand, and with the other, pointed a smoking barrel at Sam. From the look on Arnold's face, he was only just then realizing how large the fire was.

Southey turned to see his comrade hunching down, holding his arm. The wound was not fatal, but that was lucky – Arnold appeared a bit dizzy from the knee to his skull.

Arnold staggered around the fiery row of pews, ducking to see below the smoke. As he made his way to the rear of the church, by the exit, he yelled back, "Robert Southey, you are under arrest for the destruction of public and private property, the murder of innocent people, and a bunch of other things I care not to mention right now!"

Southey stood over Sam, but kept turning back and forth between Arnold on one end of the church, and the vampire looming up ahead. Torn at his options, he only moved when Sam pushed on his leg, suggestive that he should descend the aisle and go for the vampire.

When Arnold realized that the heavy debris made escape impossible, he began desperately throwing his weight into the doors, trying to push the rubble, fearful of the growing fire. He then turned to see what Southey was doing, and decided to aim his gun at the hunter's back.

"Get him!" Sam snapped his fingers and pointed toward Arnold as he yelled to the dogs. Cain and Abel hesitated only until the command was repeated again. "Get *him*!" Sam pointed at Arnold, again, snapping his fingers louder.

The obedient canines charged Arnold, who hurried to point his gun down at them, but the swift dogs quickly clamped their jaws down upon his hands. The commissioner screamed as he wrestled with the two animals.

Southey ran down the aisle, through a cloud of black, towards his devil, darkened by the shadows of fire and smoke. His heart raced, in disbelief that the moment was finally at hand. When he found himself standing ten feet away from the vampire, Southey lifted his shotgun without any resistance or trickery.

"Stupid leech. Fight back and let me *taste* it!"

The vampire stood still, watching Southey as he pulled the trigger. The shot struck its chest, tearing holes in his clothes and body. The creature fell backwards through fiery rings on the altar.

"Yeah! Burn in hell!" Southey howled, cocking his gun to prepare for another shot. He felt high; adrenaline surged through his veins.

Southey removed the silver dagger from the sheath in his boot. Prepared for the final strike, the one that would leave him without doubt, he held the weapon out and said, "Recognize *this*?" He would sever the creature's head and cut its spine – or die trying.

As Southey stepped up to the altar, with his gun in one hand, and the dagger in the other, the church door suddenly opened when firemen pried the small boulders blocking the way. Though Sam was standing over Arnold Paul, keeping the angered commissioner under control with the dogs by his side, the end was near for both hunters. Arnold sprinted for the exit, into the range of police.

Southey's mind raced; he knew it would take a few moments to finish the job, but in much less than a minute, maybe even ten seconds, police would rush in, likely with the order from Arnold to shoot to kill. Southey questioned if he really was ready to die; though he had said he would hold the creature until the flames swallowed them both, seeing the reality of death was different than picturing it in his mind.

Southey looked at the creature lying on the altar. Inviting Southey to come and end it, its voice called out to him, saying, "Come, Southey. Get your revenge...or is this not how you *hoped* it would be?"

Revenge – the word echoed in Southey's mind. Was this revenge...taking the life from a creature willing to die? Southey's head began to hurt; he was confused. Then, recalling the creature back in his cell, the one that killed Colin, Southey knew he couldn't die yet. He still had one more dish of revenge to serve...just one more savory, lustful act of violence...for Colin's sake, and then he would be done – he assumed.

But he did not have the time to enjoy the death of his devil as he had hoped, and to his utter frustration, Southey sheathed the dagger. He then pointed his shotgun at the tall stained glass window to his left and fired; as the shattered glass fell, smoke gushed out the opening. He approached the window and looked out.

At the entrance of the church, Sam was holding his arms up with his hands behind his head; his back was turned to the police, and he looked down the aisle at Southey, wondering what was going on.

Southey cocked his gun, turned and aimed up at the ceiling above the altar, firing many times in quick succession. Large chunks of wood, plaster and paint rained down onto the vampire, still lying motionless on the fiery altar. Its arms and legs were soon to be swallowed by flames, and the fresh kindling laid down by Southey's gunshots would speed up the fire.

"The flames will get him. It's ok. He's dead." Southey ranted to himself as he turned back to the broken window. "I did it... The flames *will* get him. The flames *will* get him." Southey repeated the words over and over.

He had turned down the moment of which he yearned for years – seeing with his own eyes the destruction of the beast that killed his Ellen, to die for her, to join her, perhaps. He did so not only in cowardice, but to selfishly have one more taste of that bittersweet vengeance he felt each time he destroyed a vampire.

Though he only fell a few feet to the ground from the church window, his achy body screamed in pain from the landing. It was twilight, and luckily for him, no one saw Southey land by the outer wall. He quickly rose to his feet, leaving his shotgun on the grass and ran for the black van parked in the back. To his ecstasy, Sam had left the keys in the ignition, ready for a quick escape. Southey started the vehicle, alerting nearby police, but he drove off the lot before authorities managed to get to their cars. Knowing the area as well as any cop, Southey pushed the van to its modest limits, cleverly zigzagging through small neighborhoods and making his way back onto the highway.

"I'm going to do it. I'm going to do it!" Southey laughed, as he drove back around the bay, toward the industrial park. "I'll kill *him* too! Ha, ha, ha! I'll kill them *all*!" His spit hit the windshield. "All of them!"

Southey made his way back to his apartment without police intervention; however, as he turned into the parking lot, he saw something that sent a spasm jolting through his body. A silver Cadillac with heavily tinted windows was parked next to Lance's red car.

"There's no way he…," Southey mumbled, as he stepped on the gas. "…I'm not afraid of the *police*." He laughed insanely. "If they're here then I'll kill them too! They're all *filthy* leech-lovers!"

Southey slammed the van into the back of the Cadillac, sending it rolling headfirst into a dumpster. The crashing of metal brought many onlookers to the surrounding apartment windows to see what had happened.

Southey staggered out of the van and walked to the heavy, metal door leading down into his headquarters. When his tremoring hands finally unlocked the door, he descended the metal stairs, mumbling wildly to himself. He immediately caught sight of something that emptied his bladder – Maida's body lay headless in a pool of blood in the center of the floor, and across the room, atop his desk, upon the stack of her own drawings, was Maida's severed head. Her pale face screamed in silent horror, with a gaping mouth, and eyes dug from her skull.

The door to the hallway leading to the cell was closed. Southey walked up to Maida's decapitated corpse and knelt down, feeling under her dress for the keys she had hidden, but he could not find them. It was then that he noticed the bite marks hidden beneath the blood, on her gory, headless neck.

Southey stared down at the corpse, aware that his every gesture was being scrutinized, that unseen eyes were watching him from very close by. He was totally alone, and closed his eyes tightly, with the assumption he was about to be slain.

A deep, burly male voice grumbled in the air, "Someone would like to see you, Southey!"

A dull throb, a quick, burning sting, a flash of light, and Southey went black, having been struck from behind by something laying in wait. It was over for him.

Chapter 17 – Deliverance

I expected Maida to run off and tell Southey of her discovery, about Arthur and the church, and then for him to come blazing into the cell with his dogs, his blade, his gun, anything at all; he did not need me anymore, and I knew that avenging the death of his son, Colin, weighed heavy on his mind. He would kill me as soon as the opportunity presented itself; however, there was no wrath that night. Southey was not at his desk, Maida did not come back to torment me, and for awhile, I was left to anticipate the inevitable.

Lance's corpse was not as quickly disposed of as the other two, and I stared at it for much of the night as it changed over the hours. A deepening death and a loss of blood rendered the skin of his corpse an ashen color. His mouth was frozen open in its final awkward gape, with the tongue curled back in his throat, reminiscent of his death rattle. His fingers clawed out for a monster that no longer threatened him. One of his eyelids was welded shut with a chunk of cigar ash still upon it; the other eye stared out into darkness with the realization of true horror and the certainty of his demise.

Would Lance become a vampire if left steeping in death long enough? What determined who rose to become vampires, and who mercifully remained at peace? Perhaps it was contingent upon the condition of the corpse, as Lucia once suggested. Maybe the nature of the life lived by the deceased also played a role. Maybe God chose the vampires Himself. Whatever factors suffered me into this new, overdrawn life, be it choice or chance, I grew jealous of Lance's freedom from pain. I wanted to switch places with him, to return to that peaceful place before I fell into darkness, and let him remain trapped in the cell, like the monster he was.

I tried to recall that warm light and empty space from which I plummeted into my waking, but much of my remembrance had fleeted, and like a dream within a dream, I could not harness the thought.

Daylight came. I heard the sunlight shrieking as a wispy ray reached through the crack in the boards of the sealed window in my cell.

Not much longer now, I thought. My final hours were upon me, and I was unable to rest. My twisted captor would soon return·to see what coveted knowledge Maida had extracted, and after some premeditated and sadistic torture, I would be freed from the cell through a death dealt by Southey – if all went well.

Maida came into the basement with Sam, her sketches still

waiting to be discovered upon Southey's desk. Sam looked intently at the drawings, nervously playing with his thick, grey mustache. He nodded with acceptance, and pulled out a phone and called Southey to share the news, wherever he was hiding. When she was left alone in the basement, Maida walked over to the arched wooden door, opening it, staring into the small, stony hall.

"He'll be here soon, rested and ready to deal with you," she spoke like a demonic child.

"I welcome it. I have nothing left to fear from him or you."

Maïda laughed, "So you say, but you have a lot to learn about suffering, I *promise*." She stepped into the hall, shutting the small wooden door behind her.

As Maida stepped slowly down the sloped hall, toward the door to my cell, she projected her words into my mind, riling my anger with her probing psychic eyes.

You will not die as easily as you think. Her poisonous words echoed in my mind. *Southey needs me, and because of this, I control him. I shall see to it that yours is not a merciful stroke of death, and that he makes you suffer as you deserve.*

Southey won't need you or me, once he gets what he wants. I replied to her. *And I don't think even Southey controls Southey anymore.*

I wanted to hurt Maida, to push and pull her around, but she had learned a while ago not to wear excess materials around my cell. She had no jewelry or beads, and her clothing was made of a fabric too soft and light to be a tool for my devilish manipulation; it would tear long before I could exploit it to my advantage.

Vampires are all foul and murderous, Maida scowled. *They don't belong in this world and Southey knows it. He can't walk away from his purpose. His lost love was just opportunity knocking. When he kills that thing in the church, he will find that he must go on, and I will be here to help him. I will be here to guide him.*

Maida tirelessly antagonized me, plaguing my private thoughts with her presence, and promising me many horrid things from the safety of the hall. It took many hours for Southey to finally arrive, interrupting my torment. His angry cursing distracted Maida; she broke contact with me and left the tiny hallway, entering the basement. When she inquired about Southey's outburst, he snapped.

"This is the church where Ellen had her funeral," Southey blurted at her, holding one of her sketches in his hand. "I go there every year…on the day." He shut his eyes, taking a deep breath. I felt his emotions soaring, seeping through the walls of my cell, and for a moment, I felt compassion for him. I sensed not only his intense anger, but also his incredible sadness at his loss. He acted out of love as much as he acted out of hate; the volatility of emotions streaming through Southey, as his true motivations vied for dominance, rendered him a quivering wreck. And I pitied him, and the horrible man he had become.

Arthur had not told me exactly why he chose to dwell in that church. Perhaps he was ashamed – a creature of the night, driven by guilt to a life of penance. Or perhaps, Lee was right: Arthur was afraid of Southey and hid in one of the last places the vengeful hunter would think of looking. Whatever reason for Arthur's presence, be it noble or cowardice, it infuriated Southey.

Southey continued, screaming, "He's practically spitting on her grave by being there! What a curse! It is like God *Himself* is taunting me! Who am I, *Job*?"

He pulled a dagger from his desk and held it high over Maida's head, and for a moment, it seemed to me that he was going to end her life. I felt Maida's intense fear emitting from her breathless body as she stared up at the tip of the knife, and I recalled, with pleasure, her claim that she controlled Southey. To my utter disappointment, Southey suppressed his murderous rage, refocused on his ultimate goal, and stormed from the basement, emotionally charged and anxious to go and kill Arthur, leaving Maida cowering and alone.

I was left undisturbed in the cell, waiting, yet again, for my execution, for an end to my pathetic and miserable state. Little did I know, I would be in misery for only a short while longer. Maida was sitting at the desk, shaken up, humbled, and waiting for Southey's return. I watched her browse through his papers, notebooks and data for almost an hour. I was certain she knew I observed her; I watched her eyes narrow when my presence hovered by her face, looking into her eyes – but she seemed unconcerned.

Then, perhaps having detected the same thing I did, she stood up, and with a confused look on her face, she slowly walked across the basement, looking back at the arched door, trying to figure out if the presence she sensed was a trick forged by me, or actually another vampire. I had become fairly docile from my utter helplessness and was not the one enticing her across the basement. Maida traversed the dim, silent room and cautiously climbed the metal stairs, stopping at the exit. She paused, listening to a subtle metallic noise coming from inside the steel door. Unlike me, Maida's eyes could not see the locking mechanism inside the door shifting into alignment. She was slow to react when the door quickly swung inward, almost striking her, and revealing to her the two visitors on the other side.

Bruce gazed down at Maida from the soft, non-threatening light of late dusk. He flashed a razorous, metal grin at the frightful psychic who could only stare in shock at the dark, painted creature, with a tattered corpse wrapped chaotically in black tape, staring back at her from behind a dirty, red blindfold. Looming immediately behind Bruce was Mira; her pale skin was a stark contrast to his. Her blazing-yellow eyes glimmered beneath her short, red wig, and she flashed stained and darkened fangs from behind her painted ruby lips.

Maida's eyes darted back and forth between the two impeding figures for a couple seconds, and then when she opened her mouth to yell, Bruce pressed his clammy palms to her face and pushed her backwards. Maida tumbled down the metal stairs. I heard the unmistakable snap of human bone before she fell hard onto the concrete floor, striking her head with a fierce thud. Appearing to be in a daze, she looked around aimlessly, as if blind, but soon focused on Bruce and Mira, who were descending the stairs to finish the job.

Maida's pungent terror riled me into a frenzy, but I was incapable of doing anything fatal from behind the walls of my subterranean prison. Instead, I ardently mocked her doom with the most foul and unearthly voice I could muster.

"How will you control Southey when you are dead?" My haunting words whispered into her ear, and overwhelmed and confused, she jerked her head to the side, seeing nothing. Then from the other side, I uttered, "You are going to die Maida...," I dragged out the final words into a raspy groan, repeating it over and over for her entire ordeal. "...Die Maida...die...Maida!"

"Shut up, leech!" Maida screamed as she scurried to crawl backwards across the room, limping on all fours, with her horrified face fixed upon Bruce and Mira.

"Where is he?" Bruce blared as he crept closer to her. With his right arm lowered, he dragged the point of his armblade across the concrete floor, creating a gritty scratching sound. With each simulated step Bruce took, the tape, wrapped around his limbs and torso, twisted and rubbed together with a wrenching squeak. He repeated his question, "Where is he?!"

Maida turned over and started crawling away like a dog, shaking and stuttering, "N...no. He...he isn't here! Southey is out hunting. You don't want me. Stay back!" She cried out.

With her feet grazing the concrete, Mira swooped across the floor toward the desk, and cut off Maida's path. "Not Southey you hag!" she hollered, with her dead mouth hanging wide open, and her eyes bulging from their sockets, twisting in sinister disarray. Her arm extended downward, and her long, white finger pointed inches from Maida's tearful eyes. "Where is the vampire being held?"

Bruce's patience was long spent, and standing at Maida's feet, he swung his arm down, stabbing the armblade into her left knee, through the back of her leg. Maida wailed and writhed wildly, unable to turn over with her joint held to the cement. With a handle on the human, Bruce dragged her backwards, tearing the skin of her leg. The tip of the armblade, which had fully penetrated her knee, scraped loudly upon the cellar floor. Maida clawed at the cement, trying to gain control, and leaving a trail of fractured fingernails and droplets of blood as she was pulled closer to Bruce.

Mira moved closer to her receding prey, gripping Maida's long, loose hair, clenching the locks in her dead fingers. And after a brief tug-of-war between the two vampires, Mira lifted the screaming psychic by her own hair, raising her to eye-level. Maida reached up to pry her hair free from the grip of the cold, stiff hand, but she couldn't, and with her feet over a foot from the floor, she kicked wildly and cursed in the most ungraceful ways imaginable.

"You've seen enough." Mira, holding that foul woman like produce plucked from the dirt, leaned in and clamped her blackened fangs into the side of Maida's neck; and then, immediately releasing her jaws, she bit Maida again, on the other side of the neck. Mira did not drink, but rather watched as the blood spurt from the pair of punctures. She then kissed Maida lips, painting them red with her own fresh warm blood.

Bruce stood behind Maida, watching for a moment as she flailed and bled, suspended by her own hair. Then, after poking tauntingly at her vertebrae with the tip of his armblade, he stepped back, and with a quick and brutal stroke, he severed Maida's head. The decapitated body fell to the floor, flopping like a fish for a second, then lightly twitching for a moment more, until finally, Maida's reflexes had halted completely.

Mira held up the psychic's dripping head until the final signs of life had faded from her eyes. She walked to the desk and placed the severed head, with its frozen expression of shock, upon a stack of papers.

After I savored the sweet justice exacted upon Maida, I spoke into my saviors' minds, anxious to be released. *The keys to the door…She has them beneath her dress.*

Bruce, still standing over the body, crouched and reached under Maida's dress with the hook of his blade. Tearing the fabric with a clumsy action, he removed from underneath both a set of keys, and the small brown satchel, filled with maggots. The crawling, whitish-yellow flesh eaters spilled from a rip in the bag and onto the cement. Mira and Bruce stepped back, and I heard their frightened and

ghostly screams echoing in my mind. They too knew the potential
horrors of the dead-flesh eaters.

The arched door was quickly opened, my cell door next, and
Bruce and Mira entered the cell. Lance's corpse rested lifeless upon
the blood-stained floor. Bits of my discarded arm were hosts to
feasting maggots, still present from my last torture.

"We're underground." Mira noticed immediately the inhibiting
earth behind the cement walls and above the low ceiling. "I have no
periphery vision. Everything is so dark in here."

Bruce made his way toward me with the keys in his hand. "But
not dark like night. It's different. It is almost...consuming." Bruce
unfastened the metal collar from my neck using one of the keys.
"Lee once told me that a vampire can be killed by being buried in an
open grave...that the earth will take back what belongs to it."

Mira stayed close to the door, hesitant to step deeper into the
pit. "I always had a sense of doubt, but feeling the choke of this cell,
I am now certain it is true."

"Your arm...," Bruce's voice was stripped of any ferocity as he
examined the nature of my wound.

"Eaten away," I said, as the chain fell to the floor. The skin of
my neck was discolored from the metal, and crimped from the
pressure.

Bruce's voice lowered like distant thunder, "I have felt that pain
before."

Mira looked down at Lance's body. "Who was he?"

"A waste named Lance," I replied as I hurried out from that hell
and through the hall, into the basement. "Someone who deserved to
be devoured by a vampire. One of the few just deaths I have dealt
since my waking. Lance was responsible for my murder, among
others, and based on what has happened to me, I dare say I was
reborn solely to take his life...a child of karma sent back to excise the
sinner."

Bruce and Mira followed me out into the basement. Mira said
to me, "I see that you've done some self-reflection in your spare
time. That's good."

I moved my corpse over to the desk, where Maida's pale head
rested on a throne of bloody papers. Grabbing a pen from the desk, I
held it as well as dead fingers allowed me, and gouged Maida's eyes
out from her sockets. I repeated the words Mira had said to her
earlier, "You've seen enough," and discarded the grisly shish kebob
onto the floor.

I looked up and out from the building at the surrounding area
with clarity I had been robbed of since I was put into that cell
beneath the earth; my spirit, no longer smothered by earthen walls,

was free to examine things far around me once more. I felt the presences of tenants in the apartments above me, and in the apartments of the two neighboring buildings.

"It is still dusk outside," I said, as I moved closer to the basement stairs beneath the exit door. "Did you walk here in sunlight?"

"No. We'd never have found it. Vampires can't see through daylight," Mira answered. "But we can eke our way during dusk light, if we have to."

"And the commissioner loaned us his personal car," Bruce said. "It has heavily tinted windows, taking the edge off a bit."

Mira walked toward the shelves of weaponry in the far corner of the large basement. She said, "The commissioner wanted it that way so he could transport vampires in secret, and hold meetings with Lee and other late-vampires, back when the list idea was first being tested." With her dead hands, Mira clumsily tried to unfasten one of the straps that held a shotgun to the shelf; her stiff, numb and inapt corpse's fingers failed to manipulate the pins of the tiny buckles.

Bruce was searching through the written notes, sketches and other scattered bits of information on the large, metal desk. "We knew the commissioner would quickly respond to last night's fire…"

"Mr. Paul *always* checks up on us when Southey intrudes," Mira interrupted, turning from the shelved weapons.

Bruce continued, with a grumbling tone, "He wants to cover his tracks and make sure certain things he gives us are destroyed. So last night, we waited for him to come see the damages. Luckily, he was among the first to show up, and Mira and I took him aside swiftly, and forcefully. I gave him an ultimatum," Bruce bellowed, angry that the knowledge of Southey's base had been withheld for so long. "I told him we knew he had been here, at Southey's, many times now, allowing hunters to go unchecked…a betrayal of our deal!"

Mira interrupted, "Mr. Paul denied it at first, and swore he never helped Southey. So I told him what Southey was up to, keeping you prisoner, and using that headless hag to read your mind, hunting us through you. He didn't seem too concerned, until I told him that you were with Lee when the updated list was given to us, and that it was a miracle that Southey hadn't already found out about the list."

"*That* isn't what changed his mind!" Bruce yelled, and held up his bloody armblade, saying, "It was when I held this blade to the back of his neck, pushed him down on his knees, and demanded he lead us here, or I would permanently end our deal right then and there."

"Humans take the threat of death much more seriously when it comes from the mouth of death itself," Mira added. "So, he left us his car, and directions, and we let him go."

I looked at Maida's slain corpse, and the dark red puddle which had almost stopped seeping from her tapered stump. "I showed this psychic where Arthur was hiding. If I had only held out longer, I'd have been saved without betraying yet another vampire."

"You betrayed no one," Mira assured me. "Sending Southey to Arthur was what needed to be done."

"I just wanted an end to that hell, to be killed and not be exploited or tortured anymore. And now Southey is destroying the vampire that saved me from the confusion and horror of my first night."

Bruce said, "We know you revealed Arthur to Southey. So I told the commissioner where Southey would inevitably head next. I made him promise us he would go and rid us of Southey forever. In no position to argue, he agreed, and we took his silver car and went into hiding until the time to save you was right."

I grew hopeful that Arthur might still have a chance; being the causer of all the commotion over the years, I knew Arthur would not stop Southey from taking what he wanted most. It would take an outside force to keep the mad hunter from slaying his most prized demon, be it the commissioner, the witch's curse, or something else altogether.

I walked over to the desk to retrieve something which caught my attention. The silver octopus cane, once owned by Lance, was lying on the floor. With my only hand outstretched, the wooden staff rose up into my grip, and I clenched my grubby fingers around it.

"What are you two going to do now?" I asked, as I looked at the cane I had taken once before. I was glad that it had found its way back to me. "Are you going to continue with the commissioner's list?"

"I don't know." Mira's voice trailed off into a long, whisper. "Lee sought out the deal on his own, years ago. He brought vampires together when there was no better option. The city was too dangerous to kill even discriminately. The slightest disturbances a vampire created often resulted in a swift search and counterattack by hunters, and it was unwise to linger in one spot for more than a few nights. Lee offered us an easier way. He said he had managed to strike a deal that would keep our activities underground...keep us hidden. We thought he was insane at first, but it worked. Our encounters with hunters over the last year or two dropped dramatically. It was sheer luck when they actually stumbled upon us."

Bruce grunted, "But if the commissioner takes care of Southey tonight, things should settle down for good. We would not need the list, anymore."

"We'd still have to be careful," I added. "The smallest actions can create chaos. You can't be sure who will become the next Southey. All it took for him to become obsessed with his hate, was first to love."

An alarming noise came from outside the building – first the piercing sound of squealing tires, and then the crunching metal, and breaking glass.

"Speak of the devil," I said. I gazed up and out, through the basement walls, into the waning dusk, where Southey's black van had struck the back of Commissioner Paul's loaned Cadillac. "Southey must have succeeded at the church...and now he is here to kill me!" I yelled.

With a ghostly breeze, I motioned shut the small arched wooden door leading toward my cell, as to keep my escape a secret as long as possible. "Quickly, under the stairs before he comes in."

The three of us gusted across the basement, and huddled beneath the metal stairway. The metal door above us swung open, and Southey entered, exasperatedly stomping down the stairs, mumbling like a madman. When he noticed Maida's bloody, headless corpse on the floor, his already racing heart beat even faster; his raw emotions, a collage of every frustrating thread of his plight, burned in that otherwise lifeless cellar, like a coals in a cooler. Cautiously, he approached Maida, and kneeling down, he searched for the keys she no longer possessed.

Southey did not hear me as I drew closer, drifting silently behind him with the leg of Lance's heavy cane clenched in my left hand.

Bruce growled out, "Someone would like to see you, Southey!"

I thought at first, that I was going to take his life into my own; however, I found that, despite what Southey had done to me, despite the devil I had seen whenever his glossy, red eyes stared at me, and despite the perpetual harm he had done to those around him, he was essentially a victim. I did not want to end his wasted life, nor would I let anymore waste come from it. I could think of only one thing to do with him, one decent act Southey could perform as penance. I swung the cane, striking him in the back of the head with the dense, silver head of the octopus. He fell unconscious onto the floor.

"I would have bit him," Bruce sounded disappointed, "...or cut his head off."

I looked down at the beaten beast, Southey, watching his back rise when he breathed, listening to the hammering of his stressed heart. His life had been spoiled by vampires, and he spent many years returning the favor.

Did you do it, Southey? I wondered, without a guess as to what went down at that church. Then, removing the blue-hilted dagger from his boot, I examined the clean blade.

"Do something quickly, Child." Mira knew as well as I did, that to linger was foolish. Without a doubt, police would be coming soon.

"Find some rope. Help me tie him up," I told them. "We're going for a ride."

We sloppily tied Southey's wrists behind his back and bound his ankles together. The knots only needed to hold for a few minutes. Lifting his lanky body over our shoulders, Mira and I carried Southey up and out to the parking lot with Bruce leading the way.

A moderate number of observers had gathered around the crashed van and Cadillac, and were talking amongst themselves about what few of them had seen happen. There was no way that three vampires, looking as ghoulish as we did, could have gone by unnoticed. Lacking the time to do something devilish or clever, and being fairly shadowed by the early hours of night, we took a chance, and walked through the small crowd as if nothing was wrong.

"Looks like we can't take the commissioner's car. It's ruined," Mira said.

"That would be most unwise, anyway." Bruce pointed to a car which was parked near the crumpled van and Cadillac. "The keys are in the ignition of that one." A dark red, two door car waited just beyond the wreckage.

Bruce moved across the parking lot, motioning his corpse as if he was really walking, even though the gatherers outside, and the spying tenants looking down from the three buildings' windows, could easily see many obvious reasons why they should be concerned. The curved blade strapped to Bruce's arm was splattered with fresh blood, and stale with old gore. The blindfold over his eyes defied their understanding of his movement. Worse were the numerous holes, gashes and other severe injuries which his mummifying black tape did a poor job concealing.

"Oh my God, look!" a biker-looking man in a leather jacket slurred when he noticed Bruce's monstrous corpse pass him by. Keeping his eyes on Bruce, and not yet noticing Mira and I, the grey-bearded man patted the shoulder of a larger man in a jean-jacket beside him.

"Man, you guys are messed up. Is this for real?" He asked other baffled folks, all of whom were now aware of our arrival.

Unlike Bruce, I had no tape or black paint to dampen the appearance of my wounded corpse, and my clothing draped from my body like tattered rags. Much of the makeup Lucia had applied to my face and arms had been covered with blood, or been wiped or worn off, exposing areas of my sickly-colored dead flesh. The blackened stump of my right arm was largely on display, the bone shooting far from the flesh. I assumed they wondered why the ghastly wound, or the tears and punctures from the dogs on my arms and legs, did not bleed. I gave them no visible sign of pain or concern.

Mira proudly presented a cold, pale, natural-death look. Though her corpse was in exceptional condition, her mouth and chin were stained with fresh blood, and her red hair and yellow eyes endowed her with an alluring ferocity. All it took was a prolonged stare from her, and people froze like deer in headlights.

Screams burst out around the parking lot with the announcing of our presence; but they were short cries of shock and confusion, held back from their true potential by doubt, rather than the uninhibited wails of horror from knowing the truth about what we *really* were.

Though the witnesses spread out, they did not recede too far, being too interested to abandon the scene, and perhaps feeling the safety of numbers. They all waited along the perimeter of the parking lot, watching in disbelief, as three zombie-like creatures carried, for all they knew, their deceased landlord.

As Bruce neared the Cadillac, one of its windows shattered, seemingly on its own to the human observers. A pair of handcuffs flew out through the opening, meeting with Bruce's waiting hand.

"Just in case," Bruce grumbled. "We did not tie him up very well. Those knots won't hold forever."

Bruce opted to have our getaway car ready when we got there – and not waste time by using his physical hands. A unison gasp rose from the crowd when the two doors and trunk of our getaway car swung outward simultaneously and again when the engine roared to life, without a person inside to provide an explanation.

Mira and I dropped Southey inside of the ˌtrunk, still unconscious. I shut the hatch.

"Let's go." Mira entered the car, sitting behind the wheel. "I'll drive. Someone should be seen in the driver's seat…and I'm sure we can agree that that person is neither of you."

I sat in the front seat with the posture of a dead man – my head reeled back over the seat, and my body lifeless and still. Bruce crawled into the back, lying flopped across the seats.

I listened to the muffled whispers of concern, of people's collective voices around us. Yet, not one emotionally-charged soul acted out against us, not even to save Southey. Humans tend to hesitate in the face of uncertainty, to freeze in their fear and ignorance. Perhaps that is the one reason why vampires are so capable of existing among them. As long as we remain a mystery, and not a fact, we can survive in the shadows of reality. We are walking myths.

After creating a story to haunt the community for many years to come, Mira drove off of the parking lot, and down one of the many gritty, highly illuminated industrial roads.

"Where are we going?" Mira asked, sitting upright with her arms down by her sides. Her head flopped around, with each turn of the car. Her hands idle by her sides, and her feet idle on the floor.

"Yeah," Bruce complained, lying awkwardly in the corner of the backseat, "I don't enjoy being out unnecessarily. I prefer a quieter lifestyle."

"We're going onto the highway." Remembering how the Taxxxi Cab had traveled through the industrial park, I directed Mira to an onramp. "...and north, into the woods," I told them. "I have to see something. I have to know if the witch is still alive."

The car climbed the ramp up to the elevated highway. After heading north of the city for some miles, the road cut into the foot of a verdant mountain. I directed Mira to the same place I had gone a few weeks earlier – to the side of the road where a path lingered beyond the edge of the woods. The car slowly rolled over the shoulder of the road, and down onto a small, grassy clearing. Mira shut off the engine.

"I haven't been this far from the city in years," Bruce said, exiting the car. "I forgot how wonderfully dark it could be."

"The city is not an inviting place for us," Mira added, standing still, and taking in the brilliance of night's symphony. "Why do we even linger there?"

"It is where we have wakened," I suggested. "You accept what you know first, I suppose." I lost my mind in the buzzing of the night's activity for a moment, and then said, "...until you find something better."

Bruce walked to the rear of the car, smiling at the contents hidden and stirring beneath the trunk. "We stay in the city because people are plentiful there...and there is shelter for us."

"Dwelling out here would take quite a toll on a vampire's corpse," Mira said.

"But it would do wonders for your soul," I told her. "The conveniences of the city dampen our true nature. We are not humans...we are their shadows, and we should not dwell beneath their canopy of artificial light if we can help it. We belong in untainted night, in a sea of seamless shadows...where real monsters live."

The trunk opened up. Southey was awake, but he was facing down, and did not see his three captors.

"Where am I?" he mumbled, weak and out of breath from panic. "Arnold? Is that you, you no good...Do you hear those voices yet? You'll hear them too if you keep dealing with those filthy leeches!"

Bruce and Mira hoisted Southey from the trunk, holding him over their head, so he faced upward at the night sky.

"Stop...no! Put me down," he begged, as tears ran down his face. "Where am I? Put me d...Stars?" Southey uttered, "Look at all the...all the stars."

I looked upward, toward the grey void bordering the limits of my inward vampire vision.

"Where are we?" Southey persisted to ramble out questions, despite his being ignored. "Why is it so dark?"

I led Bruce and Mira along the narrow dirt path, to the edge of the forest. From there, we traveled beneath the canopy, deeper into the woodland, tracing silently its many forking roads.

"Trees?" Southey's voice filled with concern. "Where am I? Answer me!" He cried out, "What's going on? Let me go!" Southey struggled fiercely, trying to loosen the rope, and the grip of the two vampires, but they held his ankles and wrists tightly to that his struggling would not loosen the binds.

I assumed the thought crossed Southey's mind, and that he reckoned where he was being taken. I did not bring him in those woods as a punishment, as it must have seemed to him, or to Bruce and Mira; I brought Southey into those woods as an offering to the witch – to turn Southey into something beautiful, once again.

We followed the path far into the woods, heading towards her realm, where the dirt and clay trail became overrun with grass, where massive, timbered graves kept the earth and sky from mingling, and where countless souls roamed a hilly sea of wood, bark, needle and leaf. Southey was already yelling out to the air around him, to us, but as soon as we crossed into that darkest place of the mountain, and I heard the first of many ghostly words spoken from the trees therein, he erupted with terror.

Bruce said, as he became aware of the hundreds upon hundreds of arborous souls, "I can feel them, whatever they are."

"It's the trees," I told him. I listened to the calls of the deceased; they continued to call her name, warning us of her, of the witch in the woods. Because of this, I knew her spirit still dwelt among the trees, even if her corpse had been discarded somewhere. The witch in the woods saw what I was taking to her, and the forest stirred in delight at its new addition.

Southey writhed more with each passing moment, as the phantom cries of the woods surrounded him. As he was carried along the crowded path, he jerked his body each time an overhanging branch scratched at him. When we were in the heart of darkness, and the sounds of lost voices emanated throughout the vast realm like a storm of sorrow and dread, his madness grew fierce beyond Bruce and Mira's control. He cursed and kicked so wildly, that they dropped him to the hard, clay path in an attempt to rid the last of his strength.

"Oof," Southey moaned when the wind was knocked from him. He rolled over and tried to climb to his feet, despite his inability to see in that impossible darkness. I watched with pleasure and pity as each fearful bead of sweat rolled down his clammy skin.

"Jacob…is that you?" Southey cried out, fixating his gaze in one direction. He seemed to recognize one of the voices in the woods. "A..a..alive?! I knew it. You…Help me, Jacob! Kill the leeches!"

On his own, Bruce lifted Southey back up over his head. "Is it much further?" he bellowed.

"There's a clearing right ahead," I assured them. "We are almost there."

The wall of trees ended, and a clearing of a few acres opened up before us. At its edge, where the path met a field of low grass, was a small tent with some duffel bags still inside. A few yards from the tent, a small pit had been dug, and was filled with cool ash and coals.

"This is where they came to hunt the witch," I said to the vampires.

"Looks like they left in a hurry," Bruce noted. "There's abandoned equipment over there."

The witch's small raised cabin was across the clearing, and as we made our way there, I noticed one small addition. A dozen feet from the witch's cabin was a sapling, which protruded up from a mound of loosely packed soil. Southey had mentioned to me, in that cell, that he had buried the witch next to her cabin; and that thriving sapling, which had grown phenomenally large for such a short amount of time, surely had its roots dug deep into her corpse. The witch hadn't been destroyed by Southey. She had been *transformed*, finally at total harmony with the world she created.

"We're here," I said, pointing to the ground.

Bruce released Southey's writhing body, dropping it to the earth beside the cabin.

"Are we just leaving him here?" Bruce asked.

"Cuff him to one of the cabin's stilts," I ordered.

Bruce removed the handcuffs from his pocket and fastened one cuff to Southey's wrist, and locked the other cuff to one of the four legs under the corner of the cabin.

"What are you doing to me?" Southey wailed when he heard the metal clicking of the lock.

Though still forebodingly dark, the clearing let down a bit of starlight, perhaps allowing Southey a peek at his three captors, for he stared directly at me for a moment, and I returned the gaze. Both our minds stirred with awful thoughts.

"Just *kill* me already..." Southey begged, choking on his own words – similar to the words I had said to him in my cell.

When he found himself unable to tear himself free from the cabin, Southey cursed with pure hatred, and spit at us. He squirmed like a worm, lying on his side, with his arms tied behind his back. His bulging, frenzied eyes helplessly faced the witch's sapling, which loomed several feet from his face. I saw Southey's eyes examining the small tree. His face was shaking with terror as if he saw something Bruce, Mira and I could not...something about the tree.

"No. It can't be..." He gasped, and then hollered, "We *killed* you!"

Southey shut his teary eyes, turning his face down to the earth as to not glance at the tree. But he seemed not to find serenity behind his own eyelids, and screamed, "No! I can't...can't look away. She's there!" Southey opened his eyes and turned to look at the tree again; only this time he froze, with his mouth hanging wide open and a heart drumming so fiercely, I expected that any moment his chest would explode and stain the earth red.

In that moment, we left Southey and walked from the cabin, out of the clearing and back to the narrow path in the woods. The voices of the trees did not stir upon our exiting, perhaps because the witch's spirit was not with them – she was receiving her gift from me. Any doubts I had of her receiving Southey were extinguished when, not a minute after walking along that narrow path, a terrible cry filled the otherwise still night – an inhuman shriek so stricken with fright that

I had to fight the urge to turn around and go closer. But instead of caving to my affinity and lust for terror, I simply reveled in Southey's burdened, tearful screams which reached out from a nightmare within a nightmare:

"I see her....Coming closer. Stay back! I can't...I can't get out, Jacob! I can't turn away! She's...she's....the witch...Jacob! The witch! Gahhhhh!" Southey's petrifying wails of torment shook the night until we had walked far, far away.

* * * * *

Bruce, Mira and I returned to the city, but not with the intention of staying. I was determined to leave, to wander, for a year, a decade, or forever until my ending. At least until I found what I was looking for...a purpose, a glint of hope in an otherwise hopeless existence. But there was, however, one person I needed to see before I headed out into the night.

"Thanks for coming for me," I said to Bruce and Mira, as I stepped out from the car, and onto the sidewalk of a calm, clean neighborhood I had been to once before.

Mira sat in the driver's seat, but her voice carried over to me, where I had already begun walking away from the vehicle. She said, "I haven't been here in quite a while."

"You're lucky you haven't needed to." I headed along the wide, lengthy driveway, and towards the side of a large house, with Lance's cane clenched in my only hand. The lights in the front lawn illuminated a silver sign on the building that read: Tully Funeral Home.

Bruce's voice rumbled the words, "Need or not, I'd rather remain true to form. Who ever heard of a good-looking monster, anyway? Hey, are you sure you don't want us to wait for you?" Bruce offered as I continued toward the back of the funeral home. "We can leave together."

"No, but thanks," I spoke back to the two vampires. "Go without me. Maybe some night in the future, in some other place, we will cross paths again."

Good luck then, Bruce's words entered my mind.

Goodbye Child, Mira thought, as the red car pulled from the side of the road. *We'll see you in our dreams.*

I walked around the back of the building. A small parking lot was empty, except for one, lone car. Standing at the rear door, I buzzed the intercom. A bright spotlight lit up, and a few seconds later, I saw Lucia behind the door, standing at the foot of the cellar stairs. Her faded blond hair was tied back, and she pulled a white mask down from over her mouth and nose, still working tirelessly, even in the earliest of morning hours.

"Hello again," Lucia said, not particularly cheerful, but in no way uninviting. She reached over to the wall and pressed a button; the door buzzed, and then swung open. "You look like you were pulled from a car wreck."

I descended into the cellar, and followed her into the work area. It was then, up close and under the bright lights that Lucia saw clearly the state of my corpse, and she scrunched her face a bit.

"Is there anything you can do for me?" I held up my right arm, torn and eaten away at the elbow.

"What happened? It looks like an animal attacked you." Lucia gathered her tools, and then hosed some residual blood from the shallow basin of her operating table.

"I had a long episode with some hunters and their dogs. I was lucky to walk away in such a forgiving state."

She looked up at the blackened stub of my arm, and the clean and broken bone jetting outward. "Hunters and dogs didn't do *this*," she correctly noted. "*Did* they?"

"No, they did not." I removed the tattered rags from my dirty corpse, tossed the cane down on the pile of ruined clothes, and waited for her to invite me to lie upon the table. "Maggots did this."

"Yeah," Lucia motioned at the shallow, metal tub. "That seems more like it." She gestured for me to lie down. "That's a neat cane. Where did you get it?"

I fell silently onto the operating table, and waiting for Lucia to work her magic, I replied, "I keep finding it lying around. I guess someone wants me to have it."

"It seems Mr. Southey has been stirring up some trouble." Lucia leaned over my pale, damaged corpse, and pulled a hose down, hanging overhead. She washed the away the stains of mine and others' blood. After patting my pale flesh dry with a towel, she took her finger and poked at the dozens of bite marks and tears plaguing my arms and legs. "It was all over the ten o'clock news. He attacked the police commissioner and set fire to a church. Police are saying that Mr. Southey had some kind of torture chamber dungeon in his basement."

"He most certainly did," I said through my lifeless lips. My tone must have told Lucia of my involvement in that torture chamber.

Lucia paused in her work, looking over my corpse. "Well, Mr. Southey seems to have turned up missing. There are some wild theories going around, let me tell you."

"Believe them." I forced a smile past my stiff, chapped lips. "And I wouldn't count on hearing from Southey again...unless you like to go hiking."

"I do, actually. I love it. I go camping in the mountains every summer." Lucia applied a thick, flesh-toned paste into and over my many small wounds. "It's so beautiful up there. I never want to leave."

She paused, and I knew her words before she asked me. "Ever hear of that ghost story...of the witch in the woods?" Lucia inquired.

"Yes...actually, I have."

"That legend is older than me. And I have been in those woods dozens of times, yet not once have I seen or heard a thing."

"Do you hunt?" I asked Lucia, knowing her answer already.

"Heck no! I couldn't just kill something...not unless I had to. Not unless there was a good reason."

"Well, a little respect goes a long way. You go there in peace, and you leave in peace."

"Kind of like karma, I guess?" Lucia laughed.

"A lot like karma."

After filling the many small, but brutal breeches in my corpse, Lucia brought her focus on my broken, half-eaten right arm. "I have something for this," she said as she stood from her stool. She walked to the back of the room, pulling the steel handle of a large cooler. A moment later, she came out with a long, semi-clear plastic bag, labeled with a tag. She unzipped it. "I can attach this if you want," she said as she pulled a severed right arm out. "It won't match perfectly. You're a bit fairer skinned. But it is all I can give you...and not get in trouble."

"That'll do nicely," I replied. With a simple gesture of my powers, I moved the arm as she held it, bending the fingers into a fist as if it were my own.

Lucia let a chirp of surprise and said, "That is too creepy."

Over the next hour, Lucia cut a large and useless piece of my original, severed arm, and then skillfully and meticulously fastened the donor arm, binding bone to bone, stitching flesh to flesh, and then wrapping a heavy bandage around the connection to strengthen the new limb.

"This limb should be ok, for a while anyway," she said as she began to tug and twist the arm, testing its strength. "Nothing is ever as good as the original."

"It's just a corpse. I can't feel it anyway."

"Arthur was here a few hours ago," Lucia informed me, out of the blue, as she turned to grab a small kit from the back counter.

"Is he ok?" I was relieved to find out that Arthur had somehow escaped Southey's wrath. For all the pain Arthur may have caused, long ago, he did not deserve to perish at the perversely foul hand of Southey.

Lucia returned to the operating table, and began to apply fresh make-up, powders and crèmes to my face, neck and other exposable areas. She reapplied a coat to the gash on my neck from when I was strangled with wire in another life; the tight grip of the shackle I wore had reopened the wound, and she fixed it up.

"He was badly burnt, and his torso was heavily damaged by a shotgun blast, but he'll be fine. I patched him up and he left."

I pondered what forces might have kept Arthur alive; after all, he was willing to die so that Southey could have his revenge. It seemed to me that a man as driven and determined as Southey would not allow such a failure. Did the commissioner interfere? Did Arthur fight back? Perhaps Southey was just too lost in all his hatred to realize what he actually wanted. Either way, that grisly episode was over for good.

"Did Arthur say where he was going?" I asked, curious. Not that I intended to follow Arthur only to ask him questions he could never answer – questions we all ask – like: 'Why was I chosen to be,' and 'What do I do now?'

"He didn't tell me. Just that he was going to leave now that he had no reason to stay in the city anymore." Lucia snorted a breath out through her nostrils in disgust, but smiled, and said, "You know, it wouldn't hurt you to brush your teeth once in a while. It's a cesspool of filth in there, no offense."

"The thought never crossed my mind," I said.

When she was done making me worthy of an opened casket, Lucia walked out of the room, opened a closet door, and returned with clean clothes for me to wear.

"Sorry about the jean pants and jacket," she apologized. "You're going to look like some retro-eighties punk." She laughed as she slipped the stiff, blue cotton pants over my legs. "But it's all I have that will cover you up. At least they won't tear as easily."

"I couldn't care less what I wear." I sat up and moved my new arm around. Lucia slipped a black t-shirt over my body, followed by the denim jacket. I then stood from the table, and faced Lucia with the green eyes she had given me. "How do I look?"

"Much better," she said with her hand to her chin, contemplating her work. "...but still a bit creepy."

"Perfect. Thanks for everything." I turned and headed out of the room, grabbing Lance's octopus cane from the pile of my old, bloodied rags. I headed toward the stairs that led up and out of the funeral home's basement.

Lucia watched me walk away, and then ran across the room, turning the corner to see me standing at the door, with my back facing her. She asked, "Do you know where you are going?"

"Does *anybody*...really?" I replied as I took my first step into the night air.

But she deserved a better answer, though, and not a sarcastic comment. She had been a pillar in my survival, and a thoroughly decent soul. I was eternally grateful to have had the honor of her company and care.

I stopped in my tracks, pondering the many things I could say to her, and though my vampire eyes were already studying the complacent expression on her face, I turned so she could see mine, and said, "I guess I'll find out in time."

As I walked out into the night, I listened to Lucia's calm and caring heartbeat, and I heard her friendly voice call out to me from the darkness of the basement.

She said, "Come back and visit anytime...I'm *always* working late."

That night, I left the city, alone...to search for a deeper understanding of what I was, of what I could become. There was something powerful waiting for me to find it, something I had been put on this earth to do. I would not find the answers written in some journal, in the shadows of a former life, but in the unknown horizons of my new existence.

Things had changed, most-likely worsened, but I hadn't the power to alter them, nor did I wish to. I would be only that which I knew, that which I had wakened into. I would wait in the darkness, hiding between dreams and death. I would let guilt, fear and hatred's scents lead me, and I would take the lives of the unworthy, disrespectful cretins who dishonored the majesty of life with their sinful and corrupt ways, insulting people, like Lucia, who try to make the world a better place. I would become the embodiment of a vengeful karma. I would be what the sewers of evil reap....what 'comes around' after what 'goes around.'

But most of all, like Arthur, I would defy my own purported nature, and justify my existence by turning evil upon itself.

...I would become a monster *to* monsters.

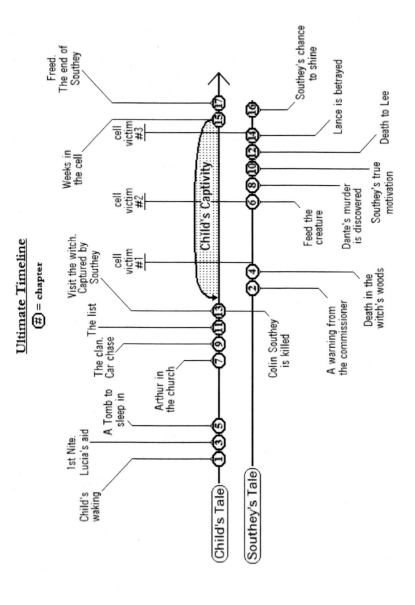

Ultimate Timeline

(#) = chapter

Child's Tale

- Child's waking
- 1st Nite. Lucia's aid
- A Tomb to sleep in
- Arthur in the church
- The clan. Car chase
- The list
- Visit the witch. Captured by Southey
- cell victim #1
- cell victim #2
- Weeks in the cell
- cell victim #3
- Freed. The end of Southey

Child's Captivity

Southey's Tale

- Colin Southey is killed
- A warning from the commissioner
- Death in the witch's woods
- Feed the creature
- Dante's murder is discovered
- Southey's true motivation
- Death to Lee
- Lance is betrayed
- Southey's chance to shine